MW01518079

Noah's A.R.C.

By David Kittrell

Copyright © 2006 by David Kittrell

ISBN 0-7414-3550-0

Published by:

INFIN∞ITY
PUBLISHING.COM

1094 New DeHaven Street, Suite 100
West Conshohocken, PA 19428-2713
Info@buybooksontheweb.com
www.buybooksontheweb.com
Toll-free (877) BUY BOOK
Local Phone (610) 941-9999
Fax (610) 941-9959

Printed in the United States of America

Printed on Recycled Paper

Published April 2007

A people must first lean back to leap forward.

Sankofa: an African concept

CHAPTER 1

Year 1935

It was just before dawn when Tentu Jubilee awoke to the proclamatory cackle of a wing-flapping rooster. Her overstuffed mattress squeaked as she rolled over the uneven lumpiness to sit upright on the edge. Slowly and methodically she rubbed at the sore spot on her thigh where, during the night, the bone would press against her flesh. All night she would roll from side to side, seeking comfort from the pain, but it always ached in the morning. She pushed herself up onto her feet. Her bones creaked as she stood. Every bending of the joints elicited a melodious praise to god. "Oh lord,' she moaned. Not from the pain. But mostly from age. "Um, um, um." It was a custom, a practiced and perfunctory proclamation to life.

Tentu hobbled slowly to the corner of the room where her favorite robe lay draped over the back of her favorite chair. In one smooth motion she removed it and slipped it on as the chair creaked from its loss. Or maybe from it's age. In any case, like Tentu it was sturdy. Just as her robe was warm and cozy or her bedroom, with its overstuffed chair and strong mahogany dresser, strong and stout. Like Tentu.

Attached to the wall above the maplewood headboard of her bed, an autographed letter encased in glass hung straight and even on the wall; beside it was a photographed portrait of its author, Fredrick Douglas, who she knew personally. On the matching maplewood bureau next to a gaudy purple based oil lamp a rectangular maplewood frame held a portrait of her family. They all stood handsomely around her and her husband Earl in their very best Sunday finery. Each face strong, proud, and black. The happiness exuding from their stilled countenance was evident even if there were no smiles. Just the proud stoicism of an early 20th century photograph. Tentu smiled and nodded proudly toward the images. In the portrait, both behind her and to her right stood Mary and Sheba, her two daughters, now living up north in Chicago. Beside her sat Big Earl, her beloved husband, long dead. Behind Earl, their son Walter.

Meticulously, Tentu went about making her bed while humming an old spiritual. When finished she walked through her bedroom door then down the hallway and through the kitchen to the back door. With each step she moved a little more freely because, as she put it, 'her bones were warmed up now'. She swung the screen door open and the majesty of the land came into view. Beautiful acreage of uniformed rows of growing vegetables, scurrying chickens and grazing hogs and cows and it all belonged to her and her family. A proud smile emerged from her face as she remembered her mother's words. "Land is power. Freedom ain't but half a thing without it." And with it, all these years, Tentu felt the empowerment the land inspired. It surged through her being defining her strength and longevity. With Big Earl long gone and herself getting on in age now, the land was solely worked by Walter who lived here with his wife and children.

Tentu Jubilee had been born a slave on the 30th of June in 1853, just ten years before the emancipation. Most slave births in antebellum times, if recorded at all, were noted in approximation like cattle but Tentu knew exactly when she was born, to the hour. Her mother made sure of that.

"Your right of passage," her mother told her. Just as she told her other things. Things most human beings knew and took for granted, but remained elusive to someone born a slave in America. Things like who they were and where they came from. Things white people deemed unnecessary for slaves to know. But Tentu knew. Her mother passed on such notions to her. Afrocentric notions of herself and her history, and the rich heritage of her people as much as she herself understood and knew it. She knew there was a heritage beyond the stereotypes presented by white people. She knew there was a history that distinguished her and her people from the animals, fields, bales of cotton and other inanimateness of plantation property and she made sure Tentu knew it too.

Now in the antiquity of life Tentu was still sharp, strong and physically adept in spite of the maladies evolved from age and the hard life she'd led. Tentu was a regal Black woman whose skin was mahogany brown. Tall and erect, she stood devoid of the consequences suffered by a life time of slumped shoulders and bent spine from bending in cotton fields or bowing in subordinate postures. Some folks whispered that she was strange. But all folks both black and white respected her. Outside her presence they referred to her in mystical quality. Some said she possessed powers of conjuring and prophecy. Many of them sought her advice because Tentu Jubilee could tell you things. Things that healed your soul. She could teach you things that made you proud, advise you in times of sickness and tell you things to help you stay well. She could teach you things about ancient Africa and the history of black people before they were slaves.

Tentu was a proud woman who loved her family and taught them well. All of them could read and write. People said her grandson, Pressman was the one. That he'd one day be a credit to the race. That he was a genius and destined for great things. But to her the most important legacy she would leave was the afro centric qualities she passed on. The very qualities and ideals her mother had passed to her. Many nights when her children were young, She would gather them to the porch and recite for them the stories of family history she'd heard as a child. Rocking rhythmically in her rocking chair she'd gesticulate wildly, animating every scene of her narration. Just as she prepared to do now with her grandchildren. The two of them scurried to the porch to position themselves at her feet. Their mother, Hattie, sat beside them in a chair.

3

"They say colud slaves was happy and didn't run way," Tentu began. "But that ain't so." The balls of her feet anchored to the floor, she pushed herself slightly to and fro.

"Lots a colud folk run away the first chance they got. Not always on the cuff either. But wit plannin and schemin. My Grandma," she stated pointing her thumb to her chest, "your Great grandma run! Every breath she took was a call for freedom. She was owned by some people up north." Cleopatra, the youngest, interrupted incredulously. "They was slaves up north, Nana?"

"Sure was Sugar. There was slaves up north, slaves down south, out west and back east."

"I thought slaves was only down south," Cleo insisted.

"Me too," joined Pressman. Tentu closed her eyes and shook her head.

"Honey, any place this side a Canada is down south! Colud folks face the same discrimination and hatred all over America. Slavery or not. Just some places more out in the open. Other places it's sneaky and under cover like a weasel in the sheep herd."

She continued. "Grandma was owned by people who thought they was good to her." She curled her lips in sarcasm. "Cause they didn't beat her. Not right off mind cha. They just could not understand why a slave would want to be free of em. They didn't beat em...Right off." She winked one eye. "Just own em." She sucked her teeth. "Ya think they's a difference to a body's spirit and dignity?" She looked at them very deeply. "Is there a difference?" she asked them not expecting them to answer. "Nary a one." She pounded her wrinkled fist into an opened hand. "Just because they ain't beatin em with a whip don't mean they ain't bein beatin down." She leaned back in her chair and rocked. "Your great-grandma's grandpa was born a pure-tee African." She gave deliberate emphasis to each word in greot fashion. "He was strong, you know, like all pure-tee Africans. He was snatched away by a roamin tribe a fellow Africans an sold to white people."

4

Cleo and Pressman looked at one another with horror. Somehow the thought of one African selling another into slavery seemed an incredible treachery to fathom, even for their young minds. Tentu noticed their queried eyes but went on. "They kidnapped him and chained him to some other men and women. Your great-great grandpa was just a young sproutlin child at the time. But he still knew he had to be free. The minute them chains was locked to his neck and arms. Like this," she demonstrated.

"He knew his purpose in life, from dat day on, was ta retake his freedom. All the way cross the middle passage he struggled, looked and planned. All the way to America. It was the rebellion in him. Soon's his feet touch dry land and the lord give him a chance to run, he did. Didn't know where he was. Ain't had no idea where he was goin cept away from white people. He knew captivity wadn't no natural state fo a human being. Specially a spiritual people like Africans." Joyously, she clapped her hands and rocked in her chair to rejoice her ancestors' efforts. The children joined in her revelry but was cut off when Tentu's eyes stopped them. She stared at them and stopped rocking long enough to whisper. "But he got caught," she frowned. After a long silence her smile returned and she winked. "When he got older, knew a little more bout where he was. He run way agin. Took his wife and chillun who he had by then." Her head tilted to one side as she added, "But then...he got caught again. Soon's he saw anotha chance, he run away agin, An it went on and on that away, till finally they kilt him." Her eyes went cold. Her lips drew tight and her voice grew sad. "Right in front a his children. They hung em. One a them chillun was my grandfatha, your great-grandma's father. Even though he saw his daddy kilt for runnin away it ain't scare him none from doin it. He knew some things was risky nuff to be worth dyin for. When he grew up. He run fo his freedom too. And stayed free his self. But ahhhhhh Lordy...he couldn't keep his family free. They was takin and he never found them. They got sold and he never seen em again. But he still was able to leave them something. The best thing he coulda

5

passed on to my momma, yo great-grandma and her sister. He left them with the will and determination to be free."

Tentu leaned in close to their small faces and spoke in rhythmic parlance. Her head swayed left to right with each word.

"Cause ain't nothin more important in this world...than your freedom...Your freedom and your history."

She grew quiet than spoke. "That was more important than life in them days and that ain't never change. It's still important to be free. Still more important den life itself. If ya caint decide your own destiny you ain't got no life at tall. Yall remember this. If ya don't get cha freedom in YOUR lifetime. Least you do is pass the spirit a gettin it to the next generation. And this!" she clapped her hands. "Is how my momma and her sista was. When they got old enough and ready they up an run fo THEY freedom!"

"Did they get caught too, Nana?" Pressman wanted to know.

"Yes, chile," she sang sadly. "They was caught...but just like they grandpappy and they daddy. They run way agin and agin."

"The people what owned em just couldn't understand why. Remember, they figgered they was good to em. So why would they keep runnin away?. Well, suh, one day the ole slave mastah ask Grandma's sistah. He say, girl why y'all run way so! Don't we treat y'all like family. She held her head up." Tentu sat erect demonstrating with her shoulders. "She look that white man in da eye, you wasn't spose to do that but she did, and said. How can I be one a yo family?. I ain't neva seen you whip none a yo chillun. I ain't neva seen none a them with chains on they legs. You ain't neva sold none of em. So how in the world could I be any kin a yourn. But If you ain't a hypocrite and I am like a family member then let me go free. Right now...She was known ta be a sprightly one now. Well suh the kindly ole family master slapped his slave family member." Tentu winked her eye. "She sho had a mouth on her!" she laughed. "That white man could not imagine who been puttin such notions in they head, but he wasn't standin for it. So he sent the two sistahs to his cousin. See, they would send or sell slaves they called 'bad', way deep down south. Thas where that cousin was. Wayyyyy down deep, in Alabama. Greatma was just a young thing then. Her sistah was a lil older. The slave mastah figgered down there the white people would beat them silly notions bout freedom out Big Sistah's head and Greatma would natchally follow. Then when that was done and dey was more seasoned ta slavery his cousin would send em back. That was a way, they thought, to brake the slave."

She took a breath before continuing. "Before they got sent, their 'good' master." she winked, "told them that when they comes back and they ever run away agin he was gonna cut off their feet!"

Down the path Walter Jubilee appeared, walking towards the house. Tentu stopped her narrative for a moment and the children turned to see their father standing at the foot of the porch steps. Tentu called her son by the affectionate name, Brother. Brother/Walter walked directly to his wife, bent down and kissed her softly on the lips. Tentu watched approvingly.

"Finished in the barn?"

"Just about."

"Daddy!"

He looked at his children. "Learnin anything?" he asked.

"Yea, Daddy; sit down," they beckoned in unison. Walter sat down on the very last step of the porch, just below Hattie. Tentu called his attention with her eyes.

"Tellin em bout their great grandmah."

"She was some kinda woman," he told his children.

"Go head Nana," Pressman urged.

"When Greatmah and her sister got to Alabama they learnt there really was a difference between a good master and a bad one. The good master was unjust but the bad master was just downright cruel. Sadistic is what they call it. But good or bad a master was still a slave master. While they was in Alabama they met up with other slaves who wanted freedom too. They all got together and run off."

7

"Did they get caught again, did they cut off their feet?"

"Wait a minute." She smiled at their enthusiasm. "Slow down an listen. They was too far south to make it to Canada so they made their way cross Alabama, through Georgia and then down to Florida, where they found refuge with the Indians."

"Indians!!" Pressman and Cleo shifted in there seats. Distributing the weight from one buttock to the other. Their excitement mounted without taking there eyes from their grandmother's face.

She went on with her story. "In Florida they settled down and built a hidden community deep in the swamps. White folk couldn't get to em long as they was down there. They built themselves a fort and some farms. Slaves from all over came down to join them. White folk finally sent Paddy rollers ta bring em back. But them slaves an Indians fought em off. This was what they called the Seminole Indian Wars. White folk lost thousands an thousands a dollars."

"Money, Nana!?!" Pressman interrupted, surprised at the advent of money into the story.

"Yes, money chile. It's what this country is all about. Havin a lotta slaves was like a good team a horses to white folks. They worth lots a money and as long as the slaves was free the white folk was out a that money. All them slaves was worth so much money the owners went to the government and got them to send the army to get their slaves back. The black folks fought hard. The Indians fought hard. But the army had better guns and big cannons and most important of all they had other no account Negroes and Indians to guide them through the swamps. Many brave colud and Indian died. Them that survived, like Greatma and her sister was beat down and brought back to slavery. They got sent back to their masters."

Tentu saw the question in Cleo's eager face.

"Yes chile," she said solemnly. "Since Big Sistah was the oldest, that white man cut off her foot. Right cross their." She drew an imaginary line across the top of her instep with

8

her finger. "He tole Greatma that she was next iffen she tried to run agin, too."

The horror in the children's eyes was testament to what their child like imaginations were seeing. They could visualize the amputation happening for themselves. Tentu forced a sad smile and continued.

"For two years Greatmah and her sistah stayed free in Florida. And in that time Greatmah's sistah had a chile. A little boy. He died. Taint zactly sure how. But he died young." Her voice began to trail off.

Tentu closed her eyes and leaned back in her chair and rocked in a slow easy rhythm. An antecedent that always meant the end of the story for now, usually accompanied by the hum that now escaped her lips. A melodious spiritual of long ago that hung in the air, melancholy, soothing and engrossing. Walter and Hattie escorted Pressman and Cleo quietly into the house and to bed.

There, the imaginary sights and sounds of their ancestors stirred as they fought and struggled for freedom in their dreams. Faceless runaways and Seminole Indians warded off snapping dogs and grimacing slave catchers throughout the night. Images that did not elicit nightmares but caused there hearts to swell with pride as they felt part of and identified with heroic people akin to themselves even in there slumber.

On the porch Tentu smiled. She knew the dreams her grandchildren would have and the pride they would feel for themselves and those who looked like them. She smiled a self gratifying smile. A self prescribed reward for a successful traditionalizing of history, heritage and pride.

*****

Things seem to be getting better Pamela Averson thought as she approached the bus station. An unsure smile graced her face as she peered through the glass doors. She could see several people milling around before pushing it open and walking inside. She headed straight for the ticket counter, struggling with her luggage along the way. The tan

9

pasteboard suitcase wasn't particularly heavy but together with the overstuffed valise under her arm it was somewhat awkward to carry. Pamela made her purchase then found her way to the front most row of wooden benches aligned in the center of the waiting area and plopped down next to a mother and her two small children. After returning their innocent smiles she turned her attention to the ever moving crowd.

Springtime always seemed such a busy time around a bus station and this Greyhound Station in downtown Baltimore was no exception. The only thing unusual to Pamela Averson was that this was still true even in the mist of an economic depression. In fact it was surprising to see so many people in the bus station at all by Pamela's reckoning. After all this was 1935. The Great Depression had been raging for over five years now. Many people didn't have the money to travel, she thought. But here were travelers. At least here, were people in the station.

On closer inspection she would have seen that out of the many people around the terminal only a few were actual travelers. Many were just lounging, some had been surreptitiously lounging here for several days trying their best to elude the single cop charged with bus terminal security. Truth be known. He didn't care. He knew they weren't travelers but squatters and distinguishing the squatters from the travelers wasn't easy. At least not if their clothing was an indicator. It was a hard time for all caste she realized. But things were getting better. Certainly things were looking better for her.

*****

She had a twenty five minute wait before boarding. Pamela decided to spend the time going over her assignment. She extracted the notes and papers neatly stuffed in her valise. Again she thought of the assignment given her by the Federal Writers Project, an organization set up under the umbrella of the W.P.A.

She had been relegated to the task of interviewing former slaves living in the south, to preserve their stories and anecdotes as a written historical record. After leafing through the papers she read over some of the material arranged for her by her F.W.P supervisors.

"In America of the 17th, 18th and 19th centuries millions of men and women of Negro descent were subjugated to a peculiar system of slavery until the end of the Civil War," she read. "It has been a well known but slighted section of American history. Someone had added in parenthesis (for many, better left unacknowledged.) However; this fact, impossible though to ignore, is attested to by the existence, at this time, of thousands of these ex slaves who still live and reside in the United States in our southern portions. Historians realize these survivors represent an untapped source of information, a virtual treasure trove of American history and experience."

"These men and women." she read on, "all well past the age of eighty can recall a lifetime of slavery by way of narration. Testaments worth more than the historic inferences of a million researchers. This occasion presents an opportunity to extract from this community of antebellum survivors information and anecdotes once relegated solely to word of mouth and folklore. Now these anecdotes can be documented for time and prosperity."

Pamela thought about what she'd just read. To her there didn't seem to be much auspiciousness in a story where Negroes were the theme. She doubted if mainstream America would even be wholly interested in the story. Especially, she opined, when the seeds of a truly American panorama of cultural grit and struggle was sprouting up all around the country now during this depression. The gaggle of white citizens who travel across the country by rail in a nomadic search for sustenance and adventure was a more rewarding story in the making, she reasoned.

The men who traveled illegally by rail, once affluent now striving to rise above the sudden poverty that was thrust upon them. "They" were the story of history in the making.

How adventurous it most be to sojourn across the open country as so many young men were doing these days, she reasoned. The pitfalls, the dangers, the tricks and skills of survival they most certainly had to learn to stay alive. The places they must have been and the many characters they must come across to befriend. To fear an acquaintance of chance, both uniformed and motley. "Ahhh," thought Pamela...that was a story beyond the simple travails of slave history. That would be an assignment for me.

Pamela's talent for writing was first recognized by her Uncle, Peter Van a well known novelist, after reading a simple story she'd written. It was a childish fable of knights, dragons and princesses but it's construction and content convinced Uncle Van that his niece may have acquired the talent he was endowed with. Thus began his tutelage of her career. He inspired Pamela to pursue her talent. Supporting her through his patronage all through college, in spirit and at times in person, to nurture her development.

After her graduation Uncle Van was instrumental in getting her the position of cub reporter on one of Baltimore's largest newspapers, the Baltimore Sun. She performed well there. Enough to gain rise on her own merit. Though having an uncle as renown as Peter Van didn't hurt.

Because of it's affluent affiliates and wide circulation The Baltimore Sun of the 1920's was considered the most stable organization in the newspaper corporate world. When the stock market crashed in 1929 financial security remained strong for Pamela. Her family was well off and there was a lot of news to report. There was no reason, it seemed, for her to worry. Her family's opulence and the newspapers stability left Pamela with a naive optimism for the seriousness and the possible duration of the crash. Benjamin Averson, her opulent Republican father, added his own sense of well being. He reinforced her attitude with his own equally naive a fortiori refrain.

"This so-called depression," he'd preach, a cigar clenched tightly between his teeth, "is merely a set back. He'd wave his hand dismissively.

"It can't last more than six months. It's an easy enough storm to weather. America," he'd preach, "is the land of surmountable adversity. It's at it's best, when times are at their worse."

That was six years ago. Since then the seventy year old publication folded and crumbled into a heap of depression era debris and Pamela's optimism had been darkened. She then joined the rest of the country in it's asperity. But now as the rest of America was being rescued so was Pamela, doing what she does best.

Pamela was a good writer and thanks to Uncle Peter Van she learned that every good writer was an astute observer of character. A good writer can compose a provocative expose from any assignment Uncle Van would say. Interesting to the writer or not, there's a story to be told and it takes a good journalist to bring it out. She smiled to herself as she remembered his advice and her enthusiasm as she proclaimed. "I'm gonna be a good writer Uncle Van." The memory suddenly left her ashamed. She'd been balking at the prospect of chronicling the life of an ex-slave when she should be preparing to make it an interesting piece of history. Could it have been their ethnicity she objected to? Pamela had little exposure to Negroes but never considered herself prejudiced against them. She never really gave them much thought at all. Negroes and the institution of slavery seemed so far and removed from her world. So much so that she remembered how surprised she was to learn that people who were once slaves, were still alive. There really was a need to ascertain this knowledge while it existed, she reasoned. Plus an interview with some octogenarian negro promised to put her talents and perspectives to the test. She now realized how fortunate she was to have the opportunity, at the same time, incidentally, it was a paying job. A writing assignment for an out of work journalist. And as a social supplemental, history would be preserved.

The uniformed driver walked passed her, walking toward the outbound door. He opened his trip book. Then without lifting his head yelled.

"All aboard!"

Pamela returned the papers to her valise then rose with the other southbound passengers. There were six beside her, including the young mother and her two small children. One of them, the little boy, reached out to help Pamela with her suitcase.

"Thank you young man." She smiled. Baring most of the weight but it was nice to allow him the illusion of being a knight in armor.

They all filed through the partially glassed doors and boarded the bus. Before stepping around the open bus door Pamela idly looked back at the milling crowd in the waiting room and shrugged. Would have been a good story though. After reaching a seat midway on the bus she enlisted the aide of a young solider across the aisle to open her window. The august afternoon was very hot. The air inside the bus was stifling. The open window did little to entice a breeze. Pamela dabbed at the sweat on her forehead and neckline. She removed her ticket from the black purse resting in her lap and gave it to the driver. He punched a hole in it, validating her ticket, then moved on to the next passenger. Pamela picked the brown valise from the floor in front of her and removed a note pad that contained the names of the people she was to interview. She read two. Addie Morgan and Tentu Jubilee. The second name she whispered to herself phonetically, listening to the pronunciation. Ten-too Ju-ba-lee. The first name was odd, she thought. The surname was odd as well but it at least was a word she was familiar with. She knew Negroes adapted the names of presidents, slave masters and events. Jubilee, she knew was associated with the negro emancipation. No doubt this man or woman got his or her name from that event.

The driver finished collecting the tickets from the passengers and returned to the driver's seat. He started the motor.

"Here we go folks," he announced. "Baltimore, Maryland to Miami, Florida. Stopping in D.C., Richmond, Raleigh and all points south in between." He backed the bus out of the boarding area stall and swung smoothly into the street. The ride from Baltimore to South Carolina was a long one and there'd be plenty time to go over her literature. She thought of a paragraph she'd read describing an epidemic of slave escapes. She chuckled to herself . An amusing delineation she thought. One band of runaways was even said to inspire mythic folklore. She wondered, facetiously, how illiterate runaways could attain such legendary status in the ante-bellum south of America. Maybe her subjects could shed some light on that story. Yes, she mused, those days must have been dreadful. A horrible experience. Overseers whipping hectored slaves, degradation, hatchet wielding black insurrectionist, flames erupting from plantations ablaze while bludgeoned lily white babies lay scattered among the erupted carnage and debris. Her body shuddered under her reverie. She laid the papers on her lap and leafed through some maps, lists and directions. Amid the list of names she came across another. Gus Morgan. Addie Morgan's husband was still alive also. Huh. She praised her project coordinator's resourcefulness. They were certainly on the ball. Information, transportation, room, board and expenses. An official introduction to her subjects would have made the registry complete, she mused while thinking back. "You'll be welcomed," insisted the coordinator, "and you won't meet with any resistance. Those old Negroes won't be a problem for an assertive white woman. Just remember your place and subtly remind them of theirs." She was not convinced such haughty intimidation was the proper way to gain a journalistic relationship. That aspect of it she decided to play by ear

*****

"A kiss!!!"
"A kiss!" shouted the crowd.
"A kiss!"
She stood upon a pedestal that held her high above the smiling crowd of adoring faces. Thousands of subjects

15

milled about in ecstatic delight whose undertones of revelry crescendoed into a hearty hoorah...for her...their adored princess. She nestled in the embrace of a handsome prince who'd rescued her from some terrible fate which she could no longer recall. But no matter. For now, no longer in distress, she beamed at him as he stood mightily...invincibly. Her grateful hordes edged her on to kiss him and reward him for his noble deed.

"A kiss," they shouted!

"A kiss!" Their voices roared more urgent!

"A kiss!"

"A kiss."

"Oh Miss. Miss!" Someone was nudging her awake. "Oh Miss." It was the young soldier from the seat across the aisle. She pulled herself erect in her seat and rubbed her eyes. "Oh I must have fallen asleep." He smiled and stood up. "Yes. The bus just made a rest stop. I thought you might want to freshen up or stretch your legs."

"Oh thank you." she said gratefully. "You're most kind. I can use a stretch. Thanks." Pamela dabbed at the sweat on her neck. She felt a rueful regret to realize her constituents call was really just a fellow passenger calling to her through a dreamy haze. She stood up to disembark with the other passengers among smiles and polite chit chat. One passenger told her they'd reached Norfolk, Virginia.

After freshening up in the ladies room and stretching her legs she boarded the bus and returned to her seat and retrieved the valise she'd left on the floor. One by one the other passengers returned to their seats. The young soldier across the aisle was already in his seat when she sat down. From the corner of her eyes she could see him. He seemed to be stretching his neck to see something. He was staring at her. Finally he spoke. "What do you have there?" He pointed to the valise resting on her lap.

"It's notes for an assignment I'm on."

"What's that?" he retorted baffled. A woman on an assignment! "What kind of assignment?" She smiled, amused at his chauvinistic confoundedness.

"I'm a writer," she explained. "I'm on my way to South Carolina to conduct some interviews."

"Oh I get it. Some Senator or Governor or something about this dang depression."

She smiled wholly. "Oh no. Not quite. I'm going to do a historical piece on ex-slaves."

His pleasant countenance vanished, replaced by sheer revulsion. "Ex-slaves!?!"

"Yes!" she answered indignantly.

"For heavens sakes! Why!?!"

"Why?" she echoed. "Well, why not? There's much we can learn from their experience," she defended trying to disguise her impatience. "There's much of that period we know nothing about."

"What in the hell can you learn that's worth anything, from those people?" She was annoyed with his bigotry but decided to debate him...calmly. Reasoning with his kind of bias would be difficult. She surely felt no obligation to defend her work to this man. Yet, she felt a need to explain herself even if it meant sparing with his prejudice. She turned toward him fully to deliberate. "There is so much history there that we don't understand," she began "Our knowledge of the period from the negro's point of view is virtually nil. We only know that they were slaves. But we know nothing of their personal lives. The way they endured slavery and how they survived. When you think about the institution of slavery and the way they were treated you have to wonder what caused them to endure in spite of it." She was almost apologetic. "Don't you find that interesting, to sacrifice and survive in the face of being the most downtrodden?" She watched for the effect her words had on him. He remained silent as his rigid countenance grew visibly harder. He looked as though he had swallowed something awful.

"I mean can you imagine. They are the last living witnesses to America's must shameful period." She silently rebuked herself for sounding, as she thought, a bit too patronizing. But as far as he was concerned she had crossed the line. "Shameful!!" he spat. "Lady, there ain't nothin for America to be shamed for. We took them people out of the jungles and tried to civilize em." He twisted his face in disdain. "They endured," he continued, aping her remark, "because white folk took care of em. Like we took care of our cattle and all dumb beast!" Then he smiled as though he'd thought of something clever. "Why don't cha write about cows and how they endure. At least they's worth something." His hate filled tirade left her momentarily off balance as he went on. "Are you one of them Communist?" he asked, thinking how ludicrous it was to study Negroes in the first place. "I bet you're one of them bleeding heart, spook loving apologist. Trying to lift them to white folks' standards. Mixing with them and all. Boy! What a sin and waste of time that'd be. Niggers. Hell!"

For the first time she noticed the soldiers southern drawl. It magnified her impression of him tenfold. Pamela turned from him in disgust figuring him a lost cause for humanity. Then turned to him again. She drew her words out in measured tones. "To you maybe...But to me they're humans with a story to tell...Now if you don't mind I'd like to concentrate on my notes." Pamela turned away from him before he could rebut. She'd had enough. His attitude was too disquieting. The soldier mumbled something under his breath that sounded like 'nigger lover'. Flabbergasted, she stared out the window at the passing scenery. How in heavens name, she wondered, could a harmless remark evoke such passion and hate. It reinforced the stories she'd heard about the southern attitude towards Negroes. She continued watching the passing panoramic view of trees and road side erections but could still feel the bigot's eyes disdainfully upon her.

Pamela was not unattractive at 30 years of age. She was average in height, thin and average looking. Her eyes maintained a youthful look of wonder above a capitulating smile. She had an awe struck unimpressive quality that deceptively hid an astute mind. Her short flaxen hair was fashioned into a flip just below her ears and above her neck in a perpetual pageboy. Now that pageboy shook as she bounced her head from side to side in disdain. How terrible, she thought for people to harbor such jaundiced attitudes She'd always considered herself liberal, though she could not really claim a relationship with any negro. Certainly she sympathized with their circumstances. She'd only known one negro personally, if one could call it that. Yet it sounded better than simple recognition. The old woman who cleaned the offices at the Baltimore paper, she thought. Someone told her that Lula was really not that old. Closer probably to Pamela's own age. She was never personally aquatinted with her; though, they spoke to each other cordially. She seemed nice. But Pamela had to admit she'd never looked upon Lula as a personality. No ones mother, sister or wife but more of a flat character. A negro fixture that cleaned the offices and greeted you when you came to work and bided you goodnight when you left. It seemed she was always there.

Pamela returned to her notes. In a few moments they were in full command of her attention. As she read, the rhythmic grind of the buses wheels, the intermittent ogling of the uniformed bigot and the undertone of conversation from either end of the bus slowly faded and disappeared from conscious view. Her experience with the bigot had by now faded into the unconscious realm of suppression, except for one aspect of the encounter that defied repression. She'd gone through a metamorphosis in her attitude about her assignment. She was now more determined to tell the story as objectively as she could. Time passed. Soon through her window a large rectangular sign came into view welcoming her to South Carolina.

*****

Aiken, Georgia is a small city. So close to the Georgia-South Carolina border it was difficult to say if it's citizens were Georgians or South Carolinians. Geographically, Aiken was in Georgia. Unofficially it's citizens were from whichever state they claimed allegiance. Even the mail was delivered accurately whether addressed to Aiken, Georgia or Aiken South Carolina. Directly across the Aiken County line stands Williston. Williston and Spritton are neighbors on the South Carolina side. Two small white dominated towns, predominantly populated by black people. It's citizenry, like the rest of America was segregated.

Four miles from the main thoroughfare in black Spritton a cluster of shacks stood haphazardly arranged at the end of Hawkins street. Their front doors were indistinguishable from their back doors except where discerned makeshift porches protruded. Built from heavy timber and brick some had tin pantile roofs. Clotheslines ran from the sides of these structures to poles planted in the ground like a network of aortal ropes with clothes drying in the sun on capillaries of line. These shacks were euphemistically called homes. In one center most shack lived George and Addie Morgan. They'd lived here since Reconstruction. The first thing George Morgan espoused to Pamela proudly was the day freedom enabled them to leave the Henry Belfield plantation "Southland" over 70 years ago and move here to their own home. George and Addie raised their children in this shack. Sent them out into the world from it and served as a sanctuary for the children when they wanted to return to it. Though once they left they rarely returned. George and his family were stable in their community and never had trouble out of the local white folk.

"Da white folkses in Spritton neva had cause to trouble dis family," exclaimed George Morgan proudly. His thumbs hooked snugly under his suspender straps. "We ain't neva had big trouble twixt da white and da colud at all lak in most places. Fact! My chillun ain't neva had cause ta fear da white folks heah. I always believed. Don't know why dey was always in a huff ta leave dis here place. But dey did. Still dey's always got a home ta come back ta. Iffen dey wants to." George's eyes didn't quite comport with his narrative. Pamela again pulled down the hem of her dress over her knees. A nervous habit she'd picked up since she began interviewing the Morgans. She found herself quite welcome in their home when she arrived two days ago. But George's eyes, she found, developed quite a habit of roving in the wrong directions that made her the least bit uneasy. It was harmless ogling she mused, as disquieting as it was. But innocent or not, in southern white eyes it was the sort of malfeasance that could get George attached to the unfortunate end of a rope. His apparent dismissal of it and Addie's complete ignorance of his actions surprised her. He...They should know better. However, it was time for work. With pen and pad in hand Pamela Averson listened intently to George and Addie Morgan's story. They furnished her with a good deal of history, biographical information and anecdotes.

At night she spent evenings in her hotel room organizing her notes with the scent of hot coffee wafting about her nose. During transcription, she found that deciphering the dialect was sometimes a problem. However, by business end she was always quite pleased with what she'd eventually gotten down.

The next day Pamela took a sip of her coffee before asking. "Why do you suppose it was so different here in Spritton. I mean, the neutral relations between Negroes and white." George waved his hand at her. "Shoot! If neutral means that white folks just leave us alone den you used da right word. It ain't that white folk and colored love each otha so much. It's jus that dey leave us alone cause we gots dat understandin. But it twernt always dat a way. White folks in Spritton was just as mean as white folks anywhere else could be. But da African Angel changed dat. He tetched em. Some folks say. Put da fear of God in em" Pamela barely missed spilling coffee on herself. She hadn't expected to hear anything as extraordinary as that. "African Angel," she repeated incredulously.

"Das right. And don't be puttin suspicion in yo mouf. I admits I caint say dat I seen em myself. But I nos reliable peoples dat has. Dey say the paddy rollers could neva catch him. Say he kilt some of em too and hepped a lotta slaves run away. Some folks say he put a spell on da white folks.

21

Made em fraid to mess wit the colud folks. Like I say, I ain't neva laid my eyes on him myself. But I sure don't argue wit what I seed dat was done. No force but a God sent angel could make white folks free da colud. And sure nothin but da supanachal unmean dese white folks down heah."

Negro folklore? Superstition? Maybe mass hysteria or imagination she surmised, passed on from an old subservient generation to the next. Whichever reason, for Pamela, it bore a common thread of preposterousness. Even ludicrous perhaps. Pamela intended to determine which. "But what about other towns. Surely if there was this angel he would have been known to and talked about by the mainstream people of other towns," she reasoned. "He would have extended his powers to protect Negroes throughout the south and not just here in South Carolina?"

"Well lak I say, I ain't neva been no wheres else but South Carolina and from what I seen Spritton ain't had no bad colud and white trouble lak dey do in otha towns since I heard of da angel. And befo dat white folks round heah was mean. When I was a boy I seen Massa Belfield shoot and kill a slave on a count a gentman loss a bet. See dey made a bet and da gentman who loss didn't have his wages. Sos the Massa up and shoot one ob the gentman's slaves and dey calls it even. Den dey sat back and had a good ole laff bout it and das probably the nicest story I could tell. So I know how mean white folks can be. Now what powah on earth coulda changed a folk so mean as dat."

*****

"Don't colored folks got schools Nana?" Pressman asked at the kitchen table. A plate of grits, eggs and fish waffling aromatically before him. "Sure we do Darlin'," she sang.

"Well, why you want me to go to white peoples school?" Pressman asked curiously between bites.

"Cause they got things ya need ta know too," Tentu answered patiently. "In fact, many of the things they got to teach was knowledge stolen from your ancestors. So all you be doin is gettin it back. Always know what yo adversary is thinkin. You remember that."

"Yes Maam."

"After you finish colud school and bonds with your own people. I want you ta go to a white school and get a idea bout the things they took from our proud past. Like the sciences and things. One school for your mind and spirit, the other one for your education. And never forget, always look to the past to judge your future. The search for your past ain't gonna ever stop, honey. There's so much about the greatness of our people that been stole, changed or ignored. Things that's good for you to know. It lifts your pride...See, white folks know who we are. It's our own people that don't know theyself. It's knowing ourselves that's the key to our future and freedom. When you know who you is there ain't nothin you can't do. A king can be spotted in a crowd even if he wearin rags, if he know hisself to be a king. That's why I keep tellin you, your history is important. It give's you a glimpse into the greatness of the people you come from. Your ancestors ruled the world at one time."

"Colud people ruled the world grandma?"

"Thas right honey. Not the way white people rule the world. Those Africans never stole peoples land or they culture. Or went round just killin and takin. For thousands of years the center of civilization was Africa and it was a just and spiritually moral society. Why, your ancestors built the great pyramids and was the first to circumnavigate the world. You come from the first and the greatest civilization this world done ever known. So always remember who you are and where ya come from, honey, cause your history didn't just start on a slave ship. Between the history of African people in the beginning and the history of our coming here to America is a lot of missin pages. Pages of world history. Learn what dey say bout it then study what you find and expose da lie." Tentu slid a tall glass of lemonade in front of him and walked away, leaving her grandson to digest that portion of wisdom along with his meal. Tentu trudged to the corner of the room and rubbed her legs, barely reaching the spot on her knee that always pained her this late in the morning. "Lordy, lord, lord," she proclaimed. sometimes it could last till mid afternoon. Sometimes till sundown. When it endured that long she called it her plantation pain, lasting from first light of morning til last light of day.

"Um, um, um." At this stage, in the winter of life, she found completing chores to be a chore in itself. But in spite of the pain she never let it hinder her from house work or teaching. By mid afternoon Walter came in. A look of excitement on his face. Earlier that morning he'd gone to the barber shop in town. A place where news and stories were served with haircuts. Walter didn't need a haircut that day so gossip was his soul reason for going. He found his mother wiping off the table where she'd been snapping string beans for dinner. Tentu could see he was eager to share what he'd heard. He wiped his feet on the mat inside the door then removed his jacket. He started to toss it over the back of a chair but the look on Tentu's face filled him with the compunction to hang it on the rack. "Mom!" he started, cutting off the remonstrance his absent-mindedness rejoined. "Guess what I heard over in Spritton." She knew he had something juicy if not important to share. He always began with, "guess what" when he did. She also knew she wouldn't have a chance to respond to "guess what".

"There's a white woman in town askin about you. Wantin ta talk to you." Her eyebrows jackknifed in surprise across her forehead. "Askin ta talk ta me. What for? Where she from?" she asked, suspiciously. "She ain't from Spritton, Ma. And she don't sound like trouble. I didn't talk to her but Herman tole me about her. He said she seems like a nice lady. Right pleasant and respectful too."

"Umm uh," she moaned incredulously. "What does she want with me?"

"Here tell she wants to interview ya." He smiled.

"Interview me!?! Bout what I wonder?"

"I don't know Ma but I think we bout ta find out." Walter turned at the sound of a car back firing outside and rushed through the door out to the porch. Tentu followed languidly, wiping her hands on her apron. From the porch Tentu spotted the slender white woman emerging from an exhaust spewing taxi with a large valise under her arm.

On spotting the old black woman standing on the porch Pamela stopped and stared at her. Immediately, she noted the regal aura surrounding her subject. She couldn't explain it but she liked and respected the ex-slave at first sight. Tentu approached the stranger with a curious apprehension. Still she extended her hand hospitably and greeted the young white woman.

"Howdy Miss. My son told me you was comin but he couldn't tell me why. Has we any business?"

"Well. In a way I hope, Maam," Pamela answered carefully. "You may have heard about writers interviewing people who were slaves and writing their stories." Tentu nodded her head. "Um huh. I heard tell of such. Are you one of them writers?"

"Yes Maam. I am."

"You plannin on maybe writin my story."

"Yes Maam if your willing to tell it. I'm sure there's lots of people who'd love to read about it."

"Why ya suppose that is?"

"Well Mrs. Jubilee. Your one of the few remaining survivors of a time hardly talked about. A life style that's long been misunderstood. The trials and tribulations of the American Negro before and after slavery is an amazing story that must be told. Your story, I've heard, is more amazing then most. People would love to hear it."

"Ya mean white folks."

"Yes Maam, I guess I do," Pamela responded warily.

"Will colud folks be readin it too."

"Of course Mrs. Jubilee this is history, American history."

"Umm hum." Her eyes squinted suspiciously; however, she was impressed with the aspect. And impressed with her guest as well. This white woman, at least, did not display any superior airs. She noticed that right away. Tentu Jubilee detested arrogant white people. The kind who always supposed they knew what was best for you, even more so than you knew what was best for yourself. Whites who looked upon you with disguised malevolence. These people she knew. On sight. This woman had a comfortable air. So, she decided, in spite of her traditional feelings, to trust her. Tentu led the way into the house. Pamela was offered a seat and lemonade which she accepted graciously. Tentu took a seat across from her in the rocking chair. Walter sat in a sturdy wooden chair beside his mother. After a long moment, Tentu asked, "where do ya wanna start?"

"The people in Spritton tell me your special," Pamela began. "You seem to be respected by everyone in town, colored and white," she added. "But first tell me how did you get such an unusual name. What does it mean?" Tentu rocked in her chair. Her eyes took on a far away look like she was watching the events of her life unfold before her eyes. "My Mother gave me that name in honor of my father's faith," Tentu stated proudly. Pamela's head cocked to the side showing she didn't understand. Tentu smiled. "See my father knew a lot of things. He was a rebel, a fighter and a prophet. He believed that slavery was gonna end one day. Colud, back then, never had such dreams. But he did. Said it couldn't last anotha ten years. Said white folks couldn't hold ta such evil forever. Made my mother believe it too." Tentu rubbed at the spot on her knees before continuing. "My father disappeared before I was born. Some folks say he was killed by fugitive slave hunters. But his body ain't never been found. My mother loved that man's memory and in honor of his faith in the All Mighty bringin slavery to a end. She named me Jubilee." Tentu laughed. "Do you know the emancipation was signed, ten years afta I was born? My father knew it would be. So, in honor of that faith she named me Tentu. Ten years to jubilee."

"Ten years to emancipation." Pamela sounded a bit incredulous. "That is an incredible prophecy."

"Does that mean it couldn'ta happened?" Tentu challenged.

"But how could he have known?"

"Like I said he was a prophet. The proofs here. It is my name ain't it."

"Yes. It is." Pamela jotted in her notebook. "Your mother had great faith in your fathers ideals, huh?"

"My mother had faith in my father's faith. And his faith was in the peoples' will to fight and do for themselves. Them white folks fretted about my fathers strength and dedication so much so, after he disappeared they kept Momma on a ball and chain till the war. Afraid she'd find a way to conger him up. Or resurrect his faith and spirit for the other slaves to take in."

"His spirit?"

"Yeah. That thirst for freedom. Them white folks didn't want the kind of fight my father had resurrectin itself in them other Negroes."

"You said she was chained till the war. You mean the Civil War?"

"That's right. Good thing it come along else my poor mother woulda died on that ball and chain." Pamela cocked her head in surprise. "A ball and chain for ten years. Surely that's an exaggeration?"

"If that means it couldn't a happen let me make it clear. Ten years they kept my momma on a ball an chain when ever she wasn't in their sight. They was so scared my daddy was comin back. They stayed waitin and prepared for his return for years. It was that fear that created the legend among the slaves. They figured if the white folks was so afraid of a black man who was suppose to be dead, he must be some kinda supernatural being."

Pamela looked at her pad. "You said your father was killed?"

"I said he coulda been," she corrected. "He was cornered by a posse with a hundred guns. They all blasted him at the same time. Must been blown ta bits cause his body wadn't ever found. Them white folks wasn't sure he was dead or not. But they wasn't taking no chances. My father struck fear in the hearts of the slave holdin white folk." Now she rubbed

27

both knees. "My father was a man. Brave and strong. A prince, he was. Some say he was an African Angel. A messiah sent to inspire and teach us." Pamela stopped writing for a moment as the words of George Morgan came to mind. She looked up from her pad and continued the interview. "Where was he a slave before he ran away?"

"My daddy wadn't ever a slave," Tentu insisted. "Not even for a day. He was born free. He was proud and he was smart. Taught my mother many things. Bout her heritage, who she was. He taught her to be a proud African woman and Momma taught it to me. Did you know the African's built the pyramids?"

"I can't say that I've ever read that."

"Well they did you know." Suddenly there was a clamor from the adjoining room as Cleo and Pressman came running in followed by their mother. The children raced straight for their grandmother and she took one, proudly, in each arm. "See these babies heah." Tentu introduced Pamela to the rest of her family. "They know it. "My father told my mother that this is the future of our struggle." She nodded toward each child she held. He told Momma that in this generation will be the future of the black race here in America and it's our job to see they know it. Now I know you wanted to hear the story of slavery days," she digressed, "but I couldn't tell ya bout where we been without first tellin ya bout where we goin and why."

"Tell me more about your mother and father," Pamela requested. Tentu put the children down and stopped rocking in her chair. Her face, again took on that far away glazed look as she thought it over. "My mother," she began, "was a solid black woman. She wasn't thin and she wasn't fat. She was muscular for a woman. She had lost most a her family violently as it was in those days."

"Were they all killed?" Pamela broke in. "Nooo," answered Tentu dragging the word out. "Some were sold and the like. Some were killed. Few if any died of natural causes. See in our family runnin away was a proud tradition and

28

takin freedom was impotant and dangerous in those days. Still is I reckon."

Tentu looked up as she remembered. "My mother taught me to keep the family together no matter what and make sure each generation do better than the last." Her voice trailed off to a whisper then she cupped one hand over her mouth in a confidential manner. "And with the little nest egg she managed to pass on, it was a might easier to do." Pamela cocked her head in an incredulous fashion. "Your mother received wages? She was able to put some away?"

"Naw. But somehow my father saw to it that she had a little sumpthin ta settle on." Tentu raised her hand to interrupt the question she knew Pamela was about to ask. "I don't rightly know how he come by it. I suspect he had a way of making things happen that caint be explained."

"Your father sounds like an incredible man. Tell me more about him?"

"My father is just as much a mystery to me...Mind you! He wasn't no Johnny come lately who wooed my mother then moved on. No Maam. He loved my mother and she loved him...When she talked about him her eyes would shine like sunlight and her chest would swell with pride. He helped slaves get free."

"Oh! He was with the underground railroad?"

"I don't know bout that but he did his part to help some slaves get their freedom before he disappeared." Pamela was writing feverishly. "My mother said his spirit had gone home to Africa...Gone home and left us with the legacy. After that she settled down. Kept lookin for a way to flee but that old ball and chain held her back. Me too I speck. So she prepared the folk for Jubilee. When it come we got this land with the money my father left. White folks left us alone and my family built their homes. All around heah. They children gots land too. That's right," she added with proud a nod. "We is one proud family."

*****

29

The following day Pamela resumed her interview with Tentu. The old black matriarch sat erect in her rocker. "Do you know that most colored is shamed of they African roots. Uh ah. They act like Africa and colored ain't the same." Pamela continued writing on her pad. "What about your husband?" she asked delicately. "What was his name?

"My Big Earl." She giggled a lost giggle from years ago. A school girl giggle that embarrassed her when she couldn't stop. "I married him when I was just a kitten," she uttered finally gaining control. "Racism had made him an old man before his time. When I married him he had the blood of a spring chicken...You know what I mean," she winked. "But life in America wore him down." She rocked her chair again and went on with her narrative. "Big Earl was a railroad worker when we met. He could really drive in them spikes with those big black arms a his. We had three children. The two girls went north. One is a nurse the other a field agent for the Colored Improvement Association. My son Walter here with me tendin the farm and guidin the children...But you knows that." Tentu's eyes were glazed over with bygone days as she almost whispered. "Hard work took Big Earl before we could rock these old chairs together. Just like most hard workin black men." Slowly a high pitched hum of an old gospel song emerged from her pursed lips. By now Pamela was familiar with the old woman and her ways. She quietly gathered her notes and made her way to the porch where Walter and Hattie sat in the cool evening breeze. She looked back at the old woman through the screen door. She was rocking back and forth rhythmically to the tempo of her song. Her eyes gently closed. On her lips a gentle grin caressed the old hymn. 'Jesus keep me near the cross.'

Pamela was receiving a social education. For the first time in her young life, the other America with which she and her fellow white Americans were unaware. These were real people she thought. Not just flat characters or back drops to white folks leisure. They were people after all. The stories she'd heard and the understanding she'd obtained filled the void of negro existence with all the shades of life. Different from white life to be sure, but only through interpretation and experience. They lived and they loved. They had hopes and dreams and they desired and rejoiced. They wanted a better world for their children and honored their families. They were human, she thought with an analytical realization. The difference was the experience. An experience that strengthened them. A lesser people would have vanished under the weight of the racism they endured. Pamela, to her astonishment, had developed a respect for them, a people she had long ignored.

The next day she made her way to Tentu's residence with eager anticipation. Today she would finish her interview. Her assignment was coming to an end. Tentu gave her anecdote after anecdote and every event became a soliloquy to the future of black America. Pressman and Cleo sat nearby listening, never tiring of Tentu's orations. Especially Pressman. He carried to heart every word he heard his grandmother say and internalized their every meaning. From this, an obsession spawned within him. Nothing would ever be more important for him than the quest for and meaning of the past and it's role in the creation of the future of Black people. That desire in him made her beam with pride for she knew Pressman would be the purveyor of her prophecies.

CHAPTER 2

Year 1980

The desert holds many secrets. Beneath its silicon expanse lies the masticated weather beaten remains of life that had once been and the historic remnants of achievements that had since past. Here and there its granulated waves are distorted with the protruding shapes of animal carcasses and the diminutive foot prints of tiny desert inhabitants that mottle it's barren face. But most distinctive of all are the gigantic triangular frames of pyramids protruding from the desert floor like colossal antediluvian eruptions. They are mysterious entities with enigmatic origins. Seemingly impregnable facades intermittently dotting the desert face, encasing all the birthright of profundity. Their tombs are staunchly forbidden to relinquish the hidden secrets and treasures within. Knowledge and artifacts sit, for thousands of years suspended in time, jealously guarded in immured silence by contraptions designed against indomitable accessibility. and if the desert and it's pyramids are the highest form of the enigmatic, then they find themselves in contention for all their majesty on earth. For they were, after all, built in place by the most pertinacious and curious beings of all...man.

In previous centuries Europeans and Arabs had invaded the deserts of Africa, dislodging the fruits of ancient African civilization. They excavated it's tombs and uncovered it's sarcophagi. Virtually confiscating much of the hidden inestimable antiquities and sacred hereditary treasures of African people with impunity. Those descendants of the constructors of these wonders viewed the European and Arab pilferage a violation but could only sit by helpless in their desecration as they themselves were scattered and dislodged from the land. So there the legacy remained. An African appendage withheld from the sons of its builders...until now, thought an elder Pressman Jubilee as he stood upon the surface of the Sudanese desert admiring the archeological virgin before him. A wonderful desert enigma...unmolested, unplundered and as yet unexploited for thousands of years. African academics as well as Black American scientist had descended upon the site, once it's discovery was made a year and some months ago, collaborating with each other in the spirit. Academically and financially exercising their putative birthright. Exploring and excavating this rediscovered heirloom.

One hundred and fifty miles outside of Khartoum the first joint archaeological effort took place. 1980, heralded to become etched into the minds of every African and African-American student of history and science as the year of their people's self actualization when Africans took possession of their own heritage.

Amidst the archeological activity Professor Pressman Jubilee continued to muse over those thoughts as he pensively surveyed the scene around the site where he stood...with pride. His felicitous expression revealed the fondness he felt for the work he and his colleagues were doing. In and around the breached pyramid, their glistening, black sweating backs rippled with muscles as they toiled with the strenuous labor of excavation. Each man's tireless drudgery went on day after day immersed in his dedication of Afro centric purpose and ideals.

*****

A driver approached the site. From his purview the converging scene of the excavation ahead played across his windshield like a cinematic movie. Overhead a gigantic sun, hovered above the staged line of miniature workmen and equipment dwarfing the encampment lying just over the dunes. At center stage laid the star, the subject, the pyramid. It's peak pointing upward toward the sky and it's overbearingly bright sun. Professor Jubilee saw the billowing evidence of the approaching vehicle in the distance. He nodded his head knowingly. The supply truck. The truck driver drove on, excavating a sandy trail of his own as he steered his truck over raised dunes, leaving swirling clouds of sand in his wake until the entire camp came fully into view. Pulling into a prepared area he stopped the truck, becoming a part of the archaeological scene himself. Professor Jubilee instructed one of his men to gather a team to unload the truck. While the truck was being unloaded other men shoveled away large portions of earth from around the site while others brushed away minuscule amounts of sand from the structures and artifacts slowly emerging from the earth. The activity was impressive. The desert sun blazed and black backs glistened as laborious sweat continued to roll. The work went on with intensity throughout the day until light began to fade from the sky. A shrill whistle sounded, inviting all to stop. A collective groan of relief rose from the work site. The grueling tasks of another day had come to an end. Men plodded down the slope toward camp. Dog tired. Exhausted beyond belief yet invigorated by dedication. They made their way with enough strength left for good -natured ribbing, laughing, and horse play as they trudged across the quarter mile stretch of sand between the excavation site and base camp.

Professor Jubilee removed his hat and beat the dust from his pants before entering the tent. His tent mate Professor Oohulu Kobolongo entered behind him. These two men supervised the supervisors and directed the cataloguing of the artifacts. They were the directors of the expedition.

"Ahh what a gloriously prosperous day eh my brother?" remarked Professor Kobolongo from his side of the tent. He spoke while removing his boots, alternating grunts between statements. "I think I will skip dinner," he groaned and fell back on his cot. A miniature dust storm erupted from his clothes.

"You're going to need sustenance Brother Professor," Pressman suggested. "My stomach agrees with you Pressman. But my poor bones. They don't give you a dam," Ohoolu quipped in a crisp Nigerian accent.

"Well mine gives a dam. So, unless you change your mind about eating, my brother. I'll see you when I get back."...He turned and shouted, "Peace" as an after thought then raised a clenched fist. "Yes Brother," Ohoolu Kobolongo grunted then rolled over. "Ojumbo."

The main encampment was a configuration of tents in rows. One row of four tents laid between two rows of ten. In these four tents the artifacts and equipment were stored. The men lived in the outer rows of ten. Each tent housed four men, making it a workforce of 80. Perpendicular to the first row of ten stood an additional row of five that housed two men each. These were the Professors and supervisors. The largest tent in the camp was the mess tent and beyond it was the largest of living quarters where a service crew of 15 lived. They fed and supplied the workforce.

Compared to some European expeditions this was a small operation. But what they lacked in size they more than compensated for in conviction. Every African and African-American here believed wholeheartedly in what brought them together. And that state of mind was the usual topic of discussion at dinner. Professor Jubilee inferred it served as a source of inspiration. For so long the antiquated treasures of Africa were unearthed and catalogued by European archeologist. Not just to understand the people and the ancient world they inhabited but to plunder and confiscate their wealth. It was to this end that the American Association of African-American Scientists collaborated with the Sudanese and Nigerian governments to put this excursion together. Through a liaison between Howard University in America and the University of Nigeria in Africa, research in the pyramidal rings of the Sudan began.

"When the British marauder Howard Carter uncovered the tomb of Tutankhamen in 1922," Professor Jubilee was saying. "He and fellow archaeologist violated the sacred antiquities that rightfully belonged to Egypt. Not the contemporary Arab Egyptians but the not so often seen descendants of Nubia whose ancestors built these majestic structures. They were the indigenous people of the land. For centuries King Tut had rested intact, undisturbed and unmolested until it was so called 'discovered' by these white men."

"That's right!" agreed Al Bendee with an enthusiastic pound on the table.

"Studied and discovered," Jubilee echoed his own emphasis with sarcasm.

"The same way America was discovered and civilized. Why is it when Europeans discover, cultivate and bring their civilization, some enduring culture is destroyed. They were just excursions in pillaging, plundering and exploitation. Obtrusive and blatant looting." That's how he saw it. To him it was the true purpose of those expeditions. "Was it for the benefit of man or for one certain kind of man," he espoused. "You only need to observe who now controls the abundant knowledge and treasures found. Strangely enough it's not the inherent people." He stabbed the handle of his spoon into the table. "They're even arrogant enough to assume the builders heritage. They will have you believe that Charlton Heston and Edward G. Robinson built the pyramids. Not the ancient black Kemetans, misnomered Egyptians but some fake Hollywood images of white superiority." Smiles broke out along the mess table though Professor Jubilee was serious and they knew it. He shook his head with disgust amid the overtones of affirmations. This irony of racism was always at the core of his disgruntled passion. "Every bit of resource was stolen from mother Africa to enrich the lives of the European. Rubber, diamonds, gold, sasso, culture, knowledge and humanity itself. Taken for the benefit of the white man on both hemispheres. They raped and pillaged then left Africa baron and depleted of it's wealth. It's cultures destroyed. The desecration of the Valley of the Kings yielded nothing for the descendants of the people who built it. It only benefited the English. Not the Africans whose artifacts lie in the basement of the British museum to this very day. Where it's knowledge and African legacy is hidden from the world."

Al Bendee added his speculation. "What would the British reaction be if a group of Nigerians went to England and dug up the English moors looking for the Celtic legends."

"Yes, yes!" applauded some of the men. "Tell it brother!" Some clapped!

"Or if some Africans went there and dismantled the Tower of London and carted it off."

"Can you imagine if the Ghanians exhumed Robert E. Lee and took his battlegreys and saber on tour for an exhibition." Laughter and a fulminating...NO! greeted the statement. "Yet," added Professor Jubilee. "I see no difference." Neither did the American Association of African-American Scientists. When word of the unexplored pyramids first came to the worlds attention, universities and scientific institutions around the world immediately sought exploration rights to dig in the spot. In response the A.A.A.A. opened its membership to scientist outside of the United States to attract scientist of African descent around the world. With its ethnic advantage a working partnership with the Sudanese government was fostered and it was decided that the A.A.A.A., or Quad A, and participating African nations would share whatever antiquities were found in the coming expedition. The treasures, the knowledge and all things recovered would be exhibited to the world, this time, by way of African distribution. For Pressman Jubilee, the spirit of cooperation between the African nations and its descendants was a great victory surpassed only by the results of the mission itself. Howard University, the University of Nigeria and the government of the Sudan under the auspice of the A.A.A.A. created a unique first-time collaboration. They were from many parts of the African world. All descendants of the great African empires, digging, analyzing and researching there own history. Ethiopian, Zambian, Angolan, Nigerian, Sudanese, Ghanian. All who believed. From the brothers who carted the dirt to the brothers examining and cataloguing the fines. Everyone gave their all with total dedication. They alone had absolute dominion over the antiquated voices of their ancestors buried in the desert and they alone would tell their story. Professor Jubilee summed it all up as he ate. "No one can conduct a sincere study of Africa but...the African".

*****

The sky was dark by the time Professor Jubilee returned to his tent. The mixture of hard work and filling food played heavily upon his eyelids. He groaned satisfaction and rubbed his satiated gut as he walked. All he thought of was his cot. Then he paused as he also thought...of the possibility of...his nightly aberration.

*****

A chill in the air mixed with a hastily approaching night. Several large fires crackled and popped along the center rows of canvas tents adding light and warmth to their fronts. A ring of heavy stones contained the flames and lent added protection against voracious sparks. Professor Jubilee took his time strolling back to his and Professor Kobolongo's tent. It was approximately 250 feet from the mess tent along the perpendicular row at the far end of camp. The sounds of camp life settling down filtered to him. The laughter, the singing, the posturing and debating all mixed with the cacophony of several different dialects. The mixture caused him a proud smile as he parted the folds of his tent entrance and entered. Professor Kobolongo's soft nasal snoring met him before the folds returned to their pre-obstructed position. Kobolongo was right. He was more tired than he was hungry. Jubilee smiled at his sleeping partner and moved quietly as possible to his cot. It felt good to work those tight dusty boots off his feet. "Boy! We sho is sensitive bout our feet." He laughed at his own stereotyped muse and after a long groan and stretch, laid down on his back and closed his eyes...At the age of 50 Pressman Jubilee was a virile black man. Even though his position was supervisory, more cognizant then physical, there was still aches and pains in the joints that savored an evenings peaceful sleep. But peaceful it was not to be.

*****

Night in the Sudanese desert has a chill as pronounced as the days are arid. Sound here would be virtually nonexistent were it not for the stirrings of man. Distinct is the din of his work and his rest and the sounds of his protection. But like many vast and seldom reconnoitered expanses in the world, many sights and sounds are yet to be explained or experienced. This desert holds such an undiscovered sensation, espoused the idle musings of Professor Jubilee as he lay with his hands clasped behind his head, trying to relax. He turned languidly toward his tent mate snoring lightly on his cot. "I don't get it," Pressman complained to himself. "No one else has heard it except me. How is it possible?" He was unaware that he was whispering aloud to himself. Still Ohoolu Kobolongo continued to sleep. "Even Ohoolu! He hasn't heard a thing. This is strange..."

The first time he'd heard it, that low and constant hum, he thought he'd simply imagined it. It was like vibration. So low in fact that at times he was not sure if he was truly hearing something tangent or not. He concentrated on it. He wanted to make sure it wasn't the internal physiologic sounds of his own body. The autonomic system in his own ears, that is sometimes audible in outer silence as Kobolongo explained it when he told him about it. But could it be that simple? Though it was barely audible it was a true sound.

For the past several nights, around the midnight hour when camp sounds faded out, a variable Jubilee thought significant, he'd pick up the strangest resonance. Not so strange in it's description but strange in it's origin. One that could not be pinpointed nor readily identified. It always came about this hour and vanished by dawn, he remembered. It seemed he'd been contemplating these thoughts for hours though it was actually several minutes, when the sound he'd been anticipating finally came to him. It's now familiar low vibrating hum was again, almost indistinguishable from the physiological noise in his own ears. He listened for a long moment to be sure.

In the semidarkness he stared up at the tent ceiling where the upper folds conjunct, nodding a slow affirmation. He'd heard the sound. It was mysterious and unexplainable. Not a mechanical sound, but a sound like pulsating energy. He sat up abruptly and swung his feet on the floor then sat still to listen. Slowly he reached down for his boots. One by one he put them on as though the slightest movement would interrupt his concentration. The sound had taken on a provocative existence for him. An irresistible entity. An elusive siren. He strained his ears toward the tent opening as though it's direction would reveal itself to him.

"You need sleep Pressman. Not a midnight promenade." Pressman hadn't realized he'd awakened his colleague. But there was no irritation in Kobolongo's rich Nigerian voice. "I'm sorry I disturbed you Brother Ohoolu," he whispered apologetically. "It's that sound again, Man! I'm baffled. It comes on like clock work and goes on through the night. But no one else has reported hearing it except for me."

Ohoolu sat up on his cot. "This is the third night my brother. You're really bothered by this thing aren't you?" He strained to hear his colleagues sound by cupping his hand to his ear. He shook his head. "I still haven't heard this aberration of yours. Tell me about it," he said quickly.

"Tell you about it?"

"Yes Brother. Tell me. Do you know where it's coming from?

Pressman looked at Ohoolu attentively for the first time. "No.. no. I don't. But I hope to find out tonight. In fact that's where I'm going right now. I'm going to try and find it," he declared. "The first night I heard it. I spent the time sitting up listening to it. I wasn't sure if it was just my imagination. You know?" His boot laces finished he moved towards the tent opening and peeped out through the folds.

"As a scientist I can understand your interest," offered Ohoolu. Pressman Jubilee pulled his head back in and continued to speak. "The second night I went out after listening for a while and walked several yards toward the pyramid."

"You think it comes from there?" added Ohoolu. He was amazed he'd slept through his colleagues midnight excursions. He thought himself a light sleeper.

"Right. It seemed to come from that way. But before I reached the pyramid." Snap! He made the sound with his fingers. "The dam sound vanished." "What!" Kobolongo reared in surprise. "It just stopped. Just like that. Gone," Pressman went on clearly irritated. "The sun had just begun to rise and as it did the sound faded away." He cocked his head pensively. "I'm sure there's a connection."

"Perhaps the sun had an affect on the frequency," offered Ohoolu.

"Yes, perhaps." Pressman agreed. He was piqued by Kobolongo's apparent interest.

"At any rate tonight I'm going to try again. I've got a few hours before sunrise and if there is a connection between the dark of night, sunrise and the frequency of the sound I'm going to beat that connection to the pyramid." He started through the folds of the opening then stopped. "But!" he rubbed his chin between two fingers. "It doesn't explain why you can't hear it." He pointed to Ohoolu. Kobolongo thought for a second. He adjusted himself on his cot as an idea came to him. Using his finger as a pointer he offered a theory. "Pressman have you ever heard of cases," he explained, "where individuals whose range of hearing are so acute that they are able to detect the slightest change in the tonal frequency in the Earth." He fashioned a sphere with his hands. "Their acute senses even enable them to predict the coming of an earthquake by sensing changes in audible oscillation. Some theorist attribute their power of prediction to sensory sensitivity rather than paranormal capabilities. Empirical studies reveal that they simply were more fine tuned to certain frequencies of sound." He watched his friend to see the effect of his words. "Perhaps my Brother, YOU!" he pointed, "like those people, are naturally intoned to the emanations coming from the sources that lie undiscovered there in the desert." Professor Jubilee digested his friend and colleagues theory then shook his head ambivalently. "You're telling me I'm about to predict an earthquake in the desert?" he chaffed. "No really Ohoolu I seem to recall some such thing. It's called William's Syndrome. You may be right. Well," he raised his arms. "Whatever it is I sure as hell want to find the source of my private ABERRATION," he emphasized the word and smiled, showing Ohoolu he remembered his earlier remark. "Ohoolu I intend to find the source of that sound tonight! There's several hours before sunrise and I'm ready to go on an investigative trek. Are you in?"

"My Brother," added Ohoolu Kobolongo. "We best stop wasting time and find the source of that sound." Professor Jubilee extended his hand with the palm up in appreciation. Professor Kobolongo enthusiastically slapped it in return.

Ohoolu got dressed and within minutes the two men were standing outside of their tent. The air was chilly. Cool enough to see ones breath and warrant a thick sweater. They both wore heavy woolen shirts. Jubilee shook off the chill then turned his head slowly from left to right, pursing his thick lips beneath his furrowed eyebrows. "There!" He pointed beyond the tents toward the pyramid looming in the distance. It towered above their position like a mountainous prodigy. It's cone shaped tip blotted out a triangular portion of the star studded sky. "That's the direction I took last night. There," he repeated. "Toward the pyramid."

"Anything else you can tell me about this sound, my brother?"

"No," Pressman answered thoughtfully, "but there is a slight difference in pitch I think." He scanned from left to right again, making certain of it's location. It seemed the sound was toying with him, teasing him as though it had a mind of its own. Being a scientist he knew it was his own efforts of concentration in league with the desert manipulating the sounds. Stay focused he told himself, leading the way into the desert. Professor Kobolongo followed close behind. To their rear, the camp was quiet. All signs indicated that at this hour they were the only ones awake. The fires dotted around the camp slowly flickered intermittently as their unattended flames continued bathing the tents in a ghostly dancing light. In the sky millions of twinkling stars blazed like neon in a heavenly metropolis. Beneath the scientists feet laid an undisturbed rugose sea of sand, stretching out toward the pyramid where the sky seemed to meet the desert. They walked ahead braking it's wrinkled pattern with cautious footsteps.

The pyramid of Adooduma stands 150 miles south of Khartoum along the Blue Nile. It was not as large as Khufu's pyramid in Giza but it was just as elaborately built. There was gold and jewels inside the ancient ruler's burial chamber but not as richly abound as Tutankumun's. It was; however much, much older than both and just as architecturally complex. Jubilee's team had managed to date its existence as far back as 4630 B.C. Hieroglyphs inside indicated Adooduma was an ancient ruler and member of the Nubian Dynasty. Portraits intricately drawn on the walls and on sleek stone slabs were unmistakably African in appearance. There was no way, Professor Jubilee exclaimed, that the community of European archaeologist could claim that the artistry and construction of this magnificent fine was a creation of some mysterious Mediterranean European people or aliens from outer space. No way could its African origin be denied...What a find!! he'd say hundreds of times. If only Grandma Tentu was alive today, he reflected sadly, she'd be so proud of it all. And so delighted with this demonstration of African cooperation. This was the first archaeological site totally excavated by people of African descent, funded by people of African descent while supervised totally by people of African descent for people of African descent. It's what Grandma Tentu had always dreamed, he thought, as he felt for the gold talisman around his neck given to him by his grandmother before she died.

Evidence of excavation lay eerily around the pyramids base in the form of neatly stacked equipment and supplies left over night. Lying there unused gave them an abandoned and ghostly appearance in the desert moonlight. Quiet and foreboding if not for their noble cause. Pressman and Ohoolu admired Adooduma's majestically constructed structure as evidence of the lost skills of antiquated black hands. The sight filled them with pride. For a moment they just stood there looking at it...basking in it. "What a wonderful unknown entity," Ohoolu remarked. But for now there was a more contemporary mystery at hand.

The entranceway was guarded by two locally provided armed security personnel from the Sudanese authorities. A long history of civil unrest in the Sudan had yielded to an uncommon compromise for the sake of African unity on the project. One guard represented the African-Arab Muslim community and the other came from the African Christian sect. "Evening sirs," greeted the Black Christian guard. "Evening Ohan," the Professors replied in unison. "Can we be of assistance sirs," offered the Muslim guard. Pressman elected not to ask them about the sound. Surely, he reasoned had they heard such an eerie sound they would have reported it. "It's okay Alif," assured Professor Jubilee. "We just want to check something out." There were no restrictions on access by any of the scientists. The guards were more cursory than a need for security. The sentinels waved them in. Professor Jubilee pulled the temporary door of heavy wood closed behind them.

"Pressman!" Ohoolu called. He held out his hand to halt Jubilee. "Pressman! I believe I can hear it. A low continuous oscillation," he described slowly. "A low toned hum?"

"Yes, yes Ohoolu. That's it. That is it," Professor Jubilee confirmed coltishly. "I can hear it," Ohoolu almost sang pointing down the long entranceway. Professor Jubilee retrieved two chemical wands from a box near the entrance and twisted the tops then handed one to Professor Kobolongo. A bright blue illumination emanated from their cylinder heads creating light to illuminate the hall for them to continue down the passageway. A pungent smell like an ancient mixture of honey and flowers greeted them in the hall. By now they were used to the sweet antiquated aroma that permeated the passageways and chambers. Jubilee found it interesting that this centuries old sepulcher maintained such an inoffensive odor. Once they reached the end of the hall Jubilee led the way left into a shorter passageway. Here the light fell upon a plywood sign that designated the area as the 'Ground level Chamber.' So called because below it was the burial chamber of Adooduma. Above it laid unexplored chambers. Adooduma had been removed and shipped, along with the gold and jewels, to the University of Nigeria when he was discovered. Representatives from Howard University and the University of Sudan would study there together. Howard University would wait patiently for their turn at housing artifacts and would always be welcomed to share in the findings of the other schools. Jubilee and Kobolongo were proud of the lack of jurisdictional jealousies between the principles. Encouraging signs of the future.

Hieroglyphic legends of Adooduma's life artistically adorned three of the walls. Here and there laid evidence of the work being done by the archaeologist and their teams. Just beyond where Jubilee and Kobolongo stood a large rectangular opening in the floor led down into Adooduma's sepulcher. Portable barricades lined three sides of the opening. Team members never had a reason to step pass the burial chamber access. Consequently, no particular attention was ever paid to that portion of the chamber wall. It was a bare smooth granite wall. Both men stood separated from it by the burial chamber access. It was practically hidden in the shadows. The only ground level chamber wall empty of hieroglyphs. It was here that the sound seem to be emanating from. Kobolongo looked to Jubilee. They nodded in agreement. They had found the source of the elusive resonant. That would have been cause enough for celebration, except that the wall was bare. Nothing was there to explain what they heard. Both men stepped around the barriers and approached the recessed wall, leading the way with their wands. The light reflecting off the large rectangular slabs revealed it completely. It's shiny granite surface absorbed the light evenly. Applying their hands to the wall they could feel vibrations. It had to be the source of the sound. The sound had to be the cause of the vibrations. It sounded mechanical. Perhaps some ancient device Professor Jubilee reasoned. He pressed his ear to the wall. Perhaps there was some hidden passageway behind it.

"There must be a room of some sort behind this wall," Kobolongo echoed his thoughts. From either side both men examined the brick wall with their fingertips, sweeping their hands in circular patterns then along the crease where the two walls met. They felt everywhere to find some clue to a way to gain entrance behind the wall but found nothing.

Ohoolu, on the left, was the first to discover a ray of hope. His finger tips fell into finger shaped grooves embedded in the crease along the seam. Three of his fingers went inside just up to his knuckles. He could just feel the ends of some kind of lever inside. "I found something Pressman!" The inner lever was there but wouldn't move. Professor Jubilee came to him. Ohoolu got a thought. "No Pressman," he waved him back with his free hand.

"Feel along the seam on your side," he instructed. Jubilee started at the top of the wall and ran his hand along the seam then downward. Midway..."I've got something!" he announced. He felt three fingered grooves on his side. "There's something inside. Like levers!"

"Right! Right Pressman." Kobolongo still held his fingers in place then relayed his plan. "On three we'll flick the levers together. One...two...three..." Flick! Simultaneously the levers gave way and the floor beneath them began to tremble. Instinctively Jubilee and Kobolongo jumped away from the wall. Above them there was a metallic click and a whirling noise like some mechanism starting up. A circular opening appeared dead center in the ceiling, inches away from the wall. They watched in awe as sand flowed from the opening like water. The entire walled structure trembled then lift itself free from the floor. Slowly it rose like some great granite panel until it disappeared completely inside the ceiling, leaving no evidence, no trace of the wall that had been there before. In it's place was a black foreboding expanse. The scientist approached cautiously, leading the way with their wands. It was an open space. A room in which their light crept into slowly, illuminating it's insides. The humming was louder now. The room was square, approximately 24 ft. by 24 ft. by Pressman's reckoning. In it's center was a large pedestal surrounded by a large ebony cage. The humming was definitely emanating from the pedestal. They were sure. But something else about it widened their eyes in surprise and delight. "Solid gold," breathed Kobolongo. "Solid gold," he repeated pacing in front of the cage. He attempted to grab hold of the cage then recoiled like a snake had bit him. The cage did not exist at all. He'd touched nothing in spite of it being there to see. It was just an image. A projection, some unexplained trick of light created by some ancient engineer. Pressman took his turn waving his hand back and forth through the aberration. He felt a strange tingle as his hands passed through the shadowy anomaly. "Did you feel a sensation?" asked Kobolongo.

"Yes!" He looked up at the ceiling and all four sides of the room but could see no clue to the source of the projection. "This is fantastic!" No matter how close they stood or from what angle they looked, it still appeared as though there were bars above, below and all around the pedestal. "How did they do this?"

"Why did they do this?" added Kobolongo.

"I don't know but at least we found the source of the sound."

"Yes. Only to find another mystery instead, my brother."

Then as if on cue the sound ceased just as eerily as it began. Only the enigmatic structure before them remained, as a riddle, in its place. "What time is it Ohoolu?"

"Not sunrise yet."

"That's strange...No matter." The discovery of this room and it's contents quickly overshadowed all thoughts and priorities. With his hands Professor Pressman Jubilee continued examining the pedestal. The alter, the legs. It was solid gold of three types. He could now feel the tinkling all over the upper portion of his body but it served as no deterrent. He went on about his investigation. The pedestal was yellow gold with a pink gold uraesus ornamented fret encircling a white gold dado. Atop the pedestal rested five uniformed rows of egg shaped objects. Six per row. Each lay nestled in its own fitted space atop the pedestal alter. Thirty in all. Each roughly the size of an ostrich egg. Pressman picked one up. It's surface was a fine black granular substance. He flipped it from one hand to the other judging its weight. Approximately 2 1/2 pounds he thought. "What do you make of these Ohoolu?" He held one up to Professor Koblongo. There was a strange vibration to the touch. Kobolongo took it and Professor Jubilee retrieved another. Kobolongo examined his. Smelling it, rubbing it and then holding it to his ear. "It has a grainy feel," he remarked of its texture. "And it feels quite dense."

"Why such an elaborate barrier?" Jubilee wondered aloud, conducting his own informal examination. "And why such an exquisite pedestal for...for black crusted rocks," he added for lack of a better term. "Perhaps encrusted jewels," suggested Kobolongo still turning it around in his hand.

Jubilee looked around the alter again. "There's nothing here to shed light on there purpose. Except for the snake patterned fret on the pedestal" he inferred. An Egyptian uraesus on an alter here in a Sudanese pyramid implied a connection to a long held belief. He, Kobolongo and others had long speculated that Egypt may have been settled by Nubian expatriates and were not just a separate African people. "There's no hieroglyphs on this thing," he stated disappointedly. "No symbols other than these golden snakes. Once we get a team on it. We'll know more."

"What else do we have here?" Professor Kobolongo held the oval object as if speaking to it. "Nothing like this has ever been found in Egypt. Especially these projected bars." Pressman was still wondering about the source of the projection. "At least that we know of."

"Perhaps," replied Ohoolu rapping the object gently on the sharp edge of the pedestal like an egg. Jubilee watched. "You suppose there's something inside? A casing of some kind?" As he spoke a small piece of the object's surface fell away. Ohoolu knelt to retrieve it and rubbed it between his fingers. It crumbled away easily. Indeed! It was a granular substance. Fine and sandy. "What do you know about that," he exclaimed as he stood. Beneath the chipped away surface of the object a faint emission of light struggled to shine through. Professor Jubilee proceeded to scratch the surface of the object he held. It was too tough to make a brake with his finger. He tapped it on the edge of the pedestal. A large chunk of black granular surface fell away. With a larger area exposed it was plain to see the crystal beneath the crusty covering. A throbbing effulgence of light radiated from the exposed portion of crystal. The sudden brilliance of light startled both scientist. The glow engulfed Pressman's hand as it strained against the granular edge of its encasement as though bursting to get free. He noticed the vitality of the outer crust was rapidly changing before his eyes. The same was beginning to happen to Kobolongo's crystal. In seconds the animated black covering turned ashen and brittle making it easy to scrape the remainder of it away with their fingers.

Each man now held a magnificent bare crystal, oddly geometric with many smooth sided segments. In an instant the two crystals burst into illuminant blue and white radiant sparkles turning the men into shadowy negative silhouetted images. Its brightness glimmered throughout the entire room. The effect lasted for all of a few seconds before imploding and drawing itself back into the crystals. "What the!?!" Both men circled the area with their eyes. "Pressman. What damness was that."

"Ohoolu. I have no idea." They still held their crystals.. in awe.

"Perimorphic." explained Pressman. "One crystal encasing another."

"One inert crystal covering an active crystal inside," corrected Ohoolu.

"Interesting. But Why?"

"Seems exposing the inner crystal or separating the energy of the inner crystal from it's outer crystal completely brakes down the molecular structure of the outer case."

"It hastens the release of inner energy. But again. Why? What do you suppose its purpose is."

"Or was...Ohoolu...listen!" The low fine pitched hum that first brought them here began to emanate from the crystals. Ohoolu raised his to his ear and listened. "I hear it. Faint but distinct." He then quickly brought it down from his head and held it out before him. One by one each segmented side of the crystal released a laser like light of energy, a pin light beam of energy seeking out its own direction. The same thing was happening to the crystal Pressman held. Then the beams of both crystals folded over on themselves creating one silver dollar sized laser like beam between them. The two beams then moved across the ceiling like search lights seeking each other out until...they connected. It took seconds to transpire, catching the men by surprise...However...It was not the finale.

*****

Kobolongo and Jubilee each felt the pull. A tugging force from the crystals in their hands. The sensation was easily traced to the beams as they cemented their connection in a magnetic grip. Their cohesive intersection came together in a silent snap, like a door slamming shut. With a silent bang the crystals drew into each other along the laser beam strip pulling Jubilee and Kobolongo violently into each other, mating the two crystals and erupting in a splash of sparkling energy. For an indecipherable moment both men experienced an extraordinary feeling of retrorse. An alien sense of orbiting oneself, engulfed in an incessant corrugated haze. A dreaminess, a displayed dreaminess. All in a consciously compiled fraction of a second. Slowly both men began to feel an encroaching normalcy. They seemed unsure if something had actually happened, or perhaps was about to happen. One thing for sure, there was a definitive difference. A change. And one look around them made it all outrageously clear. They'd found themselves outside... Inexplicably...outside...In the desert. It was dark and the air was cool. Professor Jubilee looked incredulously into the sky and back at the sand. Professor Kobolongo looked across the open desert then at his colleague. Both men felt suddenly disoriented. Ohoolu looked down at the crystal he still held in both his hands. The magnetic connection between his crystal and the one Pressman held was still in tact. They were still standing a few feet apart still locked by an invisible force along the beam. So strong, so concrete it exuded a sense of visual existence. Ohoolu moved his crystal to the right to maybe brake the beam. It worked. Pressman, three feet away, felt the pull. The broken connection of light was like a snap causing him to lose his grip. The crystal flew from his hand like it was tied to the end of a retracting rubber band knocking Ohoolu to the ground. Both crystals laid in the sand for an instant then disappeared in a blazing display of achromatic light.

Ohoolu sat in the cool desert sand completely awed by the event. Less than a minute ago he and Pressman were exploring an undiscovered section of Adooduma's tomb and now they were sitting in the desert. He looked behind him. In the distance the camps tents flickered in the silhouette of dying camp fires. "We are at least half way between camp and the site," he said turning back to Jubilee...He was gone. Professor Kobolongo spun around in a complete circle. He spun again in the other direction. Then again making a full circle in the sand. Professor Jubilee had vanished. Ohoolu stood up and intuitively started toward the pyramid. The sand made it difficult to run and by the time he reached the pyramid he was panting for breath. Ohan and Alif rushed from their station to his aid. "Are you not well sir?"

"I'm fine Ohan," Kobolongo gasped. "Has Professor Jubilee been back this way. I have lost him since we were here last." He gulped for air every few words. Ohan and Alif looked at each other in confusion. "Sir?" Ohan asked dubiously. "Look my brother!" Ohoolu said grabbing the sentry by his shoulder. "I can not explain how we have come to be out here in the desert but Professor Jubilee..."

"Brother Professor," Ohan interjected, "I am not sure I understand. How you have come to be where sir?" The two sentries again exchanged dubious looks. "You mean to say that you do not remember the Professor and I coming here tonight?" he stated roughly.

"Brother Professor. We have just now assumed the duty for tonight," explained Alif. "We have not yet seen anyone." Professor Ohoolu Kobolongo was taken more than aghast. He was on the verge of panic. For a moment he stood silently, unsure of what to do next. Finally he pushed past the guards and rushed through the heavy temporary doors. Ohan and Alif followed. Kobolongo started to beg them off but decided to wave them along. Inside the entrance Ohoolu recognized the low hum. He reached into the box near the entrance for a chemical wand. He was surprise to see the box full again. There was no sign of the two he and Jubilee extracted earlier. He made his way down the passageway with Ohan and Alif in tow. Each man carried a light source. Once again in the ground level chamber Kobolongo stopped cold. The chamber was just as he and Jubilee had found it when they first entered earlier. Barriers in place, granite wall down and in place. No sand, no pedestal and no Professor Jubilee. Kobolongo tossed the barriers to the side and rushed to the granite wall. "Ohan," he commanded. "Get over there, my brother." He pointed to the opposite side of the wall then ran his fingers down the crease in the wall on his side. "Do as I do," he instructed Ohan. "Tell me when you have felt the little holes on your side." The urgency in his voice spurred Ohan on without question. He aped Kobolongo's movements along the crease in the wall on his side. "I feel it sir! I feel

52

it!" Kobolongo instructed him on gaining entrance to the room behind the wall. Ohan did as he was told. "One...two.. three." Flip!! A metallic click and whirling noise caused them both to leap away from the ascending granite panel. Alif leered behind them in astonishment as the wall disappeared into the ceiling. He and Ohan "OOO'ed" and "Ahhh'ed" in admiration once the lights revealed the room and the gold pedestal inside.

Professor Kobolongo waved them back as he entered. There was no evidence of any prior examination. The perimorphic crystals, all 30, lay in a neat pristine row, just as they were found earlier. "I do not understand. I just do..." He was interrupted by a blaring sound like an electronic announcement. It popped and crackled enough to back Kobolongo out of the room. A flash of light followed causing all three men to cover there eyes. In an instant Professor Jubilee appeared. Thrown violently against a wall. He slid down to the floor and shook his head. "Ohoolu. We were just in the desert," he stammered. "Now we're back in the chamber? I..." He stumbled dizzily as he tried to stand. Ohoolu went to his aid. "I'm all right brother." He looked at the crystals and pointed at their pristine an undisturbed condition.

"The crystals Ohoolu! They're back on the pedestal. What happened?"

"That is right Pressman. And the light wands we used were back in their box. And we did not return together Pressman."

"What do you mean Ohoolu?"

"It is hard to explain my brother. Tell me what you remember." Pressman leaned against the wall and tried to visually recall the past few minutes in his mind's eye. "We somehow released energy from the crystals. The next thing I knew we were in the desert. Than I dropped mine or something pulled it from my hands and the next thing we were here. Including them." He pointed to Ohan and Alif in disbelief. "How in the hell did they get here." Ohan and Alif looked to each other in utter confusion.

"That is what I am saying Pressman," Ohoolu leaned beside him trying to put the event together logically. "When you dropped your crystal I remained in the desert." Professor Jubilee listened intently as his friend Professor Kobolongo recounted the rest of the events to him. When he finished they all stood, quietly reflecting over the incident they'd just heard. Jubilee spoke next. "This thing wasn't merely a quantum leap in the desert. It seems we've also lost several minutes in our lives as well. How do you account for the discrepancy in time Ohoolu?"

"I do not know Pressman but it will take a major effort to find out."

"This is an incredible anomaly Ohoolu. Adooduma most assuredly was a great man. Do you suppose our illustrious ancestor would want us to make the effort to understand the power of this find and put it to our use?"

"I'd say his spirit cries out for recognition Pressman. When do we get started."

"We'll get a separate team from Quad A to handle this," Professor Jubilee decided. "Al Bendee can take over the archeological dig."

"Yes," agreed Kobolongo, "he is a good brother for the job. All our attention will be on these crystals." Both Jubilee and Kobolongo agreed, whatever these Sudanese crystals were and whatever they would become, it would take their full commitment. Kobolongo turned to Ohan and Alif. "Brothers cordon off this area. No...The entire chamber. And not a partial procedure but the 'works' as the Americans say."

"Pressman. Our ancestors have left an incredible gift. I'm sure they're pleased that we're the ones who found it."

"Yes Ohoolu."

Kobolongo rubbed his hand along the edge of the pedestal. "A gift from our ancestors." "I wonder what it will become?" he mused. "I wonder what indeed?"

"One thing it won't become," Jubilee stated, pulling on the gold talisman around his neck, "an African artifact hidden away in the British Museum.

54

CHAPTER 3

Year 2000

Calvin Adams planned this trip for two years. Finally he was here in all his six foot, two inch regal black glory. His smooth shining dark ebony skin, muscular build and handsome face drew lots of looks from the flower and reed baring sisters standing in position around the ceremonial garden. Several of the women whispered among themselves about his good looks. A few even giggled. It was the elder sister, awaiting to escort the elder greot who remarked how baby faced he'd be without the thick mustache that bordered his upper lip. It was true. The thick bush above his lip gave him a serious look and maturity, adding to the intensity of his piercing black eyes. It had been said that his stare possessed the power to hold one in suspension like prey. Behind those eyes lived a lot of experience. Both good and bad. Not unusual in itself except for the unreadable mask of hidden rage.

It took lots of conscious effort for Calvin to control that rage. If left unguarded or elicited in some way it could be unfortunate for that elicitor. His anger, at times could be deadly.

Many black men were saddled with the same rage. Day to day simmering just below the surface of the obvious. A rage born out of injustice, discrimination and racism. A frustration worthy of it's significance. But instead of killing each other and destroying their own communities their rage was channeled into education, success, organizing and reaching back to their brothers and sisters left behind. These brothers maintain an air of afro centricity held in check by rage. That was the pay off. An afro centric air of success in the white man's world without a shred of assimilation. Calvin Adams was that kind of black man. A black success without a loss of black self. As a mission specialist for the National Aeronautics & Space Administration he was, in fact, one of the best aeronautical engineers in the business. He knew it and his superiors knew it. Yet those superiors found something troubling about this young black man. Something they called, in hushed company, an extreme sense of afro centricity. But none of that worried Calvin now. Not here. Because at this very festive occasion nothing imaginable could interrupt the elation at hand.

Calvin was very proud of his blackness and the blackness of his people. He saw it as a characteristic born of inherent ability to overcome adversity. A variable of his heritage. And here in the Kenyan village of Male he'd come full circle. The Greot of the Kikuyu tribe was now about to bestow upon Calvin the culmination of his growth to full circle. An African surname. A symbol of his lost found status he'd come to take very seriously. When he returns state side he'd have it legally changed.

Elder Mapingo slowly approached him flanked by two regally dressed matrons. They were the eldest of the ceremonial females who represented his maternal connection to the strength of the greot. All three were dressed in bou bou's of bright royal colors. Multi shades of lavender and blue. Each woman carried an armful of ekundu. Pedals fell gently to the ground in their wake. "Habari Gani yamaa na rafiki," Elder Mapingo greeted. He stood regally before Calvin, who bowed at his waist to the elder than lowered himself in deference onto one knee. An hypnotic melody slowly lifted it's timbre from the circle of women lined on either side of the party. A crescendo of melodic sopranos and altos filled the air to a beautiful orchestration of call and answer.

"Amani, amani. Upendo na umoja"

"Amani, amani. Upendo na umoja." Melodies filled the floral valley and drums pushed men and women to rhythmic jactation. Every living soul in the valley, for miles must be hearing this, thought Calvin. There's no doubt that music was invented here. The urge to bob his head to the beat was strong but he fought it. It was perfect, it was rhythmic and it was infectious. Elder Mapingo called the party to attention. "Jamaa kuinuka," he called, lifting both his arms in the air. "Brother Calvin Adams has come home. We call him Calvin Adams only for the sake of separating him from others. But our culture dictates that what a man is called is done so for the sake of identifying him. Describing him in his place of others. A man's name tells us who he is in the scheme of God's plan and allies him with the bloodline of his ancestors who's place in God's scheme he continues. A man's name is not arbitrary. It serves a high purpose. But our brother has been removed from his place in God's scheme. He has been misplaced, like so many of our children. His only link to God's plan is what he knows of the Motherland. And with that one piece of knowledge, our brother has taken upon a quest to find his way home. Somewhere here in Mother Africa dwells the spirit of his ancestors so it is with the name that I anoint him with this day that he binds the ties that link him with the spirit of his family." The long ornate ostrich feather the elder carried brushed upon each of Calvin's shoulders. "Rise Brother Kuendela Nguvu. We castigate the name that aligns you with your captors and free you with the name that forever aligns you with your ancestors."

"Kuendela Nguvu. You are reborn," announced the elder matrons together in parlando. Kuendela Nguvu rose to his feet and the crowd broke out in gleeful pandemonium. The valley was again filled with war cries and yelps. It was done.

He turned around in a circle nodding, smiling and waving at the crowd. He would no longer carry the name of those who raped his people, stole his culture and dammed his soul. Kuendela had finally emerged to live in creation as himself. A lost found native of Mother Alkebu-lan.

"Kuendela," Elder Mapingo's voice boomed in a thunderous baritone bringing his sermon to an end. "Bariki" Calvin Adams now Kuendela Nguvu beamed with pride. Unbelievably in a span of a few short seconds he felt reborn. He was actually a new man. The people around him continued singing in benediction. Louder, louder. They sang, accelerating the tempo. Dancing in a juba like celebration jig as they sang.

"Bla da bla da. Bla da bla da
English man gets an english name
German man gets a german name
Chinese man gets a chinese name
but African man his name he don't know
no ancestor, culture has he no home
He searching hard and fast to be free, Come back to thee and find who you be eeee
communication organize, Bla da bla da.

education organized, Bla da bla da..." For the newly born Kuendela Nguvu the christening ceremony was off the hook. The music, the food, the dancing, the brotherhood, the family. Everyone enjoyed themselves...Everyone except Barbara Caulden. Calvin now Kuendela's fiancee. On the exterior she appeared to be having a good time. Inside, however she was a little bit disappointed. Kuendela could see it when he handed her a hollowed out coconut shell filled with tropical nectar. A straw and bumper shoot jutted out from it's inside. She had to move the tiny umbrella to the side before she could take a sip. At least she enjoyed the cool drink. She wondered idly how they were able to keep it so cool with no obvious signs of refrigeration out here. "Your lips are smiling but your eyes don't show it baby," he cooed sitting down beside her. Her hair, her clothes, her make up everything about her was immaculate. Physically she'd make a husband proud and envied. But Calvin long sensed a problem between them. One Kuendela knew would have to be dealt with or dealt out.

"Why Calvin? Why all this afro centric name stuff. Anyone can look at you and see you're of African descent."

"I know that baby. But this is a special moment for me. Something I always wanted. You know that Barbara."

"Yes, I know. But I was hoping it was just one of those things you'd grow out of." The slight grin he had became even slighter as she went on.

"Calvin you're a successful astronaut." It was something he'd heard before. "You have a find career at NASA. Or at least you can have one," she added facetiously. "As big and as black as you are no one can help but know your a black man. This Calvin X thing ain't gonna go to well with your NASA superiors."

"First of all Barbara it's not Calvin X. It's Kuendela Nguvu . Secondly you're right I am a successful astronaut. A successful black astronaut in fact, and NASA dam well knows it. They can't afford the heat from discriminating against me because I changed my name but I ain't even playin that game. I could care less what they think about my name change. If my culture..."

"Your culture," she interrupted, "this ain't your culture Shaka Zulu. This is something from the 60's you can't let go of. And letting it go is what you need to do. You're an American Calvin. That's your culture" Her head swiveled on her neck the way only a black woman's neck could manage it.

"NASA don't want the heat this thing is gonna cause. Or this kind of culture in it's ranks and if you legally change your name they ain't gonna want you either." She raised her hands to hold off his comment. "Just listen. Cause to them you'll be aligned with...Farakan or somebody. They'll..." It was his turn to cut her off. "That wouldn't be an insult to me, Barbara. I'd be aligned to fine company. I've done my bit for NASA. I've had a good career. I've been everywhere and done everything. After the end of my tour I'm out anyway. Like I said. I could give a dam what they think. I'm going back to work with Professor Jubilee. Yes. He's offered me a position in the Quad A's. In two years I'll be back with his and Kobolongo's team." This decision was a surprise for her. "Kobolongo...My God another one. What about our plans to

59

get married. And your career. You can easily rise in the administration. You know that. You'd be a star."

"We can still get married. As far as me rising in NASA. Baby you haven't been listening...Then I suppose you never have."

"That's not fair..."

"No baby. Where my career is concerned it's true. You've got your sights set on being an astronauts wife. Rubbing elbows with the white social registry and when that's threatened you don't hear..." Barbara rose to her feet. A little too quickly. Too capriciously. "Okay. So what's wrong with wanting the best in life. Yes. I want to be an astronauts wife. Your astronaut wife." Her hands rested on her hips and a costive smirk emerged on her face

as she recalled his last remark. "White registry?" she said aloud. "Well if you want to prove you've made it. If you want to elevate your status. What better means are there. You show me a better indicator."

"That means alot to you doesn't it Barbara," he said calmly. His patient silence cooled her temper as she sat beside him again. "Yes Calvin." She picked up his hand. It was cold and emotionless. "Being accepted in the white man's world, mingling on your own terms," she was careful to add, "is the best indicator that you've made it." Her voice was soft and she believed her point strong. She looked at him awaiting a response. "Barbara," he strained to speak. "The sign that you've made it is when you can go back to your people and give them a piece of your success and give em a road map to their own success."

"Go back!!" she roared in disbelief."

"Okay! Mister Scientist, you tell me. Is it logical to go back when you've gone so far ahead."

"Baby," his voice firm but calm, "we black folk don't have the luxury of building a success just to wallow in it. We're a peculiar breed. We have a peculiar existence in America."

"Umph. Peculiar, huh. You got that right."

60

"Yes baby. Peculiar. We are born with a mission in this country. When we become successful it becomes our duty to go back and do something. To show our people something...Each one reach one...remember."

"Calvin there are programs for that..."

"No Barbara. Not where I can help. It's time I performed my duty. Those programs are just government handouts. Hush money, stipends of control. No honey. We must help our own." She threw up her hands, but not as a sign of capitulation. "Those days are over. It's not like that anymore. America has made great strides racially."

"It has always been like that," he shot back. "And in America it will always be like that. There is a need among our masses that must be met, Barbara."

"Then when will it stop Calvin?"

"When there's no more need."

"What about us Calvin. When do we enjoy what we've earned."

"It is the obligation of every African in America who has so called made it to do what he or she can to lift, in some way, the status of his or her people."

"Jeez," she yielded. "all right. But why Professor Jubilee and his people? With your credentials you can ask your price with any corporation."

"Not for me baby. For Calvin Adams maybe. But he's dead. Resurrected as Kuendela Nguvu. And he's going back to show the way."

"What about me Calvin?"

"Your place is always with your King...my Queen."

"But this king wants to live with the peasants," she whispered under her breath. But not far enough under, immediately she wished she could take it back. His momentary silence spoke volumes to her. "Well then," he began slowly, "there are other brothers in the administration. That is if race is a requirement. Otherwise there's just other men."

"Kuendela, Kuendela our brother. Come, come." Elder Mapingo beckoned with his staff. Knowingly or unknow-

ingly the wise old Greot broke the air of animosity. It was thick enough to see. Elder Mapingo walked between them with his arms looped through each of theirs and escorted the couple back to the festivities.

CHAPTER 4

Year 2000

It had been twenty years since that day of discovery. Professors Jubilee and Kobolongo had since assembled a series of teams to take on the task of evaluating the crystals. Ten years of dogged scientific experimentation, research and trial and error supervened to study and reshape them into a workable entity. An additional seven years went into yielding a means of ensuring quality and control and adapting all that had been learned about them, up to that point, into a workable application for use. Professors Jubilee and Kobolongo had named them in honor of their place of origin. They were unique specimens of odd configuration and unknown potential. A series of intense analysis and tests were performed followed by several more years of procedures designed to decipher the secrets of the Sudanese Crystal's potential and classifying their existence. Methods were devised to demarcate the extent of their power and limits of stress, their capacity and cadence. An extensive study of all possible variants of mensuration were performed and applied to ascertain every bit of conceivable information about them.

In the world of science, African science, the Sudanese crystals caused quite a stir. The United States and European science communities, for the most part, ignored them. Largely in part because the Quad A made them and their extraordinary properties less known and even less accessible to the Euro Americans misdirected sense of discovery and thirst for control, by playing down their importance.

Whatever benefits to come from these crystals would be within the soul scientific jurisdiction of Quad A. Twenty years of hard work was painstakingly put into what was now just beginning to pay off. Something incredible was emerging. A device was beginning to take shape followed by a philosophy to justify it's existence and a workable policy to guide it...Years of after class study, research and development. Years of grueling toil at every semester break and summer had finally produced a tangible purpose for the Sudanese Crystals.

*****

Professor Jubilee parked his car on the other side of the campus, away from faculty parking. A conscious decision, so that he could enjoy a stroll along the campus green that extended the distance from his parking place to the building behind George Washington Carver Hall, which was his destination. From the parking lot to the administration building a large rectangular manicured lawn enhanced the area. Beyond that, a concrete walkway between the administration building and Carver, laid a zigzagged pathway connecting the two buildings. It's pristine walkway continued along the way to lead him to where he was going. After reaching the walkway he decided against the path and ignored the "Do Not Walk on the Grass" sign and headed straight across an immaculately sculpted lawn. He always preferred walking on the grass. The quiet softness and the connection with nature under his feet was well suited to his naturalist sensibilities. He always took the time to take it all in as he walked. The smell, the green, the texture and the landscape all fit well with his sense of spirituality. He had a proclivity to nature that matched a remarkably analytical mind. He'd concentrate on and take notice of the slightest detail in things. Especially things that involved nature and it's relationship to man and God. Professor Pressman Jubileee paid attention to such things.

Tall, dark and erect, Professor Jubilee was one of Howard Universities most prolific and brightest multi-lettered physicist and anthropologist, as well as a staunch Afro centric and as he would refer to himself, a born again African. On this warm day near the end of summer, Jubilee's steps corresponded to his sense of naturalism. It was his usual habit to enthrall the spirit of the grass and trees as he walked. But on this day, once on the grass he lost all interest in it's communion. There was something else on his mind. He was fully absorbed with one thought. Today's assignation. Which would, one week from today, culminate into the fruition of all the work that had been done over the past twenty years. Today's assignation would be the final step toward that event and as his urgently swinging briefcase attested, he was in quite a hurry to get to the place where that was to happen. So focused was he that he was unaware of the tall, attractive graduate student trying to keep pace with him. The few other pedestrians who did see her efforts witnessed the rhythmic glide of this young beautiful, full figured black woman. She was a pleasure to watch. "Professor Jubilee." Her melodic voice was a far away echo. "Professor." Her voice more urgent, broke through his ambulated reverie.

"Oh Argee. Sorry daughter. I didn't see you."

"Or hear me," she smiled. "How are you today Sir?"

"I'm fine daughter. How about you?"

"I'm great Professor. I apologize for startling you. You was out of it." Her aria laughter was like soothing jazz. "Uh ah. You're Kevin now, with the jokes" he feigned displeasure. But his smile betrayed him. He slowed his pace to match hers. A gleam in his eye allowed him to pay attention to his young companion. Being indifferent to his assistants was not his style. Being accessible was.

Argee dressed casually in tight fitting jeans that were well worn but clean. A lavender shirt tucked in hugged the upper curves of her torso. She was a very shapely young woman. Full figured with classic Nubian features. On her head she wore very thin braids that draped her shoulders. At work she wore it tied back into a ponytail. "I haven't spoken to Shai yet," she informed him. "He's still at the Peoples Convention. I bet it's killing him not to be able to talk about the project."

"He'll be fine. He's a dedicated young brother."

"The last time I talked to him he said he was just as anxious to get started as the rest of us."

"What about you Argee. You ready for today?"

"Yes sir. Bilal is meeting me in the lab to go over the final diagnostics. As soon as you check them out we'll be ready."

"Excellent. Professor Kobolongo and I have some things to go over as well. When we're finished we'll meet you and Bilal back in the lab."

Argee was one of three graduate students who assisted Professor Jubilee and his team. Her sisterly attitude brought a warm sense of bonding to the team. In spite of her intellectualism she had an insipid sweetness that made her appear vulnerable. Aside from Argee and Doctor Belton the rest of the team were males. Mostly mentoring types as far as Argee was concerned. Collectively she found herself among a protective family of colleagues. She was either a little sister or a daughter. She'd been on the project for seven years now, since graduation. As an undergraduate she studied several classes under the Professor.

Argee Thomas came to Howard from Philadelphia where she was the daughter of a civil rights icon in that city. Her father, Lionel Thomas, was an active legal advocate of civil rights and a staunch supporter of the culture. Reared among Philadelphia's first family of civil rights, Argee immediately gravitated toward Professor Jubilee's afro centricity, who was also an acquaintance of her father. As a graduate student she was guided by Professor Jubilee and took on an ever increasing role in the project. Now that the work was materializing and it's application was clear it proved more and more an exciting and significant project to be part of. Jubilee picked up the pace just a little. Argee had no trouble keeping up. "I hope there won't be any problems."

"We've worked long and hard for this daughter. I also hope nothing goes wrong. And by the ancestors, nothing will. But there's always that chance. Remember, we have a model of a theory that is all but proven. Hopefully, by the end of the testing phase today and next week's run it'll be an empirical fact. Can you imagine the scope of what we will have accomplished."

She nodded. "I dream of it daily Professor."

*****

The George Washington Carver building stands central to a cluster of science and research buildings. Each one connected by a glass enclosed walkway. Architecturally, they are similar in structure with one noticeable exception. The building behind Carver. One hundred yards down a grassy incline it stands adjacent to but apart from the other buildings in the cluster. It is the only one not connected by the glass enclosed walkway. At first glance it is an unremarkable structure. Not as tall as Carver or any of it's neighbors but a perfect rectangle. Completely devoid of windows, it was often mistaken for a supply building by students and faculty, who rarely paid attention to it. It was constructed, surreptitiously along the tree line of a small wooded area at the southern end of the campus. A wary tree dense area known to students as "Howard Jungle". It's indistinct and sterile pink brick appearance belied the recondite activity that went on inside and because of it's proximity to the "jungle" the area was rarely visited by anyone except those who worked there. A welcomed feature to the building's project director...Professor Jubilee. He found the isolation suitable to the projects purpose.

Professor Jubilee and Argee approached the buildings large bland metal door. When he turned it's large aluminum handles a loud metallic click assured him that the locking mechanism had given way. It took a considerable yank to pull the doors open. He sometimes wondered how Argee or Doctor Belton managed. But they always did. Once through the security doors they passed through a small foyer then a set of double glass partitions. From this inside view the building was completely contrary to it's outer facade. It's interior is much larger than the exterior would lead one to believe. A polished tiled hallway led them to bolted twin doors. Two overhead video surveillance cameras guarding the hallway sprung to life, triggered by their entry. The final set of doors required an access code to enter. Professor Jubilee punched the eight digit code into the security box on the wall and a rectangular sign above the door erupted into lavender light as the door withdrew from the wall allowing them access into another long, brightly lit hallway, with several secure doors alined midway down the hall. Argee turned right at the first door and inserted a security card into it's electronic lock. Once the door slid open she entered and waved goodbye to Professor Jubilee as he continued down the hall. Argee entered the functional site of the building. The science laboratory. Professor Jubilee proceeded left past a framed glass door. At the next door he grabbed for the knob and before he could turn it the door opened and Professor Kobolongo smiled.

"Habari Gani Brother Pressman I've been waiting for you."

"Habari Gani my brother. Not too long I hope."

"No not long. However, Pressman you must give a look at what I have here. I think I have solved the problems we were having with the refrigeration chip in the gelatin gun." He held a balsa wood box out to Professor Jubilee. It's lid was open. Inside, was an odd looking pistol encased in styrofoam for protection. An extra cartridge of ammunition laid beside it. Pressman picked up the gun and examined it. "It looks fine my brother. Let's give it the test?"

"I am way ahead of you my brother. I have already contacted our brother and asked him to prepare our subject."

"Excellent Brother Professor. How did you solve our problem?"

"It came to me in a dream. Like a revelation."

"Is that right?"

"That is right. And it is really very simple," Ohoolu explained. "The construction was only half the problem. I have perfected the cooling process that will maintain the projectiles at a constant temperature regardless of the environmental conditions." He picked up the extra clip and pointed to a small black circle on it's bottom. "The projectiles temperature is controlled and maintained by this tiny computer chip while in the clip instead of the gun itself. A bit more expensive but practical."

"Well," smiled Professor Jubilee, "that was our problem."

"And," Professor Kobolongo smiled back, "it is solved. Surely you would have thought of it yourself. Sooner or later." Ohoolu smiled triumphantly.

"Okay my brother, let's check it out." After returning the gun and clip to it's case Kobolongo and Jubilee went through the glass paneled door. There was nothing between the men but respect and admiration. Together, they'd spent over twenty years devoted to the same dream. And it showed in their comradeship.

*****

Howard University School of Veterinary Medicine is a short walk from the project building behind Carver. It was the largest building in the cluster. As Kobolongo had stated, Doctor Robert Mushi had indeed expected them.

"Habari Gani." He smiled as he extended his hand in greeting then waved for the two scientists to follow him. He lead them down the hall to a flight of stairs. They appeared to be the only people in the building, or at least the basement, where Doctor Mushi escorted the two men to a large room in the rear. Here a large striped tiger slowly paced back and forth inside a large steel cage. The animal momentarily stopped to stare at the humans who'd entered his domain and gave them a tired roar then resumed his pacing.

"Now Pressman. Ohoolu assures me that this test will not harm my creature" Dr. Mushi spoke with the lingering remnants of a Ghanian accent.

"Is that true?"

"He'll be fine Robert." Professor Jubilee assured him. "We already know the drugs potential. What we're interested in now is the gun's ballistics and more importantly the preserving capabilities of the refrigerant chip." Doctor Mushi nodded warily. "Well. He's prepped on the back side, are you sure you can hit the correct area." Pressman removed the gun from the box Kobolongo held. "Watch me." The smell in the room caused him to squinch his nose. It reminded him of the circus when he was a little boy. He loaded the pistol with an ammunition cartridge from the box. The gun in his hand was cool to the touch as he raised it and aimed carefully at the large shaved area on the animals rear end. When he pulled the trigger he felt a sharp recoil similar to the snap of a nail gun. So was the sound it made. The animal only had time to look up in surprise before dropping like a ton of bricks. The three men rushed to the cage. Doctor Mushi opened it and they, very cautiously, approached the animal. Doctor Mushi examined him. The tiger was breathing laboriously. "He is completely unconscious," he announced. "He seems healthy otherwise." Professor's Jubilee and Kobolongo were more interested in the projectiles point of entry. After rubbing it with a dry 'Q' tip Kobolongo reported. "It has penetrated entirely. There is no evidence of truncation."

"Dry as a bone," smiled Jubilee. He handed the gun to Professor Kobolongo and released the cartridge.

"The gelatin projectiles you developed are as fine as sewing needles," he pointed out. "So I was only able to develop enough thrust to ensure accurate penetration up to 250 feet."

"That's pretty good," replied Professor Jubilee. "I think it'll be sufficient for our purpose."

"Any distance further than that the velocity decreases and the force of penetration diminishes."

Doctor Mushi remained, hovered over the tiger. "How long will he be asleep?" he asked without looking up or removing the stethoscope he held to the tiger's side. "Well that's what you have to tell us," retorted Ohoolu. Dr. Mushi looked back at his fellow academics and shook his head.

*****

While Doctor Mushi's tiger slowly and very, very irritably regained consciousness Kuendela Nguvu sat his luggage down somewhere in his bedroom. He was in a bad mood. He and Barbara had traded less than three cordial words between them on the flight back from Africa. At Kennedy Airport they finally decided to return to Philadelphia by separate modes. Kuendela turned toward the front door of his apartment after hearing a sharp rapped rendition of "shave and a haircut" followed by a latent "two bits". A lazy excursion through the apartment brought him to his door. It opened before he could turn the knob and a large black tomcat with one white front paw skirted in between his legs. Kuendela reached down and picked up the feline and squeezed it's abdomen. "X my man." He held the cat close to his face. Genuinely glad to see him. "Did you miss me?" Behind X was a tall buxom, african bronze beauty. "Hey Narda. What's happenin baby How'd X treat you?"

"X treated me just fine. Now how about a proper greeting," she pouted playfully. "Sorry my sister," he apologized just as coltishly as she extended her face then greeted her properly with a kiss on the cheek. "That's better."

Narda and Kuendela were old family friends. They'd grown up together in the same neighborhood and now for the past three years they lived next door to each other in this upscale apartment building. It was Kuendela's home away from the NASA residential quarters in Florida.

After placing X on the floor the black cat scurried into the kitchen. Narda walked into Kuendela's open arms and he added a hug to the greeting.

"How was your trip, Brother ah ah?" She feigned confusion as to the name she should call him. "Kuendela Nguvu," he said proudly. "Well that's fine. I like that. So how was your trip otherwise?...ahh Kuendela Nguvu."

"Ah Narda it was beautiful." She took a seat on the couch. "Africa is the most beautiful spot on the planet, Narda. You've got to go." She waved her hand at him. "Ancestors willing. One day my brother. One day." A dish of hard candy laid beside her on the table. She picked up a piece and unwrapped its plastic. "Where is ah...Miss Lady?" she asked with a sly smile then put the candy in her mouth.

"She went home." He shrugged his shoulders. "Tell me." She demanded patting a spot on the sofa beside her. Kuendela begrudgingly sat down and recited the entire saga. When he finished she gave her friend a compassionate and healthy dose of sympathy then slyly added an "I told you so." Not surprising Narda's good natured chiding relieved much of the anger his squabble with Barbara created. The two friends enjoyed each others company a while longer before Narda excused herself and Kuendela settled in to unpack and get some rest.

As a mission specialist for NASA Kuendela was use to the effects of time change and jet lag. He always recovered easily. He was however, unusually tired after this trip. He knew he could thank the stress of his relationship with Barbara for that. The next day he went to see her. Barbara looked particularly enticing in his favorite light blue terry cloth robe. It hugged her hips so wholesomely. Kuendela liked it. He'd always found it sexy. It was obvious she'd just gotten out of the shower. The scent of female freshness and the sexy robe, as added incentive, made it easy for him to be the one to initialize the apology. From his heart, he did. He was sure they could reconcile...Compromise at least. Give a little, get a little so that everyone got something. But, it was not to be. What begun as an apology degenerated into a mean spirited exchange of unintentional disparages. Kuendela slammed the door when he left. Anyone driving beside him on Roosevelt Boulevard could easily see the scowl on his face. He searched his thoughts for a cause in hindsight. Something to explain their differences. Maybe he was too excited about divulging his plans to work with Professors Jubilee and Kobolongo. He shared some but could not disclose all about the wonderful potential of those Sudanese Crystals. He honestly thought she'd find his working with other African scientists an exciting prospect too. He remembered Narda once saying he and Barbara were just too different. He shrugged his shoulders while punching in a jazz station on his car radio. You're a people person, Narda told him. A black people person. You're about the community. Barbara's about herself and getting in the mainstream. Barbara's beauty and poise must have lured him into a state of denial. Narda was probably right he told himself. He may have said it out loud he wasn't sure.

"Dam!"...He was sure he'd said that. So absorbed was he with his thoughts he only navigated perfunctorily through traffic. On his mental screen he replayed the scene before slamming Barbara's door. He remembered how her voice spewed venom as she spoke..."If those dam crystals or whatever they are were so dam important," she chided. "Don't you think some white man would have researched them first! And if Professor 'Black man' was so brilliant he'd be working for that same white man by now!" Calvin or Kuendela had thwarted her crossover, suburban dream and disappointed her. She didn't like being disappointed. But she had no idea how her words disappointed him. Had she been sensitive enough to notice she would have realized that that last remark not only disappointed Kuendela but hurt him as well. To him the remark was prickling, stabbing, piercing, jive and just plain fucked up! It also spoke volumes. The bottom line was...it hurt. 'Some white man would have had it first!' It was a painful statement. Kuendela was sure, as revealing as the remark had been, no amount of let off steam would ever bring him back to her now. And it would soon be a revelation to her.

*****

73

"Can you stand it my brother?" Kevin asked again for the fifth time. "Are you excited man?" he added with a flamboyant wave. It had been a week since Professor's Jubilee and Kobolongo's test with the tiger and Argee and Bilal's run of diagnostics. Everyone was excited about the next phase. Kevin's question, for Bilal though had become redundant and irritating. It was getting on his nerves. Kevin had asked the question, seemingly a million times since they started checking and hauling equipment from the back rooms to the lab for the experimental phase and his wily stare and smile showed he knew it was becoming a rub.

"I'm excited Kevin Okay. I'm excited!" Bilal was the life size image of a black GI Joe doll. A black Nubian warrior. His very muscular frame had well defined dimensions. He swaggered when he walked with the deliberate stalking movements of a jungle cat. In contrast Kevin was small and wiry with keen brown features like an ebony hawk. He had an effete manner of movement and a flamboyant gesticulating form of communication that he, often times, masked defensively with humor. As unlikely a pair could be, the effete and flamboyant Kevin and for all intent and purpose, the adonis, Bilal; however, were like everyone else on the team, very good friends. They'd spent the entire morning helping Professor Kobolongo check and double check the equipment in the laboratory and now were gathering some final needed pieces of equipment. Kevin slung the straps of a sturdy square box across his shoulder and opened the door while Bilal placed a large draped container on a four wheeled cart and followed him. Inside the container an acrylic barred cage housed a rhesus monkey who chattered away excitably inside. Kevin had trained the animal. In the past week he strengthened the classically conditioned responses the animal would need to perform it's task in the experiment. The time had also given Argee and Bilal additional time to finalize their diagnostics on the software programs they needed. Now it was all done. Both Bilal and Kevin beamed with elation. Kevin's exuberance was, as usual, a bit more visible and silently irritating to the more stoic Bilal. Still they managed to work together equitably and efficient.

Bilal came to the project, eight years earlier, by way of Professor Harold Lewis, one of Professor Jubilee's Quad A members. Professor Lewis formally taught computer science at Central State University in Wilberforce, Ohio. Bilal was one of his prized students who'd even managed to patent several software packages of his own after graduation, affording him an opportunity for a lucrative and promising career. But once he'd gotten his feet wet on Jubilee's project he was completely taken in and became totally immersed in it's goal. Just as the others had become.

Kevin's story was similar except that he'd followed Doctor Ida Belton, another Quad A member, from Chicago by way of Tuskeegee with a degree in behavioral psychology and a minor in computer science.

When Kevin and Bilal reached the laboratory Kevin inserted his security card and opened the door. He held it open for Bilal and they both entered. Bilal pushed the cart across the laboratory floor to the wall near the platform. Kevin placed the box, he carried, on a table and began removing it's contents. The entrance alarm above the main entrance chimed, causing them to look in the direction of the main door. Someone was entering the laboratory. It's chime was the same tone as the NBC networks introductory theme. "Habari Gani!" Professor Jubilee and Argee walked in to the greetings of the team members already there. Professor Jubilee stepped up to the platform overlooking the cavernous laboratory floor and took a white laboratory coat from the oak paneled coat rack on the wall. He slipped it on over a pair of blue denim jeans then stared out across the center of the laboratory floor, admiring the massive structure erected there, with his arms folded across his wide chest. The building was constructed specifically for this structure they'd all worked so hard to build. After all these years he was still just as awed by the sight of it as he was by it's purpose. As head of the project he felt obligated to remain austere. He maintained a serious expression as he eyed the device but there was genuine excitement behind his serious pallor. Professor Pressman Jubilee was a man of vision. He could see the future expeditions to come from the structure before him. This thing called The ARC. He could feel the ancient African sun, touch the ancient structures and hear the ancient voices. Once all preparations and testing phases were complete he'd be there. Standing before the fabled University of Songhay then seeing the ancient wonders of Kemet, witnessing the power and love of the wonderful and just societies of Cush. It would be the apex of his dreams finally putting a discernible face on the collective consciousness of his people. To see who they really were.

Years before when the crystals purpose had first begun to take shape, he and Kobolongo wondered if the time involved in the ARC's development would cheat them out of the experience. So many years it had taken to build. He was seventy now. Well into the waning years of his life. He was feeling the effects of age. Aches and weariness. Yet it never slowed him down. In fact, the potential for what the ARC was to accomplish sustained him, gave him a burning desire for purpose and drive. The young people he and Kobolongo had assembled over the years gave the ultimate achievement a sense of hope and promise. It was to them and the generations to come that this legacy was to be left. Like Calvin Adams, one of his most promising students who'd been an adolescent when the Sudanese crystal were first discovered. Calvin was special he knew. He'd recognized him, right off, as a brilliant afro centric. A strong young black man touched by the spirit of the ancestors. A distinction he'd sought and found in all his protégés, Shai, Bilal, Argee and even Kevin. He would mold them as African explorers, reconnoiterers. Time travelers and teachers. Purveyors of the ancient truths and he would be their guide, a discoverer and mentor.

From the rear of the platform Argee watched Jubilee's imposing figure. He was an intelligent, virile specimen of a man in spite of his age. His deep set brown eyes were fixed pensively on the structure built into the center of the floor.

One large enough to have been a basketball court. It's shining floor tiles stretched out from the platform where Jubilee stood, to the opposite end of the laboratory floor beyond the ARC. Over a hundred feet in it's entire length.

The forepart of the platform where Professor Jubilee stood, was raised four feet off the floor. Several width long steps led up to it from the floor. two thirds of it extended out from the wall while the back third was a compartment built inside the wall behind a translucent section of Plexiglas where four large supercomputers, 2\3's the size but similar in speed and capacity to the computers used at the pentagon, were arranged on it's back third inside the wall. The entire platform, when the ARC is operational, could be encased in a sliding glass enclosure whose four thick glassed segments could be lowered individually or all together. The wall on either side of the platform was ornate with various closets, gear lockers and tables with equipment and mechanical and electronic devices all suited for the project's purpose. Several monitors and project control instruments lay in strategic order around the platform. Argee and Bilal sat here, ready to power up the machines for today's operation. It was divided into two phases; The Tolerance Phase and The Azimuth Phase, the final step before the project application could be applied. For the Tolerance Phase they began running diagnostic tests as a precursor to the operation and so far all systems checked out fine. The looks they gave one another confirmed it.

Professor Jubilee turned from his vigil to look back at Bilal on the main frame computer. He nodded to the Professor in affirmation and Jubilee smiled and turned back to his view of the lab floor. Beside him stood Professor Kobolongo in traditional robe and kufi in honor of the event. Ohoolu Kobolongo was born in the British protectorate of Nigeria in a small village 125 miles into the interior from the coastal city of Lagos. Educated in British missionary schools as a young boy Kobolongo was recognized early for his intelligence but the child harbored an animosity for the outsiders who wielded so much influence over his native people. When liberation came in 1960 he rejoiced with the portion of the population that welcomed the end to British imperialism and had little love for the segment who longed for the protectorates return. Ohoolu continued his education, even through the civil wars of 1967, at the University at Ibadan. Later he crossed the Atlantic to study at Harvard University in America where, through networking with African American scholars, he met Professor Jubilee. Through their common beliefs the two men developed a binding friendship. Their common interest forged a close working relationship that later culminated in their joint organization of yearly research pilgrimages to Africa. Professor Kobolongo had several degrees. Physics, engineering, electronics, and anthropology. His smooth dark black skin was flawless. When he smiled he revealed a mouth inlaid with a set of perfectly even ivory white teeth. Ten years Jubilee's junior, he too stood transfixed on the structure in the center of the laboratory floor.

Doctor Ida Belton stood ruminating between both her male colleagues. Her jet black hair absent of gray, her brown face, smooth skin and small features made her appear younger than her 50 years. She wore a white lab coat like Professor Jubilee's. Her hands were jammed into it's pockets. "No matter how often I look at it gentlemen," she said turning languidly toward her colleagues and shaking her head. "It's still the most impressive thing I've ever seen. The dam things capabilities are too incredible for words."

"Your doing fine Ida," observed Pressman.

"Ohoolu, Pressman! If this dam thing works, it'll be the greatest scientific breakthrough in history. Something no man has ever accomplished. Black or white," she added. The corners of her mouth turned down she shook her head from side to side. "Dam impressive," she repeated. Her clear midwestern accent indicative of her Chicago lineage, especially, when saying "damn".

"We'll find out how impressive as soon as Professor Lewis gets here." They all noted the seriousness in that remark by Jubilee. "Our brother is always late," Ohoolu added. "Dam impressive," Doctor Belton said again.

At 5 foot 5 she was a feminine variant to Ohoolu and Pressman's masculine stature. Ida bit down on her black rimmed spectacles that she habitually carried in her mouth by the stem. She was a medical specialist in Quantum physics and aerospace medicine with an archeological elective. She came to the Quad A's from a very prominent and respected position at John Hopkins where she enjoyed the pioneering distinction of being the first and only black female on staff. But like Jubilee and Kobolongo, she too heard the call and felt the need of a cultural conglomeration of science.

"Well Pressman my brother. The time is almost here," chided Kobolongo.

"That's right my brother," Pressman agreed rubbing his hands together.

"It's been a long haul from the Sudan to our little project building here. The time is almost nigh." He looked back at the progress of their assistants. They were well into their preliminary preparations.

"How goes the research at the pyramids?" inquired Doctor Belton.

"Howard's School of Archeology and the University of Nigeria are handling everything. Al Bendee uncovered a lot more since we left."

"It's been a perfect alliance," added Kobolongo. "And a profitable one."

"It's a beautiful thing when African scientist work together. Now where in heavens name is Brother Lewis?" Kobolongo was showing his impatience as Professor Jubilee, the doyen of the project, struggled to maintain his traditional cool resignation.

Professor Harold Lewis, an otherwise brilliant computer scientist and mathematician suffered from a peculiar quirk of habitual lateness. The others brushed it off as just an egghead's idiosyncrasy and Professor Lewis was a consummate egghead. His life was spent buried in books and computers. Like the others, he too, craved the cultural identity of his ancestors and as dedicated and proficient as he was, here was a man who just could not arrive anywhere on time. The team was use to it by now. But today was so important that mere tolerance was having a hard time finding a comprehendible toe hold.

Kobolongo walked around to the far left of the platform and took one of several lab coats hanging there. He removed his robe then donned the coat before returning to the front of the platform and making his way to a terminal manned by one of the assistants. Bending over their shoulder enabled him to get a close look at the monitor. His finger followed the flashing data. "Yes," he nodded approvingly. "We can begin anytime now." Pressman heard him and turned around pensively stroking his thick mustache. His thick lips were pulled downward and his nostrils flared in exasperation. Ohoolu studied his colleague's expression and silently wished again that Professor Lewis would hurry. In his rich Nigerian baritone he playfully patronized him. "There is another application we haven't considered," he baited. He had Pressman's attention in the form of a questioning gaze. "It might prove quite useful as a way to insure Brother Harold's punctuality. We could leap ahead in time and meet him whenever he's late." Kobolongo laughed a deep throated, hardy Nigerian laugh. The remark served to lighten the moment for exactly as long as a moment last. Professor Jubilee responded with a quiet smile. The others chuckled aloud.

"He'll be here," Doctor Belton offered lightly. "It's not the first time. Though it may be the worst time. How do you see it Kevin? You're the behavior specialist. How about a quick analysis." Kevin rose to the occasion without looking away from his monitor. "I'd say our Professor suffered from an obsessive compulsiveness. He probably exerts too much time to the repetition of mundane tasks." Bilal nodded with a crooked grin. Argee listened with a polite smile. Doctor Belton seemed to be the only listener with genuine interest. "He procrastinates," Kevin continued with a flip of his wrist.

"And he's probably very disorganized in spite of his intelligence and academic
	achievements. He..."

"Okay," Doctor Belton surrendered. "I get it Kevin. That's very interesting," she said pivoting from Pressman's side to a terminal sitting perpendicular to the desk where Kobolongo hovered over Kevin's shoulder. Argee moved slightly to give her room to see the monitor. She nodded to the screen for Doctor Belton's attention causing her fine braids to sway. "Punch up the autonomic schematic data, Argee," she whispered. Argee read some data off to Doctor Belton's nodding head while Professor Jubilee remained silent. His attention fixed on the gigantic structure in the center of the laboratory floor. It was an immense segmented structure with a large circular center piece. A third of it's bottom section disappeared into a recessed well constructed into the laboratory floor. Extending across the recess was a five foot wide causeway that led into the center of the giant circular center piece. From Professor Jubilee's purview it resembled a colossal horseshoe. Three gleaming obelisk towers flanked it on three sides almost equal to it in height. One to the right, one to the left and one directly behind. On top of each tower were laden peaks of Sudanese crystal. Each peak reached just over the height of the wheel. Their triangular shaped tips were on a perfect diagonal alignment to the wheels center portion. Eight octagon shaped crystals encrusted the wheel's huge rim. Each crystal on the structure was aligned symmetrically and when activated, a force of energy would emit from each crystal traveling along it's aligned peaks. Reflected laser like emissions would then generate enough force and power to manage the most incredible feat of bending the very existence of dimensional barriers, forging an abyss in a very real animated existence. Here a disruption would occur in the dimensional tract, manifesting an open portal to the reality of time itself. Not the idea or concept of time but it's very physical existence. Making time's gateway a tangible entity. It was all made possible by the energy and power of the Sudanese Crystals.

If the theory on which the structure was constructed is correct, all these actions together will generate a bridge linking a continuum between the past and the present. From which one could quantum leap from the present to anywhere in and anytime of the past. 'A time chamber,' smiled Professor Jubilee proudly of the ARC. Collectively it was an anagram for Aeon Retrogression Chamber. A chamber for a dormant theoretical stage that should become tangible when activated and a portal vortex is opened by which one could transport through time.

The sudden chiming of the entry alarm broke the Professors reverie. On the video surveillance screen the image of a dowdy looking man of medium height with a light complexion appeared. He was manipulating the entrance code box. The door to the laboratory slid open and Professor Harold Lewis stepped in. His questioning eyes glared from a taciturn face. He was late again he knew. What worried him was Jubilee's and Kobolongo's possible reproof. Doctor Belton used her hand to silence a chuckle from Kevin. Reaching the platform, Professor Lewis extended an unsure hand...Professor Jubilee shook it and swung his head in feigned...exasperation. In any case he smiled. That was all the remonstrance there was time for. The team was relieved, Professor Lewis was relieved and Professor Jubilee was ready to get started. He motioned for everyone to begin Tolerance Phase.

*****

Shai was the last member to join the team. His mother was a high school teacher who spent her college years as one of those responsible for the resurgence of the Black Panther Party in Mississippi. Shai's earliest memories were of those beginnings when his mother and other council members of the Student Union formed the party, at first, to protest a planned march by the Ku Klux Klan. Then as a defensive perimeter around the home of a young African brother who beat down one of the Klan members as they swore to avenge the beating. What arose was a terrible melee. But the New Panther Party succeeded in turning back the Klan and their respective resources. Shai was right there with his mother in the midst of snapping dogs and police billy clubs. These experiences made an indelible impression on the young impressionable mind of this afro centric boy.

Shai was a historian and geologist not a technician. His knowledge of history and geology made him suitable as the project's "test pilot". As such he was a vital part of the Azimuth Phase. Yet there were some things about the operational phase of the ARC unknown to him. He remembered Bilal and Professor Jubilee explaining the gist of his role. "Let me explain." He remembered Bilal saying. "Our first transmission will be a shot in the dark. We don't know where in time or I should say 'when in time' you'll be transported to. We don't have a reference program to calculate a setting or target a time. We need a reference program to calculate from as a starting point. An azimuth. So when you go through you have to determine the time the ARC has randomly sent you to. You'll study the environment make a determination as to the era and age, take some samples and bring them back to aid in your confirmation and I'll do the rest. I'll take your data and factor it into my Azimuth Program as the unknown Factor X. A reference point that we'll equate with the power and refraction measurements it took to transport you there. With those calculations we can build the software to make a more accurate setting and decide where in time we want to begin our first expedition."

"Come here son," Professor Jubilee beckoned. Shai broke from his thoughts and approached him where he stood. Until now the young historian had been silent while the others tended to their tasks. "We'll begin with the Tolerance Phase before we come to your assignment," Jubilee explained. The Tolerance Phase was necessary to observe the unknown effects of transmission on anatomical systems. The amount of stress transmitting a body through a dimensional time portal would create and the effects thereof was of foremost consideration, naturally.

"Like the old African proverb," Professor Jubilee had said. "Not to know is bad. Not to want to know is worse." To test that unknown on a human subject, volunteer or not was out of the question so a more unwary subject was chosen. King Tut, the rhesus monkey trained by Kevin, was to provide just that means of observation. If all went well the next phase was Shai's mission. The Azimuth Phase. Professor Jubilee flicked a switch on the side of his console and the far end of the lab was flooded with a brilliant pellucid light, revealing the ARC more vividly. Doctor Belton stepped off the platform and made her way to a locker along the wall where the biological equipment was kept. She lifted the drape covered cage placed there earlier by Bilal and Kevin. After taking a few steps it's weight caused her to shift it several times from hand to hand. Shai rushed to relieve her of the burden. "Thank you Shai." She handed him the cage with a gracious smile. "I don't have much to do yet, Doctor Belton. So I may as well make myself useful." Doctor Belton smiled at him. His youthful exuberance and respectful manner elicited a maternal liking for the young historian.

Shai was brought to Jubilee's attention with an impressive recommendation from Calvin Adams. Shai's degree in history and anthropology as well as his physical fitness made him a good candidate for the Azimuth Phase. His specialties were world history, African, American and African-American history. "Honey no one's job is more vital to this program then yours," remarked Doctor Belton matronly. "And a handsome test pilot too," chimed Argee, eyeing her young friend. "A body and a brain," she added with a flirtatious whistle.

"You're a fun bunch family," cut in Professor Jubilee. "But let's get started." Shai placed the cage on the examination table and Doctor Belton removed the drape. Inside the cage King Tut was dressed in a tiny brown jump suit. He appeared perfectly calm as she reached in to remove him for a cursory examination. Professor Jubilee walked around the row of terminals and seated himself at the largest of the control consoles. Kobolongo responded from his station. "Set a configuration of 7^.77 with a hexadecimal curve of F16.4" Shai looked and listened but the jargon was greek to him. "That gives us a power setting of 12:51 degrees with a comparable position on mach 2."

"Good, good," replied Professor Jubilee.

"Okay," called Professor Kobolongo between key strokes. "All markings are down and loaded to you Brother Lewis. Awaiting your go." Professor Lewis slid into his chair beside Bilal. Bilal down loaded the data to Professor Lewis' monitor. "I'm equating a dimensional setting. It waits in the Azimuth folder for verification from you, Shai," announced Bilal. Tolerance stage is ready to go on these coordinates. All computations on reticular power will stand constant. Changing variables are real time. Shai, your reference is factor X." Shai watched Bilal. He was very serious, unlike the fun loving Kevin who was really brilliant beneath the joking exterior.

Doctor Belton finished her cursory exam of King Tut and returned to her console. "Put Tut in his carriage," she told Shai before sitting. She studied her screen momentarily with the tips of her spectacles in her mouth then removed them. "I want him tracked at normal stress settings."

"Aye, aye," quipped Kevin. He went to the ARC where Shai was placing the cage on the floor in front of the ARC's causeway and recruited him for assistance with a tap on the shoulder. Together they returned to the transmission equipment locker and pulled out a large padded container. Carefully they lift the transparent pad resting inside. The Aeon Platform was 4 1/2 feet in circumference. Metallic threads woven into it resembled a wiry spiders web. Here and there it was spotted with silicon chips that were responsible for it's function of 'transportation launch pad' to and from the ARC's destinations. Though awkward to carry it wasn't heavy. Doctor Belton followed the young men with additional apparatus from the locker. The caravan proceeded across the lab floor to the ARC. Kevin and Shai crossed the causeway ramp and sat the Aeon Platform down dircctly in front of the ARC's round center piece. Kevin then retrieved Tut's cage and placed it atop the pad. Carefully he aligned two sets of ovoid protrusions jutting out from the pad with matching perforations on the underside of the cage. A slight push locked the cage in place with a snap. King Tut moved idly inside while Doctor Belton pulled wires attached to the apparatus she carried and gently attached them to small plastic couplings on the acrylic bars of the cage. Long wires from the inner side of the bars extended to couplings attached to King Tuts chest, wrist and both sides of his head. Shai threw a questioning gaze at her. "They'll break away harmlessly after transmission," she explained. "But the couplings on his head will keep a constant reading of his vital statistics right up to transmission then reattach themselves on retransmission. Then we'll examine the differences in the readings."

"You've thought of everything."

"We hope you're right," she replied.

"What about that other device?" he inquired. "It's called a VSA," she explained while attaching it's couplings. "Vital Statistic Apparatus. It interprets, analyzes and records the biological readings."

"That's incredible," he said shaking his head. They walked back to the main platform.

"Hey! You know what, Mr. Factor X," Kevin called to Shai teasingly. "You know the past data you bring here to the present will help us set a course for the future."

"Pretty good," laughed Shai. "But tell me something," Shai began before climbing the steps. "What about the transparent platform?" He pointed back at the ARC and the pad they'd just carried there.

"The Aeon Platform," sung Argee. Her voice always reminded him of music. "That's your vehicle."

"Will I have to conceal it? Can anyone, even mistakenly, activate it if they come across it."

"Only the one holding the OCP key can activate the trans signal," answered Professor Jubilee.

"OCP?"

"Ovoid Configurational Perforation Key," Kobolongo interjected.

"Your car keys," added Kevin.

"King Tut has keys?" wondered Shai incredulously.

"Tut's gonna travel by remote," replied Bilal. "He's trained to open the cage, walk out and perform a simple task then return to the cage. When he closes the cage door re-transmission will activate automatically."

Tut peered unconcerned through the bars of his cage. Argee had named the animal King Tut while Kevin was training him for this mission. Tut was totally unaffected by the wires attached to him and the cage. Each wire had it's own tension box that would allow him to leave the cage and not get tangled. Shai cupped his hands toward the ARC. "Have a good trip Tut."

*****

Four six foot supercomputers behind the wall worked at their task. Every device on the platform was connected to it. Each system monitor and console was linked to its vast computational machinery. These electronic behemoths were the brains, the central processing units and the source of the assuring sounds of activity now coming from the wall. On the floor near the wall a hatch led into a sub-compartment accessed by an acrylic ladder that descended into the belly of the platform. Maintenance was controlled here: Air conditioning, glass partitions and electrical devices. Jubilee looked away from the hatch. "Here we go," he announced. Doctor Belton and Kevin maintained all physiological statistics vital to the subjects. Kobolongo analyzed the data and calculated quantifiable statistics. Lewis and Bilal coordinated and operated computational software program-ing while Jubilee and Argee maintained a concerted liaison between them all. Professor Jubilee flipped a switch. A blip on his screen began to pulsate silently, indicating the connection between the principles were met. "Power levels, surging," announced Bilal.

"Peak complete," Professor Lewis relayed, indicating the absolute threshold of power had been reached. Satisfied with what he saw on his screen, Professor Jubilee stood up and stepped around the console and gestured for Argee's attention. She scooted her stool over to the place where he'd been, bumping his stool aside. Professor Jubilee descended the steps of the platform and strode across the floor to the ARC, stopping just in front of the cage and VSA on the ramp. With one arm folded across his chest he studied the device contemplatively stroking his chin with the other hand. Behind him, his colleagues followed the device's activity on their screens. King Tut stared up at the Professor in primal awe. The sound of power in the lab rose to a dense hum. It seemed to come from the floor itself. King Tut was only mildly affected. He looked around for the source without agitation. For an animal he was remarkably calm in the face of the technical din around him. It was a credit to Kevin's conditioning.

"Link the power boosters to the crystal connectors," Jubilee ordered over his shoulder. Bilal carried out the order. The low, dense hum became even louder and vibrant. The Professor could feel the vibrations beneath his feet. He bent over the cage and opened it. Then pulled a small pair of shaded goggles from his smock pocket and placed them gently over Tut's head. He inspected the cage and it's occupant then closed it. Returning to the platform he traded places with Argee again. A piano key shaped button on his control board was a direct link to the maintenance control beneath the platform. Depressing it resulted in the entire platform being encased in a glass enclosure.

From threshold to absolution took less than four minutes. Now behind them, around them, under them and above them the room was filled with the whirling hum of the ARC's rising power. The scientist's donned their protective goggles. In the center of the lab the crystalline peaks atop the ARC's obelisks began to glow in oscillating luminance then burst forth in electroluminescence. A lavender beam of light, brighter and more intense, ejaculated from each peak, projecting themselves in unison from all three directions. The beams course found their way immediately to the crystals encrusted symmetrically on the ARC wheel face. Electroluminescent beams spread quickly from crystal to crystal, from obelisk to obelisk to wheel. Faster and faster zigzagging across the ARC forming a laser like pentagram. The glow was intense enough to be optically painful, even through the protective goggles. An effect none of the scientists anticipated. King Tut hunkered down in his cage with his arms across his head, chattering as though cursing his fear.

Professors Jubilee, Kobolongo and Lewis traded smiles. Years of research and theorizing culminated into the moment. Calculations, computations and the refracting and bending beams of light were their painstaking rewards. Everything seemed to be working just right. Every crystal was set and aligned to an exact degree. Every essential was in place to create the necessary and sought after reaction. A ruptured rift in the seam of the dimensional realm of time and space. Slowly the unseen light of the outer dimension began to bend and refract. Eventually the invisible dimensional doorway of time began to widen. The conception of a new reality. Though unseen it was the beginning effectuation of the miracle they'd sought. An error in the trajectory of the crystals' beams would cause a catastrophic and inconceivable disaster...but today there would be no such disasters.

"Quantum polarity," informed Kobolongo.

Argee echoed confirmation. "Quantum polarity holding," The ends of her braids swung like pendulums below the band that secured the goggles to her head, as she followed the active data on the monitor's screen.

"Hold steady at 75' mark 7."

"Down load to variable. Set Factor X," Professor Lewis instructed.

"Setting constant and filed. Azimuth. Hold setting. Factor X," responded Bilal. A sudden blast of linear light exploded then disappeared on Jubilee's screen.

"We're underway," he yelled unaware of the excitement in his own voice. Two minutes passed. All eyes were now transfixed on the ARC's portal activity. Electronic aureoles emanating from the ARC held them all in a hypnotic trance. The light bouncing from obelisk to crystal encrusted wheel spun to the ceiling. The pulsating continued with oscillating illuminations that became a circular field of energy rotating uniformly around itself. Incrementally the circular field divided into a second band of light then a third, a fourth and finally a fifth band of osmotic illumination. Blinding intensity caused the scientist to shield their eyes again in reflex. All except Professor Jubilee. He couldn't keep his eyes from the spectacle. There was something there that intrigued him. Something he saw. A theory of an effect he long held suspect and now witnessed. He stepped around his console after depressing the button to lower one of the enclosure's panels then strode across the lab, drawn to the ARC like a sleep walker. The entire display appeared perilous from the view of those on the platform, in spite of its wonder. "Professor!!" Argee yelled out in alarm. He waved off her concern. Kobolongo replaced him at his console. A high octave pitched din emanated in tandem with the ever rising illuminations surrounding the crystals. "Maintain the polarity coefficient," he shouted above the noise. "Maintained," Argee yelled. Professor Jubilee moved directly in front of the orifice of activity. Argee again yelled in protest. "Professor!!" she shouted. "Professor Jubilee!!" Again he waved her off without turning as he stepped closer, almost into the torrent aberration. He had to get a birds eye view of the process. Doctor Belton touched Argee reassuringly on the arm. Argee swallowed hard then reluctantly returned her attention to her monitor. Randomly, each scientist reported their data while Jubilee continued to stare into the center of the activity. A mixture of awe and adoration filled his face. Pulsating light reflected off the lens of his goggles. In the center of the aureole of light before him he saw an area of satin like blackness beginning to grow. It began as a small area, the circumference of a silver dollar. Then immediately expanded to a diameter of six feet, engulfing the cage at it's center. As if by magic it's aberrant visage became definably visible. "Did you ever see anything so beautiful," he said to no one in particular. His voice was choked with emotion. Behind him on the platform the rest of the team strained to contain themselves as they continued operations.

Slowly the dimensional vortex erupted into existence. It was becoming a tangible thing, stretching and convulsing as it took on a definite form. Its edges moved eerily, swirling around the blackened center. The lower half of the area was below the floor in a recess under the ramp where it was visible only to the Professor's view. Kobolongo saw an indication of it on his screen. The blackened area of turbulence possessed a definite difference in shade. It changed hue as if it breathed. Shades that converged in waves forming a widening vortex to which Jubilee leaned even closer. He didn't dare step on the ramp. He sensed a presence. As if it possessed a character all it's own. An entity reaching into an infinity. Strange, even bizarre, it was the effect he had theorized. He looked for it and he saw it. It was absent in earlier trials. Those incomplete trials had never reached this point. Now here it was, the doorway he anticipated. A tunnel, a chamber, an opening into the...Call it what one may. It was the doorway through time. He smiled victoriously. The white teeth in his mouth appeared slowly. It was the widest grin anyone could have ever seen on his face. He straightened up and gestured behind him to Kobolongo to begin ignition sequence then ran back to the control platform. Just as Kobolongo gave the command, Jubilee mounted his controls and again lowered the glass panel.

"On my mark," called Kobolongo, "9 point 16 point 90 1420 hours."

"Bio-tracking," announced Doctor Belton.

"All connections holding," Kevin informed her. "Readings stable. Tut is cool as a cucumber."

"That'll do Kevin. Just give me the vitals."

"BP stable, heart rate stable, respiration slightly elevated but within normal limits."

"It's okay," assured the doctor.

"Skin temp stable, fur secretions stable, galvanic, autonomic all stable."

"Go." Doctor Belton passed the count down to Professor Lewis.

"Systems loaded."

"Tracking and configuration," added Bilal. "Packages inter graded and systems connected," nodded Professor Kobolongo.

"Count down," ordered Professor Jubilee.

"10, 9, 8, 7, 6, 5, 4, 3, 2, 1." Argee recited.

"Pre-transmission," Professor Jubilee yelled at the top of his lungs.

"Trans phase set stored and filed."

"Contact. Perimeter scan loaded."

"Scan positive," inferred Kobolongo.

"Transport!" Jubilee ordered in a resonant voice. Argee watched as he reached inside his smock and shirt. She saw the impression of his fist bulged under his shirt. She knew he was holding his lucky talisman. He closed his eyes, raised it to his mouth then kissed it and said a silent prayer. He then thrust his hand into the control panel orifice. Gripping the handle inside he turned it clockwise. A blast of energy effloresced from the darkened center of the ARC. In milliseconds the entire laboratory was engulfed in orange-amber light. Bright but not ardent, none could resist turning and covering their faces. As quickly as the ball of energy exploded it imploded then dissipated into nothingness. A tomb like silence followed. Slowly everyone uncoiled and fixed an expectant gaze on the ramp...The cage was gone. On Argee's screen a fixed blip on the outer edge of concentric circles representing the cage was gone. In it's place blinked a pulsing cursive waiting to signal the returning connection with the Aeon platform. A few pecks on her keyboard shrunk the window around the waiting blip. The outer rings of the circle expanded from it then constricted to a bold dot. From it a long list of scientific diagnostics and equations scrolled down the screen. She alerted Professor Lewis and Bilal. "Preliminary folder to Factor X!"

"Good girl," Lewis praised. "Send it over." With one key stroke all the data on Argee's screen compacted itself into a 2 by 3 inch square then vanished. On Professor Lewis' screen it resurfaced under a label "Transparent Phase. Azimuth file". He pecked his keyboard surprisingly fast between pushing his glasses up from the bridge of his nose. "Calculate and save it," he instructed Bilal. The sounds of energy and keyboard activity ceased. Everything seem to stop at once. They all stared at the empty place where the cage had been. Professor Jubilee revealed another broad smile. Shai sat with his mouth gaped open with more than astonishment. It was now more than an anticipated theoretical event. It was now a sure possibility and he'd be next to move across time to...God knows where or when. The thought was both frightening and intriguing.

"Shit yea!!" shouted Kevin. He and Bilal slapped hands in celebration. Bilal moved around to the back of the platform where Shai sat. "What's up Brother! Give me some." He held his palms out. Shai came out of his thoughts to slap him five. Professor Kobolongo flashed his widest grin. "Pressman we did it."

"Yes Ohoolu my brother we've done this much but lets wait until Tut returns," he cautioned. "Don't kill the moment Professor," Argee quipped hugging him around the neck.

Professor Lewis and Doctor Belton continued watching the ARC. All that remained now was the Bio VSA. It's detached wires suspended in place patiently awaiting the return of Tut's cage.

*****

"Getting nervous son?" Shai wiped his sweaty palms on his trousers. "I'm good Professor. I was just wondering what it must be like and where Tut might be. It must be wicked to travel at that speed. The speed of light. Through an entirely different medium of existence." A weak smile followed.

"You'll find out soon enough brother," suggested Kevin.

"Now you know why Tut goes first," Professor Jubilee explained. "We have to learn of any physiological effects that may occur and we must know what to do about them. Shai your hide is very important to me son and we most have all the variables to protect it." He patted Shai reassuringly on his shoulder and smiled. He looked at the young pioneer pensively. Anyone on the team would have taken the chance this young brother was taking. But Shai was the one who was taking it and Jubilee greatly respected him for it and worried for him privately. "Traveling at that speed, the speed of light, I would imagine to be tantamount to standing still in the way you'd experience it. Movement would be too fast for your mind to grasp the change. Tut will go from present to past without passing through the realm of time and space in between. That's quantum physics. What that may do to living tissue. We don't know. Tut is going to provide that information when he returns. Dead or alive. Because unfortunately, Tut's skin is the only one that's expendable."

They settled back for a 30 minute wait. Jubilee and Kobolongo descended into the lower part of the platform to check on the machinery below. Argee retreated to the kitchen area and returned with a tray of refreshments. Bilal took a tall frosted glass of iced tea and leaned back in his chair. Kevin followed suit with his hands clasped behind his head. He waved off anything from Argee's tray. "I wonder where ole Tut is now?" he said aloud. "Maybe on some dinosaur's breakfast tray huh."

"You've always got jokes don't cha brother," remarked Bilal. "I don't know how you do it. I don't think Shai finds that too funny."

"It's all right Bilal," Shai replied, taking an iced tea from Argee's tray. "I was just wondering the same thing."

Argee tenderly caressed the side of his face. There was no mistaking the affection she outwardly felt for him. He smiled at her as he took a couple sips from his drink.

"Shai!" Bilal called from the ARC. "What would you do if you found yourself at some vital point in history man. Say like the Audubon in New York City." He turned his lips down pensively. "Sayyyyy circa 1960?" Shai sat down in Jubilee's empty chair. "Malcolm? The assassination?" he replied knowingly.

"Yea," Bilal swung his chair toward Shai. "You're a fit brother. You're into history and you know exactly what's gonna happen. Where the assassins are and how and when they'd strike." He took another sip. "What do you do? How do you stop it?" Shai leaned back in Jubilee's chair and thought hard. Interfering in Malcolm's assassination and stopping it would, without a doubt, be a course changing event in history. Giving Malcolm the opportunity to finish his work. To see what direction the black community would go in as a result. But at what price? Who's sacrifice? As an answer there was Jubilee's and Kobolongo's protocol to consider. "Time is like a running stream," they said. "Or a highway. Any obstruction that would alter it's course would lead to many directions, vastly changing the course of things to come. Where one course is altered it's alternative is also. What exist on one path may cease to exist in the other. No one knows where the roads may lead. Destiny is the Creators domain," said Jubilee. "It's our responsibility not to interfere in the fate that has already been laid." Shai and Bilal both swore to abide by the protocol of no interference. Still they couldn't resist the urge to fantasize.

"I...sure...would...love to stop it," Bilal replied defiantly.

"How?" challenged Kevin. Bilal shrugged his shoulders. "I don't know man. Get behind the assassins, maybe. Knife them before they could shoot."

"You'd stand a good chance to die yourself," added Shai.

"Yea. But it would be worth the chance. Maybe I could stop them before they got to the theater. Maybe alert Malcolm or his staff.

"How would you explain your information?"

"I don't know. What the hell is this.." Bilal protested.

"Just speculating Brother. I'm beginning to realize that changing the past ain't as easy as one would think. How would you get Malcolm to postpone his lecture? If that, indeed, be your course."

"Malcolm wouldn't postpone," insisted Kevin.

"You're probably right, about that and the fact that it ain't easy."

" How would you make Martin Luther King stay off the balcony. How do you get those four little sisters to stay out of the basement of the church. Do you follow Emmett Till and those white men into the woods or just kill them before they get to Emmett's uncle's house? How would you get Otis Redding to take a bus instead of a plane. Get Bessie Coleman to let us repair the engine in her plane instead of that white boy?" questioned Shai.

Bilal pounded his fist together. "We could do all that and arm Denmark Vessey too. With modern weapons!" Bilal was alive with speculation now. "We could support John Brown, David Walker. Warn all the insurrectionist about the traitors in their ranks. Get our hands on some of those racist bastards who lynched our ancestors!"

"Sure you right," sneered Kevin, joining in on Bilal's theme. "Emmett Till, Chaney. Get those white boys who killed them."

"Yea," continued Bilal. "I could really enjoy putting a 9 up their racist ass noses and making them snort a couple rounds," he snarled. "But where would I find them? How would I stay out of sight or avoid killing innocent people or like you said Shai avoid getting killed my dam self...But," he added. "I still say it would be worth a try."

"Man, if we could save Martin," added Kevin excitedly. No tellin how far he would have gone." He listed more names on the tips of his long manicured fingers. "Rosewood,

Black Wall street, Medgar Evers, Chaney, Huey, Mumia, Soledad brothers and on and on. We could save them all."

"What would happen to the world then?" interjected Professor Jubilee's protégée, Argee. "And what event would we choose first," she added. "I mean changing one course may negate the existence of other future events. Who's responsibility is it to choose. Who infers the consequence? Would we make things better, or unwittingly make things worse Would saving Rosewood negate the eventuality for the Little Rock Nine. Would advising Marcus Garvey eliminate the existence of a Martin Luther King or a Malcolm X. Could our actions create a climate that would cause the government to take even more extreme measures."

"Could save alot of our people and right a lot of wrongs," insisted Bilal.

"Or deny the coming existence of a lot of people or alter the existence of others."

"So much wrong has been done to us. We could turn a lot of things around."

"Word."

Argee rolled her stool up close to Shai. "You know the theory of the 'Butterfly Effect.' Like the Professor says none of that may change anything or it may change everything."

"I know, I know. We could even make things worse. I wonder what we would be getting into or causing if we interfered."

Doctor Belton was listening without comment until now. "I was wondering when someone would say that." She seemed to be looking at Bilal. At least he felt she was. "No Doctor Belton. I was just speculating. I wouldn't disobey the Professors protocol. You know that."

Professors Jubilee and Kobolongo ascended from the platform access. It was obvious they'd heard some of the conversation. Silence blanketed the platform...Then..."What do you say Professor. Are there any exceptions?" asked Shai.

"Yes sir," added Bilal. "Are there any events you'd change in spite of protocol?" Professor Jubilee declined the seat Shai offered and rolled one of the other stools

97

underneath him. He was quiet for a moment. Then..."Many things Bilal. I'd like to change all the wrongs done to our people. I can understand the temptation to turn the tables on history. But we don't dare alter the past. Even the rough existence we've had here in America."

"Africa too," added Ohoolu.

"You've heard the adage. Cashing a check your butt can't change. Well if we change one thing how many other things would we have to change to keep up with our sought after effect. And who decides what and how the changes should be made. Who's existence do we sacrifice. Because you know one altered event could change the existence of thousands."

"You're right of course Professor but we could change the tables for the entire race."

"Yes Bilal, with the weapons and technology we could bring to the fight. We could go into Europe and destroy the Europeans and the Arabs in the east who had been invading the Motherland since before the christen era. Of course," he added off handily, "we'd have to conquer and occupy them. We'd have to become what we now know them to be."

"It would teach them the lesson of how it feels," snarled Bilal.

"Yes. We could teach them a hell of a lesson...But wouldn't that then make us the oppressors? Is that our way?"

"No sir. It's not our way," admitted Bilal. Professor Jubilee folded his arms. "Our ancestors would end up teaching them with what we've brought. It was their way. To uplift the unenlightened peoples. It's what got them invaded and conquered in the first place. We'd teach them instead of occupying them just as the ancient Cushites did. We might unwittingly give them knowledge they would most assuredly use to some destructive ends."

"Maybe we could avoid such a result," argued Bilal.

"And maybe we couldn't. I'm not willing to take that chance. Are you?"

Silence..."But what we know we can do is learn from the ancients ourselves. From our perspective in the way of the ancient Africans. Does enslaving white folk for what they, by this time, never had a chance to do make those actions just. No. Oppressing them first would then make us the evil ones because to be sure like Bilal said we'd have to really put our twenty first century foot down on their behinds" He let the thought simmer for a moment. "What we are going to do is go back to our ancestors and watch them and learn. We'll bring back the lost knowledge stolen by the Europeans, the secrets destroyed by the Arabs and Romans and co opted and misinterpreted by the Greeks to our time." Professor Jubilee pounded his chest with a muffled thump. "We're going back to the greatest civilizations that ever existed. We're going to Kemet and Cush. Songhay and Mali. And with the knowledge we relearn from them we'll alter the paths of our own existence and lead our people of today to regain their former glory.." He looked around at the inspired faces of his young crew. The mention of the ancient wisdom's was like a hypnotic potion. He smiled. "So," he concluded, "until we come in contact with those ancestors who are much wiser than we are and whose wisdom we can use to chart a proper course for a change in our reality...Until then we remain humble. Remember, in spite of our Afro centricity we still bare the shackles of four hundred years of brain washing. Only from our high cultured ancestors can we learn the true path."

Professor Kobolongo broke in to interject. "That's why we have a protocol. We don't interfere with the path that fate has driven and we don't take lives and there's something else we must consider, especially with regard to contemporary history," he added steering the conversation toward the realm of physics. "We dare not transport back to cross exist with ourselves. That," he shook his head emphatically, "would bare consequences for us far more destructive then anything we could ever contemplate, imagine or infer. Believe me. That would prove far too fatal and dangerous to survive."

Professor Jubilee reached out to his young apprentices with his eyes. He saw their dedication, their wonder and also their rage. A conviction he was all too familiar with. He knew how they felt and he knew also that they would obey the protocol out of respect for him and all their mentors. He shrugged his shoulders. "My grandmother taught me to believe in the spirit of Sankofa. The idea that our identity as a people as well as our direction is set in the ways of our ancestors. In Sankofa we must pull back to leap forward. We have to learn the truth of our past. We cannot fix our gaze and efforts just on one point in the center of our existence here in America. We have to reach all the way back to our origin, the origin of all African people all over the world." His gaze went from one to the other. "We have a wonderful gift and opportunity family. A chance to recover the greatness of our ancestors and transport it here to enhance our present and insure our future. Sankofa, young Africans. Sankofa." They followed his hand as he gestured toward the structure. "This ARC is the tool that gives us the ability to practice that spirit of Sankofa in the most real sense. We didn't find these crystals to play God. But to reclaim the spirit of our greatness and secure the future of our people. Sankofa!" he chanted. "Sankofa!" The room was charged with enthusiasm. "Think of what we could learn from the great teachers of Kemet," remarked Kobolongo.

"Can you imagine," exclaimed Argee enthralled with the Professors' theme, "actually finding the great meaning of Her Um Aket."

"King Yusuf, Muley Ismael, Askia the Great!!" mused Shai the historian

"Hannibal, Pianki the Great." quipped Bilal. "You're right Professor..."

Professor Jubilee raised his hands to stop Bilal's explanation of penance.

"Son. You haven't expressed anything that Ohoolu and I haven't wrestled with." Professor Jubilee held out his hands to Bilal and Shai exculpating them.

They embraced him with Kevin and Argee joining to make it a group hug. Then...the moment was interrupted by a beeping alarm from Bilal's monitor. Immediately he jumped to his seat and spun around in his swivel chair to face his screen. A pulsing cursive flashed followed by the words:

RETRANSMISSION

AEON-PAD=ACTIVATED

"We've got retransmission," Bilal shouted as the others scrambled to their stations.

"VSA just kicked in over here, alerted Doctor Belton. Professor Jubilee raised to take his position at main control but not before giving Shai a reassuring squeeze on his shoulder. Shai rose from the Professors chair and Jubilee sat down. Argee pecked at her keyboard. "20 seconds," she announced. Doctor Belton stabbed at one key on her console. Data appeared. "Biological readings getting stronger," she reported.

"Well, we at least know he's alive," added Kevin.

"Power reading coming in," announced Lewis.

"I've got em.".…And so it went. The pace of activity quickened. Tut's journey was scheduled for 30 minutes and in that time he was to lift the latch on the cage door and exit. His security line and biological monitor feedings were constructed to expand and constrict with him so not to obstruct his movements. King Tut was trained to explore the perimeter to the length of his line. Without deviation, he'll retrieve samples of vegetation, soil and other inorganic specimens small enough to fit in his pouch to give the scientist a picture of the environment after analysis. An operation they determined would take 15 to 20 minutes with 10 minutes to acclimate. Now 30 minutes were up. "Okay let's bring him back family."

Argee counted down. On 1 Jubilee ordered retransmission. He turned the control handle counter clock wise. The spectacle that followed was as spectacular as the earlier scene of transmission transportation. When the flashes of energy had again dissipated…the cage reappeared. Professor Jubilee and Kobolongo with Kevin in tow, rushed to the ramp the instant the platform's glass partition ascended. Kevin was the first to observe the glistening scarlet material covering Tut's body. "Blood!" he yelled. Kevin's exclamation quickened Doctor Belton's steps. She unhooked the biological monitoring device and removed it's disc while Jubilee and Kobolongo helped Kevin release the cage. Kevin lifted the cage off the pad. It seemed heavier than he remembered but he carried it swiftly to an examination table along the wall. In seconds Kevin had the monkey disconnected from it's lines and out of the cage. He handed Tut to Doctor Belton as the other scientists rushed to the scene. Blood covered Kevin's hands. He stared at them, fearful for the animal. "Poor fellow," Doctor Belton cooed as she gently laid him on the table. She removed his little outfit. "What is it Ida?" Jubilee inquired. He could see the perplexity on her face. She rolled King Tut around several times, feeling every inch of his body, combing through his hair with her fingertips searching for the wound. "There's nothing here." Professor Jubilee looked at her incredulously. "There's nothing here," she exclaimed. "There's no wound. Nothing."

"Could Tut have killed something?" Kobolongo wondered.

"If so it was in self defense," protested Kevin defensively. "Something attacked him first."

"Or someone," added Bilal.

King Tut was visibly shaken. Doctor Belton continued her examination. "He seems stressed," she said through the tips of her glasses.

"From a fight?" wondered Argee.

"It may be the strain of the transference," offered Kobolongo." Osmotic shock perhaps."

"But the blood," someone said. "His biological-data will give me a better idea," Doctor Belton said. "Plug this in." She gave Bilal the disc from the VSA.

"We've allowed for as many possibilities as we could," offered Professor Jubilee stroking his mustache. "Further investigation will have to tell us what if anything we've missed."

"Yes," remarked Kevin. "The psychological strain at transference might have been more stressful than we could have prepared him for. Remember he is an animal and he's apt to respond with instinct to a traumatic situation. It's impossible to force him to unlearn all of his instincts."

Professor Jubilee took in the comments but only nodded. Without speaking he extended his hand to Doctor Belton for Tut's pouch. She gave it to him. It was empty. In fact it hadn't been opened at all. An infectious look of disappointment encircled the group. "Empty," uttered Argee shaking her head. Professor Jubilee handed the pouch to her then folded his arms and stared at Tut. "What happened Tut? What scared you."

"Maybe this will tell us something," rejoined Doctor Belton. The VSA began printing out it's data. Doctor Belton interpreted the fluctuating lines on the tape. "Here," she pointed. "His vitals are fine up to this point. Now see how the graph peaks suddenly. He was startled by something."

"More like scared him to death," added Kevin. "Look how extreme the jump is."

"Whatever it was it's over. Tut made it," Shai looked from Jubilee to Kobolongo. He hoped this development hadn't change anyone's mind of his scheduled transmission.

"You'll have to deal with the same thing," said Kevin. "It may have been an animal that frightened him." Professor Jubilee rubbed his chin. "That would be my guess...Ohoolu?...Lewis?"

"I agree."

"Yes. So do I."

Kevin handed the tiny jumpsuit to Professor Kobolongo for his inspection. Kobolongo and Lewis took turns turning the small outfit over and over then inside out. They both discovered there were no tears or rips in the jumpsuit. Doctor Belton was already looking at the blood through a high powered microscope. What she found was no surprise to her. "It's an animals blood," she declared. "My guess is a canine of some sort. A dog or a wolf."

"But any of those animals would have torn Tut to pieces,"inferred Bilal.

"Tut is badder then we thought," quipped Kevin.

Shai watched Professor Jubilee. He seemed to be thinking deeply. He may be having second thoughts on the mission or contemplating a postponement "I wish we knew what Tut ran into. Shai I don't like the way things are looking for you." It was what Shai feared. He spoke out in protest. "Whatever it was sir, Tut seems to have made out pretty good." Jubilee shook his head. "That's true, but there are variables we should look into just for safety's sake."

"Sir, nothing is an absolute certainty," Shai protested, "besides, I'm not concerned about the unknown variables. I accept the responsibility."

"But I am concerned about those variables!!" Professor Jubilee stood over him. "And the responsibility is mine!" Jubilee's resonant reproof boomed across the laboratory. The room went silent. But it was only his concern. Sending this young brother into God knows what was his awesome responsibility and he didn't take it lightly. His outburst may have been extreme, certainly unexpected but there was no mistaking his concern. It was his paternal side, not his academic or scientific mind. He had to admit. The blood on Tut had forced him to be more concerned but not defeated. There was no real consideration to stop the mission only caution. Everyone connected knew there would be dangers. But for Jubilee, seeing the blood on Tut gave him slight uncharacteristic cause for hesitation. Not one of these people would shirk from their duty, even if it meant risking their lives. He knew that. But, before he would cast any of these people to certain harm he'd rather go himself. For his own peace of mind he had to be sure of his peoples' safety...But there could be no stopping. Not now after coming this far, this long. It was just concern for the young lives that hung in the balance. It carried its own weight. "This expedition continues on my satisfaction. Okay!" It was not a question. "Yes sir," Shai agreed, consciously removing any hint of recalcitrance in his voice.

"There could have been any number of things," Kobolongo insisted in his crisp Nigerian accent. "No matter what, we can never be 100% sure how he'd respond to unexpected stimuli. Like Kevin pointed out, he's an animal with an animal's instincts and reflex. However," he temporized arching his eyebrows in a statement of fact., "Tut is here. So the question we seem to be avoiding but must consider, is the next phase." Jubilee knew Kobolongo was right. The project was already in motion. There was no time for second thoughts, only time for forging ahead. He nodded in agreement, exhaled deeply and turned to Bilal. "What's the reading on the perimeter threshold?" he asked exhaustedly. Bilal looked at his monitor and applied a few key strokes.

"Perimeter threshold shows a negative reading sir," he verified. "No biological contaminants. Tut came through all alone." Professor Jubilee wished there was more physical pieces of data to analyze before sending a man through the ARC. More intrinsic data, something concrete to ensure Shai's safety. He shook his head to loosen the nagging feelings of doubt King Tut's bloody jumpsuit brought to mind. Though blood analysis did indicate it wasn't Tut's. He shrugged his shoulders. He had to admit. His friend was right. His emotions were getting in the way. Besides, as the youngsters said. Tut did come through unscathed. He ceased his pondering. After so many years of sweat, toil and dedication, how pragmatic would it be to postpone now. With one last moment of introspection Professor Jubilee made a decision. "I appreciate everyone's enthusiasm. I'm well aware of your commitment. It's the reason I chose each of you." He spoke directly to the young participants. You know how important this project is to me and I know how important it is to you. But you must understand, children, that my only concern is not just the success of the project but my ultimate responsibility is your safety. Especially you Shai. He watched the strain of concern on each of their faces. "I bare the weight of all the decisions." Shai tried to second guess the Professor's thoughts with another interjection. Professor Jubilee cut him off with a hand gesture. "Relax son. We've come to far to let this obstacle hold us back now. I just want you to understand my concerns..." His already deep baritone was enhanced further by his prior cogitating. The room was silent.

Professor Jubilee cared. Maybe, it seemed, too much. Everyone knew it. But no one except Professor Kobolongo knew how he feared compromising the mission because of it. Shai feared his concerns would postpone the mission. Kobolongo saw it differently. He had confidence in Jubilee's sentiments. It was that atmosphere of caring which fostered the dedication and loyalty of the team as well as the respect for Jubilee's ability and brilliance. Professor Jubilee conferred Shai an exculpatory smile then turned to the rest of the team. "All right family lets move on to the next phase." He looked to Professors Kobolongo and Lewis. They nodded in concurrence. Professor Lewis clapped and rubbed his hands together. "Let's go brothers and sisters." He threw his hands up in mock exasperation. The probes show there's a safe threshold in the target perimeter. So let's hop to it." The group dispersed to their stations with returned optimism. Shai disappeared through a door beside the platform that led to where the expedition gear and supplies were kept. When he returned he was dressed in a black denim jumpsuit with protective goggles slung around his neck. Professor Lewis placed a plastic object into a corresponding utility pocket in Shai's suit. The pencil length apparatus was T-shaped at one end and shaped like a two tined pitch fork at the other. "Your OCP key," he explained. "Bilal will brief you again on how and when to use it."

Bilal escorted Shai to the causeway and briefed him. They were joined there by Professor Jubilee. "You've got an hour to explore," he instructed. "If for any reason you have to abort in an emergency before that time is up, don't hesitate to retransmit. Now, we can only track you on transmission and retransmission. So in between, you're on your own." He rubbed his chin as he thought of more instruction. "Don't leave anything behind. Stay out of sight of the locals, if any, and take care. Stay alert Shai and be careful." The Professor grabbed his young explorer by the shoulders and added in a concerned voice, "I don't know what else to say son..." He shook his head. "This is history Shai...Black History. May the Creator and Ancestors be with you." They grasped each other heartily then without another word Professor Jubilee returned to the platform.

"Be safe my brother," Bilal bid his friend then embraced him the way only black men do. Argee approached and hugged him lovingly. "Take care Shai." She kissed him on the cheek. "See you in about an hour. Okay?" He nodded, she smiled and turned leaving him on the causeway. Shai looked around him. Behind him loomed the imposing figure of the ARC. Before him laid the serious activity of his colleagues encased in their glass sanctuary. An ambivalent wave of apprehension passed over him. He felt flushed with fear and anticipation causing him to tremble. Professor Jubilee gave him a nod of confidence then raised a clenched fist. The gesture had an empowering effect on Shai. It seemed to ease his hesitance. He finally knelt down and snapped the OCP key into place then stood up. "Readjust the perimeter threshold," ordered Professor Jubilee. "I know that's right," chaffed Kevin. "I'd say Shai was a little bit taller than a rhesus monkey." Bilal made the necessary changes to the program. All the procedures for transmission were now complete. Argee looked again at her friend. He looked at her and adjusted his goggles, flashing his most convincing smile. His gold tooth glistened beneath the laboratory lights. He nodded to her in a coded regard only she understood. Argee felt an ambivalent pang of sorrow and joy then stoically began the count down on Professor Jubilee's command.

"10, 9, 8, 7, 6, 5, 4, 3, 2, 1."

Professor Jubilee reached into his shirt for his pendant then whispered a silent prayer. "Transmission!" he shouted then turned the operation handle. There was an explosion of red violet light followed by a similar implosion. A multi shaded brightness consumed the entire room. The changing intensity of light made Argee squint momentarily. In that moment her view of Shai was altered several fold from clear to vague in strobe like frequency until all activity subsided.

An eerie quiet prevailed over the entire lab. On the causeway validating Argee's final change in perception was the silent empty space where Shai had been standing before vanishing into the ARC's vortex.

CHAPTER 5

Year 1852

The largest plantation in Aiken county, South Carolina was owned by Colonel James Randolph Richards. A tall broad shouldered descendent of a Scottish gentry. The 'Colonel' as he was called, held strict reins on a sprawling plantation. Like many of the affluent plantations of the south it existed as an autonomous and self-contained unit operating on the backs of the two hundred and thirty black slaves who maintained it. For the slaves, it was a contrary life to their masters. Their lives of servitude were lifetimes of toil without reward from the cradle to the grave. Thankless work from sun up to sun down with no gain, no resource or no opportunity from generation to generation. Conversely, Colonel Richards and his family's life was comfortable. For them and their fellow southern class families, life was full of gentle breezes and magnolia blossoms. Ensconced in luxury, opportunity and the fortuity to reach as far as ones dreams and ambition or family money could take them. For them life was the pleasant side of kismet unlike the slaves whose lives were it's ugly contradiction. Yet in spite of their misery, their reticence and their aching bodies the slaves on Angora plantation worked hard. They produced the products and maintained the comfort that provided the Richards family with their opulent life- style. All with little thanks and less consideration. But even an opulent life style had it's tribulations.

Keeping the childlike mentality of the slave in line could be so exhausting, yawned Colonel Richards as he stepped through the portico leading to the porch of the main house. He looked out toward the long pathway of neatly manicured fir trees that lined either side of the winding path leading from Angora's main entrance to its main house and made a mental note of the broken cones strewn about beneath many of the trees. He'd have his slaves pick every one of them up, he mused. This was the path taken by his visitors and he prided himself on the grandeur of his estate. He was, in fact, awaiting a visitor at this very moment.

The view from the ornate rail was, for him, awe inspiring. He lit his long black cigar and exhaled a puff of smoke with pride. Off to the side, on an intersecting path, he watched some slave children playing around the uniformed line of trees. In his mind their play and seeming gaiety only lent itself to the panorama of the perfect plantation scene. For him their ragged clothes and bare feet was an enjoyable juxtaposition to the backdrop of the plantation. It seemed to be their natural state. Then he frowned. The downright unpleasantness of the recent number of escapes intruded his pleasant reverie. The seeming countenance he saw in those slave children made the idea of escape all the more perplexing. Why, he thought. Why do they do it? Then in contrast his oldest daughter Jenny, on the path opposite the little negro children gathered flowers from the house garden. He allowed himself a smile. Her head was covered by a pink chiffon bonnet that matched her multi layered dress. Corroboration, he concluded. Proof, that his eyes could see, that the opposite in caste was the way God intended it all to be.

Angora Plantation was admired throughout Aiken County. A source of county pride and imitation for the well-to-do elite of South Carolina.

'Angora' Greek for market place was a multi-facetted plantation surviving on a rotating cash crop of tobacco, cotton and rice. Large separate crops were rotated seasonally to prevent exhausting the land so that every season was a profitable one. Tobacco on Angora's field was a secondary crop to it's primary crop of Carolina cotton and rice. During the season while the cotton field's soil was at rest, Angora tobacco provided a tidy income in reserve.

Soaked from perspiration and wearing ill fitted clothing, the slaves of Angora worked in the several square acres to the rear of the estate beyond the family's main house. Far from sight but not far from objectionable, Richards family members would often promenade to the fields to take in the reminder of the labor that maintained their cozy life style. The sight of slaves hard at work in the field was an inspiring picture to behold. The good southern folk contended that their slaves were fortunate to be given good God fearing work to civilize themselves. But this argument did nothing for the citizens of the county to explain the élan with which the slaves were taking their freedom of late. It seemed so odd to the whites that these, otherwise slothful people would exert so much energy into running off into the wilderness. Away from good soul enriching work and the masters protection and benevolence. In the past, a few slaves managed to flee but were quickly apprehended. In most cases as expedient as a few days or at the most, weeks. Of late there had been a noticeable rise in the incidents of runaways in the county and these fugitives have remained on the run for months. An unusual length of time for a Carolina slave to be at large. Some were never caught at all. Lately there seemed to be a continued rise in attempts. An epidemic the citizens said. Even now! there was an Angora slave woman who'd been on the run for several weeks now with a young boy. She was a trusted slave whom the Colonel never believed would violate his trust this way.

Concern over the sudden increase in slave decampment showed on Colonel Richards face. Concern for both the cost to his reputation as well as the cost to his financial assessment. Not to mention concern for the effect these absconders accomplishments would have on the rest of the slaves themselves. The successful fugitive could serve as an inspirited influence to the others. Just the other day the Colonel reminded his overseer of this and impressed upon him to make a solid example of any slave recaptured. One that would make a lasting impression on the remaining slaves by way of consequence. Just a deterrent. He had no desire to enkindle any other such foolish notions of liberation. A slave imparting his or her own freedom was a thought that thoroughly appalled Colonel Richards. The sneer on his face belayed his reverie.

A small covered carriage now made it's way through the ornate gated entrance. It's horse trotted handsomely to the front of the main house where Colonel Richards stood between two gleaming columns. A dark skinned driver sat atop the cab dressed in a black tailed coat and stove pipe hat. A well dressed white man sat patiently in the carriage while another tailored servant opened the carriage door. Colonel Richards strode down the wide marble steps to greet his visitor as did several other slaves in attendance. The visitor stylishly emerged from the carriage. The two men greeted each other cordially as perfect gentleman while the servants fussed over the carriage doors and steps. Even the horse got the royal treatment, as the white men ascended the stairs to the porch where a drink awaited each man on a silver server sitting between a set of high backed conversational chairs.

*****

"I believe these darkies may have put some organization to this resistance James," the visitor was saying several minutes later. Colonel Richards leaned his head back and blew a long column of cigar smoke then stroked his beard as he contemplated the statement. "Latimor. I just don't believe that," he stated firmly. "Negroes lack the mentality to organize a network that could effectively orchestrate a resistance. I don't believe them capable of accomplishing the kind of cooperation it would require without the guidance of a white man. So mind you, there must be some dammed abolitionist in the area offering leadership and guidance to these heathens." He digressed. "But whatever the manner of orchestration and whatever fool abolitionist traitor is orchestrating it, finding an end to this criminal behavior is what's imperative." He pounded his fist on the quatrefoil railing. "And an end must be found quickly."

"Sheriff Picket has doubled his efforts," remarked Latimor, "though my confidence is with the McPacker boys. When it comes to tracking the coloreds he's the one that can track this epidemic back to it's origin." His face turned grim with contemplation. "Some of the residents are wary with the thought of these vile nigras roaming the countryside, Colonel."

"I am in sympathy with you friend. These thieves of liberty and the great southern traditions have to be extinguished so that the tranquility of our southern way of life can be restored." A curling trail of smoke encircled the Colonel's head. Those convictions were shared by all the slave owners in South Carolina who'd been affected by and feared this...epidemic.

"Utterly horrendous, shocking and dismaying behavior. Now Colonel I have a proposition for you." Latimor changed the subject with a perfunctory smile and the expert guile of a business man. "I'm hoping you have just the kind of nigra I'm looking for. For sale." Rubbing his beard as the conversation turned to business the Colonel put on the poker face he reserved for just these occasions. He leaned in to give his guess his complete attention. "I'm looking for a slave with a special aptitude James. One with enough learning ability to become a clerical apprentice. Of course," he added, "he must not be given to flight. In fact he must be more trustworthy and conditioned than most. For this slave apprentice will be given much freedom about the premises and bare a lot of responsibility." Colonel Richards raised eyebrows betrayed his continence and showed his aversion to the idea. "That is a tall order Latimor, sir. You yourself have intimated the innately diminished intellect for such aptitude." Latimor listened patiently then smiled. "You will remember, sir, I also intimated that with a superior hand to guide the way they are capable. I reiterate, this negro must exhibit a certain penchant for grasping the technical intricacy of ministerial work." Colonel Richards leaned back in his chair, smoking in silence but graciously lending his attention to his guest. His proposal meant this negro would have to learn to read and write. Colonel Richards expression faltered for the second time. One may as well teach a fox to guard a hen house. To men of his profession educating a negro was out of the question. It was just too dangerous a tool to give.

"Of course," Latimor added as if reading the Colonels mind. Then repeated matter of factly. "He must be absolutely stable and not given to flight."

"Such a nigra who is both educated and stable can only be one of two things." remarked Colonel Richards, this time leaning forward. "Extremely loyal or thoroughly intimidated. We've just discussed the present climate in the county, Latimor. A negro with such abilities would not be viewed kindly. Nor would the man who taught him,"

"Yes James," Latimor totally ignored the Colonel's last remark. "But we both know that with the right incentives and the proper aptitude the work itself would prove a proper enticement. Besides a negro possessive of all the amenities I've laid out would not only be kindly looked upon but assuage the matter as an enviable commodity as well." Latimor smiled cordially before interjecting. "And it is with this that I have placed the proposal before you as well as several other businessmen in the county." Colonel Richards position began to weaken. "James," Latimor shift gears to appeal to Colonel Richards vanity as a slaver. "Finding a nigra with this kind of apprenticeship aptitude will be a difficult commodity to find but a challenge for the more resourceful and imaginative slaver among us. It will take a keen eye to ascertain." Colonel Richards took the bait. "Exactly what duties will you have this extraordinary servant perform?" Latimor was silent for a moment as though he was forming his reply. Shaking his finger toward his host and readjusting his sitting position he explained. "I intend to teach him the bulk of the clerical business. I'm going to make him a thorough book keeper. Of course he will have to read and write as well as calculate."

"What of the law!" protested Colonel Richards.

"As an extension of my business he will be well within legal bounds," he explained with a wink. "And as I said he must be stable. Broken," he emphasized honestly.

"All right go on."

"Then I will lease his services to others who might find themselves backlogged with clerical duties. Which most often happens. Revolutionary, unorthodox? Yes but a valuable asset," Latimor added rubbing his finger tips together.

*****

The Richards family lived in seeming playful perpetuity, oblivious to the misery and suffering of the people in the slave cabins near by. Inside the mansion, house slaves moved about like automatons, shackled to the soul purpose of maintaining the Richards family convenience and comfort. They wore Richards family hand-me-downs except those who wore uniforms and those were handed down from slave to slave. The white overseers who lived with their families on Angora also lived a full life. Living, loving, learning, and growing in worldliness and all its possibilities. Like most white Americans of 1852 they too enjoyed the American birthright. The slaves they oversaw lived a vacuous life. They were rode hard upon by their drivers who enforced an endless repetition of mental repression. These slaves who were driven by their masters had one saving grace. They had an ability to turn themselves off emotionally by suppressing every natural instinct that defined life. To go about their duties, to appease the whites and do so without the obstacle of emotion, without feeling...denying the pain. They suffered the obtruded indignities of not being seen as human. They were chattel, livestock, inhuman. For them life was a respite until death. Colonel Richards and those in immediate charge held actual power of life and death over the slaves as well as the quality of that life, and when it came, the austerity of their death. Such was the life suffered by Sara, one of the many enslaved Africans on Angora plantation. Her life was a living testament to the rapes, whippings, degradation, intimidation and horrors inflicted on her young 23 years. Twenty three years of daily toil...even on this day. A day when Sara had given birth to a young son. Overseer Jim Smith permitted her to convalesce for two days. Not out of concern for Sara's well being but out of concern for her work potential and upkeep. On Angora there was the same concern for pregnant cows and horses.

Sara laid on a hard wooden bed softened by a blanket thrown over burlap bags. Edna, the slave midwife who aided her, now prepared to leave to attend to other duties. She laid a bag in the corner of the cabin. "Here some peanuts and yams Miss Clara took from Massa kitchen. It all we got ta give, but it hep keep yo strenph up." Sara nodded mutely. "You rest up nah," Edna instructed. She looked down at the tiny bundle in Sara's arms then at Sara and fought back a tear. "Seem like a brand new life would cause a body praise. But all it does is make me sad. Lawd keep ya little nigga," she said looking down into the tiny brown face. "Cuz you gonna need all da prayer you ken git. Dis life ya come ta ain't what ya think it gon be." With that she left Sara and her child alone. Sara held the brand new life she'd just created close to her bosom. Tears welled up in her eyes and a pang of sympathy knotted her stomach. The words Edna left behind ruminated inside her scarf bound and exhausted head. Instead of joy over the birth of a new life there was only sadness. A sadness that expressed itself in tears that flowed freely down her embittered face. The cold realization that this beautiful child had only a miserable existence to look forward to was just too much to bear. Slowly she grew consumed by a vehement hopelessness that grew steadily until it engulfed her completely in a miserable reality. "No, no, no," she cried to herself. "...Not my baby." Her head swung from side to side. "My baby, my baby," the words were far away. They didn't seem to be coming from her own lips. Both the hopelessness and the chanting cry grew, ingesting her...consuming her totally. Her surroundings melted into oblivion as the words became an all empowering cry. "Not my baby, not my baby," she chanted. "Not mine!!" Her movements were the actions of someone else. She joined in as a participant...as a spectator. She watched...curiously as the spirit of woman pulled herself up and got off of her cot. It wasn't her moving across the room. Nor was it her picking up the bag of peanuts and yams. Nor was it her who carried the baby out of the cabin. It was an aberration, a spiritual image, an empowered Sara. No one saw her steal across the grounds except the lone figure of a slave woman who nodded numbly in her direction.

Sara disappeared through the uniformed tree line bordering the plantation then edged her way along the graveyard dividing the slave cabins and the back road. Here she crossed and entered the fringe of the woods. When she finally became aware of her own movements, it was she, who trudged the woods, crossed the clearing and entered the forest. She who, with desperate thoughts of freedom for her and her child, was empowered with God's own divine will. Her eyes widened in panic and her heart and breathe quickened as she found herself moving deeper into the woods. She was surprised she'd gotten this far unseen. Quickening her pace, she began to run. No extra clothes, no plans, and no provisions, just the peanuts, yams and an impulsive dash for freedom. There was no turning back. Determination on her face swelled in her heart. Her's was a soul defined to no longer be that of a slave. Not her. Not Sara. And surely not her baby. She'd now rather die as well as kill the child before surrendering their lives to bondage. Sara smiled proudly. She discovered she possessed a sense of conviction. It's fervor coursed through her veins, not to be denied. She trudged further and further away from the plantation widening the distance between her and captivity. The taste of freedom now seemed so insatiably natural. She stumbled, almost dropping her baby. Amazingly, she wasn't tired, she was invigorated...Euphoric. It seemed so easy. Why hadn't she done this before. Others had. In fact it was just last week when Kimbe ran away and now it was her. But where will she go?...Kimbe...she thought again.

117

Sara leveled her pace to a moderate stride. Intermittently she turned to look behind her. She was still alone. It was freedom or death now, or as she once heard Master Richards say some white man once said, liberty or death. How good it sounded. She kissed her son. So sweet was her newfound taste of freedom. She pushed on, exhilarated, in spite of her postnatal condition. For the first time she felt responsible for her own destiny. The decision to turn left, move south, sit down, get up or look ahead was hers now. Hers alone...She was delighted and giddy to the point of intoxication. It was all up to her. She started to laugh. Softly at first then out loud. "Hush up fool," she warned herself. Still she continued to smile. She stopped walking for a moment and looked into the tiny face. "We gonna be free baby." She kissed his tiny brown face..."or we gon be daid." She moved on.

*****

Colonel James Randolph Richards was a ruthless and pious hypocrite. A slave master who could quote God fearing principles of christianity while mercilessly ordering the brutal beating of a helpless slave. He would sell his own eponymous mulatto offspring despite the desperate protestations of its tormented, bonded mother. In a white greatcoat he made his way across the plantation. A curling stream of cigar smoke trailed behind him in his wake. He strolled through the slave cabin area to reach the field. Two of his children played there with several young slaves. They were running in a circle. The white children's pink bonnets were tied tightly to their golden tresses. White linen handkerchiefs covered their mouths and noses to keep the swirling dust out of their throats. It was hard to discern who was chasing who as they ran in the same circle. It was just as hard to discern the slave girls from the slave boys. They wore only shirts that hung just below their crusty knees. Not even the length of their hair could help to tell the difference.

At the end of cabin row Miss Clara raised a call for early dinner. The large conch shell she blew into held a distinct and familiar sound for the youngsters. They instantly broke away from the circle leaving the white girls pouting after their retreating backs.

Of the scores of slaves on Angora, 32 were children. From every direction, it seem to Colonel Richards, the little dirty black urchins appeared, running toward the sound of Miss Clara's horn. Those old enough ran with the younger ones in tow to gather around two fourteen foot wooden troughs filled with broken bits of cornbread. Miss Clara shooed them away from the troughs toward three buckets filled with water. "I declare." She clapped her hands. "Yall wash dem dirty hands in dem buckets fust. Lessen yall wants to eat dirt too. Now git!" They dutifully obeyed without question. Afterward they took their position around the troughs as she poured in buttermilk from an oak wood bucket. "Humph!" Colonel Richards huffed to himself in disgust. "That better not be good drinkin water you got them pickinninys washing in Clara!"

"No suh. Massa Riches," she replied with the least bit of sarcasm she dared to display. He thought to check her for what he thought he detected in her tone, but let it pass. He had other matters on his mind. Unconsciously he rubbed at the front of his greatcoat. At the place where he received a wound in the war, as a young veteran, under General Andrew Jackson. Even through his clothing he could feel the coarseness of the abdominal scar he'd garnered from the near miss of a British bayonet during the New Orleans campaign of the War of 1812. Begrudgingly he remembered the bayonet of a British soldier and the Negro volunteer serving with the American forces who deflected it. Though Colonel Richards wore the mark of his patriotic adventure proudly. He seldom espoused the tale of the battle, even to willing ears, without neglecting the bravery of his benefactor. To him there was a quiet shame and dishonor for having to owe his life to a common negro and because of it, gratitude seldom found it's way to the countrymen of his wartime savior. Instead he reviled them in his memory.

As the Colonel made the short walk from the cabin area to the tobacco field he barely spotted a male slave inside a clump of bushes privately relieving himself. His back was to the Colonel. Colonel Richards turned around his walking stick to strike the man with the blunt end of the handle. "Oh oh!" yelled the slave turning to see the Colonel. He was terrified. "Get your black ass back in that field boy!" he snarled, then calmly blew a thick trail of smoke at the slaves fleeing back. He smiled. There was no look of outrage on his face. Just a satisfied smirk at a little fun. After all, the slaves were told to do their business close to the field, then cover it. But Colonel Richards could rarely restrain himself from the opportunity to exert his superiority when the opportunity arose.

"Mr. Smith," he yelled as he turned the corner of trees. The large field came into view. Jim Smith, a tall gangling man with a pinched red face hurried to his employer. Jim Smith worked for Colonel Richards a little more than six months. He was an able overseer who was recommended to the Colonel by a former employer, Colonel Richards' cousin. Jim Smith came with excellent recommendations. Angora's last overseer was unceremoniously fired and physically booted from the plantation after failing to put an end to the sudden rash of escapes. Though the escapes still continue, Colonel Richards cousin assured him Smith would bring closure to the problem, given a chance.

Since coming to Angora the Colonel had grown to admire his new overseer for his hard but clever mind and his roughshod handling of his slaves. He'd proven himself a good task master. That admiration would die a disappointing death, however, if Jim Smith's sexual penchant for arrogant Negresses were known. The Colonel would not be pleased with his methods for dealing with what he called 'high minded nigger women.'

"Yes sir Colonel," he puffed when he reached him. This was no social call. Colonel Richards fixed a serious paler for his subordinate. "Any word from McPacker on the matter of my property?"

"No sir. He was doing a job for Wilson. He seems to think these slaves may have made off together. But I ain't heard from him yet."

"Mr. Smith." He blew some smoke. "I don't take kindly to my property liberating itself. Or my employees allowing them to do so."

"Colonel.. I" Colonel Richards interrupted him with a wave of his cane. A constant trail of smoke laced around his head as he clenched his cigar in his mouth. "That Kimbe took the boy. I want some privilege taken from them all, in her regard. And if there's another run away I want something even more serious done in THEIR regard." He then pointed his cigar at Jim Smith. He couldn't have looked anymore sinister. "And if there are anymore escapes beyond that. It will find YOU lacking in some unfortunate regard. Do I make myself clear Smith." Jim nodded, "yes sir." Remembering how his predecessor was cracked over the head with a riding crop before being fired.

"Colonel, you hired me to do a job. I'm good at it and I'll do it sir," he added, tired of his own obsequiousness. "Now I have an idea them nigras are gettin help."

"I've heard some say they may be organized," added Colonel Richards. He removed the cigar. "What do you say Mr. Smith."

"I say I'll get to the bottom of it and put a stop to whatever it is. You've got my pledge Colonel."

Colonel Richards smiled and replaced the cigar. He knew Jim Smith was aware of his obligation to remonstrate his subordinates. It was sometimes the way employers got results from their workers. Being an overseer, Smith knew that. So, Colonel Richards knew when Jim Smith promised results it was not out of intimidation over the reproof. No, he could count on some devious and useful measures from his new overseer. There would be results. Changing the subject he asked about the pregnant slave. "I was just about to send Clem over to have a look at her."

*****

121

Sara's escape had yet to be discovered when Josh slipped away from the field. The overseer had refuse to give him permission to go when Edna told him of the birth of his son. Not during the busy time of day, the overseer said. It was all Josh could do to contain himself from leaving anyway. But now dusk had come and the work was slowing down. Work was not done but Josh took the opportunity to steal away and see his new baby...God's little miracle. His young Solomon. That was the name he and Sara planned to give him.

Sara's cabin was close to Miss Clara's. He could see the children's feeding trough as he emerged from the field. The smaller ones were long gone but the older children were still there cleaning the long wooden troughs after dinner. He didn't see Miss Clara. But she had no need to be there. The older youngsters knew what to do. With a chest full of pride Josh burst into the cabin. A large welcoming grin on his face, expecting to see his son nursing at his mother's breast. Josh's prideful smile dropped to a nervous quiver when he entered. Miss Clara and three younger women were the only occupants.

"Wheah's Sara!?"

"Hush up fool," remonstrated Miss Clara. Her bony finger pursed at her lips. The disappointment on his face softened her tone. "She gone Josh."

"Gon!?!" he shouted dumbly. "Didn't I say hush!" she rose from the chair. Her withered face barely met Josh's chin. In a hushed voice she explained Sara's disappearance. The three women looked nervously at one another. Concern for Sara in her post delivery condition and the new born was plain to see on all their faces. They were the ones who notified Miss Clara. Josh stood in the doorway in a state of catatonia. There was something he felt he should do or say, but he had no idea what it was. "Wheah she go?" he blurted hysterically. "Josh," Miss Clara called softly. "We gotta get hold now. Sara just up an left witout a plan. We gotta keep our heads togetha." She pulled him to a chair. "Leavin on the spur, like she did, her chances ain't to good a reachin north.

We got ta figger a way ta hep her. She ain't got no plan. If she did, she'da tole me sumptin." All the occupants in the room listened intently as if she was drawing them a map to heaven. Among the slaves her voice was the voice of experience and wisdom. "Now. Guardless what she thought when she left heah. She know ta go ta da Point. Now we know Kimbe theah and Kimbe'll know what to do bout Sara's condition."

"Do she know wheah da Point at?" one of the girls inquired.

"Don you worry none. She know the story jus as good as you. You oughta know that Mae." Miss Clara turned to Jessie, the girl beside Mae "Jessie you git down to da field and fetch dim Negroes fo dey come out. Tell em we got some singin..."

"What's goin on heah," came a voice from outside, startling the group. The white man entered. Josh stood up dumbfounded. "Suh!?!" He tried to cover his alarm by mumbling something incoherent but it was too late. His eyes darted nervously about the cabin. "You heard me boy...What's goin on heah goddamit," Clem insisted. "Whatcha doin up heah?" he looked at Josh. "It ain't quittin time in the field yet!" He pushed past Josh and slammed the door to the cabin so hard It shook the walls inside causing an herbal reef hanging on the wall to fall to the floor. His beady eyes scanned the cabin. He looked from Miss Clara and Josh to the others. He knew someone was missing. There should be a convalescing woman here with her new born commodity. Josh started to stutter some response to his question but Clem's mind was long past it now. "Wheah's the wench and her pickininny?" he demanded. Josh and Miss Clara stared at each other then averted their eyes to the floor in unison. Feeling the tension in the air a few more slaves gathered around outside the cabin. Beads of sweat mottled Josh's brow. Miss Clara looked nervously at the milling crowd. "You hard o hearin boy...I said wheah's the nigger winch?" They both looked at him obsequiously. Stupidly, Clem thought. He looked from one to the other, blowing in exasperation. "Get the hell out a the way." He pushed violently past Josh and Miss Clara, knocking the elder woman to the cabin floor.

Clem marched off to the main house kicking loose each clump of grass in his path. He dreaded notifying Colonel Richards but he had no choice. Better to get it over with he reasoned. Jim Smith met him on the way. "Well, how's the wench?" Jim Smith asked. "Can she work?" Clem could smell Jim's afternoon whiskey rising from his body. Hunching his shoulders, he gave Jim the bad news. "Goddamn the Colonel's gonna have our asses!!" Jim swore.

"I was just on my way to the main house," Clem said almost apologetically. Jim Smith scratched his head and waved Clem on to his duty. Clem continued on to the main house. Watching him, Jim began to have second thoughts. As the head overseer he'd be the focus of Colonel Richards wrath. He hurried across an adjoining path to intercept Clem before he reached the main house. Quickening his pace, he overtook Clem and pulled him back towards the cabins. "No need in alarmin the Colonel, Clem. She can't get far wit that little nigger bundled under her arms." He sounded more demanding than suggestive. Then he toned down the authority in his voice and smiled. "Go on over to Spittle Rock and get them McPacker boys. They should be back from Wilson's job by now," he said, patting Clem assuredly on the back. "I ain't too keen on upsettin the Colonel either," Clem said knowingly.

"But, wouldn't it be wiser to tell him before he finds out later."

"That's why I want to move on it right now boy. We act fast enough the Colonel ain't got to find out."

"Well," Clem sighed, glad to be relieved of the responsibility. "You're the boss."

"That's right!" Jim sneered. "Now git. And tell em if they bring her back before sun up, they'll get a quarter more than the usual rate. I'll pay their wages myself. And you go with them," he added. With a nod of his head Clem turned toward the stables to get his horse. Jim called after him..."Bring her to my cabin when ya get back," he ordered. "Don't go arousin the main house. You hear?" Clem waved his arm without turning around then climbed atop his horse and galloped off to Spittle Rock.

*****

Few, if any, house servants knew of the cave at Fall Point Mountain. Some field slaves knew of it. Of those, few had ever actually been there, though all who had escaped with Miss Clara's assistance certainly had been. And of those captured none ever betrayed it's location. Sara had a vague idea of how to get there. 'Look to the falls and keep walkin,' was the old mantra that pressed her ever eastward. Eastward toward a mountain whose waterfall spewed from a hollowed depression at it's top flanked by mountain peaks on either side. It was an unusual feature of topography known to the whites but whose real significance was known only to the blacks. Fall Point Mountain's waterfall was an unusual anomaly of nature. It's magnificent waterfall spewing from it's top was also fed by a stream of water from inside, while it's cascading falls from the cut above completely hid the mouth of the cave that spewed it's inner stream, making it the most prized of hiding places ever. Together these tumbling torrents poured into a flowing basin at the mountain's base. Aft of these falls and perpendicular to the upper stream that fed it, the ground swelled to two twin peaks that dropped into an atmospheric abyss on either of the two sides of the mountain, pushing the stream through it's rocky valley. Beneath it's cliff on the rear, an abutment, six feet below the ledge extended a mere five feet from the mountain side before dropping off into the bowels of Fall Point. One would have to be very careful not to fall from this meager platform. Just to be on the ledge seemed insane. There was no where to go...except down. Unless you were aware that to the left, where the width of the ledge was a bit wider, a crevice existed. An aperture that by the grace of God, conceded an entrance into the back end of a hidden cave whose inside expanse was large enough to comfortably hold an auditorium.

The cave was fabled among the slaves having been discovered by an old runaway who was chased to the ledge of Fall Point by a posse of paddy rollers. With no other way out the old runaway leapt from the ledge to what his pursuers thought was his certain death. They never bothered to look over the edge to see or try and recover the body. The abruptness of the drop was evidence enough that their pursuit was over. However; had they looked they would have seen the desperate black man clinging to the wall of the abutment for dear life. The old runaway slave credited providence with delivering him from certain death by revealing to him the five foot berm before he jumped. The stream he found inside the praise worthy cave provided him with fresh water. At night he hunted small animals around the base of the mountain. From then on he spent the remainder of his life as a mythical legend. The whites who heard the story of the Fall Point Mountain phantom considered it superstitious nigger dribble. To them the ghost slave who wandered the mountain by day and the nigger imagination by night was simply the desperate memory of the old runaway who jumped to his death at Fall Point. But to the black slaves the legend was real and well known. The accidental good fortune was omitted for good reason from the white folks version. Sara knew the legend well. She could surely find the falls. It would be a good place to hide, to rest and to revel in her new found freedom.

*****

By the time Sara reached Fall Point it was getting dark. She had travailed an arduous journey with her child to the base of its rocky mountainside. Slowly and cautiously she edged her way along the slopes until she found herself atop the rocky side of the mountain. As she struggled with each step she thought about Miss Clara. She admitted, now, that her escape was hasty. She knew she should have talked to the old woman first to gage the timing of her act but she couldn't help herself. It had all happened so fast. She justified her impulsiveness by abstracting an old maxim. 'Always follow your first mind.' She smiled weakly then thought about Josh. A rueful ache tugged at her stomach. Maybe she should have waited for him. But would he have come with her? Josh could be so slow and unsure of himself sometimes. Well, she shrugged. Me and my baby are free. Here and now. It's our time. Yes, this was one time, she thought, she could look back and sneer then forge ahead. It had been a difficult journey for her and Solomon. Getting this far without being captured and navigating this rocky crag without falling was a feat worthy of praise. Riskiest of all was the jump down to that thin and unsteady looking ledge before her. She knelt at the cliffs edge silhouetted against a large full moon in the night sky contemplating the jump down. The ledge seem so narrow. She felt herself losing some of the confidence that had driven her this far. She shook off her fears. Kimbe had made it. So could she. Kimbe would be down there too. Somewhere hiding. With that thought in mind she bent over her knees with Solomon cradled in her arms and hung her head out over the ledge to whisper down into the shadowy crevice.

"Kimbe." She paused, waited for a reply then called again.

"Kimbe...please."

"Kimbe!" Whispering louder with more force and desperation.

"Kimbe!!" Her voice was almost a shout.

"Sara?" came a cautious disbelieving voice from deep inside the crevice. "Sara...that you?!" Slowly an arm...a shoulder...then a bandana covered head partially snaked its way out through the aperture. "Sara! What cha doin up heah!?!"

"I run Kimbe! I got my baby and I ran!" she exclaimed in excited breaths. She gently handed the child down to the still flabbergasted woman. "I never got word that you was comin out heah," she said, cradling Sara's child in one arm.

Before going down, Sara checked the tie holding the bag of provisions securely to her back then slung one leg over the ledge and then the other, scraping her knee. Carefully she lowered herself down onto the berm then followed Kimbe inside. The cave was dimly lit by a small fire. Moonlight creeping in through the opening added its own faint illumination. Kimbe, tall and medium built, stood in it's shadow cooing the tiny infant. The flickering flame reflecting on different spots of her mahogany brown skin gave her the odd illusion of strobe like movement. She eyed Sara up and down. "You sho you ain't been follid?"

"I ain't been followed, nobody even know I'm gone." Sara answered stumbling weakly. Still holding the baby Kimbe rushed to her aid. Part of Kimbe's right foot had been amputated at the instep but she was surprisingly agile in spite of her impediment. The wooden staff she carried as a cane only aided her in a small way. She ambulated mostly by sheer will and determination. She helped Sara as she slid weakly to the ground. Sara propped herself against the wall then held her arms out to receive her baby.

"Chile you look like the devil," Kimbe remarked placing Solomon tenderly into the young mothers arms. Kimbe poked her staff into a small fire beside the stream. "I got a few vittles," she offered, raking some yams from the edge of the flame. She handed one to the young woman. Sara bit placidly into the vegetable and nodded to her own sack of vittles left beside the cave entrance. "I feel like the devil too," Sara remarked languidly looking around the cave. For the first time she took in the total vastness of her new sanctuary. At first she had to shout to be heard over the constant roar of the cascading waterfall but she quickly became acclimated to it's din. Now it was hardly noticeable. In front of her the slender stream rushed by. Back in it's shallow end, distal to the mouth of the falls, Sara saw a small boy splashing around in pursuit of a toy wooden boat. Kimbe followed Sara's eyes to the boy. "Mind now Noah. Don't you go splashin too close to the deep end," she warned. "You fall down that water fall that be the end a you boy!"

The stream rolled along lazily toward the mouth of the cave. As it approached the drop the water picked up momentum changing into a rapid. Here the water became suddenly deep as well, creating a current Kimbe knew Noah would be unable to resist. So she kept a watchful eye on the boy whenever he was in the stream. "Yes Maam," he complied matter of factly. He waded back even closer to the shallow end. "I got ta get afta that boy all the time bout that stream," she complained, looking back at Sara. "I know children gets figidity sometimes and I hate keepin him cooped up in this cave. He needs to be out runnin and playin in the grass and climbin up in the trees, like boys suppose ta."

"I know," intimated Sara sardonically. "Not fetchin water buckets for field hands and nasty overseers."

"Yea," moaned Kimbe glumly. "Lord, I'll be so glad when Bessie gets heah and we make our way up north." Kimbe navigated to a corner of the cave to sit down next to the meager supplies then shook her head. "Lord it sho is hard bein colud ain't it." She laughed lightly trying to ease the atmosphere. A fellow runaway was always welcome. It was the cultural way of the family and necessary for survival. But now her concern for the younger woman returned. She could see Sara was unsure of her next move and Kimbe knew how uncertain the first few hours of escape could be. She'd been there before. "Sara you welcome ta travel wit me and Bessie when she gets heah." Kimbe didn't bother to wait for a reply she just went on talking. "We got a sure fire plan and dependable connections ta get north ta Canaan. Soon's we get word from Miss Clara." She looked at Sara curiously, she still seemed nervous and unsettled. "Chile how'd you get away from Angory anyhow?" She picked up a yam for herself then offered Sara more sustenance. Sara waved off her offer and lowered the strap of her dress, exposing firm, milk filled breasts. She commenced feeding her infant. Little Solomon ravaged his mother's nipple. It was plain to see the baby was hungry. "Thas right baby. Eat it up," Kimbe quipped. "Ain't no white baby gonna get that good mother's milk."

Sara seemed to settle down some. Calm enough to recount her escape. "I know'd you'd still be heah," she said, "I saw Bessie when I was leavin. I knew you wadn't gon no wheah witout her."

"Thas right," Kimbe nodded in agreement. "I gotta wait fo ma sistah. I been waitin for a while now and I ain't heard nothin from the plantation yet." She exhaled exhaustedly. "I caint leave till I do." She wiped at the sweat rolling down the back of her neck with a soiled cloth. "This waitin part, doin nothin got to be the hardest part of all." Sara nodded knowingly. "You might as well wait wit me," Kimbe offered again. She pointed to her son who had since given up his wooden ship for sleep under a coarse woolen blanket. "He's sleeping like the child that he is. We can all make ourselves comfortable heah until then."

"No Kimbe," Sara stated firmly. "I'm gone soons I gets some rest." Kimbe looked at her beneath raised eyelids. "What's yo hurry chile."

"I hear of a family north of heah who heps colud get up North. I'm gone get my baby there soon's I can. They call it the underground station," she informed Kimbe proudly. "I know bout the underground," Kimbe stated, "and it runs good with the right plan and organization. You can't just upset the way things run Sara. To many people have put there lives on the line to make it work. That's why I'm waitin for Bessie and Miss Clara's word."

"That's why 'YOU'! waitin, Kimbe," Sara said all too coarsely. "that plans built around you not me. I done all right so far on my own plan."

"But just up and leavin ain't no plan. There's things about this business you don't understand. Things important for you to know to survive."

"Like what?" Sara asked sharply. Even she couldn't explain her own boorish tone. "Miss Clara gettin word to us out heah? How she gonna do that, Kimbe?"

"See Sara, thas what I mean. That fool hard headedness ain't gonna get you or that baby far. You don't know nothin. At least not enough and theah a whole lot more to runnin than jus walkin off the field. You say you heard of a house where you can get shelter? Well when you expects help from people in this game you have to make sure a they safety too. Do you know if it safe to go there now, Sara? Do you? You know if the paddy roller out lookin for you right now? No!" she answered her own question. "But Miss Clara can find out and arrange all that and let you know. There's a reason why so many of us been gettin away lately. Thas because a lot of people took care to do a lotta plannin. All you have to do is take heed, wait and listen."

"What you mean listen." Sara's tone was indignant.

"Listen for the singin comin out a the fields," Kimbe replied. "That's how you get word out here Sara. They tell us what we need to know, right under them white folks noses. Ya better stay awhile and learn sumptin Sara. Figger out what cha CAN do. Best to wait an see." Sara had never heard this before. But "Hum hum hum," was her incredulous reply. Her indignation remained, propped by an arrogant pride. "There been people who made it without as much," she retorted with a shake of her head. "But not as many who made it with," Kimbe retorted. She was, by now, thoroughly vexed with the girls hard headed attitude but endeavored to prod on. "Sara you stay get some rest. By the time we get word you oughta be stronger," she went on exhaustedly.

"An better able ta travel."

"But you is waitin fo Bessie," Sara argued.

"Don't you worry none bout that. Bessie'll be here befo long." Sara looked at her thoughtfully and shook her head again. "I got freedom in my feet NOW!, Kimbe," Sara insisted, stumping her foot emphatically. "I caint stay heah waitin. I gotta get to that house sose I know I'm on my way." Sara's eyes narrowed to determined slits. "I ain't goin back to slavery Kimbe I ain't. I can't take the white folks meanness no mo. I'm goin and I ain't stoppin till I gets up north."

131

"Thas what we want too Sara. But ya gotta be careful chile not reckless. Mistakes out there can get yo butt killed. Or worse right back on the plantation."

"I ain't worryin none to much bout that Kimbe. And you right, nothin could be worse than goin back to slavin, not even death." The look in Sara's eyes sent a nervous chill through Kimbe's stomach. "What bout Josh?" she managed to stammer. Sara dropped her head. "I been waitin long enuff," she almost whispered. "Josh'll surely come fo ya." Kimbe thought she may have touched a nerve. But Sara rebounded. "Josh ain't gon run no wheah and you knows it."

"But his chile out heah. Might be nuff ta,"

"Kimbe, I caint sit here waitin fo what he might do. I got ta figure what I know he most likely do. An he ain't most likely ta come heah lookin fo me. I got dis far by myself. I can make it the rest a the way jus the same." A tear formed in the corner of Sara's eye. "Dem white folks is so mean," she related in a shaking voice. "So very, very mean Kimbe. I caint go back dere and I caint take my baby back to that kinda life." A tear in Kimbe's eye showed her sympathy to Sara's lament. "I know Sara. But I ain't talkin bout goin back. I'm talkin bout takin care an bidin time. Chile thas the only way to get away and stay away. To move slow an careful. Now ya need ta stay here wit me, Sara. Don't go jus yet." Kimbe exhaled in exasperation. Sara's new found determination was as visible as the fierce stubbornness in her eyes. Sara was determined and hell bent on leaving and leaving now. Kimbe smiled weakly trying to hide her exasperation. She shook her head. "I know Sara. They sho make life hard fo colud people."

*****

The McPacker Brothers, John and Virgil were the best fugitive slave trackers in the county. Their business sense and tracking prowess was inherited from their father, Angus McPacker who immigrated to the United States with his father, William from McGinely, a small village in the northern province of Scotland, The new immigrants settled down in the northwest territory of the new world and flourished as trappers and traders of beaver pelts, trading with the French and British outposts in the area. After serving with General Mad Anthony Wayne during the Revolutionary War Angus, now with his own young sons, switched from trapping beavers to tracking run away slaves. One night Angus, perhaps inured by the meekness of the beavers he used to trap, cornered a runaway slave and was killed by him. With their father gone John and Virgil continued the family business. John, the oldest took charge as manager. His spoken english was mixed with the Scottish tongue of his father. His younger brother Virgil, large and strong but not too bright provided the brawn and spoke exclusively in the broken hillbilly drawl of the south. Virgil admired his older brother and always without fault followed his instructions dutifully. They lived unassumingly on their small farm tended by John's wife and two sons. The McPacker's mother and even younger brother, Harry lived there as well.

Both brothers entered the farm through the rickety wooden gate, followed by their tracking dog and black assistant, after returning a runaway slave to the Wilson plantation. John believed they'd find the Richards slave and her 9 year old with the Wilson's slave but he was wrong. She and the boy were not to be found. John's beefy red face was lined with anxiety. He didn't look forward to reporting to Colonel Richards empty handed. There wasn't even a line on the direction they'd continued in. John and crew had tracked them as far east as Fall Point Mountain where they'd apprehended the Wilson's slave at it's base but lost the trail of the mother and son somewhere at the summit. Losing the trail the way they did perplexed him. All the trail signs were prominent in the beginning. They were so obvious all the way to a stream half a mile from Fall Point. There they disappeared. He expected to second guess the woman. Maybe pick up her trail further down stream on the other side of Fall Point. But on the other side there were no signs.

No signs at all. Those niggers can be crafty at times, he thought to himself. But they've never been so crafty or unpredictable as to evade him. He shook his head facetiously. A woman and a child. "I am truly kittled, by Eire," he admitted to himself with his pet phrase.

"What's that John?" Virgil thought he'd heard John say something.

"Them nigra's Virgil," he replied scratching himself inside his pants.

"It tis as though they toppled from the edge of this world."

"Don't chall worry none, John. We a git that nigra an her pickininny."

"It just seems to be gettin harder to track em Virgil." John turned and scratched his head under his dusty, sweat soaked hat. He had to squint his eyes to look down the road as he talked. There was a rider galloping toward them. "Who's that John?' Virgil asked, squinting. John looked and recognized him by the way he rode. Even before he came into clear view he knew who it was. "It's Clem. By the Saints," he complained. He surmised Clem was carrying a demand from Colonel Richards. He probably wanted a report on the nigger woman and her son. "How'd he know we was back?" There was an implicative manner to Clem's urgency. Something in the way he rode that suggested his visit meant more than Colonel Richards' wanting a report. They watched him as he rode up to the house. His horse kicked up dust in every direction. Clem dismounted before his horse came to a full stop. "McPacker we got us anothern." He gushed forth in excitement. John was barely able to understand him. "Another nigger's run off?" he asked without feigning disbelief. There was no believing the gall of these niggers of late. "By the Saints of Eire you boys over there need to brake them notions out them nigger's heads once and for all. Afore you know it you won't have a slave left." Clem couldn't tell if the man was serious or having fun with him. Big John McPacker frightened him. Him and his Irish brogue. Not a cringing fear but a weariness that made him uneasy. It may

134

have been the ruthlessness the man was known for. Especially with Blacks. He was just as capable of being ruthless with white men. He found John's brother Virgil not as frightening, in spite of his burliness. As long as John was calm Virgil was no threat. But when John exhibited his wrath, it was Virgil who often acted out his brothers aggressions.

John McPacker upended a wooden bucket and sat on it, then pulled off his boots and socks one after another and brushed the dirt from the bottom of his feet. He bent over his chunky frame making himself grunt as he spoke.

"By Eire, I think I'll talk to the Colonel about contracting our talent for breaking the runaway spirit. The only way to put a stop to these doings is to make kithe the notion that running away will only bring them harm. Once I brake the black devils, by Eire there'll be no need for me to track em down. They'll be deviled to run away again. I may put myself out of business," he laughed. Clem timidly interrupted, "McPacker, Mr. Smith would be obliged if you'd get right after the niggress. She's only been gone little more than six hours."

"Mister Smith? Aye."

"Yea. The Colonel ain't been told yet," Clem continued sheepishly, measuring the effect of his words on John McPacker. "Mr. Smith wants you to find her before it becomes a need to tell him." McPacker slapped his thigh and grunted. "I see. Don't wish to rouse the wrath of the ole Colonel huh. Well by Eire the lack of sleep you wish me to endure is gonna cost ye extra lad. Also we been employed by your Colonel to track another winch. This reprieve in tracking will also call for an extra expenditure."

"Mr. Smith thought as much. So I am authorized to grant you a quarter more."

"Double!" demanded McPacker.

"Mister Smith only authorized..."

"Mister Smith be damned. "Added risk and resources nets added cost." Clem shrugged his shoulders. After all Jim Smith wanted the job done through covert channels. He had no choice but to agree. "Good! By Eire. Now lad, if you'll be good enough to tell me all the particulars we'll be on our way." Clem hoped to go along with them. After filling McPacker in on all the details of Sara's escape, he was surprised when there was no opposition to his request to tag along. Clem went on briefing the trackers while John and Virgil stood a few feet before him giving their full attention. Not saying a word but absorbing all the facts.

*****

When Virgil turned to ready the horses Clem noticed the man sitting on the ground for the first time. His eyes were closed and he was breathing laboriously as though asleep. John McPacker walked toward the man and kicked him in the thigh. Dust flew from McPacker's pants. "Get up Willie. Get your arse up now!" he ordered in a contemptuous tone. "By the Saints of Eire you'll be sure to earn your keep today! Get up!" Willie sprang to his feet. A terrible soreness was delivered to his brain as his aching feet touched the ground. The pain professed the inequity of the men's traveling arrangements. That said the white men rode horse back while Willie Chaser, the black slave tracker, peregrinated along side the dog they used. The large black man went about his preparations quickly. His thick matted nappy hair, thick lips, wide nose and rich ebony skin typified his pure African heritage. The dissolution in his eyes typified the state of perdition relegated him by his white masters. An identification tag hung around his neck identifying him as a chaser or tracker. His quarry, ostensibly were his fellow human beings. More precisely, his victims were his fellow Africans. Obsequious Willie Chaser went about his task perfunctorily. A turpitude likening him to a bloodhound. A tracking dog, who this day set his scent, along with his masters, on Sara and her new born son.

*****

At work day's end the slaves began tending to their personal needs and congregated in endeared social isolation, at least for a time, from the sight of their enslavers. Each slave community defined its own focal point of activity. On Angora, when weather permitted, a large contained fire in the center of the rectangular configuration of cabins served as the social gathering place. That's when religious and social unburdening was provided through song and interaction. Branches of hickory and fir burned scarlet in a flaming pyre while miniature explosions of crackling sparks burst from it like fireflies in the night. Tired and pain racked slaves gathered around the flames to sing and release their terrible frustrations in song. Trouble bearing, God imploring, soul wrenching songs with coded lyrics in a perfect blend of rhythm and octaves carried their melodious chorus and messages skyward. Resonant voices made ready to herald heartfelt lyrics toward eagerly searching ears hiding and listening among the southern mountains...until the overseers suddenly forced them to cease. Smoke bellowed towards the heavens and a thousand stars while the frustrated group of men and women begrudgingly obeyed the orders to disperse. They did so in every direction. Their tired bodies casting bent silhouettes against the flickering lights dancing upon the cabin walls. Languidly they made there way back to their cabins after being thwarted from purporting their songs. They still wore the clothes they'd worn in the fields. Dirty clothes on perspiring bodies seeking an airy refuge from the thick atmosphere suspended about on a claustrophobic night. Some of the women carried babies, some led small children by their hands while others walked sullenly along side their men. Every face in this parade of bondage wore a sardonic mask of discouragement.

Jim Smith stood in front of the community fire with two armed assistants. With both hands on his hips he imperiously finished his execrative speech, apprising them there would be no more singing tonight. Shooing them away like flies. Unaware of the action he'd scuttled. "Run along now!" he yelled at their retreating backs. "There'll be no more a y'all wailin tonight...Ought ta be gettin some sleep." He turned to his companion and laughed at what he thought was a clever quip. "There'll be plenty work to be had tomorrow. Now get!!!"

By order of Colonel Richards, Jim Smith removed their singing privileges in response to Sara's escape. The slaves were otherwise inured to these petty castigation's. But singing had never been prohibited on Richards plantation before and it was a problem. Tonight's vesper had a surreptitious meaning that made the white man's intrusion more of an inconvenience than they could know. The grumbling in the mist of the white men's laughter meant far more than the loss of religious or social fellowship. Through Miss Clara's direction the group had planned to sing a song of hope tonight. Those abstruse lyrics, they knew would have given both aide and comfort to Sara and Kimbe's waiting ears.

The song Miss Clara was prepared to lead the people in tonight would have warned that Sara's disappearance had been discovered. It would have implied a lot more to the women than the explicit words told. That enigmatic information would be well beyond the purview of the whites who thought their black adversaries too ignorant to develop intrigue. Like Miss Clara always said. "Colored folks ignorance was a tool for outsmartin white folk." But even the pretense of ignorance could not account for white folks outsmarting them by default. Hearing a song within 24 hours of escaping was an important tool to a runaway. The resonant caroling of voices over cabin walls can carry a lyrical melody for miles. Lonely black ears in swamps and caves searching for freedom had found instruction and solace in those decipherable words for years. Refrains like "Go down Moses," "Goin over yonder," "Goin up to Canaan" could instruct the listener to avoid detection by going south, east, west or north. "Wade in the water" would warn them that dogs were on their trail. Every plantation amazingly had the same unique encryption and their own bonded doyens to orchestrate it's secret compositions.

At Fall Point Mountain Kimbe and Sara sat anxiously in silence waiting to hear the voices. Some word to alert Sara that her disappearance was or wasn't discovered. Kimbe awaited a message that would herald the coming of her sister Bessie. But there was nothing. A beginning portion of a song had started but then vanished before it could be identified. The song was over before they had a chance to encode anything.

Jim Smith and his cohorts watched until the slaves disappeared into the night. The smell of cheap whiskey mixed with the white men's condescending laughter as they turned to leave, singing to mock the slaves, with their own anacreontic ditty. Josh, Miss Clara, Minnie and Bessie distraught, made their way back to Miss Clara's cabin. Concern for Sara and the baby vehemently etched on there worried faces. Seeing the group congregate around Miss Clara's cabin didn't concern Jim Smith. In fact he blew a sigh of relief because he knew her as the slave community matriarch and respected her as someone who could be called on at times to quell disturbances in the small shanty. A voice of reason on behalf of the whites. Jim Smith even had plans for enlisting her services, if all else fails, to help put a stop to this run away situation. At the very least her cabin could serve as a place where slaves would feel free enough to be spied upon.

Satisfied that all was quiet and under control the three white men retired to their prospective homes. Still laughing and amused, they congratulated each other with hearty slaps on the backs as they disappeared beyond the fires radiant threshold. Miss Clara stood in the doorway of her cabin watching the white men fade into the darkness. A hate unseemly to the aura of an old woman permeated from every pore. She was an old slave. She'd been on Angora since she was a very young woman. She served many functions as a field slave and a stint as a house servant but now her primary job was tending the small slave children while their mothers were in the field until they themselves were old enough to go. She was a gaunt and effete matriarch with no children of her own. Very black and very wrinkled she held the respect of all the slaves, and an ostensible respect from some of the whites who came across her at the Richards plantation. Miss Clara turned back to the group assembled in her cabin. Minnie, a wiry brown skinned slave of Sara's age who'd spent most of her free time with Sara approached the already lit fire place and grabbed a charred tipped stick for a poker and stoked the fire. "I wish I'da know'd she was goin run. She shoulda at least tole me sumptin," she said into the flames, stabbing the fire angrily. "

"Less people know the better chile you know that," stated Miss Clara slowly making her way inside. "Some us ain't so tight lipped. Some don't even need to be ase to tell nothin," she accused prudently. "I just hope she a wait," added Josh. "She ain't hear no singin she might think she ain't been found out yet. You know how she is." His voice shaking.

"Yea," agreed Minnie. "Sara ain't never had no patience."

"Hard headed is da word," chimed in Josh.

Though no one had yet mentioned it, everyone thought about the child Sara carried with her. Josh was the father and everyone knew and silently humored his concern. He nervously paced in the corner while the others claimed seats around the one room cabin. Miss Clara, now standing over an iron vat sitting on a stool in another corner of the room brushed away foamy bits of floating fruit to expose a brownish liquid fermenting beneath the foam. Ladling the sweet juice she sipped some. "Ahhh! Not just yet." She shifted to her rocking chair, sat down and began rocking slowly. "I reckon she done caught up wid Kimbe by now. Eh Bessie?"

"Yes Maam," replied a tall, muscular woman with very dark skin. "I reckon they both sittin up deah at Fall Point Cave. I bet Sara bout as whipped as she can be after havin nat baby and climbin all the way to da Point."

Miss Clara sighed. "I reckon so. But Sara strong and young...and more so she's determine in God's will."

"Id'a thought she'd wait till she was a bit stronger," claimed Josh. "She so hard headed. She could be out theah somewhere in the woods bleedin ta death."

"We done worked fo these peckahwoods befo right up ta and afta havin babies. Ain't no reason she caint find da strength to work a little fo her freedom after havin her's," averred Mamie, a dark brown skin girl who'd followed the group into the cabin. "Dats all well and good!" spouted Josh angrily, "but we ain't figured how we gone get word ta her. Dem peckawoods don stopped us from singin. So what now..."

"Now just hold on Josh," interjected Miss Clara. She softened her tone to show her patience. "We know ya worried. But calm yoself. Sara ain't gettin but so far wit dat baby. If she was to be caught she'd been caught by now so she must ta got ta Kimbe. Kimbe waitin fo Bessie and you know she ain't going no where till she hear frum her. So calm yoself.. Sara's in good hands."

Foot steps outside the cabin caused Josh to cut off an apology. The others turned towards the door. A squat and shabbily dressed black man humbly entered. "Pardon me..," he said removing a crumpled hat from his head. "Miss Clara heah?" Everyone got the impression he already knew the answer. "Miss Clara.., folks.. Sorry fo bustin in on ya.. I jus got heah and I heard yo voices in heah. I'm Caesar. My old master was in debt to yo Mass Richards. So her I is as payment." "I hear yall done had some runaways."

"Thinkin bout runnin away yoself?" asked Josh incredulously, eyeing the intruder askance.

"Naw nigger, just makin small talk and gettin aquatinted."

"Thas a funny question to start wit," challenged Josh.

"Calm yo manners Josh," Miss Clara intervened. "Come on in Caesar," she beckoned from her rocking chair. "Don't mind Josh he jus a little fussy sometimes."

"Oh thas all right Miss Clara," Caesar giggled slapping Josh familiarly on the back. Josh squinted daggers at him.

Caesar made his way further into the room. Miss Clara eyed him to size him up. "How'd you know to look fo me?"

"Mr. Smith tole me you could get me settled."

"Uh ah," Miss Clara rubbed her chin. "What kind a man was yo ole masta. Was he mean."

"No Maam," said Caesar, wearing a broad smile. "We had it pretty good at Mass Charles. He a good man."

"A good man huh?" Miss Clara laughed. "Son I caint imagine a good man ownin and givin way people like they was a horse or a dog or sumpthin." Caesar looked from face to face as they all laughed. He couldn't understand what was so funny. "No Miss Clara that good ole masta ain't gonna give up a good horse o a good dog. But he sho ain't gon sweat ova givin up a good nigger," added Minnie in her high whining voice. Caesar was beginning to feel insulted. Seeing the affect their humor had on him Miss Clara changed the venue. "Caesar, some of our girls ain't with us right now and we feelin bad cause we caint hep em. But we can pray for God to hep and guide em and have mercy on their souls...Will you join us in a prayer for them. We was jus bout ta pray."

"Why I spose I be glad ta..." replied Caesar reluctantly. Together the small group quieted and knelt together while Miss Clara led them in prayer. They all closed their eyes and recited her fervid plea for Sara and Kimbe's safety but her eyes remained open and never left Caesars face.

*****

With Miss Clara's help Kimbe and Bessie prepared their escape weeks ago. They'd plan to meet at the end of the workday and make there way to a pre-proposed weigh station along the underground. But after days of planning, Mrs. Richards thwarted Bessie's part by assigning her to some unexpected chore. Kimbe remained at the rendezvous as long as she could, long enough to know Bessie wasn't coming. By then Kimbe was committed and well past the point of return. She knew if she continued to wait at the edge of the vacant tobacco field she was sure to be spotted. There was no choice. She took Noah and ran. She prayed her sister would soon be able to seize another opportunity. That was a week ago, and still she waited. She was consigned, however, to wait. No matter how long it was going to take. This wasn't Kimbe's first. She once stayed free for almost a year. It was there while hiding among indigenous people and other runaways in the Florida swamps that she conceived her son Noah. But her freedom didn't last long. Kimbe was recaptured and punished severely for being obstinate enough to want her liberty. But, even punishment would not deter her from her longing for liberation and whenever she saw the same spirit in a fellow bondsman, she nourished it...welcomed it with open arms. Now she recognized it in her unexpected companion.

Sara had been in the cave now for 32 hours. Her anxiety mounted strong. Together with her condition her nerves were racked raw...It made her restless and anxious to move on. Kimbe watched as impatience ate away at the young impulsive girl. "I ain't heard nothin else so far," commented Sara. Just a few bars were heard before the song abruptly stopped. "I wonder what coulda happen?"

"Wait anotha day," suggested Kimbe. "Miss Clara knows we here. She'll see to it we hear somethin."

"Kimbe I caint wait anotha day."

"Remember you just had a youngin.."

"Yea, I just had a youngin. But shoot! Goin right out ta work in the fields wit a brand new sucklin don't mean nothin ta dem white folks. So I sho ain't gonna let it stop me from gettin my freedom. Anyways," she waved her hand, "I feel just fine." Kimbe wanted to keep her there. Sara's impulsive and impatient ways were known to many around the plantation they once called home. "I can see that Sara. You think this baby ready for..." Sara cut her off with another wave of her hand. "Same go fo this youngin a mine Kimbe. I think it's time fo us to go on ta Caanan...or glory," she pounded a free hand on the ground for emphasis. "One thing fo sho. I ain't gon back ta Richards plantation. Sittin here, is like waitin fo the paddy rollers to jump down on me." She looked around the cave. "I gotta keep movin." She shook an index finger at her hostess. "Maybe you oughta do the same Kimbe. YOU oughta come go wit ME!" Kimbe remained silent and just looked at her. "I'm gon be free," Sara declared stomping on her heel, then stretched her free arm to the heavens while the baby nursed. "When I left, it was like a call from glory, Kimbe. Like God was showin me the way."

"Sara you always jumpin at things gal. Sometime ya gotta think things out. God lay the spirit on you but he spect you ta use some sense. Don't mess it up by movin on blindly. I ain't sayin God ain't workin in ya but its smart to look at each step befo ya leap."

"When God lay the spirit on me he mean fo me ta see it through. Not sit ponderin whether he mean go this way o that," argued Sara. Solomon never let up his voracious attack on his mother's breast. Kimbe listened to Sara as Noah sat between her legs on the sandy cave floor, staring at the nursing infant.

*****

Except that night had come and gone, neither woman was aware of what time of day it was. One thing they knew for sure. The sun was high above the mountain. The air was warm and dry and Sara was determined and ready to go in spite of Kimbe's protestations. Kimbe decided to change tactics. "The last underground train group going north was the one me an Bessie was spose ta be on," she reported. "I don't know when the next one be. But I do know Miss Clara gonna let us know when that is. You caint go to them peoples farm till then Sara! It might not even be the same one." Kimbe wasn't talking about a train literally but a symbolic gathering of runaways who would gather periodically at a predetermined place. A station. Usually a farm. From there to be led north by a conductor. Someone whose express function was to lead them safely out of the south to freedom in the north along a pre-planned route of hidden paths and safe houses. Sometimes these trains would not leave for weeks and they hardly ever left from the same station twice in succession. Kimbe stared at Sara to see if she was taking it in. Sara's expression gave no clue of concern. She kept looking at her baby. Convinced of her empowerment. "You hearin me Sara," she harkened. "You go trudgin off in them woods the paddy rollers gon get you sho."

"Kimbe, dey don't even know I'm gon yet. You said yoself Miss Clara would warn us if there was trouble. We ain't heard nothin so must not be nothin. Thas why I gotta go befo dey fine out I'm gon."

"Sara you don't know that!" This girl is so hard headed Kimbe reflected, gritting her teeth. Her stubbornness was as infamous as her impulsiveness.

"Kimbe," she began slowly. "I know in my heart its time fo me ta go." She appreciated the older woman's concerned. She hoped her tone conveyed that point sincerely. Kimbe felt at last that it was useless. Reluctantly she capitulated. Sara's mind was made up. She gave her three potatoes, a knife and a blanket for the baby. At least she could help her prepare for this unwary journey. Sara gathered the supplies and eased out through the cave entrance. Kimbe and Noah followed with the baby. Sara scaled the ledge on her stomach onto the berm she turned and extended her arms. Kimbe handed the child to her then climbed up herself. Again she took the child from Sara. Once more Sara repeated the climbing maneuver to the next ledge then turned again to receive Solomon, asleep now, and bundled in the blanket. After following Sara onto this last ledge Kimbe and Noah only dared to accompany her and the baby to the small trail leading along the upper stream and down the side of the mountain. Here they said their goodbyes.

"Be particular," Kimbe warned her without trying to conceal her concern.

"I'll be careful," she smiled. "You do the same." She looked at Noah. "Take care o yo Momma boy You hear," Sara playfully mugged him across his chin.

"Yes 'em," Noah replied weakly.

"I'm gone be free," Sara called to them happily as they turned out of sight. She shifted the weight of the infant to her other arm then with an eerie laugh, repeated the refrain… "or be daid."

*****

Sara's one hundred and ten pounds of fortitude and determination pushed along the trail leading to the base of the falls while Kimbe and Noah returned to the cave. Kimbe held her son tight against her bosom and shuddered. Her eyes filled with conviction and tears. Noah could sense it. Something imperceptible to his young mind but it was there, growing in his collective conscious. It was more than a mother's embrace it was an energy of will and fortitude. Fear and courage created a strange mixture of forbearance and determination. How much will does it take to overwhelm the changes that seem irreparable. To Noah, a Black child, his mothers aura of embrace conveyed a history of malady and affliction. A collective disparity of fear, hopes and tears. So much more than a nine year old mind should be required to digest. It was an impossible hope for a black child to hold but a simple perception a white child would find as a birthright.

*****

John and Virgil finally surmised the best direction to search. East of Angora. Willie Chaser and the dog tracked a hundred yards ahead as the McPacker's trotted leisurely behind on their horses. Clem tagged along quietly. About four miles out, halfway across a small clearing the dog picked up it's pace. "He's got a scent by Eire, Virgil!" Willie Chaser struggled to keep up with the animal. His chest heaved as his lungs filled with oxygen and his heart pumped furiously to carry that precious air to his limbs. The horsemen maintained their pace, keeping the trackers on point within their sight. Just beyond the clearing lay a thick patch of forest accessible only by a small path leading into it. A few yards inside the forest just off the path, Sara sat, resting with her son. The strain of child bearing and the stress of escape turned out to be more than she'd anticipated. She sat by a tree to catch her breath.

She was barely visible from the path's entrance and completely unseen from the clearing. But she could see and hear Willie Chaser approaching. She wasn't too alarmed by his sight. Perhaps he was another brother in liberation. Then she spotted the dog just ahead of him and the horsemen in the distance behind him. She became frightened. They were all part of the same dangerous entourage. She knew that now. It was bad enough that her freedom was now threatened by these horsemen, but they were being led to her by one of her own. Fear gave way to ire that abolished her exhaustion. She laid her baby against the tree then brandished her knife. Sara turned the large blade over and over in her hands anticipating their moment of arrival. In her judgment the dog would reach her first. That should give her enough time to gut the animal, then escape through the thick brush. The animal picked up it's pace. From her vista in the brush she watched him trot closer. She readied herself flexing the knife. Not too tightly yet not too loose. If she could just get that dog out of the way quick enough she could then do something to throw the men off her trail. Sara braced herself and wished for the first time that she'd stayed in the cave. Why hadn't Miss Clara warned her these men were out looking. Maybe they weren't looking for her. But what would that matter. One fugitive was no different than the other to a paddy roller or his dog and his nigger. Sara bared her teeth in anger. There was no time for regrets only time for fierce determination.

The dog broke away from it's black companion. Sara crouched down ready to pounce...When...suddenly!...she was startled by a strange noise behind her. A whirling sound. Loud, yet not blaring. She turned to it. The din crescendoed into a flash of light and energy that almost knocked her down. Like being engulfed by lightening. Then...something came out of the light. It seemed to materialize from it. It was a strange unearthly form...It was like...an animal. A strange, eerie animal that looked almost human but smaller. It's large bulbous black eyes were the eyes of a demon. A sight she'd never seen before. A demon from hell. The demon wore clothes. A one piece brown outfit. A pouch hung from it's side, probably for gathering the lost souls it collected. Long coarse hair jutted out from it's sleeves and neckline. It's face was covered with hair and it's eyes were black and too large for it's face. Such a hideous thing was surely from the very depths of hell. Instinctively she let out a yell. Then from her periphery she saw the dog closing in on her. But instead of attacking her the dog charged past her. Straight for the demon. Even the dog knew the devil when he saw him. But this devil was afraid. The demon ran back toward what appeared to be a small cage. For some reason it couldn't get inside it. The dog chased the thing around the cage, barking ferociously. Sara took advantage of the incident and attacked the dog. The threat the fleeing demon posed was now small compared to a dog who would surely return to his masters business. With more speed then she realized she possessed she was on the dog, plunging her knife deep into his side just as he wrestled the demon to the ground. Blood sprouted everywhere. The dog turned toward Sara to counter attack. But turning is as far as it got before falling over incapacitated from the gapping wound in it's side. It's head made a feeble attempt to rise but the dog's body would not come along. He just laid there panting and bleeding profusely. Sara knelt beside the dog gasping. She hadn't noticed the demon had escaped while she struggled with the dog. Nor did she notice the flash of light and energy erupting from the demon's cage before it all vanished into thin air. When she looked it was gone...Without a trace. As if it had never been. The entire incident was terrifying. Too much to bare. Frantically Sara scampered to her son and scooped him up. She ran as fast as her legs could carry her. Sheer terror motivating every step. Willie stepped off the path into the area where Sara had been hiding. He was bent over trying to catch his breath when he caught sight of Sara's blurred image bolting through the brush. Before pursuing her he saw the lifeless body of the dog laying beside a blood splattered tree. He rushed to the animal and knelt down beside it, lovingly stroking it's head while life's fluid flowed from it's body. Rueful tears of pain flowed from Willie's eyes. Seconds later he heard the hooves of his masters' horses approaching. Willie ran out of the brush to meet them. "She kilt ole Hound suh. She kilt him," he cried painfully. "By the Saints of Eire. After her Willie," commanded John McPacker. "After the nigger wench." Willie took off in Sara's direction. John McPacker dismounted to see the dog for himself. Virgil and Clem remained on the path. There horses circled impatiently. John returned to the path and mounted his horse.

"The wicked slattern slit him from tail to gullet Virgil." There was an obvious sign of hurt in his tone. "The heartless wench. "I'll slit her from arse to breast plate."

"Remember boys. She's Angora property," warned Clem.

As the riders guided there horses in Sara's direction another silent blast emanated from inside the brush. The disturbance was only marginally perceptible to them but apparent enough to their horses to make them buck. John was thrown from his mount. Willie seeing his master thrown to the ground cut off his pursuit to returned to his masters aid. "Go on fool," John yelled from the ground. "Get back after the wench." Just as quickly as he responded to his masters plight so did Willie obey his masters direct. Virgil dismounted to assist his brother after calming his own horse. Neither man could fathom what had spooked the horses. Nor had they noticed the figure that appeared...just out of their sight.

CHAPTER 6

Year 2000

"10, 9, 8, 7, 6, 5, 4, 3, 2, 1." Argee's count down was like an echo fading in the distance. Barely audible among the whirling and humming of the ARC as it powered up. "Transmission!" was all Shai heard before sight and sound merged into one. In one instance he could see his colleagues plainly, functioning busily at their controls. In the next their images collapsed into a thousand specks of molecular beads. He was experiencing peculiar sensations. His mind seemed to be torn from his head. His body felt deatomized like the fulminated image of his spectators. Shai spun wildly, jaculating in opposite iterant waves of retrorse. He was vaginated, crumpled into a thousand portions of light then violently and abruptly snapped back together and all sensations ceased, replaced by a hasty and silent calm. A death like calmness. Shai opened his eyes slowly then blinked hard and removed his goggles. He looked around slowly. Gone were his colleagues, the laboratory, the terminals, the computers, the building, the ARC. Everything! In their place was the greenest of foliage and the unmistakable sounds of nature. A butterfly danced before his eyes. Behind it a stage of trees, bushes, grass and flowers lay in picture postcard serenity. A soft gentle breeze stroked his face. For an instance none of this made sense. Then it hit him. A forest! His mind yelled out in an epiphany...He'd made it! He'd actually made it! He had crossed over into another time another dimension!! It worked, his mind shouted. He was there...He was...Where?...When? None of it was apparent but he was undeniably in some other place. At some other time. He knelt down to remove the ignition OCP all the while scanning his new surroundings. "Where the hell am I?..." he asked himself. "What era?...Neolithic?...No," he inferred scanning the vegetation around him. "Maybe pre colonial. Post colonial..." Cautiously he stepped away from the platform. "I'm a TIME TRAVELER!!" An amusing phrase, he thought. Imagine. Back in time. But again when and where became the question. That's what he was here to find out. Wasn't it? That was his mission. He smiled for one more euphoric moment then got to work. He had to find something. An artifact or geologic sample that Professor Kobolongo could examine. Something to substantiate the date or era for Bilal to formulate Factor X. Which way to go? It was a coin toss. There was no procedure, no technique or contingency to go by.

Shai decided to walk east. He thought of the blood stains on King Tut's jumpsuit and a wave of apprehension washed over his exhilaration. There was no animal life form about that he could see, still he walked cautiously. Almost crouching. His head rotated like a tank turret, watching the slowly passing terrain. The foliage was thick. Lots of trees and brush. He'd walked several yards before stumbling over something. He looked down and what he saw made him jump. The body of a blood covered dog laid at his feet. It's wound was still wet and oozing serum. Immediately, he again thought of Tut and the monkey's return transmission. The blood of a canine, Doctor Belton had said. Shai looked at the dead animal's wound. It was long and deep. Too long and too deep for a rhesus monkey's claws. "Tut couldn't have done this."...Could he?" Suddenly loud, anxious voices came to him from somewhere in the woods. Instinctively he crouched to a kneeling position and froze. The voices seem to be coming from the other side of the tree line. He couldn't see them but he heard them distinctly. "Never mind me boy." Said one voice in a harsh tone, "get that nigger wench!" The words chilled Shai's blood. "Dam!!! Antebellum America? Slave drivers!?!" A staggering feeling overcame him. His instincts griped him and turned him toward the platform to run. The pit of his stomach flipped. The words reverberated inside his skull, more in exasperation than intellectual submission. The thought made him shudder. Shaking, he had to remind himself. The mission. After all, it could be any era of American history. Just hearing the word 'nigger' didn't necessarily mean slavery. It could be a year ago or the day before his transmission. Anytime from the fifteenth century to his own time. His confidence returned with his curiosity. He needed more precise data. He turned back toward the sound.

He could barely see the three men on horse back through the forest cover. He was sure they couldn't see him. The men galloped in apparent pursuit of something or someone. He crept closer to the path to get a better look. Then followed them, staying to the rear and parallel to their movements. He inspected them as much as his purview would allow. There was no doubt now. Their style of dress, the type of gear on their horses, their arms. It was a fact. This was late 18th to mid 19th century. He knew now it was antebellum for sure.

The horsemen stopped 50 yards from where he'd first spotted them. They appeared to be looking at something or someone just ahead. Shai dared to creep closer to get a better view of what they were eyeing. Up ahead he could just make out the figures of a man and a woman. The horsemen were watching them. The man and woman were black. The black man seemed to be making threatening gestures toward the black woman and she was backing up apprehensively. The black man cautiously stalked her. The woman appeared wild eyed. She held something up in each hand. Shai strained his eyes to make out the objects. What he saw struck a nervous knot in the pit of his stomach. She was holding a baby in one hand, upside down by it's ankles. In the other hand she brandished a knife. Her burlap smock and sweating chest heaved up and down with bated breath. Her sweating face was twisted in rage. Her hateful eyes were ablaze with anger below her furrowed brow. "We'll die first!" she warned coldly. Not a trace of hysteria or hesitation in her voice. There was no doubt she meant what she said. She continued to back up and her pursuer continued to follow...Why was she so fearful of the black man?...The paddy rollers. They used black men to help track down their runaways. The thought angered him. Why would a black man aide the slave chasers. Why would a fellow bondsman help the very people who held him in bondage. Should I interfere? He wondered. Surely rectifying this one incident, helping this one black woman wouldn't make a difference in Jubilee's protocol. Would it? But his reverie was broken by the most hideous scene he could have imagined. Without the slightest hesitation the woman raised the baby by it's little feet level to her own eyes. Then raising the knife she quickly and callously ran the blade across it's tiny neck, then dropped it's lifeless body to the ground. All the while her hateful gaze never left the face of the black man stalking her. It was as though she was mocking him with the infants death. The macabre sight stunned all the spectators in their tracks.

"By the Saints of Eire," cried one of the white men in a horrified voice. Shai's legs grew weak and his knees trembled. It was all he could do to keep his guts from spewing and his legs from buckling. The black man remained frozen in place as the woman let out a blood curdling scream and pounced on him with the ferociousness of an animal. Before he could react she plunged the knife into his abdomen. All the way to it's hilt.

"My Lawd," yelled the man when she withdrew it. Her face bore a hideous grin of satisfaction as he staggered backwards and sat on the ground moaning. She straddled the helpless man and grabbed a handful of his nappy hair then swung her arm back to deliver the final coup-de-gras across his neck. The largest of the white men dismounted and pointed a long rifle at her. He warned her to stop. "Drop that knife wench or I'll blow a hole in yer black ass."

"Mass Virgil," begged the black man breathlessly. "Get this wildcat nigger offen me!!" He tried to hold the woman off with one hand and hold back his oozing guts with the other. The eyes of the woman astraddle him caused him to blink in fear. They warned him vociferously. This woman crossed a line that she'd never concede. A line of freedom or slavery where conviction never teetered. Too late, he saw conviction, in her eyes that he'd never seen before. "No quarter, evil whitman, no quarter!!" she yelled and leaped from Willie toward Virgil. At a back stcp he pulled the trigger of his shotgun, point blank. The force of the blast caught her in mid air and threw her back upon the ground. Her eyes continued to blaze hatred as she struggled to get up, still holding the knife, determined to fight. The second blast smashed into her chest and laid her prostrate on the ground.

"By the Saints you've killed her, Virgil" scolded John McPacker.

"The crazed nigga was hankerin to kill me John!"

"Colonel Richards just might kill us all," protested Clem.

"Sometimes these things cannot be averted, young Clem. The facts are well kithe to the Colonel boy," John reasoned sarcastically. "Sometime an oxen takes ill. A horse takes lame. A dog goes mad...And a nigra gets killed. Ha ha." He shrugged his shoulders. "They happen Clem my boy. They just happen."

From his spot in the woods Shai was appalled by the monologue he'd overheard. It sickened him as much as the grizzly scene terrified him. Never had he been in the presence of such hateful ennui. The men were completely foreign and indifferent to the act. "Massa Virgil!! Massa John!" cried their wounded companion. Then as if by illustration the irritated looks of the white men fell upon Willie then ignored him by returning to themselves. To the ears of the idle chit chatters the pleas seemed to come from far away. His voice, however, succeeded in drawing their attention and they again turned their focus on the fallen negro. Inexplicably each man found Willie Tracker's cries irksome. "Massa please. Please, I believe I'm bleedin ta death suh!" The fear in his voice was matched by the terror displayed in his eyes. For a moment nothing was said.

Except for Willie's panting gasps for air there was silence. Willie's eyes widened with mounting terror and for the first time he recognized his true standing in the eyes of the men he believed might reciprocate his loyalty. The revelation frightened him even more. "Massa. Please!"

Virgil remounted his horse and looked to his brother John for instruction. John forwarded his command to his younger brother with his head and eyes. Virgil pulled his horse closer to the bleeding black slave. "Yall gonna take ole Willie to Massa Doc Jeffson?" he pleaded. "Ain't cha suhs!?! Please!!" Willie's eyes bulged from his sweat drenched face. His voice was hoarse and screeching, hinging on a desperate terrified octave.

Shai was awash in pity for the man and rueful for his own inability to help him. He watched Virgil guide his horse even closer to his wounded slave. He looked down on him disdainfully. Willie Tracker writhed at the horses feet as Virgil sneered and withdrew his sidearm. "Yall don fer Willie. I don't see what we can do fo ya." Looking back at his brother smiling he chided, "we caint waste no mo time and money on you when we can always jus gets us anotha nigra." His nonchalant air and tone caused Shai to tremble both in fear and rage. The white man would have probably shown more concern for the plucking of a chicken than the taking of this life. This black man's death elicited no more than an impassive twitch of the nose. "Willie," Virgil quipped callously. "You just don't understand these things. Nothing ta fret over. It's just business."

The humor wasn't lost on Willie Chaser. "Please Suh!" he begged. His voice full of trepidation. "Willie's all right. I can get up Suh, please." Willie made a vain and pathetic attempt to pull himself erect but was thrown back to the ground by the force of the gunshot from Virgil's revolver. With one shot he'd put an end to Willie Chaser's protestations. Shai was soaked in perspiration. He wanted to run from them. He wanted to run at them. But all he could do was stand there, frozen in his spot. His heart bursting with hatred and horror. For a moment he thought the men could

155

hear the wild thumping in his chest. Cautiously he backed himself deeper into the forest and watched the men as they rode past him. They trotted down the path then leisurely galloped across the clearing. He was amazed by the cavalier manner they exhibited after having committed such heinous butchery. When they were out of sight Shai stepped out onto the path and approached the corpses on wobbly legs. So ghastly a scene he'd never seen before. The tiny near decapitated body of the infant laid beside it's mother. Her chest and abdomen were splattered open like a smashed watermelon. Perpendicular to them laid Willie Chaser in crimson soaked clothing. His eyes open wide in disbelief, even in death, of his master's treachery. Shai felt a sickly churning in his stomach. He stood for what seemed like hours before easing around the scene. A vertiginous stumble nearly cost him his balance as he spotted a tarnished metal tag around Willie Chaser's lifeless neck. He stooped to remove it. The blood stained leather tie securing the tag was difficult to brake. It took a violent tug to snap it free. Willie's head jerked with the force of the pull, causing air trapped in the dead man's larynx to escape. The ghoulish moan startled Shai for a moment. He stopped to regain his composure before reading the inscription on the tag to himself.

Willie Chaser
Property of McPacker Bros.
Aiken Co. S. Carolina

"No doubt," he commented to himself aloud, "post colonial, ante-bellum, slave driving, white racist ass America." He was still trembling. He remembered the weapons the white men used and the clothes they wore and the horrible situation it all inferred. It caused a pain deep within him. An antiquated ache in his collective conscience. He inspected the medal further, scratching his cheek then his chin. His face itched all over. Nerves he thought. He looked again at the three black corpses ghoulishly arrayed around him. The woman's dress didn't tell him much right off but the man's clothes were similar to the revolutionary style of the American colonial period. "Hand me downs." "This has got to be pre-civil war. Early fifties I'd say or maybe even the late forties. The info on this tag can be checked at the Library of Congress Archives." A sudden breeze again brought the encroaching stench of death to his nostrils. Sudden urgency crept its way into him amidst all the horror and he turned to leave. "I got to get the hell out of here!" He started back to the Aeon Platform.

*****

The three horsemen rode in silence until Clem hysterically broke in. "What in hell am I gonna tell the Colonel," he shouted. "You tell em the truth by Eire," said John growing annoyed with the man's whining.

"I shoulda went on after her instead a lettin that dumb nigra spook her thata way," Clem went on this way for several minutes, ignoring the tiresome looks of his companions. Reaching a weary point, John McPacker swung his hat at the young man. "This won't do boy," he scolded. "Gather yerself. What is done is done and I do not intend to ride the distance to Angora listening to your belly aching."

"Belly aching by Erie," Clem spouted sarcastically. Mispronouncing the man's pet phrase. "Dam fool..."

"Mind y'all tongue LITTLE CLEM," warned Virgil, drawing the words out. He and his brother had enough of the little man's whining. They were already disappointed, knowing Colonel Richards would be reluctant to pay full price. If at all. It was not a dead or alive job. It was not even a valid job since the Colonel was unaware of the job in the first place. Well, Jim Smith will be liable. He would personally challenge Jim Smith if he decided to renege.

Clem knew the brothers to be dangerous by reputation. He'd crossed the line with his rub and had no desire to be acquainted with the brothers parlousness through experience. Besides he had the added problem and grisly task of getting a wagon and returning to retrieve Sara's body. If that giant oaf

Virgil would have simply subdued the girl instead of opening her chest like a gutted pig he'd be carrying her back unconscious instead. There was also the added task of escorting Jim Smith to an audience with the Colonel, and explaining this sordid affair. At least, he thought to his relief, it was Jim Smith's decision not to inform the Colonel of the escape. Not his. That at least was a burden off his back. But what of the lost property.

"Well, seems the only thing to do is blame the winch's death on Willie," he said aloud. "By the Saint's Clem boy, you may have something there." On that they all agreed. "We even had to kill Willie defendin ourselves," added Virgil laughing and feeling clever for his contribution.

"By the Saints," John yelled, pulling back on his horse. "We left Willie's property tag on his body. No need to forge another," he explained turning his horse around. Virgil and Clem turned their horses to follow. Together they rode back to retrieve the metal ID tag from Willie's vilified neck. After several minutes of leisurely trotting they again reached the clearing. On the other side of the clearing near the tree line they spotted a lone figure in the distance fading into the trees. "Another nigga!" shouted Virgil. "By Eire, they're running away without fear or worry!" added John, taking after the walking figure at a full gallop.

*****

Shai made one more observation of the landscape. The horsemen were halfway across the clearing before he spotted them. Their sight added strength to his legs and he dashed through the line of trees to make his escape. Momentarily he found himself running in the wrong direction. Panic stricken he stopped and spun around trying to reorient himself. "That way!" he shouted and ran. John and his companions were at the path dismounting from their horses while Shai fumbled for the OCP key as he fled. He dropped it, recovered it and continued to run. The forest looked the same in every direction. He was afraid he may be running in the wrong direction again as his pursuers closed in on him. Just ahead he spotted a landmark. He was close to the Plexiglas Aeon Platform. At full stride he raced toward the pad and slid in on it like a ball player at home plate. In one smooth motion he inserted the OCP and locked it in place. The sound of the platform powering up filled the forest with a low pitched hum. Shai stood erect on the platform just as the three men were upon him. He braced himself to repel his pursuers. It was imperative that he remain on the platform and throw them off. Clem reached him first and put his hands out to grab him but was knocked to the ground by a solid punch from Shai's right hand. John McPacker rushed in behind Clem like a raging bull. With the force of a freight train he knocked Shai off the platform just as a burst of electrolumi-nescent energy engulfed the entire area in effervescent light.

*****

Professor Jubilee and the others anxiously manned their controls. Each one hovered over their particular station with worried anticipation. Perturbation was the overall mood throughout the laboratory. No one expected any serious trouble but the element of danger and mishap was an ever present and real possibility. Professor Jubilee warded off his anxiety with premature visions of projects to come. 'Time expeditions' he called them. To ancient Africa, Nubia, Kemet and Judea. All first considerations on the project itinerary. Second. To experience the grandeur of empires like Mali, Timbuktu, Zimbabwe, Dahomey and others. To view the wonderful universities of Sankore and Carthage. Third. To meet and draw knowledge from the greatest like Pianki, Hannibal, Imhotep, Nzingka, Ramses, Melenik and the Kandakis. Fourth: the coming of the European and the beginning of the destruction of African civilization. Fifth. Expeditions to the days of bondage in America. Pre and post Civil War. then ultimately the late 19th and early 20th centuries. Post Reconstruction, Jim Crow. The plate was going to be full. Professor Jubilee closed his eyes in rapturous expectation. All that was needed now to begin the expeditions was the completion of the Azimuth Phase and the Factor X computation of time setting.

Argee returned from the kitchen area with a tray of coffee and soft drinks. Kevin took the tray from her and placed it on an empty desk top. Argee passed the cups around. Bilal declined a cup choosing to remain vigilant by the ARC.'s causeway. He hadn't left the spot since Shai's transmission. Professor Jubilee paced back and forth sipping coffee. Doctor Belton and Professor Lewis remained at their prospective stations. Professor Kobolongo sipped fruit juice and jotted data in his log book. All principles employed their own means of waiting out the period...Suddenly Kobolongo's monitor showed activity! "Aeon Transmission." He put down his pen and tapped some keys on his keyboard. Doctor Belton sat her cup down. "I've got something!" Her voice shook slightly as she received indications on her screen that the VSA had been activated. She bit on the tip of her glasses and noted the empty spaces in the data blocks on her screen. Her voice trembled with consternation. "There's no biological readings." She looked anxiously at Professor Jubilee. He was busily pecking at the keys on his board. "Perhaps there's a malfunction in the VSA."

Argee joined Bilal at the ARC's causeway to receive their friend. With practiced scrupulosity the rest of the team spun into action around their controls, tracking Shai's transmission and aiding the retransmission procedure. "Retransmission!" Professor Jubilee shouted to indicate the Aeon Platforms return. Now inured to it's blasts of energy they watched the ARC's action until transportation procedures ceased and the Aeon Platform appeared...without Shai...The platform...was empty!!!!

Everyone was stunned. An anguished cry escaped from Doctor Belton's lips. Her glasses clattered to the floor. Argee fell faint against Bilal. He held her steady. Professor Jubilee disengaged the ARC's controls and slowly rose from his seat in disbelief. When the platform's glass screen ascended the operators rushed to the causeway, seemingly in one motion.

Doctor Belton's hands flew to her mouth in distress. "Oh my God!" Argee stood in Bilal's arms trembling and sobbing. "Where the fuck is he!!?" Bilal blurted over her shoulder. Kevin bent over the Aeon Platform feeling the empty space where Shai should have been standing. Disbelieving the emptiness, he answered slowly. "I don't know."

"We have to be calm," reasoned Professor Jubilee holding Kevin's shoulders to steady himself. He had to be composed. Shai's survival depended on it. Professor Kobolongo continued to scan the monitors, displaying his own equanimity. He ran through the diagnostics looking for any information that would explain what had happened. Professor Jubilee knelt down to examine the platform. He noted that the OCP device was still locked in place. He detached it. "I don't understand. Somehow he was removed from the platform after activation."

"Could it have been animals?" inquired Kevin. "I mean...like.. pre-historic animals."

"I...don't...know." replied Professor Jubilee with an uncharacteristic stammer. Professor Lewis knelt beside Professor Jubilee. "Is there anything on the platform that will help?" Taking a magnifying glass from his smock pocket Jubilee examined the platform closely. "There's soil here. It may tell us something." He brushed some of the soil onto a card he took from his pocket and handed it behind him to Kevin. "Take it to the archeology school and have some forensic people analyze that for it's organic composition. See if there's time to do a complete analysis. It's the only data we have. We don't have much time to act."

"Much time for what? Pressman what are you thinking?" inquired Doctor Belton.

"What are we going to do?" sobbed Argee.

"Go back for him...Shit!" Bilal exclaimed. Professor Jubilee stood up, imperturbably, speaking to no one in particular. "Bilal's right. And as soon as we can replenish the power...I'll go."

"No!!" Doctor Belton shouted, discomposed.

"No! No!' echoed Argee.

"No sir," averred Bilal, more composed. "That's not what I was thinking sir. I meant me!!"

"I know what you meant son. But what I mean is that it has to be me. I can't send any one else..."

"As you said my brother. Bilal is right," interrupted Professor Kobolongo walking towards them. "And he is right on both accords. You're speaking emotionally Pressman. Come now. You are more rational than that. It has to be one of the young folk, Brother. You know that." Kobolongo went on to cut off Jubilee's further protest with a wave of his hand. "I know you feel responsible Pressman you always do. And you're always worried. But your responsibility is here at the helm. This job is for the young brothers."

"Yes sir. I'll go," offered Bilal

"I agree with Bilal, Pressman. He is the most fit...What do you say?" Kobolongo caressed his friends shoulder. Jubilee looked at the others. They were all in agreement. Pressman closed his eyes and reluctantly agreed. A small bit of embarrassment passed over him. He knew they were right. Professor Jubilee gestured for Bilal's attention. "Before you go I have something for you." Bilal stepped up on the platform expectantly. He was ready to get under way immediately. Professor Jubilee extracted a box from an open panel in the wall. In the box was the prototype for the gelatin gun he and Kobolongo devised. The others knew of it but no one expected it to be used at this stage of the project. He removed the gun from the box and handed it to Bilal. Electromagnetic propelled chemical gelatinous projectiles. They were not engineered for killing. Instead they were meant to instantly incapacitate any living target. Man or animal, large or small. A button on the handle grip switched it from single shot to automatic. Without another word Bilal took the ignition device from Professor Lewis and the gelatin gun from Professor Jubilee as the rest of the team returned to their stations. Argee counted down while Jubilee again fondled his lucky charm and gave a silent prayer. "Activate and Transport," came his order...in minutes...Bilal was gone.

162

Bilal materialized at the other end of transmission, unbeknownst to him, in an American forest of 1852, with gel gun firmly in hand. At the ready. Set on automatic. The area was quiet and serene. Bilal turned a cautious 360 degrees, darting his eyes in compartmental succession. Taking each scene into memory. He saw only trees and foliage. Nothing suspicious. Nothing, at first, that would explain Shai's disappearance until he saw a gold colored object on the ground beside the platform. He picked it up and examined it. It was a metal tag with an inscription etched into it. He placed it in his pocket. The ground around the site, he observed, was disturbed. "A struggle went on here." He ran his hand across the boot like impressions on the ground. Their jumbled configuration made it obvious what had happen. "Shai was jumped! Fucking bastards." There were a lot of indications on the ground to be read. Several footprints turned in different directions at varying depths, clumps of grass dislodged and a long impression that could have been made by a fallen body. Intermittent grooves in the dirt extended from the impression as though someone or something had been dragged away. A lump welled in Bilal's throat as he imagined the iniquity Shai must have faced. "What in hell happened!?!" he inquired to the trees.

Bilal made mental notes of his findings as he walked around. Straight ahead laid a clearing just beyond the tree line. Cautiously he moved towards it. He came across the blood drenched body of the dead dog. It seemed the animal had been disemboweled. Probably with a knife. "What the hell went on around here. What is this place?" he added in desperation. Several feet from the dog he reached a path just below the clearing. A neckerchief strewn in the center of the path lay in the mist of several hoof impressions. "Horses?" The path was a well worn roadway lying just inside the tree line from the clearing. He kneeled to inspect the cloth. Just before he pick it up he caught sight of something further down the path. Clutching the gun in a sweaty hand and pocketing the neckerchief he started towards the aberration. Bilal's heart fluttered wildly in his chest. He moved closer...Then stopped dead in his tracks. The two massacred bodies completely astonished him. They laid on the ground in a grotesque frozen dance. A macabre sight. It made him wince. It was so appallingly repugnant. He'd never seen such a ghastly sight in his life. Flies buzzed around the widening pool of blood and festering wounds. The male's head was abnormally swollen. His unraveled intestines jutted out from his gaping abdomen with its scarlet entrails glistening in the light of the sun. The female's torso was hardly recognizable as human. Her chest was clawed open like a detonated watermelon. Her face was frozen in an eerie, hideous smile as though mocking her fate. Her lifeless eyes stared vacantly up at him. Most sickening of all was the near decapitated baby laying beside her. The infants tiny throat was cut into a ghoulish grin. Bilal staggered backward. He couldn't hold the nausea churning in his stomach. He regurgitated all the undigested material in his gut, spewing it over the legs of the male corpse.

Bilal's face was covered in cold sweat. He removed a small cloth towel from his back pocket to wipe his face. It was the neckerchief he'd found on the road. Repulsively he threw it to the ground and staggered backwards. He'd had enough. It was time to get away from this grisly spectacle. "How does Shai fit into this mess?" he wondered. Bilal looked around fearfully. "Where are you man?" This was way over his head. There must be more information to be found. Something to use to get a fix on Shai. Before turning to go he noticed the broken leather tie around the dead man's neck. He wondered if the tie could have secured the medal tag he found. Was Shai bringing it to the Aeon Pad? He turned weakly to go back up the path, light headed, dizzy and dripping with sweat. He decided to make a full 1/4 mile sweep in all directions around the area of transmission before leaving. Forty five minutes later he'd managed to find his way back to the place where he'd started and took one last look around. Almost two hours had passed since he'd first arrived. He was more than ready to return to his own time.

As soon as Bilal reappeared in the laboratory he ripped off his goggles and stepped weakly from the Aeon Platform. He was suffocating from the horrendous sights he'd seen. Professor Jubilee and the others rushed to him for a report. In an emotional tone he recounted the full and horrible details of what he'd found on his expedition. "Neither of the bodies was Shai," he assured them. "Something very bad happened out there though."

"McPacker Brothers, property of," Professor Jubilee read out loud while examining the medal. He handed it to Doctor Belton. "Willie Chaser?!" she read incredulously. She looked at Professor Jubilee, placing the stem of her glasses in her mouth for a pensive moment, then removed them. "A slave?"

"I'd say so," Jubilee answered. "Argee," he called turning to his worried assistant. "When we're finished here I want you to go to the Library of Congress and dig up anything you can find on these McPacker's."

"Wouldn't it be faster to go online to their site."

"No daughter. I want you to dig into their physical records. If there's any information on them it'll be there." He read the rest of the information.

"Aiken County, South Carolina. Check from about 1830 to 1862. wouldn't you agree Professor Lewis?" he added. "At least."

"Daughter, we'll need slave records, deeds, birth certificates..."

"Birth certificates," Argee interrupted, skeptically.

"Yes, daughter...For the McPacker's."

"Yes sir."

"Professor," called Bilal, "after tabulating the X factor date. Would it be possible to transmit ahead of Shai and intercept him? Do you think that's conceivable?" Kobolongo thought, then looked to Jubilee for his recommendation. "Pressman. What do you think?"

"I don't think so. That could be a problem," he explained.

"There would be an adverse reaction if positive and negative dimensional forces crossed each other in the same dimensional state.."

"We would be transporting the ARC to overtake itself. And that could have very grave and ill effects. It may cause a serious invaginated effect. I only want empirical action on this. Nothing theoretical."

"I agree," said Professor Lewis. "So do I," added Doctor Belton. "We can't afford to take chances." Kobolongo turned to Bilal. "Compute to real time, son." Professor Jubilee buried his head in his hands. Lifting his face he wore a woeful expression. "Getting Shai out of this is going to be tough," he lamented. "But it's to be our highest priority. We're going to need someone with real survival skills on this."

"Going back to antebellum America," Professor Lewis remarked, shaking his head, "is going to be like going into a foreign country alone to extract POWs. Movement would be constricted. You'd be unable to mix unobserved with the locals and they would be extremely hostile and threatening to you."

"Maybe worst," added Kevin.

"What we need," added Doctor Belton, "is a Harriet Tubman.

"What about going back, recruiting her as a guide? Might be worth a try," suggested Bilal. He was still visibly shaken by what he'd seen "She knows the drill and the layout of the land better than anyone we could employ."

"That could be a problem Bilal. We don't know if this is in her time or not. Besides revealing ourselves to her might be too much and too consequential," reasoned Professor Jubilee.

"Sir. We've got to do something!!"

"We will son!!" Professor Jubilee grabbed his shoulders. Then softened his tone. "We're going to do everything. You know that Bilal." Jubilee turned to Argee. "Daughter. We need all the data you can muster on the McPacker's and their time. We need all we can get about the county. And we need someone who can track Shai down and bring him back safely. And family," he rubbed his chin confidently, "I know just the brother we need."

CHAPTER 7

Year 2000

In a conservatively paneled conference room at city hall in Philadelphia, an informal inquiry had been going on for at least an hour. The stance on either side of the question at hand was staunch and stoic. Neither side seemed willing to yield, though one side dealt from and relied heavily upon a position of authority and conservatism. The other side considered itself politically and consensually in the right and because of it's stand the latter stood at an advantage.

Seven men sat at the long mahogany conference table. Two policemen and their representatives on one side. Kuendela Nuguvu and his attorney, Simi Ali on the other. The judge, Leonardo Hicks, sat at the head refereeing the proceedings, ready and willing to pass final judgment. Behind him stood an array of his various support personnel. "I'm appalled," remonstrated Judge Leo Hicks. His pinched red face was frozen in a mask of genuine disgust. His corpulent physique overwhelmed the head of the table, giving him the appearance of some immovable obstacle. He wore his judicial robe over a dark suit though it was really unnecessary for this informal inquiry. But Judge Hicks was a man of tradition, and a proud judiciary with liberal philosophies. "A man of Mr. Adams' stature and influence has no business being harassed and accosted on a public street as a result of his preference of attire. We have long looked down on this kind of profiling."

"But sir! It's reasonably understandable for an officer to be suspicious when he sees a person who obviously looks out of place..."

"Silence!!" scolded the judge. "This is the end of the 20th century. We have thoroughly out lived those old and tired prejudices." Judge Hicks' tone was stern. Neither rising or falling in timbre. He maintained a stoic monotone. Plainly, he was thoroughly irritated. Anderson, a representative for F.O.P, the law enforcement union, appealed. "Judge Hicks!! Mr. Adams struck a police officer."

"In self defense," contended Simi Ali. He leaned in closer to the table and turned his head to the right where Mr. Anderson was sitting so that his response could be directed to him personally. "Being a policeman doesn't give him the right to unlawfully and without provocation strike another human being. On the contrary. He should remain professional at all times. A law enforcement agent, Your Honor, is a servant of the people. And," he continued. "Should a man. Any man, be he policeman or not, unjustly strike another person, that person has the right to protect himself." He emphasized his words to drive home his point. "Being a policeman does not exempt him from that point of law."

"Your Honor...," Anderson began but was cut off again by Judge Hicks.

"Gentleman please. I've heard enough. I think we can mitigate these proceedings quickly if we can all agree the fault is equitably shared by all parties." He leaned back and pulled his robe tight against him. "Though the policemen's actions," he continued, "in pulling over Mr. Adams could be construed as questionable." The policemen looked at one another. Judge Hicks silently halted a gesture of objection from one of their representatives. "A citizen must demonstrate a proper respect for an officer of the law," defended the F.O.P counsel, "even if that officer's tactics seem to that citizen to be questionable. A mere citizen is not always in a position to be the best judge of those tactics."

"If by demonstrating proper respect," interjected Simi, "you mean obligated obsequiousness you're a century too late."

"If an officers procedure begs a question there are proper venues to voice complaints. There is no need for, and a citizen has no right to, take the matter into his or her own hands." The two officers they represented smiled between themselves. "Proper venue. You mean a deaf venue," scoffed Simi. "Your proper venue also leaves a lot to be desired. The community where improper behavior elicits the most complaints is the district where those complaints are most ignored. I'm sorry my community has little faith in you and your venues."

Judge Hicks raised his hand to put a stop to the lawyers squabbling so that he could continue with his ruling. Esteemed and respected albeit a freshman juror, Judge Hicks was sincere about ending this equitably. Most of all he felt a duty to halt the incident that possessed the very real potential of becoming an embarrassing affair for his city. How he wished the police would put an end to these underlining racial provocations. After a lifetime of respect for the law an antiquated core of good old boy officers seem to keep him in an uncomfortable compromise. He banged his gavel for their attention.

"The court in accordance with the city has exercised it's prerogative to prevent an escalation of hostilities by acknowledging that the behavior of Officers Collins and Williams was somewhat overzealous. We extend appreciation to Mr. Adams and his counsel for their gracious acceptance of a simple apology." Kuendela turned to smile. He was satisfied. If he had pressed for a full civil action there was no certainty he'd win and he didn't need the money. Or the notoriety. He was however more than pleased with humiliating the policemen. Unbeknownst to them, he and Simi had reached an agreement with the city previously. Judge Hicks was simply going through the motions, trying to smooth the city's feathers as much as possible. That was OK with Kuendela. He enjoyed the cops perplexity.

"Not just an astronaut," elucidated Collins, "but an L.C. astronaut." Kuendela released the startled Williams. "L.C. astronaut. What the hell's that?" asked Williams rubbing his neck. "Lunar Club," answered one of the cops. "It means he's been to the moon, you ass hole!" Collins cast an abhorrent eye to Williams. Disappointment showed on Williams' face as Kuendela returned his baton to him. Williams was puzzled. This was just a drug dealer. He was sure of that. This nigger wore no suit, how could he be a professional man or an astronaut for that matter. He wasn't buying it this easily. What astronaut dresses like this. Besides weren't they scientist too?

"Wait George. How can you be sure about this guy? IDs can be forged you know. Man this nigger..." It was the first time he said the word out loud. The look on Kuendela's face chilled him in mid sentence. It was not an emotional hate, embarrassment, or irritation. No. It was a cold look of warning and concern.

"Anthony. No one black or white can forge these things." He gave it back to it's owner. "Mr. Adams. These things happen unfortunately. Sorry man." He turned to leave. Officer George Collins was ready to try and forget this thing. "These things do happen officer. But for some reason only to black men!" Kuendela replied implacably. Officer Anthony Williams was unimpressed but pragmatic. This may clearly be no nigger to goad into an altercation. But he could still have his uppity ass for disarming him. But clearly not now. He may have to kiss his ass today but he'd get a hold of the D.A. and file some sort of charge tomorrow.

When a reporter picked up the story Officer Williams complained to the F.O.P, against Collins' protest, and tried to file an assault charge. Kuendela and Simi countered with their own complaint. The city had no desire to spar with a notable black astronaut. The notoriety was unwanted and unwelcome.

At the very apex of the municipality the decision was ironed out. Officer Williams and Collins were left out of the process. That was fine with George Collins. Not with

174

The officers were ambivalent. Collins was ready to forget the whole thing. Williams felt betrayed. His face was hard and sullen. The arrogant niggers attitude and smirky grin grated every nerve in his being.

"After hearing all the witnesses and the participants," Judge Hicks continued, "I'm satisfied that Mr. Adams acted in self defense. As for the act of provocation on the policemen's part, I believe apologies would suffice to quell any sense of infringement on Mr. Adams civil rights. Now let's adjourn gentleman. This case is dismissed." Without another word Judge Hicks rose from the head of the conference table and exited from the chamber. A small entourage of attendants and stenographers followed close behind him. He let out a sigh of relief, glad the proceedings were over. Placing the event as far back in history as possible was fine with him. He hoped psychological profiling of policemen would weed out racist officers and the re-orientations in civil interaction training, especially racial exchanges, that emerge from this agreement will work. These kinds of exchanges between the police and the black community demeans the fabric of liberty in this country, he mused begrudgingly. But, as he entered his own chambers and closed the door behind him he admitted to himself, with a sigh, the reality of history assures him that this will not be the last of such incidents.

The group around the table rose, ensconced in a low murmur of conversation. It was plain to see the disrespect and ill feeling the four lawmen had for the two black men. Their sneering white faces made no attempts to hide their disappointment. Kuendela Nguvu stood and embraced his attorney Simi Ali. Both men were immaculately dressed. Both men were tall measuring 6'2 a piece. Where Kuendela, in his mid thirties, was dark skinned, youthful and powerfully built. Simi was brown skin, portly and approaching a comfortable middle age.

The officers had no intention of following the judges recommendation for apologies. The black men knew that. They found the officers indignation amusing. So much so, they made no attempts to hide their smiles. Which only served to infuriate the officers further. Which in turn made it that much more difficult for the black men to refrain from laughing. The officers expected the wrath of the judge to fall on Kuendela in spite of his status. Instead they were embarrassed. Everyone in the room began filing through the conference room door into the foyer. When the group reached the main hallway a small cadre of reporters rushed over to them. Immediately they were lit upon by the media and separated into two groups. Kuendela and Simi with one group, the officers with the other. Each conveyed their version of the events that led to the incident and their interpretations of what took place in the informal inquiry. Kuendela recalled them this way.

It was two weeks ago while driving home from Barbara's. The scene between them had been very heated. An angry scowl masked his face as he stormed from her apartment. He was not; however, the type to transfer his anger onto some inculpable innocents he may happen upon. He kept his anger focused yet plain on his face. And so it seemed to the two policemen who pulled him over after he'd driven passed them. To them Kuendela looked menacing and hardly appropriate for the surrounding community he was traveling through. They found him out of place in the elegant expensive car and his dress unsuitable to this upscale predominately white, residential area of Northeast Philadelphia. The few blacks who did live in the officers district didn't look like this. Kuendela's black satin trimmed kufi, matching shirt and pants, and fashionable gold rimmed sunglasses were very suspicious to the pair. "We better pull this spade over," suggested Officer Williams. "He could be a drug dealer or something. These spades don't drive cars like this legitimately without a suit and tie." Was his rationale. Officer Collins went along with his partner reluctantly. Anyway, he thought, the logic wasn't entirely soundless. Plus they could harass an uppity black. And if they feed his name to narcotics and it pays off, a few extra points to their standing wouldn't hurt their careers or reputations a bit.

Two other patrol cars joined in support when Kuende was pulled over. The tall elegant black man was cooperativ and rather refined in his manner thought one of the back ups Officers Williams and Collins found him cocky, too uppity when he stood outside his car. Arrogance was added to the tally. Officer Williams was especially perturbed. "Let me see some identification," he demanded. A silent Boy!!! was clearly evident in his tone. Kuendela handed his wallet to the officer. Williams took it and handed it to Collins without looking at it. "You know what a car like this cost?" he asked. Again Kuendela perceived a silent "boy" in the cops inquiry. Kuendela rolled his eyes skyward. "That's a silly question. Don't you think so officer? Since I'm driving the dam thing. I must know what it cost. The car is mine okay. If you'd bother to look at the registration you'd know that!"

"You're a real smart one. Aren't you boy?" he stopped himself too late.

"Let's have a look inside," he sneered. He made a move pass Kuendela but was stopped by the black man's protest. "On what grounds?" he demanded.

"On the grounds that this badge gives me the right," he snarled and pushed Kuendela aside. "That badge don't give you the right to put your hands on...," Officer Williams swung his baton before Kuendela finished his protest. Years of training caused a lightening reaction. Before Williams completed his act Kuendela countered and Officer Williams was disarmed. Clearly he was embarrassed. Kuendela held the baton tight against Williams' neck after spinning him around. Back up officers moved in to smash the assailant. "Hold it," yelled Officer Collins. "Everybody! Hold it!!" The outburst froze the officers in their steps. "You can let him go Mr. Adams." Kuendela looked surprised as did Officer Williams. "Let him go Mr. Adams. Please, this has all been a terrible mistake." Astonishment graced the faces of all the officers and the now small group of spectators attracted by the scene.

Collins held Kuendela's wallet open and swept it pass the faces of the back ups. "I'll be dam," one of the officers said. "An astronaut!"

Anthony Williams though. For the first time a new partner looked appealing to him. The irony was not lost on Simi as they were swamped by reporters. He and Kuendela enjoyed making the city squirm. Actually they were letting the city off easy.

"Isn't it just a cop out?" asked one of the reporters.

"We're satisfied with the arrangement," replied Simi. "There's no agenda here. We embrace Judge Hick's decision and we accept it for what it's worth." He winked at Kuendela. "Judge Hicks ordered the F.O.P to apologize to my client," Simi informed the group of reporters massed around them. Simi looked to Kuendela and winked again.

"Have the police released a public apology yet."

"The city has," replied Kuendela. "But not the F.O.P. And should it come we won't accept it anyway." Every reporter seem to have a question at the same time. On the tail end of the chattering one reporter's question emerged audibly. "Why is that brother? What's that mean?" He was a reporter from the city's black publication. The New Observer.

"It means Fred," began Simi, "that any apology from the F.O.P would hardly be sincere. False sentiment doesn't interest us."

"Simi," Fred began. Reciprocating with his first name to demonstrate their comradeship to the other white reporters. "The police Chief has announced plans to reeducate his officers to proper interaction techniques and racial sensitization, as well as ferreting out racism in the ranks. Is this what interests you." The winks among the blacks did not go unnoticed by the white reporters. It was obvious Fred was privy to information they didn't have. they now traded looks of their own.

"Yes," replied Simi. "We met with Judge Hicks and Chief O'Leary yesterday. They agreed to publicly acknowledge the need for such training and investigating within the department. But you know this Fred. Your paper has an exclusive on the decision doesn't it." The looks among the white reporters were now coupled with some choice comments. The mutterings drew the attention of the reporters surrounding the police officers. They abandoned them to join the media mob around Kuendela and Simi. Officers Williams and Collins were just as surprised by the knowledge of public announcements. "My brother." Kuendela held out his clenched fist. Simi banged his own fist against it. The two men proceeded down the hall, still followed by the questioning mob. Outside Simi looked at his friend and placed a hand on his shoulder. "I'm proud of you, my brother," he said smiling.

"Why is that?"

"You went through the entire proceedings without losing your temper?"

"You trying to say I can't control myself, Brother Simi?"

"When confronted by this shit, Brother Nguvu, that's exactly what I'm saying." Both men laughed. Kuendela's temper in the face of discrimination, bigotry and such was no secret to either of them. "We must be cool in the face of the enemy brother. You of all people should know that," Simi stated seriously. "It's the reason we went through this today." Kuendela's smile vanished. "The reason we went through this today is because those two cops thought I was the one they could fuck with. If that cop got his feelings hurt because his face was smacked it was his fault." Then in a lighter tone he added, "besides today's outcome and the look on those cops faces was worth the trouble." He stuck his hands out. "I must agree with you there brother." The laughter returned to both men as they slapped hands in a gesture of farewell then parted company, leaving the group of reporters filing out of the municipal door in their separate wakes.

Kuendela removed his tie and jacket as soon as he reached his car. He placed them in the back seat then slid himself under the steering wheel in the front seat. Just before reaching the expressway his cellular phone rang. He placed the phone to his ear and spoke. "Peace."

"Peace Brother Adams," came the voice at the other end. "This is Professor Jubilee. How are you son?"

"Professor Jubilee!" There was genuine respect in his voice. "I'm fine sir. How are you?"

"I've seen better days son."

"You can't stop a stepper Professor. And you can out step them all."

"I've been reading about you in the paper. You've been doing some stepping of your own."

"Yes sir," he laughed. "We went through a lot of trouble just to wipe the arrogance from the faces of two racist cops. But it was worth it." He laughed again before adding. "Plus it was fun too."

"Yes. Things haven't changed much. Not even for a famous astronaut." Kuendela noticed the hesitance in Professor Jubilee's tone. He went on apprehensively. "Well we're still just niggers to a lot of them Professor. How's the project going? I can't wait to join you. Soon's my tour is done."

"I'm glad you feel that way son. I'm hoping you have some time left before reporting back to NASA."

"As a matter of fact," he stated slowly, "I have. What's up?"

"Son we need your help. A lot sooner than we expected." Grim feelings replaced his initial elation. "What's the problem Professor?"

"Calvin." Kuendela started to correct Professor Jubilee. But something in his old Professor's tone showed this was no time for vanity. "I've been trying to reach you all day son. There's been a serious problem here and...we really need you," he stammered. Jubilee's tone concerned Kuendela. The Professor just didn't sound like himself at all. Kuendela began to worry. For the Professor to sound the way he did something terrible must be happening with the project. What could he do? "Professor," he said respectfully, "I'm at your beckon call sir. You know I'm always your man. What do you want me to do and when do you want me to do it?"

"I knew I could depend on you son. Can you come down here as soon as possible?" Kuendela thought for a moment. "I can drive down in the morning, sir. If I leave early I can beat that morning work traffic on 95. How's that sound?"

"Wonderful son. Meet me in front of the building behind Carter. You know the lab. In fact!" he added as an after thought. "Call me as soon as you get on 95 and I'll brief you over the cellular."

"You got it Professor. It's all good." Kuendela started to click off the phone but was stopped by Professor Jubilee's voice. "Oh and thank you..ah.. Kuendela, I'm sorry I didn't remember son."

"No problem Professor."

"I really appreciate this son. Habari Gani."

"Ojumbo, Professor." Kuendela clicked off his phone and drove straight home to his modest and well kept apartment building in the Mount Airy section of Philadel-phia. The five story building was lined with a geometrically manicured lawn and pruned cypress trees. In the rear were private parking spaces set in concrete overhangs jutting from the building. After parking his car Kuendela entered a door at the edge of the buildings rear. Ignoring the elevator he took the steps two at a time to the second floor and walked through a large self closing pressurized door. Once on his floor he walked pass his own apartment door to the one next door and knocked. Narda opened the door. She clucked her tongue against the roof of her mouth and shook her head knowingly. "You're gonna abandon poor X again aren't you?'

"Not abandon Narda. Think of it as an extended visit with you. His and my favorite neighbor."

"Oh, weak flattery. Please" She bucked her eyes at him. But there was no question, she would cat sit for him. She was always willing to help him. Just as she knew she could always count on him. That was the kind of communal tribemenship they shared. Be it a small thing or a large thing. But she just couldn't let it go without needling him. Just a

178

little. "This is not the happy cat sittin service you know. Keep this up and X is gonna forget who you are."

"A cat never forgets," he smiled.

"That's elephants," she laughed. Kuendela gave her a door key and turned to go down the hall. "What about Barbara?" she called after him. "You still got it bad for her. Don't cha?" Kuendela turned slowly and shrugged his shoulders. "Take care my Brother," she said before closing her door.

After dinner he wasted no time getting to bed but sleep was slow in coming. Jubilee's frantic call consumed his thoughts. He couldn't forget the sound of desperation in his mentors voice. He tried imagining what the problem could be but it was impossible. There was no lack of talent or ingenuity in that group. Their scientific knowledge exceeded his. There's hardly anything he could add to fill a void in that group. But he opted to capitulate and let it go, for now. Sleep was the best contribution he could make in preparation at the time. As difficult as it was going to be he tried to sleep. He tossed, he turned, he forced himself to lie still. Finally for an unguarded moment Kuendela slipped into a fitful sleep. His last conscious thought before falling asleep was what would Barbara say if he changed his mind about his career.

As long as Kuendela could remember, he wanted to be an astronaut. He remembered as a child getting little inspiration from the teachers he had in school. To them it was unreal for a black child of that time to think seriously about being an astronaut. One arrant educator went as far as to find it preposterous. But he continued to dream and like many ambitious black children he could always count on his mother and community for inspiration. "Ain't nothin a white man can do that you can't do baby. She'd say. A far cry in diversity from women of Barbara Caulden's elk.

In college he met his greatest mentor, Professor Jubilee. Under his tutelage he received academic instruction with urgent ambition. Professor Jubilee inspired him the way no teacher, black or white had ever inspired him before. It was Professor Jubilee who persuaded him in adult life to follow his dream. After enlisting in the Navy and spending seven years as a Navy pilot he applied to NASA with the encouragement of the A.A.A.A. The experience for him, they knew, would later be of invaluable service to the project somewhere down the line. They watched Kuendela's progress with great hope and expectation and was equally as proud of his accomplishments at NASA as they were with his performance at Howard University. At NASA there were complaints made by some white applicants who couldn't make the grade. They complained that Kuendela was given an edge through affirmative action. None of them ever considered Kuendela's superior grades and aptitude. "Racism, hate and fear of the Black man," Professor Jubilee would tell him. "Don't let their bigotry deter you son. It's sour grapes" Kuendela went on to NASA undaunted by sour grapes. He became an excellent missions specialist. One of only a few African Americans to hold that distinction. During his career he found further distinction by way of a special service award when he rescued a fellow astronaut who's equipment malfunction in the lunar craft imperiled an entire crew. Kuendela saved them from a doomed fate of lunar abandonment. Kuendela's quick thinking and coolness in the crisis enabled him to access the situation and rectify it to a successful outcome. The incident was legendary among the astronauts and scientist at NASA. However, unknown to the general public. At least for the next 20 years, when the mission becomes declassified.

Kuendela was indeed well respected at NASA. Name change not withstanding. Concern gleaned the agency halls when his plans to anoint himself with an original African name became known to NASA. They seemed to be worried about the unsure ramifications of his impended afro centricity. NASA was unsure of how to relate to a proud and aware black man but Professor Jubilee had a remark for it. "Racism, hate and fear of the Black man," he'd say. "Sour grapes."

"A true adventurer with equanimous character," was Kuendela's byline in the black press. "A skillful professional who's abilities will overshadow any racist paranoia surrounding his stoic Afro centrism." How NASA would react to Kuendela's plans for early retirement remained to be seen. Barbara's reaction to it was unfortunate he thought, but not at all an indicator of NASA's response. His contribution to the ARC's progress, he lamented, will adequately suffice his loss tenure at the Space Agency and fortunately the loss of Barbara as well.

*****

As a student, Kuendela then Calvin Adams, assisted Professor Jubilee in the early days of the ARC's development. The Professor found few of his early assistants as adept in physics as Kuendela. Now, years later, they anticipated his coming involvement with the ARC team after an early retirement from NASA. Yet, no one foresaw that Kuendela's expertise would be needed this soon in the project for this horrible emergency. Now with the morning sun only two hours away he'd be more involved than he could have ever imagined.

*****

Philadelphia at 4 am in the pre dawn hour was dark and dismal this cool, crisp October morning. At this hour little activity is seen and the traffic is sparse. A bus passed by him with only three passengers. Their tired faces showed the strain of getting up at that time of day. Kuendela's face was focused and alert in contrast. He enjoyed the wee hours and the thought of what may be happening at Howard University had his system running on all pistons with anticipation. He again thought of Professor Jubilee's frantic call. The Professor was no hysterical personality. Yet, there was desolation in his tone. Kuendela remembered talking to him only a month ago about the program. He was elated over the progress they'd made and the plans to run the first phases of testing. That had to be it Kuendela thought. Something must have gone wrong during the test phase. But what? He pulled onto the Schuykill

Expressway's entrance and followed along the inside lane to Center City. The volume of traffic had increased by a few more cars. He made a left turn onto the General Pitus bridge and followed Interstate 95 pass the airport. In his rear view mirror he saw the Philadelphia skyline dwindle behind him as he left the city then entered on through Chester. Almost an hour later a sign announcing the way to Baltimore appeared. He picked up his cellular phone and dialed the Howard University exchange. In less than a minute the operator transferred his call to Jubilee's lab. Someone answered on the first ring. The cognizant voice of Professor Jubilee came through ready and eager to give him the crux of the horrible incident that now required his presence. By the time Kuendela ended his call he knew most of the particulars of Shai's disappearance and Bilal's short excursion to the past. He thought of how incredible it was. Professor Jubilee and the team had done it. They'd accomplished the most incredible thing imaginable in spite of the terrible event that followed. They actually transported Shai, and Bilal, back in time. He shook his head. He'd been aware of the work for years but the fact that it actually happened, that someone had actually retrorsed to the past was INCREDIBLE!! He remembered how, while studying aerospace engineering at Howard, he'd signed up as a project assistant on the ARC project. He came to share Professor's Jubilee and Kobolongo's dream of time expedition, and like the others never betrayed it's existence. His cousin Argee followed in his footsteps to Jubilee's class and in no time Professor Jubilee had inspired her, just as he'd convinced Kuendela to share the dream. Argee then in turn brought in her friend Shai on Kuendela's recommendation. Now Shai was trapped somewhere in time and needed his help. Trapped in the most dreadful era imaginable, in America, for a black man. Argee is probably taking it hard Kuendela thought, for sure. They'd always been close. Whatever it took Kuendela vowed, Shai was coming home. The very thought of what he must be going through made him shudder. The further he drove the more concerned he became. He silently prayed. "Hang in there Brother. Hang in there."

CHAPTER 8

Year 1852

Shai opened his eyes but his olfactory senses were first to coherence. He winced at the smell. A dank and musty odor like an old, wet condemned building mixed with the raw odor of perspiration and the pungent smell of decayed flesh. The combination was a sickening potpourri that made him nauseous. The odor snaked its way through Shai's nose and down his esophagus. It collided with the walls of his stomach and boiled and churned causing him to swallow hard. He tried keeping it down, but the peristaltic action in his throat was out of his control. He vomited and wretched until his stomach cramped. Drenched in sweat and partly covered in his own vomit he tried to wipe his mouth with the back of his hand. It was then that he realized the extent to which he was chained...'CHAINED!!' The word reverberated inside his head...'CHAINED!!' His heart began beating wildly as fear charged his autonomic systems. Inside this unfamiliar darkness each thump in his chest was amplified tenfold in his ears as recent events came to memory like a wild nightmare. He looked from one dark corner of the room to the other desperately trying to make sense of it all. Where am I? In a jail! WHERE!?! What am I gonna do? The sound of his own thoughts was like the voice of a terrified child. What's happened to me? His imagination was running rampant. He tried hard to get a hold of himself. With his back against the wall he wormed his way up until he stood erect. The clanging of the chains gave an eerie accent to his every move. He strained his eyes to inure himself to the darkness. The shape of his surroundings took on a shadowed image. He was imprisoned in a cramped barn like structure. Then his ears came into play. He thought he'd heard voices outside. He stood perfectly still, straining to hear. The voices were barely audible but it was confirmed. They were voices. One voice sounded familiar. His heart pounding in his ears made it difficult to understand what they were saying. He tried again to steady himself so he could better discern their words.

"By the Saints of Eire Colonel." rolled one voice, "you would not be thinkin o takin advantage would ya now?" It was the voice of the man in the woods. Shai pursed his lips to smother a gasp trying to escape his throat.

"On the contrary McPacker. I consider my offer rather equitable. After all. I employed you to retrieve my slaves with an adequate advance. Yet of the four I employed you to recover, you only captured one. Then you surreptitiously conspired with my subordinate to go after another without my knowledge. Why? It befuddles me to think...But that is of little issue at this time. Because now I find that you have managed to allow your nigra to slaughter her. Tsk, tsk Mr. McPacker." Shai found the man's tone shallow in spite of the outrageousness of his charges.

"True sir, and my apologies." McPacker began slowly. It seemed to Shai the men were bantering over some trifle, not human lives.

"It was not due to negligence I assure you. But to the consequential misfortunes of my profession. However Colonel that nigra in there would well compensate you and more for the loss of a mere winch! Even at the meager price I've presented. He's strong and he's intelligent, forby sir."

"Compensation? True sir. The full value of the boy should equate me the full value of my lost property. But more as you intimate. It remains to be seen."

"Ha ha Colonel. Surely you can't equate full value of that young strapper with equal value of the weaker and ignorant wench," countered McPacker.

"Yes my good sir. Attributes he has. But you must admit to me that his spirit and erudition presents a potential liability. Take notice the quaint occurrences of escapes that has been a plague on our county. Perhaps he is a northern nigger agent of the abolitionists who are causing us this malady. Hmm." He rubbed his bearded chin. "The likely cost of forcing domestication on him will surely have to be taken in account. I must commission someone to brake him sir."

"Commission someone! Aye Colonel. You kittle me sir. I am by kithe the best breaker in this county. And you know it sir. Surely you know also that I'm at your service."

"As an added incentive?" added the Colonel slyly.

"By the Saints Colonel you are a most rapacious man...I am at your service sir," he laughed. "Besides you cannot deny the potential here."

"Potential for what sir?" replied the Colonel dubiously. McPacker reared on his heels as the game continued. "Is it not true Colonel that the barrister Latimor is seeking a slave of singular ability?" Colonel Richards removed his cigar slowly, careful not to reveal his expression though he was truly impressed. Latimor's proposition was known only to the elite of southern businessmen, or so he believed. "I congratulate you McPacker. Your inferences are reputable to be sure. However. Might I add that you are not a broker. And since this nigger has obviously never been in bondage before, this transaction is felonious at best."

"Colonel. You have me sir. You are the most remarkable of the trade. I'm honored to be at your service. We can assist each other. I have the skill you have the commodity. By Eire it is the making of a mutual enterprise."

"McPacker you amuse me. I do enjoy bartering and we are both in a sporting mood. But no matter how far from pernicious the remark, cajoling will not change the price."

The two voices broke into raucous laughter. Inside the barn Shai's blood turn from ice to molten lava. "The bastards are haggling over me. And playing a game at it. Ain't this a bitch." He was enraged and horrified.

"Thirteen hundred dollars," he heard the one called Colonel say. "Just the price of my lost property wouldn't you say," he added slyly

"We have a deal sir...with braking forby?...Tis a fine art." laughed the rolling voice of McPacker.

The transaction between the men could be construed as light hearted and jovial yet despicable. Shai fought to control his tremors but could not calm himself. Listening to them, as he stood there in the dark, seemed like eaves dropping on plans for his own execution. Outside, Colonel Richards interrupted his guile smile to delight his cigar. From inside the barn Shai heard him calling to someone. "Boys, come in with me." Then he changed his mind. "No!!" he yelled, "fetch him out here." He gestured with the cigar. "I hate the smell of that shack," he added wrinkling his nose. The door opened and two white men burst in. Shai turned rigid and braced himself. They grabbed him and he resisted only slightly. "Come on here boy," one of them said. Roughly, they jerked him from the wall. A third man came in and unlocked the chains then forced Shai's wrist together and replaced the chains with metal cuffs. While the two other men continued to hold Shai the third man then placed a metal collar over Shai's head, then locked it's brace around his neck. The collar had three metal stems projecting from it. At the tip of each stem swung a bell that jingled when Shai moved his head. They shoved him out the door. When he stopped stumbling he was standing toe to toe with Colonel Richards. The sudden introduction of sunlight made Shai squint his eyes and lower his head. When his eyes grew accustomed to the light he forced himself to look Colonel Richards directly in his eyes with as much hate as he could muster. Colonel Richards took a frightened unconscious step backwards. Immediately he regained his composure. The arrogance!! The Colonel expressed his protest with his eyes. Shai continued to stare at the bearded white man. He reminded him of the stereotypical plantation owner. A Simon Lagree. He looked like all the pictures he'd ever seen of a slave owner. What kind of man is this Colonel, he asked himself. He studied the man briefly. A tall white man with a 2 inch thick black beard splashed with blotches of gray. It completely hid his upper lip. A protruding black cigar revealed the location of his mouth. Cigar smoke encircled his brown stove pipe hat. It matched his brown great coat. Poking through the end of each sleeve were white ruffled shirt cuffs and to complete the ensemble, a large gold pinky ring adorned the hilt of the little finger of his huge right hand. Shai was taken aback by the mans size and demeanor. There was no doubt he was the head man here. Shai jerked his head sharply to the right. He recognized the man standing next to the Colonel. It was the same man who attacked him on the Aeon Platform. He too was large, but he seemed subordinate to the Colonel. Still, Shai could tell he commanded a measure of respect none the less. Even from the head man.

"Arrogant nigger aren't you boy," snapped the Colonel. "Take this dam contraption from his neck," he ordered one of the men who dragged him from the barn. "I want to get a good look at him." Someone unlocked the metal collar and removed it. SMACK!! Colonel Richard's hand viciously assaulted Shai's mouth. He then grabbed Shai's chin and turned his head from side to side to examine his face. Shai could taste his own blood in the corner of his mouth. "He smells putrid," sneered the Colonel, examining his latest acquisition. Eyes, nose, mouth, lips. Even the teeth like he was examining a horse or a cow. The smoothness of the Negroes skin and healthy flawless glow impressed him. He'd never seen a negro so well groomed and healthy looking or so articulate according to McPacker's assessment. There were stories about the Negroes up north who spoke as well as a white man and being as well groomed as white men but he'd never seen one before now. He looked almost human, the Colonel thought to himself. A glitter of sunlight reflecting from Shai's mouth was of particular interest. He squeezed Shai's cheeks together with one hand to force his mouth open into an "O" shape so he could get a better look inside. "My," praised the Colonel. "What have we here? a

Gold tooth?" This boy certainly amused him. He felt the tooth with his index finger. Shai's resistance caused him to squeeze his jaw harder and shake Shai's head to weaken his resolve. He was awe struck by this nigger's golden tooth. Another one of the boys characteristics that he'd never seen in a negro before. "Where in hell did this come from boy!" Shai remained silent.

"I'm Colonel Randolph Richards. Son!!. I own you. I say again. Where.."

"Own Me!" Shai broke free of the man's grip and spat the words out like a bad taste. "Motherfucker you're crazy. Own me! I'm nobodies fuckin property! I'm a man." he managed to shout. He felt stronger. "A fuckin man.." WHAP!! The slap caught Shai totally by surprise. "You've got a lot to learn boy. A lot to learn. First lesson is you don't speak until you have permission to do so. And then you say only what you're required to...And you dam well better take your eyes off my face!" Shai arrogantly continued to stare. Wiping his hands on a handkerchief the Colonel turned to John McPacker. "You have a challenge before you McPacker. This boy has fire."

"No challenge that can't be won, by Eire," he snarled. "True he has fire but that will prove to be a good thing once he's properly in his place. Afore I'm done he'll be a messan."

"Where are you from boy? Boston or Philadelphia? What in hells name are you doing in God's country? What do you know of these escapes that have been plaguing us of late? Answer me boy!" He slapped him again then continued to interview Shai without a response. Colonel Richards then trying another approach changed the timbre of his voice. "Niggers are free up there they say. Personally I think a free nigger is a worthless one. There is nothing you are fit for if it is not to serve your betters."

"If there is a better man than me. He ain't here." Shai retorted, determined to show arrogance Colonel Richards eyes stretched in surprise then he slapped Shai with the back of his hand. This time the force of the blow staggered him.

Two helpers held Shai stationary while Colonel Richards back handed him again and again. Shai struggled against the two men holding him. The Negroes resolve both impressed and frightened them at the same time. Colonel Richards, not being use to such insolence, decided to end this session for now. He needed time to muddle all of this. He hoped McPacker could work his training magic on this bad seed of a negro. Though silently he admitted to himself that he was impressed with the boys fire. Still it was intolerable. "Take him back inside the shack," he ordered. The men obediently returned Shai to the shack. Colonel Richards dabbed at the perspiration on his face with a white linen handkerchief. "A singular negro wouldn't you say McPacker? His fair skin decries at least the third generation blood of a white man I think. It would explain his articulate and bold manner."

"Bold in deed sir. Worst I've seen. And I've seen many. But don't worry. It is his black blood that curses his veins and brings his station in life. It will take some doing but he'll brake. They all brake in the end, by Eire."

"Singular indeed," Colonel Richards repeated absently. "But it's that singularity that when broken is going to make him a profitable commodity." The two men laughed as they walked towards the main house. "He is dressed rather peculiar," observed McPacker. I can not say that I've ever seen the likes of it."

"He's sure to have never been a servant."

"I'll wager that by Eire. Servants have a broken look that our young nigra here lacks." He nodded his head. "He's free and learned to boot. A dangerous mixture in a nigra."

"Dangerous to be sure," added Colonel Richards flicking an ash from his cigar with his pinky finger. "An absolute waste. In the north there are those who have confused the nigras natural station in life and christian business with humanity. Misguided they may be. They are ignorant to christian values. They forget that to save the nigra we must guide and control him. Just as we have led the cattle to their true purpose." Colonel Richards lectured with the end of his cigar.

McPacker smiled. He enjoyed the dialogue. It wasn't often that he enjoyed a verbal exchange with the likes of business men of the Colonels ilk. "There is no wonder that you are the superior in the county Colonel, By Eire. You've the philosophy."

"It is no trick to know Gods planning." Fair exchange was no robbery. For just as pleasing to Colonel Richards was McPacker's adulation. Together the men stroked each others vanity as they sat in the retreating sunlight. "Take our boy," the Colonel went on. "He is spoiled by learning. Some abolitionist has tainted him and now he exist misguided. Confusion of this kind in these people breeds arrogance. Arrogance gives rise to insurrection and that benefits no one. Though his aptitude makes him a valuable apprentice his value is worthless if he doesn't know his place. If he is to be worth anything he must be broken." He smashed his fist holding the cigar into his other opened hand causing a long ash to fall. Softening his tone for effect he eyed McPacker rigidly before adding, "then mended to his station."

"Yes by Eire," agreed the tracker/breaker. "And he will be Colonel. I'll see to that by starting on him first thing early morn."

*****

The walkway leading to Angora's main house was framed by a meticulously kept garden. It's manicured greenery grew perpendicular to a row of white grecian columns where the two men mounted white marble steps leading to a freshly painted white portico. A uniformed slave attendant ushered them to two over stuffed chairs on either side of a small mahogany tray-table. Mary, a very black, short and portly servant rushed out from the house as soon as they were seated. From her apron pocket she produced two cigars and handed one to each man. Timorously she wrung her hands while awaiting an opportunity to further serve her master's pleasure. "How bout some lemnade, Massa Riches? Freshly made suh." As she spoke her extraneous gestures

190

matched her animated movements and high pitched voice. "Thank you Mary. No. Tell Jasper we'll have some brandy."

"Right away Mas Riches suh." She paddled away wearing an endless perfunctory smile forever elusive to her eyes. A smile forever amenable to her subjugator.

"McPacker," Colonel Richards said through three rings of cigar smoke.

"Where do you suppose that boys from? And where," he added thoughtfully, "was he going."

"Would you mean that philosophically Colonel."

"Very amusing," he replied dryly, "but not very helpful McPacker. Seriously what's your opinion?" he demanded impatiently.

"You know Colonel. I've heard tell of darkies from Africa immigrating to Boston. Just as white people immigrate from the grand continent."

"But why would an expatriated nigger come to the south."

"You've long suspected the abolitionists were behind these recent events, Colonel. Could he be one?"

"I've considered that John. But that's a mission for a misguided white abolitionist. Not a nigger. They'd be afraid of being returned to their station of nigritude."

"Well by Eire. I'd say it's the fate that's befallen him." Both men broke into rippling laughter. Colonel Richards stopped to ask a question. "What do you make of the gold tooth?"

"Ahh by the Saints Colonel. Admittedly, had I noticed a golden tooth when we found him, it would not be their now." He thought for a moment. "I must confess I don't know. The Africans have been known to adorn themselves with precious metals."

"Yes," he agreed smiling. "That tooth would make him a novel house servant. The man who could impress his guest with a servant whose mouth is adorned with such regalia would be the envy of all the south."

"You are the envy of every family in the south Colonel."...Jasper, a thin gaunt negro dressed in resplendent house servant finery entered with their brandies. They took their glasses and sipped slowly as Colonel Richards continued with his impressions. "He is rather articulate," he intimated. "Some fool has ruined that nigger with a white man's education. Could be you're right McPacker. It's beginning to sound more and more like the work of the abolitionist."

"By the Saints, it's blaspheme. No doubt the bugger can read to boot."

"Its a sin and a shame." Richards inhaled deeply. "We must brake him. Return him to the station God meant for him and his kind." He stood up and walked to the edge of the porch. With both hands on the railing and a foot in the quatrefoil he blew a plume of cigar smoke. "Tomorrow. First order of business." He held an index finger in the air. "Give these niggers another healthy dose of fear." Two fingers pointed at McPacker. "Leave you to your task." Three fingers back in the air. "Third I'm putting Jim Smith to the task of finding these abolitionist dogs. We must put a stop to these escapes." John McPacker rose to bid Colonel Richards good day.

*****

Nighttime had come. Shai laid on the cold ground chained in moonlit silence. Over and over he tried convincing himself Professor Jubilee would find some way to save him. He had to have faith and confidence in Professor Jubilee's abilities. Maybe they were close by at this very moment. But deep inside, he felt hopeless. How could Professor Jubilee find him. How could they possibly locate him here in this god forsaken era. He tried hard to weigh the possibilities of a rescue. But in his gut he was pragmatically pessimistic about his chances. How would they track him. How would they get to him? How would they get him out? It would take an army to rescue him. Overwhelmed by exhaustion, by fear, his head fell to his chest in despair. He swallowed a hard despondent lump that settled like a stone in the pit of his stomach. The creaking and sudden movement of the door interrupted his reverie. His head snapped up and he stared at it in the dimness. Slowly and deliberately it swung open. A mans hand appeared and it's fingers wrapped around the doors outer edge. It was large, thick veined and callous...and it was black. The intruder pushed his way completely into the shack and quickly closed the door behind him then stood in the shadows. Features of his face were hidden in the darkness. Bright moonlight coming in a small window behind him cast a silhouette around the large frame of his hulking body. "Hey deh boy!" he whispered before tip toeing closer in quick cautious steps like a burglar. Shai cringed against the wall in uncertain anticipation. The stranger knelt down before him and shoved a wooden bowl of tepid water in front of him. Shai cursed the chains for clanking when he grabbed for it.

"What Massa you hail frum, boy."

"Massa!? aped Shai. "No my brother. I don't have a massa. I'm from..." he stopped himself. "I'm...from...Africa," he stated falteringly. "You a Afkin sho-nuff?"

"That's right." Shai took the bowl.

"You don sound lak no savage ta me."

"Savage!" Shai managed a terse laugh. "Won't you get in trouble bringing me this water?"

"Shoot. Massa Riches and Mr. Jim Smith don know what go on round heah at night..." he said proudly. "Josh is my name," He sat another wooden bowl down in front of Shai. Cornmeal mush. But to Shai it was a Thanksgiving feast and this friendly stranger was like a long lost relative. Shai was happy for both. "My name's Shai, Brother Josh."

"Brother? Humph, lak a parson huh?. You be a ligous man Sha."

"No Josh. Just a spiritual Black man. Like you. That's why I call you brother. We're all family you know, of the same race."

"Afkin huh," he looked at Shai quizzically. "I reckon dey's jus lak colud folks." Shai managed a friendly grunt.

"Just lak colored folks Josh," he aped. Josh looked at his beneficiary curiously. "You sometin else man. I gotta go now. But I be seein you agin...Okay? Brotha." He tipped back to the door chuckling. Into the night he stole away just as stealthily as he'd come. The door closed quietly behind him. Shai stared at the door for moments after Josh had gone. He already missed the only friendly face he'd seen since arriving in the past. "I've got to stay cool," he told himself. "Got to get my shit together and hold out...Got to be strong...Black...Remember my African heritage." The words came quickly as he tried to ward off the impending fear hovering at the edge of his psyche, threatening to overwhelm him, drown him in panic and hysteria. Somehow I've got to get back to the transmission site. If the Professor comes looking for me, that's where I'll have to be. Stay as close as possible to the site without getting myself killed. How easy or hard it's going to be remains to be seen.

Shai wondered how far he was from the transmission site. He had no idea how far the men had taken him. His best guess came by judging the time that elapsed from the moment he was captured to the time he inferred it took to awake in the shack. What he came up with was that he still had no idea where or how far he was from the site. It was frustrating. It may not even be the same day. He may have been transported in a wagon. He may have been carried. The added inferences depressed him. Again he felt helpless and overwhelmed. He tried shaking the feeling off. Then he remembered his watch. He strained to feel for it. But...just as he feared...it was gone.

*****

The morning routine at Angora was dreary for the field slaves and no picnic for those who worked in the house. It was a dull, monotonous, back braking drudgery. Since first light most of the field slaves had been out in the fields working. The house servants were busy in the main house with household chores while others still, tended the everyday machinations of the plantation. A few slaves were on loan to the shipyards at Charleston and the gristmills in Suffolk County. But for sure, every Angora slave was at work doing something. "Go up and make sure those steps are dusted proper." Mrs. Jane Richards instructed Mary. Barking her commands, as always. A dignified looking woman with gray streaked brunette hair. She was the only one who seemed to genuinely enjoy the morning bustle.

Mrs. Richards was dainty and elegant as most genteel southern women of means were. She stood at the bottom of the staircase fanning herself with a perfumed handkerchief. She was heavily over dressed in fine linen and silk as was the traditional apparel, even in the morning, for the belle of South Carolina's society. Jane Richards was a haughty woman who easily vacillated between frangibility and autocracy depending on the color and social standing of her company. When not reigning over her servants she could be possessed of the softest femininity imaginable. The very wistful image of southern flowery. She could be given to tears over something trifling like a broken rose peddle but bare enough fortitude to brave witness to a slave being beaten within an inch of his or her life without so much as a flinch.

When it came to her home she was persnickety. In the household, Jane Richards delegated all authority over her house servants and she prided herself on running a tight and efficient household. She ran the house like a general, handing out orders and discipline, and the servants were her troops. Each female servant in her army wore braided cotton kerchiefs around their necks. It was Mrs. Richards idea. A way of distinguishing the female house servants from the females in the fields and an effective means of intimidation. When a slave did something around the house that Mrs. Richards deemed naughty she could pull on the noosed end of the braid and choke the lazy gal. Whenever other southern women saw the braided kerchief they knew the wearer was an Angora slave. One of Mrs. Richards girls. Jane Richards thought it gave them a mark of distinction that she believed they wore proudly because they represented her. But Mrs. Richards never looked into the soul of her servants. If she had she would have known how preposterous her sentiments were. To them she was a vial creature whose forced will upon them was only eclipsed by the hated neckerchief she made them wear. To her, her gals were flat characters just as nondescript and indiscriminate as blades of grass in the field and as about as important.

Today's regimen, like every other day consists of cleaning, inventory of household supplies and planning the family meals for the entire day. Mrs. Richards orchestrated every step. When she finished giving orders to the cooks she directed the endless parade of chamber maids, servants and laundresses in their duties. Giving an assignment here, making a demand there. "Janey girl I declare." She pointed a scolding finger at a young diminutive black woman carrying a heavy chamber bucket down the steps. It's thick wooden panels made it awkward for her to carry as well as its heavy weight. "I declare sometimes you girls can be just like little children," she scolded still pointing her accusing finger. "I told you to wash the masters riding outfit first, then come back for..." Janey simply tuned her out. She knew her duty and knew the lady of the house was never satisfied. No matter what the servants did. It was never right. "Land sakes chile." She turned her attention to a tired sallow mulatto with an arm full of laundry who still managed to curtsy obsequiously. "Yes Maam Miss Riches." She scurried off as soon as she received her instructions. Mrs. Richards looked totally drained after the morning ritual. The sight of her would lead one to think she did all the actual work. "Lottie get that butter churned before noon now! My goodness you all is so lazy. I declare!" She barked and scolded her servants as if they were children. In her mind they were. She spun on her heels from servant to servant directing her force like a military strategist.

Outside Colonel Richards stood on the porch above two white men standing sheepishly on the walkway below the quatrefoil balcony. Anger etched a grimacing stone like mask on the Colonel's face. He'd intended this talk to be a pep talk to inspire his subordinates but his anger had quickly gotten the best of him "I'm losing my patience with you two. Your a good overseer Jim but I hold you especially responsible. For Gods sake man they're just dumb niggers. How can you allow so many of them to run away. I pay you to put the fear of God in their black hides and keep them from fleeing and I pay you Clem to assist him." Clem's eyes were anchored to the ground.

"It's your affair to see that they are here to produce, Jim. Not forming alliances and intrigue to run into the forest to divert my profits for their apprehension." His voice was guttural and foreboding. A prophecy Jim Smith had no desire to see come true. This epidemic could cost Jim Smith his job as well as his reputation. Colonel Richards thumbed the collar of his outer coat and took a long deep drag from his cigar to set him back on track. "They can distrust each other," he began through a cloud of smoke. "But they have to believe that no one can care for their needs except us. We white men. Understand! They have to believe. They have to know that insurrection is a sin before God. That running from this estate is the worst act of treason that one can perform. And anyone who entertains such an idea is a betrayer of no end to all. Angora is their liberty gentlemen. Where they are free to serve. This is all the world they need know." He projected his tirade like a fiery preacher standing on a pulpit. Emphatically he pounded his fist on the railing for dramatic execution. "I've lost too much property Jim." His tone softened to entreaty. "Somehow these niggers are getting away from here and not being recovered." He shook an index finger at the two men. "There must be a common entity here. Someone is helping them and I want you to find out who." He returned to a fiery oratory. The veins in his neck bulged. "And I promise you that their abolitionist asses will hang by their nigger loving necks! Now get to the bottom of this quandary or you and your family can replace them runaway darkies in the field!"

197

Jim Smith stood speechless. He knew he wouldn't be expected to work in the field like a common negro but his job and standard of living was surely hanging in the balance. Runaways were nothing unusual on plantations. Every plantation has had them. But Suffolk County's proud heritage was that they were always recovered. Now inexplicably two Angora slaves remained at large beyond the usual recovery time and there seemed to be more and more attempts everyday. Other plantations in the area were reporting the same occurrences. Jim Smith knew that Colonel Richards and the other plantation owners had valid reasons for concern. A terrible trend was occurring in the county and it had to be eliminated.

*****

Colonel Richards' wrath would be the end of it for him. Clem had already been chewed out by Jim Smith after the fiasco with Sara. He was bound to get chewed out again. Everyone seemed to be up in arms over this thing and it seemed he was the one to catch hell over it when the bosses needed to unload their frustration. What he didn't know was that Jim Smith had a plan in the works that just might offer some relief to this situation. One that hadn't been tried before. An unorthodox plan that smacked of the kind of intrigue Clem couldn't understand but could dam well appreciate. After being dismissed by the Colonel, Jim Smith and Clem started towards the rack to mount their horses. "Clem ain't no doubt about it. There's an agent of this dam underground railroad that I've been hearin about at work here in these parts. And we're gonna get em."

"Agent of an underground?" asked Clem, puzzled.

"Yea boy. The underground. That's what they call the outfit that helps the darkies escape. And I'm gonna uncover their hides before long."

"I hope so Mr. Jim. I sure would like to see it stopped." They rode off toward the fields.

*****

The slaves on Angora Plantation went about their tasks in the fields like perpetual labor machines stuck in miserable repetition. By mid morning the sun was already unbearably hot. Jim Smith slowly paced the area atop his horse, watching over the slaves in the field. Occasionally the mood would strike him to single out someone slothful and he'd crack his whip over the back of the unwary slave. Clem paced the field on foot. Whenever Jim Smith saw fit to brake the monotony by cracking someone, Clem would brake out in sadistic laughter. Every so often Jim Smith would stretch his neck southward as though he was suspecting something or someone. Finally he caught sight of a wagon trudging slowly up the road. He mopped his brow with his handkerchief and broke out into a wide grin. The slaves, seeing the wagon approaching broke their rhythms of labor long enough to watch Jim ride toward it. He met the wagon at the edge of the field. When it rolled pass, Bessie was the first of the workers to recognize Sara's ghastly image, uncovered and sanguine stained in the back of the wagon. Her tiny infant lying horribly beside her. Sara's arms were stretched toward the sky, stiff with rigor mortis. Even in death she seemed to be reaching desperately towards the heavens for freedom. A loud gasp escaped from Bessie's throat when she saw the grotesque sight of her friend. She clutched at her heart and dropped her basket then covered her mouth in despair. Tears welled to fullness in her eyes then fell down her cheeks. The other slaves left their labors unfettered to run to the edge of the field. They followed the death wagon part way up the road and Jim Smith made no attempt to stop them. He allowed them to follow the wagon with impunity. He wanted the blood stained cadavers to relay a message. The looks of shock and intimidation on their terrified faces told him his message was read. As he rode along side the wagon he shouted something to the driver to drive home his point, spitting his words out sardonically. "I hope every nigra that runs away from here comes back in the same condition.

199

Just like this little wench and her pickininny." Shaking a scolding finger he spoke directly to the gawkers. "You nigras mark this sight well. You hear me!"

He smiled. This was not the end of his machinations. No...He had more plans of deterrence up his sleeves. Each slave looked to the other with a hopeless despondency in each eye...and a miserable weight on every shoulder.

*****

A gray overcast had just begun to lift when the morning sun made it's appearance. John McPacker arrived at Angora and found Shai lying on the floor of the shack, exhausted from another fitful nights sleep. McPacker stood over him menacingly to intimidate him. Shai stared up towards the white man and willed himself to remain defiant. He was determined to present himself as a formidable adversary. Though John McPacker held the advantages, Shai had only his will and a weakening determination.

"Boy! Know this." The white man kicked him stiffly in the thigh. "There is one thing to be sure. You WILL prostrate yourself before your masters." He bent down on one knee to look into Shai's face. Eye to eye. Nose to nose. "By Eire, you know exactly what I am saying to you. You're no dumb nigger I'll grant you. But by the Saints boy you are a nigger. A slave to be sure and I won't tolerate you at any other station. I'll wager you're smart enough to know that." Shai stared up at him coldly. McPacker's hulking frame loomed over him like a giant. He stood up then reached down to Shai with a large beefy red hand and slapped him violently, knocking him over. Shai recoiled and sprung from the floor like a rattle snake. The large white man was taken abback by the man's agility. But hampered by the chains, Shai was an easy target to knock down again.

Again and again Shai lashed out at every affront. Again and again McPacker knocked him down. Finally Shai remained on the ground, gasping for air. His resolve weakening. Shai had neither the strength nor the will to resist the white man any further. "Now if you've a mind to cooperate with your betters we can go on...Ya black arrogant heathen." With that McPacker struck Shai in the side with the most furious kick he could muster. It was greater than any previous blow Shai had received and the pain shot across his body in every direction. Excruciating pain. It left him choking for air and rolling in a ball as far as his chains would allow. For a moment Shai thought he'd black out. He wasn't sure that he hadn't.

"Now maybe you're ready to receive proper instruction."

"Proper instruction? Man kiss my ass. "Shai could barely squeeze out the words. "The proper manner of slave behavior boy...But before this is over you will be kissing mine and any white man's arse, by Eire. Would ye say."

No reply.

"Have ye a mind boy!?!"

No reply. 'Slave behavior!' The awful meaning of the words was an act of rape in itself. Slave!...ME!?! The thought...the idea...the concept, if it wasn't so harrowing a thought it would've deserved a joke in reply or the most sarcastic remark imaginable. The statement seemed to suddenly and shockingly define the meaning of this most distressful predicament. He wanted to cry. What's going to happen to me, he feared. Suddenly shaking...What am I going to do?..."Well boy!?! Still no reply. McPacker kicked him again. HARD! and he asked him again. And again received no reply. This evil pretense went on all morning.

By mid afternoon McPacker and his two assistance emerged from the shack sweating and exhausted. McPacker dismissed his helpers then made his way to the main house to apprise Colonel Richards of his progress. He found the Colonel sitting on his porch with Jasper serving him his second brandy. Permission granted, McPacker ascended the marble steps and approached Colonel Richards with an evil, satiated grin affixed to his face. Without speaking he held out his hand. In his palm was a slightly bloodied handkerchief rolled into a soiled, sanguine linen ball. "My God McPacker, what conferment is this?"

"Tis a present for you Colonel. From your most recent acquisition." Colonel Richards found this drama all too peculiar. He stared at the bloody cloth. "Well you don't expect me to soil my hands with that. Do you man? Open it." McPacker slowly unfolded the cloth with a mock gesture of court side cordiality. Inside was Shai's imbrued gold tooth. Colonel Richards recoiled from it in shock at first then summoned his composure. He smiled crookedly at McPacker. "Mary!" He called for the corpulent black slave and gave her an order to clean and stow the grisly extraction away. Mary cringed at the sight of it. She carried the handkerchief away from her body between two finger tips. Jasper brought out another snifter of brandy and Colonel Richards invited McPacker to join him in a celebration of progress.

*****

The next day McPacker arrived with the morning dew. A formidable slave tracker and breaker, he was consistent and precise in his work. He believed every slave had individual dispositions but as a group they had collective strengths. These variables he dealt with and used to his advantage in tailored fashion. He had a method to his work that followed a precise procedure. After learning the temperament of the slave he was working on and the identities with which he empathized, McPacker would then work on redefining those entities. Once the slave was stripped of those strengths he would replace them with total dependence, ultimately gaining total obedience. He knew Shai was strong willed, proud and intelligent. Points he would have respected had Shai been a white man. But points now he must manipulate to brake him. Not only was this man black, he also seemed unfamiliar with slave etiquette, albeit out of sort with the ideas of negro attributes...He was for all intent and purposes, alone. A similar condition held in common with his kidnapped fore bearers, McPacker mused. Loneliness and terror was his most reliable tool in shattering ones resolve. Also, it helps when you don't consider your adversary human.

*****

Colonel Richards and McPacker walked to the shack together discussing the attributes of effective slave breaking. Virgil and two other assistants followed close behind. "It's his identity which must go first," explained McPacker. "A connection with an ancestry is the most important thing to deny these people. Our forefathers, with much foresight, severed the definitive ties to their origins. But it tis for our part that we continue to deny them any folklore or culture. Such that it is."

"I don't believe that they have maintained any useful semblance of their primitive homeland," interjected the Colonel. "It is for their own good that it is so. It is only what they have made for themselves that can define them as their own people. I am not even aware of what he calls himself. Are you?"

"No. But it tis of no concern. We shall decide on what he'll be called and calls himself, by Eire."

Shai laid on the floor inside the moldy wooden shack, cold and weak. His swollen face pained him. He wondered if he would be able to withstand another blow to the jaw after having his tooth pried from his mouth. God his jaw ached. He heard the men approaching the shack and was too sore and frightened to pull himself to his feet. What in hell else could they do to me. The door opened. Virgil and Cyprus rushed in and jerked Shai to his feet. McPacker and Colonel Richards trailed in behind. Before them stood a pitiful sight that elicited no pity from either man. The Colonel noticed how weak the young black man was and ordered the two white men to help him remain standing. "What's your name boy?" he asked rolling his head from side to side like an inquisitive puppy. Shai peeked at him through swollen eyes.

He could barely see the man before him but struggled to answer the question. "My name is Shai," he said weakly.

"You have some bearing for a colored boy and you are almost as articulate as a white man! Where are you from? You've never labored on a plantation, have you?" Shai painfully clenched his eyes in disgust. "You've much to learn about temperament, boy. You are intelligent and it could very well be an asset to me and a saving grace for you. Or it could very well be a liability for you. The choice on weather it be easy or hard is the only choice you'll be allowed to make. Son it could be a very good benefit to exploit your intellectual services," Colonel Richards went on enthusiastically. "A revolutionary idea. It may well create a novel way to employ my most adroit slaves." He congratulated himself for his cleverness.

"You mean you want to lend me out. Show me off like some trained monkey. Well you've forgotten one thing," Shai spoke up. It was painful to speak. "What pray, would that be," snarled Richards growing increasingly perturbed by Shai's arrogance. "I'm no fucking slave!" McPacker stepped in to slap Shai but Colonel Richards stopped him. "Do you suppose yourself on a social par with white men?"

"I suppose myself on a par with any man. Certainly you. You fuckin hypocrite. All you dam whites whose business is hate and whose religion is bigotry." His voice sounded hysterical, even to himself. He tried to laugh but it was too painful. "You call yourselves christians. You call yourselves civilized." He couldn't stop himself. "You rape, you steal, murder. You're an earth borne disease...A plague on the planet...You...You're the fucking barbarians." Shai was in tears. "You're a destructive devil who would destroy everything...In the name of God...That's blasphemy as well as barbaric," he shouted referring to one of McPacker's remarks.

"You dare speak of God," Richards snarled. "You. A member of a heathen, ungrateful race. We white men rescued you people and had to forced you into civility..."

"You call this civil. Stealing babies from mothers arms. Torturing and killing helpless unarmed men and women. Denying them the very liberty you profess to hold so dear. Shit...! I call it cowardice! You speak and swear by liberty and you sanction the very opposite. Your entire institution is bullshit. Pure BULLSHIT!!...Nothing less than plain ass hypocrisy. Just like your fuckin constitution." Tears streamed down his cheeks. "All lies...and Bullshit!" He spat every word with venomous emphasis. "You got the nerve to call my people savage. You and your kind are the savages. You dare deem me 3/5s of a man. Most of these white motherfuckers around here don't have the intelligence of a flea. But you'd still, hypocrite that you are, claim I'm innately unequal to a white man." Shai schemed pedantically to challenge him intellectually.

McPacker couldn't believe the Colonel allowed this impudence to go this far. Even Shai had a feeling he was pushing the limit of what he knew was his place in this time. But Colonel Richards was some how amused as much as angered, even impressed with the arrogant but intelligent young nigger. But enough was enough. Only so much arrogance could be tolerated. On second thought no amount of arrogance could be tolerated from any negro. "You've been a most attentive student to the white abolitionist who groomed you boy," he sneered. "But no amount of white man's learning will ever put you in equal standing with a white man. And our constitution speaks of you as you are. Property. You're less than a man in a white man's eyes and you have no rights I'm bound to consider." Colonel Richards spun angrily on his heals and stormed from the shack. John McPacker stepped in front of Shai. "By the Saints of Eire, it is shameful what those abolitionist have filled ye with," he said disgustedly.

Virgil and Cyprus continued to hold Shai by either arm while John unlocked and removed his shackles. John McPacker leaned in inches from Shai's face and spoke slowly and deliberately into his eyes. "You've courage tis true. But it tis now to business. To begin with," McPacker informed him in measured tones, "Shane or whoever you claim to be, is no more. From this day forward you will be called...Joe...By Eire that's it...Joe."He looked to his companions then back to Shai. They shook their heads in approval. "Do you understand me...Joe?" He turned again and winked at his assistant as though he'd said something clever. Shai turned his head and grimaced in response. "Shit," he swore. For the first time McPacker punched him with his clenched fist instead of an open hand. The two men held Shai steady. The pain was unbearable. McPacker lightly massaged Shai's chin between his thumb and forefinger, studying him. Then stepped back and looked Shai up and down

"We know there's intelligence in ye. But I want to know how spry you are. Jump up and down so that I can measure your sprightliness."

"Fuck you," Shai sputtered. McPacker's face was sprayed with each syllable from the blood streaked spittle that ran from Shai's lips. McPacker punched him again. The blow nearly rendered him unconscious. Virgil and Cyprus propped him up again. Shai gargled unintelligibly. "Fuck you motherfuckers!!" he screamed hysterically. He barely recognized his own voice.

"To be sure you'll soon be reciting that name to me, Joe. Now say it after me." McPacker's voice had risen two octaves. "You say. My name...is Joe...and I am a slave." He dragged out every syllable. Shai's only reply was a silent struggle to stop the tears of frustration from rolling down his cheeks. McPacker hit him again. Shai's face had taken so much abuse the pain was numbing. His head drooped and John McPacker lifted his chin. "I'm waiting lad." Shai's answer was a mad mixture of crying and laughter. "Man fuck you!! Fuck you!!" He screamed deliriously. "Bring the nigger outside Virgil!"

John McPacker stormed out of the shack "We'll give him a lick o the nines. By Eire that'll oil his tongue."

*****

206

Miss Clara's cabin was all abuzz with talk of the slave from Africa. Josh, having been the only one, as yet, to have actually seen him commanded the attention of everyone in the cabin with his narration of their first encounter.

"He talk jus lak white folk," he was saying. "He talk lak he had some learnin."

" Heard tell African people didn't know how ta talk,' suggested Bessie.

"Wheah on earth did ya get thet foolishness Bessie?" blasted Miss Clara. Bessie shrugged her shoulders. "I don't know Miss Clara. Everybody say dey's savages."

"Nobody but white folks would have you believe sumptin lak that."

"How you know he got learnin? asked Caesar, ignoring Bessie and Miss Clara's dialogue. "I saw it in his eyes. Mayhaps he can write."

"In his eyes?" Caesar spat incredibly. "Get on way from heah."

"Nobody need you to make it gospel," replied Josh defensibly.

" Maybe he can write me a pass, huh Miss Clara," mused Bessie. "Hush up gal," warned Miss Clara. Cutting her eyes accusingly at Caesar. She hadn't noticed the look of interest he returned her.

There was a kind of intelligence in Caesar's eyes. Not the kind Josh saw in Shai but the kind of intelligence that warranted heeding. A deviousness that bared watching. Since he first came to Angora, Caesar had constantly asked questions about runaways and their means of escape. Field slaves considered his questions a reasonable query. Such questions coming from someone with different eyes would be harmless. But to Miss Clara such eyes as Caesar's left her somewhat wary. She had seen many eyes in the faces of many people, black and white and learned to read them well. To Miss Clara, the inquisitive slave did not fit the bill of a runaway. To her he emitted the aura of a treacherous rat. Or what the master called a trusted house servant...and those she didn't trust. Trusted house servants could be untrustworthy brothers in bondage she always said. Not knowing Caesar personally was no lack of proof of intent either. It did nothing to unease her sense of accusation. Incrimination of him lingered somewhere in her gut and she learned long ago to be a good listener to the soul. But intuition was not the whole game. She'd done some investigating of her own on their new brother in bondage and discovered he'd been a coachman on a Clarkville Plantation. His hands were smooth though he professed to be the new blacksmith apprentice and his back was unscarred. He smiled too readily, even among his own people. Plus, experience had taught her, coachman and house servants were rarely so interested in running away as he was. She knew if anything they could be counted on to alert the white folk. No. even though Caesar worked with the blacksmith at Angora now, he was still a servant of the house to her and until she had evidence to the contrary she opted to remain wary of him.

"Mayhaps he can hep you meet up wit yo sista." Caesar suggested to Bessie...too cynically Miss Clara thought. Noise from the outside interrupted any chance for Bessie to reply. "What's that commotion outside theah?" she asked. Bill, an elderly slave stuck his bald head in the cabin door. "Miss Clara. Dey's gonna whump that nigga frum Afreeka!"

"Lord have mercy," she prayed. The cabin occupants ran out the door.

No matter how terrifying, a whipping always brought out plenty of spectators. And if they didn't come Colonel Richards would order them to observe it anyway. Though curiosity and inquisitiveness were just as powerful lures.

"Bessie!" Miss Clara beckoned her back inside with a gnarled index finger.

"Come here gurl." She lowered her voice almost to a whisper. "Chile I done tole you to stop talkin bout Kimbe round that poppy eyed nigger."

"Miss Clara he as me a question."

"It don't mean you got ta answer it. Now mind me gurl. That boy'd run ta dem peckahwoods as soon as the words got out yo mouth. Soon's he get somethin to tell he gon tell it. Now you mind," she scolded. Bessie fell silent for a moment, then replied. "You right Miss Clara."

Miss Clara always knew what she was talking about. There was not a slave on the plantation that would dispute it. Especially Bessie.

"You know I am," she averred. Her voice fell to a consoling tone. "Bessie, listen to me. I think its time you ketch up wit Kimbe. The longer her an that boy wait on Fall Point the dangerous it get. And you know Kimbe a wait on you come hell o high water." She let the words sink in. Then winked her eye.

"Beside. There's a train a comin." Bessie smiled. "You mean..." Miss Clara held up a finger to stop her then stage whispered. "You know jus what I mean. Now it's comin so you mind. Heah? Now's the time. Wit them folks givin all dey attention to dat pooh chile frum Afrika, it's a good time fo you ta get. Whilst the white and colud is busy. Cuz when dis whippin is ova and things quiet down the white folks'll take they shame face back to the main house an drink an laugh. And the colud folk'll hide in they cabin fo a while." She placed an assuring hand on Bessie's shoulder. "So, long's we keep dat nosey nigger out da bizness," Miss Clara pointed her head toward the door. "You can get ahead, two three days maybe. By then it'll be a meetin called to the underground station house. And from theah somebody gonna lead all yall up north." Bessie looked long and unsure at Miss Clara. "I wish you all would come too Miss Clara." Miss Clara shook her head. "Naw. I'm too ole chile.. Anyways these white folks ain't workin me none and somebody gotta keep a eye out fo the colored round heah." Bessie searched Miss Clara's eyes. "If they eva find out how you hep people run away they gon hang you for sure, Miss Clara."

"Don't you worry none bout dis ole woman heah.. I been round long nuff ta teach the white folk what they don't know," she stated arrogantly. The women laughed a nervous laugh. "Hey ladies what you all laffin bout." Caesar's reentry into the cabin startled them. Miss Clara's eyes closed to contemptuous slits. She wondered how much he'd heard.

*****

The cat-o-nine tails is a formidable tool of persuasion in the hands of a man who knew how to use it. Virgil McPacker was just such a man. It's short oak handle with finger grooves could be held securely in hand. Nine leather straps or tails attached to its head were knotted at the ends to deliver the maximum sting. When the tails were wet the cat-o-nine was an even more effective device for torture

Two men drug Shai from the shack and tied him face down to a large wooden X shaped plank. Both his wrist were secured to its upper end with twine. His ankles were bound to its lower end, leaving him spread eagle, face down with his head dangling between the X's V shaped center. John McPacker ripped Shai's shirt from his body, exposing Shai's bare back to his tormentors then knelt beside his prostrate figure. John McPacker leaned close to his ear. "Again lad," he whispered cynically. "I command you...to recite...your new and proper name...Like this." He changed his tone to ape the inflection of a docile servant. "My name his Joe suh and Imma slave." Shai strained to lift his head as far as he could to look into McPacker's face. His voice was weak but he held his resolve. McPacker pressed his ear close to Shai's lips to hear him. Barely audible, Shai struggled to mouth his refusal. "Go...to...hell" Shai's face bore the most pugnacious expression he could muster then struggled to laugh. Virgil swung down on him with the cat-o-nine. The burning sting radiated throughout Shai's body. The spectators on the scene gasped with each stroke of the nine While Virgil's muscular arm swung the whip with deadly precision. Each lash made Shai constrict against the binds on his wrist and ankles. His 21st century sensibilities were a poor match for Virgil's 19th century condemnation. The stinging pain was just too much for him to bare. Soon Shai's consciousness was cloaked in darkness, temporarily freeing him from the ordeal. he floated in an enveloped state of limbo but still his mind could react. He saw an image coming toward him. A large shining wheel, spinning rapidly, creating a circular blur. From it's center emerged a hand. It reached out to him. Behind the hand appeared a face, barely visible. It was a face familiar to him. Soft pleasing and ebony. It was Argee. Behind her, large buildings stood silhouetted against a metropolis skyline. From it emerged many faces. Jubilee, Kobolongo, Lewis, Belton, Kevin, Bilal. Their faces swirled in clock wise fashion. He felt relieved. Finally in their company. He was happy again, safe and secure...Then...their images faded as other sensations grew palpable. He then sensed a voice. One he hadn't heard before but still rapturous. It chanted in a staccato rhythm. He blinked his eyes open as the voice grew louder. Instantly his senses reminded him of where he truly was. A hapless knot of despair welled in his heart and eyes while silent tears began to fall.

Miss Clara had been praying over the young man's unconscious body since the male slaves summoned her to the cabin after the white men drug him there bruised and bleeding. She was applying something to the wounds on his back that caused a sharp sting. It made him jerk. "It smarts some don't it," she said soothingly. Her voice was the most pleasant sound he'd heard since coming to this god forsaking era. "It'll ease some directly."

He was laying face down on his stomach, His back ached something awful and it pained him to move his head but he was determined to see the face of the woman whose voice was so soft and maternal. It was important for him to put features on her charity and an outline to her kindness. He wanted to be able to hold her image in mind during the times that he knew were sure to come. Her angelic grace was the only tangible existence of compassion left for him to hold on to in this inhospitable world. She was an old woman, very black and wrinkled. Her gaunt and weather beaten face was full of dignity and grace. Her smile showed a sincerity and concern that made her beautiful. Her eyes held the flame of wisdom that told him instantly he was among family.

"Folks, colored and white call me Miss Clara," she said softly.

"Thank...you...Miss.. Clara..." He could barely speak. It seemed an effort to merely move his mouth. "They say you called Joe." The suddenness of his agitation startled her. "No.. no!" he exerted weakly. She had to strain to hear his protest. "My...name...is Shai." Her smiling response had the effect of assurance and he was able to settle down. "You rest now Shy...Miss Clara heah now. You jus rest." Her voice was so soothing and reassuring. Another woman's voice came in. It too, was gentle yet firm and young like Argee's.. He couldn't see her face but she sounded beautiful. "Miss Clara," called the voice from the doorway. "It's gettin on dark now."

"Yes, yes, yes," Miss Clara chanted in parlando rising from the make shift bedside. "Lizzie," she ordered going out the door, "tend ta dis chile's back."

Lizzie took Miss Clara's place at Shai's bedside and continued tending to him with the same tenderness and care.

Miss Clara navigated through the darkness to an isolated clump of trees a short distance from the cabin. She found Bessie nervously leaning against a tree wearing a cotton linsey woolsey dress tied tight at the waist. A rope of yarn served as a belt. Her eyes darted from side to side A greasy cotton scarf covered her head and a burlap bag was flung over her shoulder hanging carefree across her back. "Ya got the red peppa fo the dogs?' inquired Miss Clara. Bessie shook her head yes.

"Rubbed yoself wit onion juice?" Again Bessie mutely affirmed. Miss Clara's inquires took on the itinerant tone of a checklist. An old hat at the game of freedom taking, she took her business very seriously. She went on to instruct and advise her charge with a pointed index finger.

*****

"Remember chile. The only enemy you got in the forest is hunger and white folks. Yo stomach, you can take care of natcherly. You can always find food. But white folks and paddy rollers," she waved her hand while clucking the roof of her mouth, "you betta off stayin way from. Don trust none of em." Bessie took in every word as she sat her sack down. Miss Clara held her by the shoulders as she went on. "Ignorant white folks you can fool, cause they think you too dumb ta fool em. Smart white folk. Dey think it's they duty ta trouble ya but they think ya at least got enuff sense not ta try and fool em. Dey think ya too scared. But deys all ready ta be fooled just the same. She looked at Bessie in solace. "Thas yo bes weapon gainst em if ya finds yoself in a corna. Bessie be careful. You go on and find Kimbe and her boy. Yall stay put an lissin. We'll do our part ta guide ya through song. Tell ya when the underground bout ta move and where. And remember," she pointed to the sky, "the handle of the big dipper always points north. See it?" Bessie looked skyward and nodded her head slowly.

"In ya travels, if ya come up on a house or cabin wit one a dem colud ornaments in front, you know what make fun of colored, wit big blubbery red lips, a great big mouth and big buck eyes keep a steppin. Don't go dere. But If dat gardin jockey got regular lips and eyes lak a human being, it could mean ya can get help dere. Mayhaps be a abolition family live theah. Theys the onlyist people who would have a colud ornament what look human. Even though; still be careful." She smiled and looked around cautiously, then back at her charge. "I love you Bessie. But I hope I neva sees you again." She nodded her head towards the woods. "Go on chile. Gon and be free. I'll be prayin fo ya."

Bessie snatched off the linen kerchief she wore around her neck. She remembered how Mrs. Richards labeled her and the other girls with this badge of degradation that identified one as a house servant. Miss Lady thought was so honorable. When Bessie was banished from the house for what Mrs. Richards called high faluten arrogance, she forced Bessie to continue wearing the kerchief even in the field as a sign that she'd been demoted in favor. How ridiculous that old phony was, Bessie smiled. Being in the field wearing it was a proud badge of defiance to her. But now that she was taking her freedom it was only a reminder of her servitude. She flung the thing to the ground then looked longingly at Miss Clara. Bessie hated saying good bye to the old matriarch but freedom awaited. She was eager to taste it. No matter how frightening a step it was to be...FREEDOM!!!!!!! All the things she imagined she'd have to endure to keep it will be worth it. She inventoried the things Miss Clara told her tonight and the things Kimbe had told her before. It was a lot to take in and remember. But she'd remember...for...FREEDOM!!!! Bessie put her arms around Miss Clara's shoulders and kissed her lovingly on both cheeks. "FREEDOM!!!!! Miss Clara!...Freedom!!!!" Then she disappeared into the darkness

CHAPTER 9

Year 2000

Howard University in the autumn, the air is clean, crisp and charged with intellectual anticipation. Dying leaves serve as a back drop born in contrast amidst a new semester. Fresh faced eager young students scurry to class and a new learning experience. That's how Kuendela remembered it when he was one of those fresh young black faces. As an alumnus he felt a special pride in seeing and feeling it all again. Walking the campus reminded him of his days in Professor Jubilee's physics class. He and his fellow students always looked forward to fridays in that class. That was when physics was set aside and Professor Jubilee would instead opt for an extemporaneous lecture about life. Black life especially, historical black life in particular.

"There was once a village," the Professor would begin his soliloquy. "It sat near the Zambezi river where a dense jungle separated it from the great plains. Everyday a braggadocios old bird would come to roost upon the fence around the cattle pen while the men and young boys tended cattle. All morning the bird would go on and on about his exploits on the great plains. Ostentatiously he'd flap his wings and strut the fence as the boys and men gathered around him. He'd brag in graphic detail about his encounters with the lions on the plains and how within an inch of his life he thrashed the biggest and baddest of the mythical kings of the jungle. One day, finally, after hearing this story at length, many times, in countless variation, a young boy asked his father. "Father. I've never been on the plains but I have seen the lions from afar and I don't understand. How is it that this old and diminutive bird can best such a strong and mighty animal?"

"Son," his father replied, "we've only heard what the bird has to say. We have yet to hear the lion's story." Professor Jubilee would smile. His eyes would gleam. "Today young Africans we're going to hear the lions story." His voice would begin in a mild tempo only to rise in timbre and grow strong with conviction. "You can call an Englishman white or a Frenchman white but it doesn't tell you who they are or where they come from. We are all black and that identifies the color of our race but it doesn't say who we are. Our history," he'd state, "did not begin on a slave ship. Nor were our ancestors wild uncivilized savages before meeting the white man. On the contrary, when the whites lived in caves your ancestors had for thousands of years before lived in great civilizations. The Greeks first came into contact with your ancestors before the days of Sparta and praised them as the most beautiful beings they'd ever seen."

He'd pace the room proudly. His back straight and his deep baritone booming. "When they saw those tall beautiful, regal black men and women, they thought they were gods." He'd shake his head. "Herotodus, their own so called father of history, bared witness to our ancestors greatness and recorded it. The people he met called themselves Nubians. The Black Hebrews called them Cushites. Herotodus called them Ethiopians. People kissed by the sun. White folk would have you believe that civilization began with the Greeks. But that's not true. Maybe the assimilation of it's concept began with them but not the concept of civilization itself. That all began with your ancestors."

"Herotodus, Plato and all the others came to Alkebu-lan or what we now call Africa, to study. To learn the high sciences of civilization from those altruistic black men. And how did the Greeks repay them for their benevolence. After 300 years the whites returned to Africa with the likes of Alexander, misnomered the Great, and others to pillage, plunder and steal that which the Africans had freely shared with them. They wanted it all and would say later that they originated it." By now the class would be mesmerized. He'd gesticulate dramatically. "Picture if you will," he'd say. "A time and place when the Greeks walked on all fours and the European groveled on the dirty moors, beating their women over the head with clubs and dragging them into caves." Professor Jubilee would pound his fist on the desk. "At that time in Africa our ancestors lived in an orderly society with just and moral laws. They studied the stars and the movement of the earth. Our ancestors," he'd point, "gave to the world the concept of right and wrong that gave way to religion. Our ancestors built the pyramids and first charted the stars. Let me tell you something," he'd digress. "Christopher Columbus believed the world was flat like all Europeans of the time. It wasn't until he came in contact with Moorish seaman, who'd always known that the world was round, did he come to learn the truth. And of course," he'd add facetiously, "being white he's credited with," he held his fingers up in quotes, "it's so-called discovery. Ancient Africans circumnavigated the world way before the whites began their maritime plundering. The Africans built monuments to their grandeur and fame everywhere." By now Professor Jubilee would be speaking at the height of passion. His pride beaming. "Our ancestors created the greatest cultured civilization the world has ever known. The African high culture's achievements have yet to be surpassed by any other culture. Then or now. In our ancestors society there was no word for jail because no one had ever gone to one. There was no word for orphanage because no child had ever been abandoned or left behind. There was no understanding of an old folks home because no elders had ever been thrown away. This planet was ours. We lived one with nature and the creator but lost it. We dropped the ball family. We became corrupted by the influence of the white interlopers from the north. We allowed our heavenly land to be taken by the invaders." His pace would slow. His expression staid. "Young Africans we are a spiritual and benign people. No match for a feral and unprincipled breed. But imagine if we could relearn, could uncover, the high culture that was taken and erased from us. We could reclaim the greatness that was ours. Throw off the self destructiveness we've degenerated to in this wretched, decadent, barbarian society. It is not the way the creator meant for us to live." His prideful face would be tinged with rage. "Yes! I said decadent! and I called them barbaric. If you can show me one place the whites have gone on this earth where the indigenous people or nature itself did not suffer, if not completely destroyed. I'll take those words back." There was almost a tear in his eye. "Young Africans," he'd say somberly, "You must look to your past to regain yourselves. You are heir to the greatest and oldest civilization that ever existed upon this earth."

Kuendela remembered Professor Jubilee falling silent for a moment to let the sense of his claims sink in, then stretch out his arms to caress his class in a conceptual embrace. "You are the people kissed of the sun. In your collective conscious the potential of the ancients high culture and intelligence lie dormant like a sleeping giant within your spirits. Waiting to be awaken. You were created in the creators image and the earth and all that is holy upon it. Is yours." Kuendela took a deep breath, sucking in the smell of fresh grass. He smiled and shook his head as he remembered Professor Jubilee's enthusiastic monologues and the zeal with which he delivered them

"Beautiful, wonderful Cush, Kemet and Nubia." he'd say. "Somalia and Zimbabwe. There were universities, scientists, kings, brave warriors and beautiful queens. They trekked the entire globe and built things that, even with today's technology, cannot be reproduced." The Professor's eyes would shine, his shoulders would pull erect and his devotion would nestle in his student's consciousness and ferment in their blood.

Professor Jubilee had devoted his entire life to teaching science and bringing the glorious history of Africa to the fore. Every year after classes broke for the summer he'd take off to a different site in Africa. To dig, to research and to uncover the truth of the existence and grandeur that was ancient Africa. That, Kuendela knew, was the driving force behind the discovery of Professor Jubilee's crystals. The first year Kuendela spent as an assistant in the ARC program he remembered the Professor as a perpetual motion machine. During the development phase of the ARC each new breakthrough fueled his fervor to go on to the next. He was hungry for the wonderful cultural reality he knew he'd find in the ancient world. "Ahhh," Kuendela thought with impassioned reverence. Those wonderful days of learning and those friday sessions. How empowering. The memories were warm. But now! He felt sadness for this unfortunate setback, for the Professor and for Shai. He shuttered to think of what Shai must be going through.

Kuendela made his way through the mingling crowd of students to the George Washington Carver Building and down the grassy slope to the glass and concrete structure in the rear. The doors of the building slid open automatically when he approached the front entrance. Behind the opening door stood Professor Jubilee, smiling. "Kuendela!" He greeted him with out stretched arms. "Hotep."

"Habari Gani Professor," Kuendela said smiling.

"Ahh Kuendela." Professor Jubilee shook his speckled gray head. "As you know son, news is not so good. Ah Ujambo," They embraced with genuine respect and affection. Kuendela noticed his old Professor looked worn and haggard but still managed to maintained an air of control.

Kuendela entered the building as Professor Jubilee led the way through the tiled hallways and security doors. Finally, after traversing a last long glimmering hallway one floor down from the entrance they reached the main laboratory. The team was hard at work when the two men entered. Work ceased and the team turned to see the Professor leading the tall black man into the room. Kuendela stepped up on the opened platform and greeted everyone warmly. Doctor Belton rose from her table and caressed him, giving him a personal welcome. Argee rose from her station to hug her friend and cousin. "How's Barbara?" she asked. Kuendela nodded flatly. "How are you doing?" he asked. "I'm worried about Shai."

"I know Princes." He kissed her on the cheek. "The Professor told me all about it. That's why I'm here. I hope I can do something about it."

"If anybody can Cuz, you can. You've been my hero since I was a young girl. You know that? Just be careful okay. I don't want anything to happen to you too."

Kuendela was indeed her hero. Ever since she was a child she looked up to him. He was like a big brother. Argee, herself, was a shy but intelligent young child. Being the cousin of the popular Calvin Adams made for little difficulty in finding friends. He'd been her idol and protector. And she his silent beneficiary. Kuendela/Calvin was always there for her. His strength was her comfort. His broad shoulders available to cry on and his patient, understanding ear to talk to. His appearance now gave her hope, in spite of the air of sadness and anxiety hanging over the room. Kuendela could feel it. The climate was palpable but understandable he told himself. It was unnecessary, though, to mention it. Just as it was unnecessary to assure the group against it. He was ready, that was all to it. He was a man of action. Few words were necessary at this point. It was time to get down to business.

"When do we start Professor?"

"We have already begun my son. We'll make transport transmission tomorrow after a final briefing. Today I want to show you what we have and the preparations we've made. Then you get some rest. You're going to need it." As he spoke he led Kuendela to the center of the laboratory floor and presented him with the ARC. Kuendela had seen it before, in several different stages of development but this was his first look at it's complete form. He was impressed. "Well done Professor."

"Thank you son," Jubilee almost whispered. "But. Until Shai returns. I'm afraid it's just a moot acknowledgment. A reminder of a tragic legacy." Kuendela placed a reassuring hand on his shoulder. "Don't worry sir. We're going to make sure the ARC has a proud legacy to claim."

Professor Jubilee stood silent for a pensive moment then gestured for the other Professors and Doctor Belton to follow. He led them and Kuendela through an electronic sliding door down a short hallway to a large conference room. It's walls were uniformly adorned with afro-centric art work, posters and plaques that contained words of wisdom by such notables as Malcolm X, Martin Luther King, Nat Turner and W.E.B. DuBois. Some had historical quotes from J.A. Rogers, Doctor Ishakamusa Barashango and others. Between them, spears, shields and other forms of African motif were stylishly arranged to hang from the walls for inspiration. Several burning sticks of incense tied together filled the air with a sweet aroma accented by the sound of Coltrane's jazz coming from speakers mounted on the walls in each corner of the room. Melodious waves of saxophone music floated softly in the air among whiffs of jasmine. The group of scientist settled in around a mahogany conference table to confer, relaxing as much as the ambiance allowed. Professor Jubilee authoritatively took his place at the head of the table in a large contoured chair overlooking the groups discussion. Kuendela listened attentively as Professor Jubilee laid out the particulars of the ARC and its capabilities. Doctor Belton, Professor Kobolongo and Professor Lewis each took a turn relaying pertinent data and information relating to their disciplines on the project. After seventy five minutes of conferring Professor Jubilee wrapped it up with some important conditions on three exposed fingers. "One; I can't stress enough how important it is that you not interfere with historic events. We don't want to contaminate the flow of history anymore than your presence will cause. It's our highest degree of protocol. Two; Don't bother trying to convince anyone of your true origin. We don't want to take the chance it would be recorded somewhere. And three; Leave nothing from our time behind." Kuendela nodded. "I got it Professor."

Professor Kobolongo tapped the table for attention. "I want to explain what will happen and what you may experience when you enter the ARC Kuendela. It's going to put you through a displaced vortex of time on this side. I would imagine the sensation will be similar to the multiple G force you've experienced in a shuttle take off but with an added sensation of invagination. Bilal described it as going in through your back." They laughed.

"It sounds funny but it's as best a description as one could give."

"Bilal reported no adverse physical effects during transmission," Doctor Belton interjected. "I'm sure you won't experience any either. So we can assume that Shai transported without untoward physical effects as well."

"Any questions on what you've heard so far son?" Professor Jubilee asked. "What's to prevent my materializing in a tree or a wall or something?"

"We'll transport a pre-perimeter threshold scanner ahead of you. Standard procedure," replied Professor Lewis. "It's a device we call cat-whiskers. It will analyze the perimeter of your transmission site then relay its findings to the main control for recommendations. When the site is clear we can transport you." Kuendela cocked his head to the side thoughtfully. "Why is it necessary to close the portal after transmission," he asked. "Why can't the corridor remain open? That would have eliminated the need for Shai to activate his return since he was only making a test run.

"Good question," mused Professor Lewis.

"Yes. It is," agreed Kobolongo in his crisp accent. "So let me explain. Aside from the obvious threat of someone or something contaminating the portal. There is a much more important reason. The window to the corridor consumes a tremendous amount of energy Kuendela. The Sudanese crystals can only expend enough energy for an initial dimensional thrust. To maintain such an expenditure for an infinite length of time would drain and ultimately disintegrate them. They would have no opportunity to rest and regenerate their power as they need to after transmission." He completed his explanation with a hands up gesture.

"So someone or something prevented Shai from using his O.C.P." inferred Kuendela. "No," replied Professor Lewis, "His platform was activated. Someone or something prevented him from transporting with it."

"How will I conceal the platform?"

"You won't have to. We know from Bilal that the transmission point is in a thick wooded area. Also the platform is transparent and most importantly," Professor Jubilee added. "The platform itself undergoes a unique reaction with the change in molecular dimension. Once you've reached the other side it will become extremely dense in composition."

"We are not yet sure why it happens," added Professor Kobolongo. "But an African elephant could not move it."

"One more question." Kuendela pointed an attentive finger. "How close to Shai's time of transportation will I be?" Professor Jubilee leaned back in his chair. A week or two. Not much more. One thing for sure you will arrive after Shai. Not before, we're sure of that. Transmission occurs in real time. The time that Shai spends there lapses parallel to our own time with little deviation. Your journey will be like overtaking the echo of Shai's existence in the time of transmission. The theory of dimension we're operating on, as you know, is like the remnant of a far off star that has exploded long ago. Now from the earth it is still visible even though it no longer exists. The stars image takes that long to travel into the earths purview. Time is much the same way and it's that image of time, that dimensional echo, that we will catch at a precise setting. What increment in that setting? We're unsure."

"This is gonna be some space ride. I've been gone from the project too long."

"You're here now son." Professor Jubilee flicked the switch on the intercom on the table and spoke into it's diaphragm. "Bilal. Come in. Bring the gear Professor Kobolongo stored in the equipment locker." In less than a few minutes Bilal entered the room carrying a large suitcase. Kevin came in behind him. Bilal laid the case on the table in front of Kuendela as Professor Jubilee rose from his seat and gestured for Kuendela and the others to rise. Bilal opened it and spun it around to Kuendela's view. Inside were several pieces of equipment arranged neatly in their own fitted spaces. Professor Kobolongo withdrew something that reminded Kuendela of a large star trek phaser. It was, as Professor Kobolongo explained, the automatic gelatin pistol much like the prototype Bilal carried on his transmission. This one had a lot more sophistication. Positioned inside the case around the gun's empty impression were eight extra climatic chip controlled clips of gelatin projectiles. Kuendela accepted the pistol from Professor Kobolongo. "It's cold."

"Yes. It maintains a constant temperature. The sudden change in temperature it undergoes when it enters a warm target dissolves the needle like projectile instantly rendering the target unconscious. On automatic you can bring down a large bull elephant. Watch the recoil," he added. "It takes a lot of force to propel these gelatin darts with enough thrust to penetrate heavy muscle tissue." Professor Lewis took up the mantle and pointed out each piece of gear in turn. A first aid kit, chemical light sources, survival kit with various tools, high powered vision scanners and other pieces. Corresponding carrying packs for each piece were secured to the inside of the top lid of the case. "Bilal will go over each piece of gear with you." Professor Jubilee informed him. "Also, here." He handed Kuendela a small digital audio recorder. "This is your mission log. I want a precise description of every activity you encounter. We'll download and transcribe it's data when you return. Bilal take over."

The four Quad A members excused themselves as Bilal went over each item in the case with Kuendela. Kevin then handed Kuendela two sets of body armor compressed into a carry all shoulder bag. That was it until the morning. Sleeping quarters were prepared in back rooms for the entire crew. The women shared the best of the facilities. Of course, Kuendela opined, Barbara would have plenty complaints though. The Professors accommodations were nice and comfortable as well. Kuendela decided to rough it with Kevin and Bilal. Their conditions were frugal but functional. Much like an army barracks. Before retiring for the night Professor Jubilee designated 7 am as Kuendela's transmission time. With that the crew settled into their accommodations for the night. Those who could, found anxious, fitful sleep.

*****

Shai had been beaten daily with the cat o nines. Following each beating McPacker would order him to recite that degrading refrain and each day Shai would refuse. McPacker's patience was wearing thin. The young black man's resolve was much stronger than the slave breaker realized. But experienced breaker that he was, he knew no ones resolve could withstand this pressure indefinitely. So McPacker increased his castigation in severity and duration to the point where Shai required at least half a days convalescence to regain consciousness only to be awaken and put to the lash again. So it went. Shai's back was soon mapped with ugly, painful scars. He was beginning to doubt he'd survive when suddenly there was a reprieve. The beatings had stopped. Why? Shai didn't know. He was left alone in the small dingy shack to ponder that question for an entire punishment free day. No beatings but still shackled. There was no illusion that this would last nor that he could out last his oppressors once the beatings resumed. He could only wonder when it would begin again and how much more he could take. He was doing his best to hold on. He felt he'd begun to reach the point of no resolve. There was nothing left in him. His eyes had become vacant of the determination that sustained him over the past two weeks. There were signs of despondency showing in him as he fell into restless sleep with an ever growing loss of hope of ever being rescued.

In the morning, scattered rays of sunlight found him sitting on the dirt floor staring vacantly at the wall. He reeked of sweat and filth. His putrid clothing was crusted with soil and waste that clung to his aching body. Every joint and muscle radiated pain with every movement. His gums, swollen and aching from his extracted gold tooth pained him to tears. It even hurt to moan. His eyes had now lost the bare modicum of a human soul. All that remained was a vacuous image of himself as sunlight knifed its way through the now opening shack door casting warm rays on his gaunt and sullen visage. McPacker slithered in holding his nose. "By the Saints boy," he taunted. "Phew! Such a feculent state...Ha...Ha...Ha...Not so high an mighty now. Are ye?" Clem and another man entered behind him. They pulled Shai to his feet and McPacker unlocked his shackles. Shai noticed a wickedly suspicious smirk on McPacker's face. "Your Master's about to take a short jaunt across the estate...Joe. He's most anxious to have you help him up on his horse. Assuredly, he'd enjoy a relaxing ride before lunch and I'm sure it would please him if you were to demonstrate your eagerness to assist him. Give him your concern, and well wishes." Every word was slow and deliberate. Shai stared ahead, blankly.

"I think the fight is just about gone from em," Clem observed wittily . He and the other helper, Foster, snatched Shai out of the shack with a violent pull. They pushed him across the grounds to a barn then shoved him inside and forcibly sat him down on a wooden stool. Quickly they bound his arms and legs. Shai put up an exhausted and ineffective protest. McPacker entered the barn holding a small box in one hand. He carefully extracted a large winged insect from it, pinching it's wing between his two fat fingers. It's one free wing fluttered wildly. The thing was barely visible in his large beefy hands yet he was surprisingly gentle in handling it. Deliberately he placed the insect beside Shai's head. Shai could hear the insect's buzzing as it desperately tried to flutter itself free. Shai flailed his head from side to side to escape the irritating sound. Clem and Foster held Shai's head steady while McPacker inserted the bug into his ear then covered it with the palm of his massive hand to prevent the bugs escape. With his other hand he brought up a brush dipped in a hot mixture of molasses and melted wax and splashed a generous coating over Shai's ear. McPacker then placed a soggy wet burlap bag over Shai's head to intensify his distress. The trapped insect's buzzing and claustrophobic wet bag served to create excruciating and adverse sensations. An added mixture of water and molasses poured over the bag made it more difficult to breath.

The soggy, sick smelling, sticky darkness increased his anguish. The clever trio now stood back and waited for their terrible machinations to work. The desperate buzzing, the shrinking acerbic sack and dwindling oxygen seem to reverberate Shai's distress tenfold. All these elements mingled to do their dastardly work until finally it elicited a blood curdling scream that came from deep in his throat. But his cries only fell on deaf and uncaring ears as the men feigned ignorance and laughed. The torture seemed to go on forever. Shai struggled against the bounds that secured his hands and feet and threw himself off the stool onto the ground. It was a vain attempt to relieve his aguish. Rolling on the ground gave him no relief as all his recalcitrant zeal seem to vanish. All resolve disappeared. Shai could now only plead with the men, begging them to relieve his agony. But they continued to watch and laugh. The torture, sensory deprivation and restriction continued. His horror increased becoming more and more maddening. He began wailing in insane pleas but on dispassionate ears. Soon the insects sounds of struggle became intermittent as it waned in it's final throws of death...and as it died, so did Shai's will. Shai was whipped. His resolution was completely gone and Shai...resigned to his fate became...a slave. He cried out in defeat. All dignity...gone...In a subdued stammer he recited the fawned refrain over and over between sobs. "My name is Joe. I'm a slave! My name is Joe. I'm a slave!" Every phrase was a shameful dagger plunged deeper and deeper into his anguished heart. The white men led him from the barn to the horse stables in agony. He was a sleep walker in a surreal nightmare. Master Richards stood by his horse knowingly.

He watched the once vital black man approach him in a catatonic trance. Shai was drained, tired and bent. Like...Joe...the slave would be. Clem and Foster guided Shai/Joe to a kneeling position beside the horse. They all stood around triumphantly as Shai cupped his hands to give Master Richards a boost up on his stallion. Shai stared vacantly at the thick mud covering Colonel Richards boots. It now covered Joe's hands. Soiling them in degradation and shame. Shai ceased to think and to feel. It was the only way to acknowledge his new identity and survive his agony. Joe found it easier that way.

Astride his horse, Colonel Richards instructed Clem to take Joe to the slave quarters and assign him a cabin and duties until he could be prepared for his application of apprenticeship on loan. Colonel Richards was excited. He was anxious to inform Latimor that his order could now be filled. "He'd make a fine smith," suggested Clem. "He's a good learner I can reckon."

"No," Colonel Richards looked at Shai with a smile. "I have well suited plans for him," he told Clem, still looking at his new appurtenance. When he turned to Joe he pontificated, "an honorable post awaits you Joe. You will thank me for my faith in you. A slave with such an aptitude will fair well at the trade. Maybe even an apprenticeship. A revolutionary idea, and a good one," he thought triumphantly. Joe continued to stare at the mud on his hands. He barely recognized them or his own voice as he mouthed the words..."Yes...master."

*****

In front of the rice mill at the southeast corner of Angora, west of the tobacco field, slave men and women stood in isolated groups flailing rice. Straw hats protected their heads from a brilliantly concentrated sun whose rays beamed, hot, down upon them. The brims of their straw hats cast relieving, minute shadows over their tired bloodshot eyes, providing them the only shade available. Inside the mill other slaves gathered rice for threshing and pounding. Some of them gossiped as they worked, some sang songs and others merely flailed in silence. George, a short muscular black man and his working companion labored in silence until George finally spoke. Darting his eyes from left to right to insure no one was eavesdropping he spoke in parlando with the rhythm of his flail. "I'm outta heah tonight. I got my stuff stashed by the ole graveyard wheah Mas Riches pappy is buried. Got it all worked out." He stopped to wipe the sweat from his brow. "Dey'll neva think of watchin thet place. You know how white folks think. Dey don't speck no nigga to be messin round no graveyard" He chuckled at his cleverness. His companion continued flailing rice stalks in silence but he took in every word George said. He hated this work. But he had to be here. The two men continued with their chore without another word.

*****

During count, from his perch at the edge of the mill, overseer assistant Luke discovered the number of females in his work force had again decreased by one. He snatched off his hat and beat it against his thigh in disgust. "Another nigra gone!" Throwing his arms in the air he stomped off to report the loss to Jim Smith.

"Which one?" Jim Smith asked flustered.

"Bessie."

"Bessie?!" Jim Smith scratched his chin. "Mother and daughter eh? We shoulda been keepin a close eye on that one. I never thought she'd follow in her mother's footsteps." He snorted as he realized he'd said something clever, referring to the loss of Kimbe's foot. "I always thought Bessie was a good girl. Not like her mammy. That Kimbe been a trouble maker long as I've known her." Jim Smith's eyes glazed over in a perverted cast of lust and rage. "This time we better let the Colonel know." Luke shook his head in agreement. He had no intention of making that mistake again. Jim Smith rode out to the west end of the plantation where he found Colonel Richards with a friend, trotting along his orchids, atop his favorite horse.

The leaves were turning brown as they began their autumn conversion. Jim Smith's information hardly altered the Colonel's expression as he considered the news pensively. "Ride out and take over McPacker before he gets off the estate. Inform him that I want him on this trail immediately...And this time Jim," he added firmly, "I want this girl back alive!" Jim Smith spun on his heels toward his assignment. "And Jim," the Colonel called after him. "You're proposal for getting at the root of this problem is intriguing. I like it." Jim Smith nodded affirmatively. Colonel Richards fished a cigar from inside his greatcoat and lit it before turning to his companion. "My God! This is an outrage! We can't operate an efficient enterprise this way. McPacker and the other county trackers have been stretched beyond their limits to track down these fugitives. They truly have their arms full. I curse the misguided white traitors who have aided these Negroes to abscond. Desperate means are needed and I hope Jim Smith's plan provides us with answers and relief."

*****

Jim Smith caught up with John McPacker at the horse stable where a stable slave was tending to his horse. "By the Saints of Eire! The Colonel is fit to be tied I'll wager."

"One would think so," Jim replied, "but he hardly seemed put out. I think he foresees some relief."

"Aye. I'm not sure that I am kithe to the meaning of that Jim. But if I were a betting man, I'd wager the Colonel may have been dignified outright but the man is boiling inside."

"Maybe. But things are due to change," Jim said slyly. "I would have thought you'd be in a rage yourself to have the added burden."

"Aye. Tis a full order indeed."

"If you're in need of help I'm at your service."

"Thank you but no Jim Smith. I've not reached the braking point yet. A man doesn't fly in a rage over that which he loves to do and Smith, my lad, I love what I do." McPacker laughed. "These black heathens of late make the most challenging game I've trailed in a long time and if any man can rise to the challenge, Jim my boy...Tis I."

*****

The family cemetery on Angora was an isolated area south of the main house, opposite the slave quarters. It was purposely constructed there by it's planners, from the lower end of the main house to the main road, in plain sight of the slave quarters. In this way it served both as memorial and deterrent. In the latter, with slave superstition in mind. They surmised the cemetery's position would protect the main house from any nocturnal stalkers too afraid to cross it's eerie ambiance at night.

The Richards family graveyard was a desolate and foreboding place in contrast to it's manicured lawns and uniformed, sculptured headstones. George had stashed his supplies at the base of Stuart Richards' headstone, the Colonel's father. They remained there unnoticed and unfettered from the previous night. It was an ironic cache for his gear he laughed to himself, since white folks believed it such a frightening deterrent for slaves. In that, it was a clever hiding place. He knew his supplies were safe there. George tiptoed quietly around the rice field, going the long way around then cutting south through the tobacco field using the stalks for cover. Avoiding the oil lamps that gave light to the area around the main house he made his way through the final end portion of the field to the cemetery gate. He squatted there and waited until midnight, then carefully dug up the shallow pit where his supplies were buried. George turned around for a last look and gave the main house a facetious salute before sprinting across the graveyard back across the field toward freedom.

Twenty yards into his flight George was tackled from behind by Luke. He hit the ground with a heavy thud. George put up a good fight in spite of being taken off guard. Had Luke been alone there was no doubt the powerfully built black man would have overcome his light weight aggressor with ease...But Luke wasn't alone. His party of five overtook and beat George about the head and body with wooden clubs. George bellowed discursive protests to his punishers as his only means of resistance but to no avail. Without enough arms to protect or shield himself from all the well placed blows, George was quickly subdued. His arms were heavy and numb from the trauma. He could barely hold them up to protect his head. His back and sides ached with pain. He laid there suffering in silent, painful agony. George remained limp while the men dragged him off to the punishment shack. After he was shackled and locked down for the night the six white men raced to the main house to report the thwarted attempt to Colonel Richards, who was waiting with the plans engineer. Jim Smith could finally vaunt the success of having prevented an escape. He smiled broadly. "You have my confidence." Was all the Colonel said in response but it was all Jim Smith needed to hear. His plan was now surely blessed by his employer and he felt the pangs of anticipation to carry on with the rest of it. Jim Smith thanked the Colonel for his praise and made his way down the lower end of the main area to a perfidious figure in the shadows, awaiting his praise and reward for his role in the affair.

"Good lad Caesar." Jim Smith vigorously rubbed the middle aged negro on top of his head. Caesar reveled in his new found glory. He smiled, not wanting the moment to end. "It's all dat nigga talked bout whilst we tended rice Mister Jim." Jim Smith beamed. "I told Colonel Richards I had a handle on these escapes that would pay off." He felt equally proud of himself. He too claimed glory to revel in. Grasping Caesar by the nape of the neck, he captured his attention with an icy stare. "Caesar," he said coldly. "You're gonna be my prize agent. You're gonna get me some word on how them women got away and who helped them and how they plan on getting up north."

"Sho suh, sho." Caesar acquiesced. Jim Smith rocked confidently on his heels. "Caesar. I know just how you gonna do it. There must be an abolitionist workin here bouts somewhere." He poked Caesar in the chest to the rhythm of each word. "You're...gonna...help...us...find...him and put...a...stop to this thing once and for all." He replaced the fingers in his chest with a firm hand on each of his shoulders as he looked his agent in the eyes. "Now! I'd be mighty grateful Caesar...Mighty grateful and generous to ya," he added after a fleeting moment of silence. "All suh," Caesar grinned. "You know Ole Caesar is always yo man fo a job. Iffin anybody gonna hit a stop to dese doins it gon be you. An Ole Caesar a do his part ta see ta dat." Jim Smith smiled coldly. "Thas why I always say, Caesar you the best boy I ever had. You do me proud and I'm always gonna do right by you. Now you carry yourself on. This thing go right, I'm going to fix you up with that pretty little nigra gal up at the main house. Maybe you and her bring us some good christen pickininnys. Huh?" he laughed. A bright sunshine smile brightened Caesar's face as he thought of Jessie the pretty mulatto house servant. Caesar embroiled Jim Smith with a mastered sycophantic laugh to verify his pleasure in his masters offer. "Ha ha Mister Jim, go on." Caesar patronized him in a puerile voice and gesture. "Caesar is on da job suh." After an animated salute he faded back into the shadows and Jim Smith hurried to the main house to discuss the next phase of his plan.

*****

Outside their crude rustic quarters, a group of slave men and women stood in a closed circle. Their heads were extended atop stretched necks singing in perfect harmony towards the heavens. Their voices were strong and resonant. They praised, they sang and they rocked as Miss Clara led them in choral rhythms of vibrant tones.

"O Canaan, sweet Canaan. I'm bound for the land of
Canaan.
I thought I heard them say, there were lions in the way.
I don't expect to stay much longer here.
Run to Jesus, shun the danger.
It's gettin mighty late when de guenea hen squall.
An ya better dance now if ya gwine ter
dance at all.
If you don't watch out you'll sing anudder tune.
Fer de sun'll rise an cetch ya
if ya don't go mighty soon.
An de stars is gettin paler an de ole gray coon."

*****

At the main house, Jim Smith and Colonel Richards stood on the portico porch. "Well Jim. No need in stopping their singing tonight eh?"

"No sir...and they're not even aware that at least one of their kind has earned them some recreation tonight." They laughed heartily together until Colonel Richards broke the jocularity with a serious tone. "Good job," he praised his chief overseer. "You have both my esteem and highest regards Jim. For the first time in weeks I foresee some relief in this affair." Colonel Richards leaned back and blew a plume of cigar smoke towards the sky. "Ahh. It is a trying experience to hold reign over unruly slaves and it is tenfold when they are further tainted by the influence of benighted white men. What sort of white man lends a blasphemous hand to the servile masses? A hand at the peril of his own brothers."

"I'm at a loss Colonel." And truly he was. For if there is an agent of abolition at work here in the county, a white man. He or they had committed the worse crime imaginable. Colonel Richards flicked a long ash from his cigar and smiled to lighten the mood. "That ole coon's eyes must have bulged like tea cups when you seized him, eh Jim?" Jim

234

Smith laughed. "Ahh There's more in store for the lot of em Colonel. The end to this bothersome affair is near. You can rest assure." Colonel Richards bent his ear in the direction of the sweet choral melodies filtering from the slave quarters then looked towards them pensively. "Those wretched people," he reflected. "They have the most beautiful voices to enhance the most infantile lyrics."

"Well. As long as they're happy Colonel. No one is more content then a happily singing nigra slave."

*****

Kimbe and Bessie's reunion was bitter sweet, marked with endless hugs and kisses while Noah joined in. "I neva loss hope," Kimbe cried. "I knew you was comin." Bessie wiped a tear from her sister's face. "Dogs or wild white men couldn't a kept me away." Silence. Then..."Did ya ever see Sara, Mah?"

"Yea I did. She came heah and I tried ta get her ta stay and wait till you got heah or at least til word come from the plantation. But left heah anyhow in a all fired hurry. You know how head strong that gal is. I sure hope she made it. Did cha hear anything?" Bessie lowered her eyes in mourning then looked back at Kimbe. "She didn't make it Mah...They brought her back in a wagon. Her and her chile...Dead." Hurt and sadness swept Kimbe's face. Her joyous mood quickly turned rueful as she thought of Sara's fate. She couldn't help but wonder if there was anything more she could've done or said to have changed the impulsive girls lot. Bessie saw the question in her sister's eyes and placed a consoling hand on her shoulder. "There was nothin you coulda done Mah. Sara's mind was made up. Like you said. You know how headstrong she...was." The implied tense choked the air with a silent sadness..."Don't blame yoself," she said finally. "You done all you could do." Kimbe smiled gratefully. She knew in her heart she was persecuting herself unjustly. Sara's pertinaciousness was legendary. "Yeah Bessie I know. It's jus so sad. If only

235

I'da..." Suddenly the women's attention was diverted by the sound of harmonic voices drifting along the breeze from far off. The sound of the waterfall obscured the words but the choral voices were unmistakable. Kimbe held her staff for Noah to remain then motioned with it for Bessie to follow her through the crevice.

A fading yellow sky announced the end of day as Kimbe and Bessie climbed out of the cave onto the crest of the berm where they could hear more clearly. The harmonic sounds of many voices were easily recognizable to the two women. They bounced from canyon walls to flow across the forested valleys. The coded words from Angora's choir came to them clear and succinct. The women listened intently, scrutinizing each word for it's surreptitious meaning.

'O Canaan, sweet Canaan. I'm bound for the land of Canaan...'

"There gonna be a underground train movin north in a day or two Bessie." She looked into Bessie's eyes with a weak and worried smile as she deciphered the next line. 'a lion's in the way...won't be here much longer...shun the danger, run ta Jesus...' "Somebody a rattin on niggers back theah."

'...when de guenia hen squall. An yo betta dance now if ya gonna dance at all...' Kimbe strained her cupped ear to hear more then frowned. 'If you don't watch out you'll sing anudder tune. 'Fer de sun'll rise an catch you...If you don't go mighty soon. "Somebody out lookin fo us." '...de stars is gettin paler an de ole gray coon.'

"They'll be here searchin round the falls befo noon." She pinched her chin between two fingers as she thought for a moment. ""We got time ta gather supplies befo dey gets heah. Then we'll wait fo dem ta pass. Dey won't find dis cave. Thas fo sho. Then we can go to da meet."

"I bet I know who that nigga is das rattin back theah." Bessie slapped a fist into her open hand. "Miss Clara warned me bout dat nigga."

"Well that Judas won't eva know nothin bout dis place. Ole Miss Clara neva tell him. She let us know what we needs

236

ta know ta stay ahead a dem paddy rollers too." Kimbe leaned forward on her cane. "We gonna be less den a sunrise ahead of em. They ain't on to our hidin place but you best believe they on to our trail." She rocked back and forth with both hands on her cane as she looked up at the sky. It was becoming a deep, rich black satin blanket in a heaven encrusted with thousands of twinkling diamond stars. A constant breeze left the night air cool. She closed her eyes and inhaled deeply becoming one with the atmosphere. "Smell dat Bessie?"

"Smell what Mah?"

"That!" She spread her arms and pointed her staff toward the heavens.

"Freedom girl...Smell it?" She turned to Noah, now peeping out through the crevice opening. "What bout you honey. Can you smell the freedom?"

"Yes Maam," he answered after a long inhale. "Smells good." Kimbe laughed a deep throated cackle of a laugh.

"We ain't theah yet," Bessie warned. "We still out hidin."

"Yea we hidin sure nuff. But we free ta hide at least and whas in ever we do. We free ta do it. Ain't no white folks out heah to oppress us, or rape us o work us fo nothin. Tellin us what to do and what not to do, An soons we get ourselves ta Canaan we be freer still."

They stared at the stars together. Kimbe reared back. "Bessie I'm goin down ta check my traps. It ain't gonna be safe to check em afta tomorrow. So I might as well get whatever we got in em and you get ready fo monin."

"But the paddy rollers Mah."

"Don't chall worry. I can get along mighty good on dis heah stick. I be back afore dawn." She cut Bessie off before any added protest. "You tend ta Noah till I get back and be ready to go onto Canaan when I do. There's a farm of friendly white folk northeast a heah who tend the underground station. We'll be makin our way dere tomorrow after the paddy rollers go by."

"Bessie watched as Kimbe made her way down the path that follows the stream to the upper face of Fall Point. Kimbe navigated the mountain terrain expertly with her thick wooden staff. She turned and bided goodbye. "See ya soon." The sound of her voice against the rumble of the rushing falls could barely be heard as Bessie saw her disappear down the path.

*****

Noah curled up on a mat of burlap strips and leaves to sleep along the interior stream while Bessie laid a few more sticks of wood on the small fire. The fire was a real comfort against the dampness and draft. It could be maintained without fear of discovery inside the caves vast expanse and small entrance. The inner stream flowed along the caves bank and emptied into the back of the falls as water from above reverberated in a constant roar. At nine years of age the constraints of fugitive life offered little recreation or stimulation for the young boy. But the stream. The stream had become Noah's favorite place to play. He enjoyed lying in the shallow end along the bank, kicking his legs and playing with his wooden boat. Kimbe warned him constantly against going out too far in the stream to it's rapid end where the current was so strong it could easily wash him away.

*****

In Noah's young life he'd known little of the bondage he and his mother fled. He'd just become of working age when they escaped. Just before plantation protocol would have introduced him to his laborious station in life. His short stay on the plantation however was not spared of all the precursors to subjugation before Kimbe whisked him away. He'd spent his time there the way all slave children at Angora spent their toddling years. Playing, exploring and remaining virtually innocent to the harsh realities that awaited them as slaves. Until then they played and lived as children. It was when the slave children were encouraged to play with the white children that they first received their indoctrination. Colonel Richards sanctioned the interaction as a carefully planned preconditioning to their caste. When working age was upon them the fraternizing was discouraged.

Noah and his slave brothers and sisters preferred the company of their own to the condescending company of the white children. Even at that young age the stigma of racism and white superiority found it's way into the interactions of their young lives. When slave children played together their games were happy and creative. They invented consonance of amusement for themselves. Games that only the innocence of childhood could create in the bleak hardship reality of a shanty slave community. But with the white kids the black children played an infantile variation of the grown up life around them. They played at master and slave. All the slave children played this game at one time or another with the white adults approval and soon the white children's insistence. Playing at antebellum was just as cruel and degrading as the grown up thing. It emulated the asperity of slave life with an eye for the vicissitudes foretold of the future. It was accurate right down to the whippings. The adult whites who witnessed the play acknowledged it with a statement of amusement. It was "oh so cute."

There was a game, however, that Noah did enjoy playing with the white children. That was pioneers and indians. This game he really loved. Not surprising, so did a lot of the slave boys. Noah, like them was always cast as an indian and played this part with enthusiastic reality. They would ambush the white children and playfully slaughter them. It was the only time they could beat the tar out of the white kids with impunity, much to the chagrin of the white adults. This game, they never saw as "oh so cute". One day Colonel Richards and a visiting friend witnessed the slave children's indian aggression over the young Richards pioneers and was too embarrassed at their defeat to punish the little pickininnys outwardly so he simply forbade the game from ever being played again. Noah sure enjoyed pioneers and indians.

*****

Bessie and Noah fell asleep huddled together beside the fire. In the morning the sun made it's showing when they awoke. Kimbe still hadn't returned. Bessie knelt beside the stream to wash up. She plunged her face into the cold refreshing water. Noah headed up stream with his boat to play before his aunt prepared them something to eat. He sat down at it's edge and placed his boat in the water to sail. The current pushed it passed the tips of his outstretched toes and Noah scrambled towards the center of the stream to retrieve it. Bessie momentarily lost sight of him while she splashed water over her neck, shoulders and arms. The cold water felt so good. But the momentary lapse was too long. The rushing current drew the small wooden boat into it's rapid. Noah failed to notice the changing depth in the water as he rushed out too far to save his beloved toy. Nearing the sudden dip, he lost his footing in the swell. He struggled to regain his footing but the rush and pull of the current was too strong for him to resist. Before he could let out a cry for help he was swept to the mouth of the waterfall by the sudden pull of the rapid course. Bessie was just lifting her face from the water when she caught sight of him. Without hesitation she jumped into the stream. She too misjudged the depth and pull of the water and was thrown off balance by the same current that trapped her charge. Together they struggled against the ever pulling current. Neither of them strong enough to withstand it's pull. Both child and sitter were expelled from the mouth of the cave into Fall Point's rushing cascade and hurled down to the basin below. Bessie let out a gurgled scream as they dropped in rapid motion. She couldn't see Noah as she tumbled through the water but she heard his terrified scream. The fall was quick and sudden. At an instant they were plunged into the falls basin. As soon as she hit the water she was struggling to break through the surface to spot Noah.

Her head turned in every direction. Twice she spun completely around, frantically searching for him. She spotted his bobbing head emerging from the water between her and the bank. Noah drifted buoyantly. She splashed her way to him in fright filled panic, calling his name. Over and over she yelled to him but got no response. She had a difficult time pulling him to the bank and dragging him ashore. His limp body laid across her outstretched legs. She cradled his head and rocked back and forth in distress. "Oh God," she wailed at the top of her lungs. "Oh God no!...Nooo!! Noah! Noah! Please...don't die!.. Please...don't die!"

*****

Virgil's large beefy hands reached for it for the second time. Luke, teasingly, held it out in front of him then snatched it away from his grasp. Laughing, he went on dodging Virgil's efforts as the large man chased him around in a jagged circle. Virgil's moon shaped face flushed red with anger. Finally he grabbed the smaller man roughly by the neck and flung him to the ground. Luke surrendered between chuckles. "Uncle, Virgil, uncle!" He extended his hand submissively to hold the bigger man off. "Well give me the dad blame time piece then, Luke." He took the watch then offered Luke a hand up.

"You got this thing from that nigger you and Clem caught in the clearing below the Point?" Luke inquired as he rose from the ground. "Thas right. Never seen nothin like it. It's the dad blamest piece I ever run cross. Look at that." Virgil pointed excitedly to the black cloth band. He twisted it around several times and stretched it to demonstrate it's flexibility. "Watch this here." Virgil refastened the velcro ends then tore it open. Luke flinched from the tearing sound it made. Neither man had ever seen features such as these on anything let alone this strangely miniaturized time piece. Neither could they explain how it worked or why it worked the way it did.

"Where do you suppose that nigger got this thing. I ain't never seen nothing like it. It don't even have a time piece...How do you wind it?"

"Don't need to. This dam thing ain't stop runnin since I had it and it don't even tick. And this thing here holds it to your arm," he explained, wrapping the watch around his wrist and attaching the velcro snaps. He held his arm out, displaying the watch proudly. "It just sticks together. Just like that."

"It's so small," remarked Luke. "That there's a white man's piece," he stated. "Ain't no nigger spose to own such a thing."

"Hah, probably stole it," Virgil inferred still admiring his new possession.

"John seen it? He know you got it?"

"Heck no and you ain't gonna tell em either." All the time the two men dialogued a large stoop shouldered, muscular black man patiently observed them. Despite his muscular physique, his constant submissive gesturing had manifested into a slouched, stoop shouldered appearance. He was overly dressed in a dusty great coat and vest. A scraggly beard hung from his face with intermittent patches of gray revealing his encroaching years along with his kinky semi bald head. The top of his bowed head glittered in the sun. Willie Willie or Two Willie, as he was called, had been purchased after Willie Chaser was killed. Two Willie replaced Willie Chaser as a tracker, or as Virgil laughingly referred, 'a second dog'. Two Willie patiently held the reins of their horses while Virgil and Luke dallied over the watch before the dawn's expedition was to start. As the sun slowly emerged from the earth's horizontal floor to introduce another day's dawning, the two white men finally ended their talk to mount their steeds. They started off at a slow and measured pace. Two Willie trotted on foot ahead of them with the new tracking dog.

"Dam Virgil. We gonna need more men to track all these dam runaway nigras," Luke complained. "John off trackin one. We a trackin anotha."

242

"John says they's all in one place. He thinks their all headed the same way instead of flitterin around in different directions. All we gotta do is find em. If there be too many of em, we can go back to fetch a posse." Luke nodded his approval of that idea. Virgil respected his big brother John McPacker. John had made the decisions and done the thinking for the pair since they were young boys. Their relationship was just right for the business they were in. John supplied the brain. Virgil supplied the brawn. There mutual hate and disdain for their quarry and their love of the unpleasantness they inflicted made the brothers the best fugitive trackers in the county. Luke was their friend and tracking partner. His pragmatic approach to things sometimes provided a congruous balance between Virgil's impulsiveness and John's obsessiveness whenever the two brothers operated apart.

"You know Luke," observed Virgil. "You're a dam sight better company then that dam Clem, boy."

By mid morning Virgil and Luke had covered several miles, backtracking east from Angora toward Fall Point. Up ahead Two Willie began gesturing.

"You think them two's on to something."

"Betta be on to sumptin," exclaimed Virgil. "This nigger was bought from a tracker out west. He spose to be one of the best nigger trackers they is."

"We'll see."

"Seems to be headin for the base of Fall Point Falls," observed Luke.

"Yea. Not far from where we tracked that otha gal. I tell ya Luke them nigras is holed up in these parts somewhere. Their tracks always lead in this direction. And this ain't north."

"Yea Virgil, but before you go thinkin you solved this thing, remember: niggers naturally head for water."

"In the east?" asked Virgil skeptically. "You'd think they'd follow the streams west and then head north..." Luke tried more analysis. "Remember, they use ta head south to Florida. So the north ain't the link we always thought it was." Two Willie's trot became more intense. Virgil yelled for him to slow down while he and Luke dismounted to follow. "We're close to the Falls now," Virgil observed. "We better tie these horses and track around the Point on foot." Luke laughed and slapped himself on the leg. "Ha ha! I got a feeling we bout to bird dog us a slave trail...We gonna bag us a nigger wench today."

"We'll track down this nigger gal," Virgil assured. "Her trail'll be the warmest so far. We stay on it...She'll lead us to the rest of them darkies.

CHAPTER 10

Year 2000

Morning came quickly for the group of scientists. Professor Jubilee shook Kuendela awake at 7 am then left him to rise on his own. He was surprised he'd slept at all let alone so soundly. He didn't remember falling asleep, only thinking that there is sure to be a lot of hate he'd never seen before on another man's face in antebellum America. That thought transcended to Shai's experience and the hell he must be going through. The very idea of the racist inspired horrors they must be committing him to made him angry. But he would have to keep his rage in check. He thought of Simi's advise on the steps of city hall. His words were prophetic. He'd have to keep his cool to help Shai. After all, if my forefathers were strong enough to hold it together then so should I. I only hope Shai was dealing with it. Be strong young brother was his last thought before hearing Professor Jubilee's voice and feeling his gentle nudge. Kuendela threw his feet over the side of the bed to the floor and shook the sleep from his head. He still couldn't shake the anticipation of the coming mission or the thought of mistakes that could happen. The miscalculations and misreading. But in spite of the unknown variables he'd have to face. He was ready. Professor Jubilee popped his head back through the door. "We'll get underway soon. That is," he added, "if Professor Lewis shows up."

"He stepped out?"

"For a moment. Supposedly," Professor Jubilee said incredulously. "Same ole Professor," Kuendela chided, stretching.

"Son, I hope you got some rest."

"A little Professor. But I'm ready." Professor Jubilee was the one who looked tired. Kuendela could see the man's exhaustion behind the concern on his face for Shai. And now for him.

"We'll meet in the conference room in a half an hour." Thirty minutes later Kuendela walked down the hall to the conference room where, except for Professor Lewis, the others were already seated. Breakfast was on the table. Fruit, vegetables, eggs, grits, fried fish and beverages. The bowls were just about to be passed when Professor Lewis walked in. They ate in relative silence. Each entertaining his or her own thoughts. Intermittently, sparse chit chat began. "Get any sleep?" asked Argee of no one in particular.

"Not much," replied Kevin with a flamboyant wave of his hand.

"None what so ever," answered Doctor Belton.

"Ehhh," was Bilal's sleepy reply.

"I'm too worried about Shai to sleep," added Argee. "I can only imagine what's happening to him."

"It's best just to have faith," comforted Doctor Belton.

Bilal wiped sleep from his eyes. "Shai's a strong brother, Argee. If anybody can hold it together, he can."

"I certainly hope so." Her concern through the night brought anguished lines across her tired face.

"I'm worried he might become despondent," inferred Doctor Belton. "He doesn't know if we can reach him or not. He must feel completely alone and helpless by now."

"He'll hold on," insisted Bilal. "He has to."

Professors Jubilee and Kobolongo had left the room during the verbal exchanges and now returned. Jubilee sat next to Kuendela and placed the square metal ID tag on the table in front of him. Kuendela picked it up and flipped it over. "Bilal found this. It was the only evidence in the immediate area that could help us."

246

"Was it near the bodies?" asked Kuendela. His eyes still on the metal tag.

"No. It was in the transport area. Right beside the Aeon platform as a matter of fact," informed Bilal. "See the names?" Kuendela read them aloud. Also etched in an arc shape across the top below the strap hole was the name Aiken County. "Was there any information on these McPacker's in the county records?" asked Kuendela, still studying the tag.

"Argee found something on them in the Library of Congress archives. The records show the McPacker's were fugitive slave trackers."

"Paddy rollers!"

"Yes and slave breakers," added Professor Lewis.

"They did a lot of work for the most affluent plantation owners in the region. Aiken, Suffolk, Norfolk counties" Professor Jubilee paused for a breath. "In their assets are listed two black slaves they used as trackers to trail run aways." Immediate disdain broke out on Kuendela's face. "Can you imagine," he sneered. 'Trifling coward bastards."

"We can't judge outside of their shoes," reasoned Professor Jubilee. "Remember the lure of Willie Lynch. For many of our ancestors the psychological effect of captivity created many adverse behaviors. So let's let that go."

"Yes sir. So in 1848 they purchased a Willie Chaser and his property number was Number 180." Kuendela turned the tag over again and read the number etched on the tag, out loud. "One eighty."

"That's right but in 1852 another tracker was purchased from a negro broker in the neighboring town of Spittle. His name was Two Willie. Tag number 181. The broker purchased Two Willie from a western fur tracker."

"The term sounds revolting doesn't it? Good research cousin." Argee smiled. "Argee always does a find job," added Professor Jubilee. "There's lots of useful information here but these tag numbers were the most helpful."

"They certainly had a thing for the name Willie. Didn't they?"

"Yes. Such a pity for that poor brother Bilal found in the road," interjected Professor Kobolongo. "He has to be their tracker, Willie Chaser. His death had to have precipitated the purchase of Two Willie in 1852. There were no other consecutive numbers found. So one eight one was the only other tracker they employed."

"So if the brother in the road was Willie Chaser," inferred Professor Lewis. "Shai must be in the 1850's. Fifty two specifically."

"Yes but suppose this tag had been lost for some time?" reasoned Kuendela. "Granted," replied Professor Jubilee. "But from what we have this is the best inference we can make. You see, Shai must've been bringing that tag back for factor X dating."

"Azimuth?" recalled Kuendela.

"Correct, son. It must have fallen in the struggle. When Bilal came back he reported that the area appeared to have been disturbed by some sort of tussle. And since a new slave tracker was purchased. PLUS! the fact that the data shows the McPacker's went out of business the following year." Professor Jubilee bowed with his hands outstretched to applaud his inferences. "1852 must be our transmission date."

"How'd they go out of business?" asked Kuendela.

"Seems one of them was killed by a run away slave." Kuendela nodded his head. "Guess one McPacker couldn't carry the family business alone huh?"

"Apparently not. The two largest slave owners at the time in that area were Colonel Randolph Richards and a Henry Belfield." Professor Jubilee tapped on the mahogany table. "I think your search should start with those two plantations." Kuendela nodded again.

"I found out," added Argee, "in some letters and journals from the Richards family archives, that there had been a rash of run aways during the early days of 1852."

"You think Shai could have something to do with all those escapes?"

"Stands to reason," interjected Kevin. "If Shai's there I'm sure he's trying his damnedest to escape."

"Believe it or not," said Kuendela carefully. "I hope he stays put."

"Why's that?" Argee asked surprised.

"Because if he's on the run it's going to be that much harder for me to find him."

"Makes sense," agreed Kevin shaking his head.

"But you can't blame him if he's trying," put in Bilal.

"Bilal brother I would expect it. But I really hope he stays close by. Remember. Shai's not of the time. Antebellum is a helleva culture shock for a proud brother of our time. My guess is he's being seasoned for one of McPacker's clients. If McPacker has him he's being sold on the slave block."

Professor Jubilee retrieved a map from the papers on the desk. "Here's a map circa 1850. It shows Southland the Belfield place and Angora the Richards plantation. Trent a plantation owned by the Jackson family and some smaller places." Jubilee handed the map to Kuendela then looked at his watch. The hands were closing in on 9 o'clock. "Well son," he looked at Kuendela. "You ready?" Kuendela gathered his gear. "Yes sir. Ora Pro Nobis," he added smiling. Professor Jubilee smiled back leading the way from the conference room to the laboratory. "Ayende."

Bilal and Kevin assisted Kuendela in garnishing and organizing his gear. After a long check off they escorted him to the causeway. Argee handed him some food supplies. He slung the straps of the bag across his back. "Trail mix and tree bark?" Argee smiled then mouthed a muted good luck and kissed him on his cheek. Everyone was in place, ready for Transportation transmission. Kuendela donned his goggles and inserted the OCP key then formed his fingers into an O to signal he was ready. From the view of the operation platform he posed a formidable image. His stance beneath the ARC's wheel exuded a complete picture of confidence. All his nervous anticipation was now gone from him. His mind was totally transfixed on the mission at hand.

The black denim jumpsuit hugged his body snugly, outlining the rippling muscles beneath the cloth. Baring his clenched teeth, he gripped the gelatin gun in a steady hand, holding it at the ready. His jaw muscles moved with each clenched contraction.

"Quantum polarity," yelled Argee.

"Setting is 75″ mark 7," confirmed Professor Kobolongo.

Power up began. The energy from the crystals atop the obelisk towers began to dance in alternating currents. Less than a minute passed as the power mounted. The electric and laser emanations grew in intensity as the din combined with the electroluminescent display. Inside the enclosed platform Argee's voice hung audibly above the sound of the surging power.

"10, 9, 8, 7, 6, 5, 4, 3, 2, 1"

"Pre-transmit Perimeter threshold."

"Perimeter threshold activated. Contact made."

"Scan positive."

"Transportation Transmission!"

Professor Jubilee touched his charm and said a quick silent prayer. "Engage!"

"T,T!"

From Kuendela's purview it could only be described as an explosion. Like evaporating in the center of an atomic blast. He was pulled apart without pain by mammoth imaginary fingers and for a fleeting moment he perceived a familiar sensation of flight, reminding him of a space shuttle launch. He was in space again. Outer space, inner space, flying, soaring. The feeling was euphoric. He was flying beyond himself...Then suddenly without cognizance...It was over...All sensations came to a halt...For the first time he realized his eyes were shut.. tight. He blinked them opened. Then closed them again. Slowly he raised his eyelids letting light in through his goggles. The sights around him were at first strange and unknown. A serene silence enveloped his ears. Then it dawned on him. The laboratory was gone. As were the people and things in it. Silence gave way to unfamiliar sounds that became familiar. Objects came to him that for a moment seemed unknown. A forest!! The realization came to him like an explosion. Startling and relieving. It all became clear. The softly rustling leaves, the buzzing insects, chirping birds and hidden animals. He'd made it. It was incredible.

A strong breeze brought him out of his reverie. It seemed like early morning. He could smell the dew. Feel the dampness. The yellowing color of foliage suggest the end of summer but that was not important. Not now. Kuendela removed his goggles and turned a complete 360. There were groups of trees and clumps of grass with bald patches of brown. He adjusted the weight of his pack on his shoulders and stepped off the Aeon Platform. After holstering the gel gun he removed the OCP key and secured it in a utility pocket designed especially for it in his jump suit. Remembering Professor Lewis' comment he was curious about the density of the platform. He knelt down and tried lifting it's corner off the ground. It wouldn't budge. it was like trying to remove the curb from the sidewalk. "Damn! Nobody's walking away with this thing." He stood up and fished a compass and map from one utility breast pocket. With his finger he traced the direction of Trent, Southland and Angora. Looking out over the forest he could just see the top of Fall Point jutting above the forest canopy. Consulting the map against his compass he did some minor calculations and found his position southwest of the water fall. He stabbed his finger into the sketch of the mountain falls on the map. "I'll be able to watch all the approaches from here," he told himself. "It'll make a good reference and base point too." He exhaled an air of frustration and appealed to the atmosphere. "Where are you Shai? You've got to be in one of these three hell holes brother. But which one?"

The climate was warm. The heavy bags he carried only added to the heat. A mountain water fall would be a perfect place to view the entire area and stash his gear. He folded the map and returned it and the compass to their respective pockets then started east. He noted the clearing Bilal mentioned. Fall Point should be a few miles beyond it. "Hope this map of the time is correct." He made mental notes of the surroundings for referencing and carved crosses into the barks of several trees for land marks near the pad. He walked cautiously through the forest sensing an innocent aura in the environment. A discernible freshness hung in the air, probably due to the absence of any nearby pollution. Except for that, the South Carolina forest of 1852 bore little difference to the forest he knew in the year 2000. But just before he reached the clearing the sweet smell of nature gradually grew putrid. A few more yards and he stumbled on to its cause. There by a blood splattered tree laid the stiff decomposing body of a large black and brown dog. Flies and maggots were busy devouring it's open abdomen. The smell of decomposing flesh hung in his nostrils for several feet, making him wrinkle his nose until he stepped across the path and onto the clearing. There the fresh floral scent of nature again filled his lungs.

From the clearing Kuendela got a fuller view of Fall Point in the distance. Carefully he walked across the open field. Ever mindful of the surrounding tree lines. He had no desire to run into fugitive slave catchers, though he was ready to handle himself if he did. Remembering Willie and Two Willie, he had dubious feelings about meeting another black person as well. Slave or free. Having an ally would be helpful. But they'd have to be the right sort. A freedom fighter or some run away he could trust. But would they trust him? In these days the chance of betrayal and the need for caution was so great. More than he could imagine. Or was it. Wasn't the stakes just as high for him and Shai? He was in a place where his life was less valuable than an ant or a fly. Where he had no rights. Here he was inhuman. Nothing. He shook off those dreadful surmises as he walked and made cursory plans. First order of business. A base of operation. Next, surveillance. If he can't spot Shai in either of the large plantations with the high acuity laser optic binoculars the project supplied him with, he'd have to make contact with someone. Their just would be no way around it. He'd have to connect with some future African American. Some 19th century slave. One of his forefathers and enlist them. One who might have seen a strange arrival to the county, an unusual slave. The grape vine of 1850 could be no different than the grape vine of 2000. Probably faster. It was a chance he might have to take. Surreptitiously of course. If one of those strange reports turns out to be Shai. Whip! Bam! Boom, back home.

The openness of the clearing keyed his awareness. The unfamiliar aura of the environment kept his edge sharp. The distance from the woods where he emerged to the thick cover of trees on the opposite side seemed like a thousand miles. Step by cautious step he moved until he reached the tree line across the clearing. The mountain was no longer in his line of sight. He checked his map and compass then proceeded southeast. He came to a stream that his map indicated led to the falls basin. He followed along it's winding bank to a curve where a clump of trees obstructed the view of the stream and bank beyond. As he made his way around the curve the water fall at Fall Point gradually came back into view. Straight ahead above the fast moving stream about a half mile further. He saw it. A rumbling, roaring water fall. Foamy blue torrents tumbled from it's mountain summit to mix with the gentle rolling watery abyss at it's basin. Kuendela followed the moving stream to the falls base and stood at it's bank to take in it's beauty and vastness. Almost story book in appearance with it's crashing falls and spatial bank. A large white butterfly fluttered across the face of the falls. Even in its minuteness it made the scene picture perfect. Suddenly something was tossed from the mouth of the falls. Two objects that seemed oddly out of place. The entities took Kuendela by surprise. There sudden appearance comically spoiled the post card setting. Maybe they were logs or something, he thought as they tumbled. He watched them hurl downward and turn twice before crashing into the water. Just before impact he could have sworn he'd heard a scream. When the largest of the objects emerged from the water there was no doubt. He was sure of it and just as sure that it was a woman's voice. A black woman! She spun around in the water before splashing toward the smaller object that was now emerging between her and the bank. She was struggling towards the bank with the small object in tow. Kuendela could see that it was a small boy. He dropped his pack and rushed to the bank where the woman was dragging the limp child ashore. Her uncontrollable wailing stopped him in his tracks. The boy was dead. He'd drowned.

"No!" she screamed. "Noah, don't die!" Kuendela felt a pang of sorrow at the sight. She had no idea she was being watched. Probably, she didn't care. The boy's head cradled limply in her arms. She sobbed, she wailed and she rocked. Then she saw Kuendela. For an instant her face was frozen in fear. Bessie had no idea where the large black man had come from. He seemed to appear out of nowhere. Her next reaction was to protect her nephews body and she did, as best she could by holding him even tighter. "It's okay, sister." He tried to speak soothingly to her. He displayed his hands submissively to assure her there was no danger. "It's okay," he said again. Her eyes softened. For some reason she lost her apprehension. Miss Clara's words of warning died inside her skull. She found his completely alien manner non threatening. There was something about him that put her at ease. He seemed trustworthy. Why? She couldn't articulate but this man was no enemy. He was family. "It's okay, sister." His voice was soothing. There was something friendly about him. She surrendered herself. Kuendela approached her slowly but decisively. "Let me help him."

"You can't help him!" she cried "He's dead!" The realization gripped her in panicked tones. "He's DEAD!!" Tears flowed. Kuendela bent down to take the child and Bessie surrendered his body. He laid the child prostrate on the ground and shook him roughly, testing for alertness. "What's his name?"

"Noah."

"Noah!!" he yelled. There was no response. "Hey! Noah. Little brother!!"

"He's dead!" she sobbed.

"Not if I can help it." He laid his cheek against Noah's lips. Felt no sign of breathing. Next he felt the carotid artery for activity then listened to his chest. Still there were no signs of life. Without wasting another second he lifted Noah's chin to open an airway then positioned his head to resuscitate him by administering CPR.

The whole affair was an odd set of behaviors to Bessie. The stranger was so adamant in his rhythm of movement. She watched mesmerized, without interfering. Kuendela kept perfect alternating rhythm. He blew gusts of air into Noah's mouth causing his bony chest to rise and fall with each breath then straddled the boy's soaked body and pressed down on his chest in a constant pumping motion. For a full five minutes he repeated the bizarre procedure without braking stride until finally Noah began coughing and spewing water from his mouth. Bessie fell back with both hands over her mouth to muffle her screams. Never had she witnessed such a thing. There was no doubt in her mind her nephew had died as a result of drowning. She knew what death was. She knew it when she saw it. She remembered listening to his chest and feeling no breath from his mouth. There was nothing. She knew how to test for the all too obvious signs of death and Noah had displayed them all. She'd seen enough of it to recognize it's sad registry. But!! Here was Noah. Back from the dead. Brought back by the skill of this wonderful and mysterious stranger. She'd seen it with her own eyes. It was a miracle. She raised her hands to glory to proclaim providence for this divine blessing. "Merciful Jesus!" she professed. "Lord a mercy!"

Noah sat up with a stir, still spitting water. Kuendela tried to restrain him. "Whoa little brother! Take it easy. Don't get up so fast." Kuendela held him down. Noah responded by wildly flailing his legs and arms. Kuendela knew the youngster was distressed after having life returned so suddenly. He smiled at his efforts and released him. Noah got up and rushed to Bessie. They hugged as though they'd been apart for years. Bessie found her voice.

"My God Mister!!...you...you saved him!"

"Noah," she looked directly in his eyes. "Honey you was dead. This man brought you back from God's judgment. I just can't believe it." She turned back to the stranger. Her expression though joyous was full of inquiry as she tried to articulate her gratitude for the miracle she'd witnessed. She looked at Kuendela. Deeply. Her head cocked like some questioning spaniel. The smile on her face slowly faded as the full weight of it all crashed down on her and her eyes spewed forth with tears. She reached for Kuendela's hand and pressed it close to her cheeks. Kuendela could feel the tears flood the palms of his hands. Noah turned to look up at the tall muscular stranger. It began to dawn on him what all the fuss was about.

"Thank you...Thank you suh." A full fledged smile returned to Bessie's face and she caressed Noah again and planted kisses all over his young face, embarrassing him. "Le me go Bessie."

"You must feel real good," she stated happily, "You too shame face fo me ta kiss you in front a this man." She smiled. Her hands on her hips. A look only a loving black nourisher could give. Kuendela laughed and sat back on a stump. The boys protest was a sure sign of health. However he wished the boy would take it easy. For a minute at least. Then it occurred to him. Jubilee's protocol. But surely the Professor would not have wanted him to sit back and let the young brother die. After all, he rationalized, he didn't take a life, he saved one. Kuendela removed a heavy jacket from his sack and motioned for the boy to sit down. Then he draped the coat over him. Noah was still soaking wet and the heavy jacket felt nice and warm. Next Kuendela removed a tightly rolled compact blanket. After unraveling it he gently draped it over Bessie's shoulders. It was the softest material she'd ever felt in her life. She was dripping wet but warm and snug in the green canvas cloth. She rubbed the material over her face and closed her eyes enraptured by its softness.

"Now this is a happy reunion," Kuendela laughed. She smiled. Kuendela eyed her closely. She was beautiful. Her very dark skin was smooth, almost creamy. Her eyes were a

light brown and her Africoid pug nose was slightly tilted above full pouting lips. There was still a look of bewilderment in her eyes as she looked back at him but he could see a strength of will deep inside them. He was staring at her intently but she didn't mind. Here was a man who
appeared strong yet gentle. His baring was regal, kingly and compassionate. A colored man unafraid. Not that all colored men were afraid. On the contrary. Many were brave and strong just demented in a strange way. Broken even. One would have to be to endure the hardships of slavery and survive the insanity of degradation. Forcibly taken from ones family, your wife ravaged by some drunken devil. Mother's and father's dignity striped before your very eyes. Children violated with impunity on any number of contemptible levels. It was any wonder that they lived on at all. But this strange black man had strength beyond those indignities. He was beyond enduring them. It was strength and self control in the face of overwhelming adversity. It was the survival of the people. It was the day providence would ensure the wrath of two centuries of degradation and wreck havoc upon those who perpetuated the pain. In this man she saw that day had come. Yes. that's what she saw. She could not articulate the order, the concept or the idea. But indeed she felt the existence, the presence. With this strange black man, she was safe. Kuendela finally broke the silence. "How did you two manage to fall from up there?" he pointed to the falls. "What in the hell were you two doin up there?" Bessie ignored the question and continued to stare at him. "You ain't from heah," she decided, wiping her eyes and sniffing.

"That's right," he replied guardedly. "I'm not. What's your name?" He changed the subject. "Didn't I hear him call you Bessie?"

"Yea, thas right." She extended her hand. "Bessie. My name's Kuendela."

"Kin who?"

"Quin della," he replied phonetically.

"Kindella?"

"Close enough," he laughed.

"I'm Noah!" projected his legatee proudly. Bessie put her arms around Noah's shoulder.

"I know little brother." Kuendela shook his shoulder playfully. "Bessie already told me your name."

"How'd you do that?" Bessie asked, still staring at him.

"Do what?"

"How'd you do it? How you bring Noah back like that?

"Just a little trick I learned in school."

"You mean you been ta school," she asked unbelievingly. "A place fo learnin?"

"Yes."

"Hush yo mouth. What school learn you somethin like that? He was dead," she protested.

"No, no he wasn't Bessie. He was just unconscious."

"Un who."

"He was knocked out," Kuendela explained.

"Well I don't know. I jus know what I saw. Can you read an write?"

"Yes I can." Things were getting side tracked. He wanted to get back on course. Kuendela held up his hands to slow down any further inquiries, to begin his own. "Bessie. How'd you get up there in the falls." He pointed up again. Bessie explained only part of their ordeal. Miss Clara's warning choked off the part about the cave. Recounting her story brought back all the fears and insecurities of her bondage. She thought of Kimbe but continued recounting her plantation horrors. She knew he could relate. He was surely a runaway too. Bessie wondered where in the hell he came from. "Wheah you run from Kindella?"

"Run from!" He hoped he didn't sound curt. "I'm not a runaway Bessie. I'm not a slave." That didn't completely surprise her. "Miss Clara says there's colud abolitionist up north. You one ain't cha," she guessed. Miss Clara's warnings teetered on dissipation. She felt secure enough to say the words to him now.

"You wit the underground Kendella?"

"No Bessie I'm not," he replied cautiously. He didn't want to spook the sister. But her curiosity was peaking. She drew her head back. "Wheah you from then?" Kuendela knew the question would come sooner or later. Still he was unprepared for it. He couldn't tell the truth she would never understand. He decided his answer would contain some figurative truth, at least. "I'm an African from up north," he stated proudly. "You a Afikin!" noted Noah surprised. "I neva seen no Afikin."

"Little brother you see an African every time you look in the mirror." Kuendela realized the boy may not have seen a mirror before or knew what it was. Bessie eyed him. "You still ain't say. You a free abolishin man. I jus know you ain't one a dem colud who always runnin to white folk wit colud business." The blanket that draped her was now open and dangled from her shoulders. Long tangled black curls sprouted beneath the scarf she wore tight around her head. She had an untarnished innocence. His eyes scanned her smooth chocolate hued skin then met her light brown eyes. In spite of the ordeals she most assuredly had to endure her skin looked remarkably soft and moisture smooth. Flawless and radiant. She maintained a natural beauty. Kuendela was attracted by her sharp African features. Her beauty seemed innately enhanced, she was very handsome for a woman. Unhampered and tenderly resilient. She had an appearance that black women of his time sometimes failed to remember about themselves.

As she returned his stare her lips parted to speak revealing ivory white teeth lined evenly behind her full lips. He could see the shape of her muscular build beneath her bedraggled, roughhewn dress. It hugged her every curve. Sunlight shimmered from the droplets of water clinging to long silky hairs covering her legs and thighs. Kuendela shook his head to chase away the distracting images. "Somethin wrong?" she asked quizzically. "No Bessie." He smiled once more, she was a beautiful black woman.

"Well which is it?" Her voice was tense. "Yea, Yea. I'm searching for my brother," he explained. He was kidnapped by some white men and sold to a plantation around here. I'm trying to find him and when I do I'm going to help him escape." Bessie exhaled in relief. "I'm sorry bout yo brother. Them paddy rollers snatch a lotta people from up north I hear tell. You know where he might be?" Bessie felt more secure. The man was a compatriot. "I have no idea. I just know he's in this county somewhere. I guess I'm going to have to search all the plantations in the area."

"You could end up a slave yoself if you ain't mindful. You know what you gon do if ya see him?"

"Not yet. My only plan is to find him. Then I'll decide what best to do. He may even be on the plantation you left," he shrugged. The magnitude of his quest began to bare on him. His statement revealed to him just how large a task it actually was. But it was not...impossible. Was it? She saw the expression on his face change. She would be blessed, she thought, to be able to repay his deed with some help. "How long he been took?"

"Within the last week or two."

"Dere was two come inta our plantation bout a month ago. a Afikin boy Mista McPacker bought ta Massa..."

"McPacker!" Kuendela recalled the name. But the two slaves could be anybody. McPacker did service the area so it would not be unusual for him to broker slaves in the county. Still it would be a place to start. He fired several questions in succession. "Did you talk to any of them? What did they look like? Did the African tell you his name?"

"One was Joe, the Afikin and the other Caesar. Josh talked to Joe."

"Joe and Caesar!!" His hopes were dashed. "Josh said Joe had book learnin. Probly like you.," she added as the thought came to her. "Whas yo brother's name."

"It's not Joe," he replied dishearteningly. "Caesar couldn't be yo brother. He ole. Miss Clara say he one a them rat niggahs. But that Joe. He wasn't scared a Massa o nobody. When ole overseer grabbed at em he tole em to take his hands off em." Her tone demonstrated the pride she felt for the spirit the unknown rebel showed. But that quickly turned to anger when she remembered the first time the young black man had been put to the lash.

"When I saw him Miss Clara was tendin the scars on his back."

"He was whipped?" Kuendela's own anger mounted.

"They beat him bad cause he stood up to em."

"Do you know if any slaves have been brought to any of the other plantations?"

"I ain't nevah even been to the otha plantations." The words made his heart sink. She felt a pang of pity for the large man's disappointment

"Lawd!" Her hands flew to her mouth as she remembered something. "I don forgot Mah! I plum forgot, she gonna be worried somethin awful." She turned to gather Noah. Kuendela grabbed her arm. "Wait!!" Bessie motioned toward his gear, dragging one of the two packs by the straps herself. It was heavy. "You come and lay low wit us, man. Paddy rollers a neva find you where we goin. We'll help see if we caint find out somethin about yo.." Her words were cut off abruptly by the sudden sound of someone approaching. Bessie waved for Kuendela and Noah to follow her into a clump of bushes resting between the hillside above the bank. "My God," she whispered. "What now." The trio bent down to take cover in the bushes. They could hear a man humming as he came near their position. Kuendela quietly separated the bushes to peek through. He saw a black man walking into view wearing tattered clothing and a tattered hat. He looked tired and weary to the eyes spying on him while he stooped at the waters edge and cupped his hands to take a drink.

Kuendela thought perhaps they'd found another ally. Another runaway. Bessie read the expectation in Kuendela's eyes and placed a hand of caution on his shoulder. He gave her a reassuring nod and rose slowly from their position. So not to alarm the stranger he approached him cautiously and carefully. "Psst." The stranger heard. The voice expanded his eyes to saucers. His hands still cupped and submerged froze in the water. He slowly turned his head around toward the sound of the voice, pulling his bulging eyes along. Kuendela hoped his black skin and hyperbolic smile would put the man at ease. But the opposite effect was achieved. "Massa Virgil! Massa Virgil here!' The man yelled at the top of his lungs. "Heah she is!" She!?! Kuendela turned to see Bessie standing exposed, targeted by the strangers finger of condemnation. Kuendela's smile melted into scornful indignation for this black man's treacherous outburst. The tattered informer grabbed at Kuendela while bellowing for his master's assistance. Kuendela planted two solid punches on either side of the man's face with lightening speed. He went down in mid protest without uttering another sound. Just then the two white men emerged from the trail the black man had come from. One white man had a large hulking frame the other was of average build. The average sized man held a side arm. The large hulking frame brandished a musket rifle. In a blur Kuendela produced his gel gun from it's holster and tumbled across the ground throwing either man off. He then unfolded into a kneeling position and squeezed off an almost silent projectile. It only made a whooshing sound before immediately rendering the average size man unconscious. As he hit the ground the hulking musketeer raised his weapon to fire but Bessie leaped on his back. He spun her over his shoulder and held her in front of him. Wildly, he swung a heavy fisted hand down on Bessie's head knocking her back into the bushes. Regaining his aim at Kuendela he endeavored to fire...too late. Anger surged through Kuendela. He grabbed the white man's weapon with both hands and rocked it back and forth with the man still clinging to it. Using the white man's leverage against him, Kuendela swung left and right, rocking the rifle out of his grip while flipping the large man over his back. The white man tried to pull himself up while simultaneously reaching for the large hunting knife sheathed at his side. Kuendela grappled him in one smooth expert motion and spun the big man around leaving his head locked in his muscular arm. With a grunt he broke the trackers thick neck effortlessly. As the white man fell dead Kuendela panted exhaustedly in anger. Perhaps it was the sight of the large man molesting Bessie, he couldn't say.

It was like the surge of anger that engulfed him when he witnessed two white teens pulling on the dress of a distressed black girl as a teen in Philadelphia. On that occasion it took a couple police officers to save both white boys from certain destruction. And the time he came to the defense of a smaller and younger black ballplayer being choked by a larger, older white teammate. The vicious whipping Kuendela gave his older teammate got him suspended from the game. The obvious similarities in the characteristics of the victims and an equal disregard for the well-being of the perpetrators was there then as now. It was an impulse he'd worked hard to repress and keep under control. He was wondering. Had it returned? Blacking out was the way Kuendela described the behavior. He'd once said it was a consciousness that emerged unexpectedly. It was an impulse he might have to defeat all over again to do his job. At the very least, in order to abide the protocol laid out by Professor Jubilee. He had done the unconscionable act of taking a life.

Professor Jubilee's words reverberated from frontal to temporal lobe. Don't take a life. The words of protocol echoed. But it was too late. He thought of Noah, who would have died had he not intervened. Had destiny somehow been changed by these two interference's. One life taken against protocol and one life saved. In spite of Professor Jubilee's warnings there was nothing to be done about it now. He acted on impulse and he'd have to worry about the consequences latter. He remembered Simi's warnings again. He would have to be more vigilant. Take control of his anger. He made a mental note to do just that. "If possible," he whispered to himself.

Noah rushed to Bessie from his hiding place in the bushes. She laid sprawled over a clump of bushes like a discarded overcoat. She was just coming to when Noah helped her to her feet. Bessie shook her head to clear it as they staggered to the place where Kuendela stood...in a trance.

*****

263

The scowl on his face was a mixture of amusement and contempt. His hands rested defiantly on his hips while he surveyed the aftermath of his handiwork. Bessie held on to him as though they were old friends. She found security there. She closed her eyes and embellished the feeling. Noah joined them and found the same haven within the tall black man's shadow. "You saved me Bessie." He looked down at Noah. "You too Little Brother. Thanks." Kuendela playfully rubbed his head. His hair was beginning to dry. Noah broke away from Bessie and his hero. "Shoot I ain't do nothin. But man," he praised with childlike exuberance, "you sho whumped them paddy rollers good!" Noah gesticulated offensive movements on imaginary foes while continuing his praise. "You went whump and wam...!" Every movement accompanied the wildest of narration for his newfound paladin.

Kuendela looked over at the sprawled bodies. There was a dead white man and two unconscious but live witnesses. One white, one black. He looked at Bessie and Noah. These are the black people he'll be leaving behind when his quest is done. He wondered about the consequence his actions may cause his new colleagues. They'll be the ones to face the white folks wrath. He felt Bessie's arms constricting around him and believed she could read his discomfort. She loosened her hold and looked into his face. "We best git from here."

"You sho whumped em good boy! You sho did." Noah continued to commend.

"Let's check out our intruders." Kuendela decided leading Bessie to the bodies. "They all dead?"

"Naw. Just him." Kuendela turned to her and noticed her face.

"You're gonna have a nasty bruise on your cheek Bessie." She touched the tender spot on her face. She hadn't noticed until now. It was sore, but nothing she couldn't stand. Kuendela bent over the bodies of the white men and began searching them. On the dead man's wrist he discovered an unusual item. "A wristwatch? A 20th century wristwatch?" He removed it and examined it closely. A wide grin broke out on his face. "It's his," he exclaimed in excitement. "It's Shai's watch!" There was no doubt about it, he was on the right track.Bessie peeped around his shoulder. "What's that?" Kuendela quickly placed the watch in his pocket and stood up. "Do you know this man Bessie?" he asked, ignoring her question. She looked down at the man on the ground. It was her most vivid look at the tracker since the melee began. "Oh my!" She covered her mouth. "Thas Mista Virgil! He one a dem paddy rollers what tracks runaways." She scurried over to Luke's prostrated figure. "He a overseer. And that one," she pointed to the unconscious black man. "He track colud fo white folk. Now thas a rat niggah!" She snarled at his repugnant figure then pointed back toward Luke. "You sho he ain't dead?" she whispered then gently kicked his legs. "I'm positive," Kuendela replied still looking through the dead man's items. There was no identification among the things he found, just items of survival and other inconsequentials. Bessie came back to Kuendela's side. "Um, um, um. Mistah Virgil McPackah." She spit on his expressionless face. "This is McPacker!?!" Kuendela asked. "Is he the man who brought the slaves to your plantation?"

"No. It wasn't him. It was his brother Mistah John."

Kuendela dropped the items in his hand and pulled a small notebook from his utility and leafed through to a page. "John McPacker," he read. Then looked at Bessie. He's the John McPacker who tracks for the county?"

"Yea. For Colonel Richids, Belfield and everybody else in the county. They say he a hard man ta have on yo tail."

The watch, the tracker McPacker. The medal Bilal found. It was all more than coincidental. This man was at least one of the men who prevented Shai's transportation transmission.

"Bessie is there anyone who can tell me about the new slaves McPacker brought to the other plantations."

"The only person who can tell ya that is a white person...Or Miss Clara," she added sheepishly. "Who's Miss Clara?" Silence... "Bessie!!" Kuendela was desperate.

Miss Clara was adamant about her anonymity. But, Bessie thought. He just killed a white man. Miss Clara couldn't deny him help now. "Bessie!?!"

"Miss Clara's the one who helps people get they freedom. She lives on the plantation I left."

"Bessie...You have to help me. You gotta take me there to meet her? I've got to have her help."

"You crazy man! I just left Angora to get free not ta go back."

"Bessie. You snuck out you can sneak back." He realized what he was asking her to do was tremendous! He'd gotten them into enough trouble killing the white man. Now he was asking her to forgo her plans for survival to help him. But he was desperate. As desperate as he could possibly be. He needed a guide! Kuendela locked her eyes with his and held them. "Bessie these are the bastards who snatched my brother. I'm a long way from home. I know absolutely nothing about these plantations. I need your help. If Miss Clara can find out how many slaves have been bought in the last few weeks and where they are, then I need her help.

There was no mistaking the desperate anxiety in his voice. Bessie thought for a minute. She'd have to help him. There was no doubt of that. This very special black man helped her and Noah. Miss Clara would surely approve. He was certainly no threat to the network. If anyone could aide him in finding his brother Miss Clara could. "Yea I'll help ya Kendella. I'll take ya to her. If she caint find yo brother he caint be found."

Hope!! The old adage was true. One good blessing demands another. All the people he could have happened across in this century, he happened on the very person best suited to help him. She was strong...and beautiful. Things looked promising for him...so far. Kismet was uncanny as well as ironic. It was reasonable to worry that Shai might be sold again. They had to act fast.

"God is on our side."

"Sometimes I wonder," Bessie said wearily.

"Kinella...look!" Noah pointed.

"Ahh maybe we can get some info from our brother here." Two Willie was just coming to. He rolled over and moaned. Kuendela straddled him and grabbed his tattered collar, pulling his head up off the ground. A gold colored medal tag attached to a rawhide string around Two Willie's neck fell out his shirt. Kuendela noticed the number stamped across the top. '181' A broad smile stretched across his face. From Two Willie's point of view the contempt in the man's eyes eluded his smile. The hatred and disgust Two Willie read there was almost tangible and it stabbed into him like a dagger.

"You filthy, lowlife bastard," Kuendela snarled. "I should kill you." A light spray of spittle showered Two Willie's cowering face. "Where is your master John, you bastard?" Two Willie tried stammering some reply. Kuendela shook the breath from him then asked again.

"He...he back at da farm."

"How many slaves has he caught in the last few weeks?"

"Mistah nobody tells me a thing. I don't ass bout nothin and dey don't tell me nothin." Kuendela's eyes grew colder. Any sympathy that could have emerged for the man was now hopeless. "You bastard. How in the hell do you sleep at night." Two Willie stared up at Kuendela in horror. This man was insane. Two Willie was sure of it and he was on the ground at the mad man's mercy. Maybe he could humor him. "Wa...wait suh," he stammered weakly. "I ain't do nothin. I jus do ha masta tells me. You know how it is."

"You ain't do nothing," Kuendela aped, growling. "You traitorous rat. No you ain't do nothin but lead your own people to slaughter. I should kill your ass right now!" What Kuendela said rang true for Bessie as well. But strangely enough she had empathy for the pathetic man's life.

"You don't even know who you are. You mother-fucker!" Bessie watched Kuendela spew his disgust. "That worthless rat ain't worth killin Kendella." He turned to look at her, still clutching Two Willie's neck. His head flopped like a chicken. "We gotta get. I got ta see Mah." She didn't want to be here when the white man awoke. Kuendela would probably hold him hostage for information. There was no doubt the large black man was ready, capable and willing to do just that.

"You lucky bastard. I guess I won't be killing you." The words held no relief for Two Willie. He saw something else in the black man's eyes that made him wince. He found out what it was. Kuendela reared back his fist as Two Willie watched and swung down, smashing Two Willie on the jaw, putting him out once again. The scene amused Noah so much, he jumped up and down in delight. Kuendela stood up and tossed the tracker's weapons into the stream. Bessie wasted no time gathering Noah then led Kuendela toward the trail. He hoped his companion was as stealthy as she was beautiful. The woods would be teeming with bounty hunters and vigilantes by nightfall. They ascended the path to Fall Point. Bessie snapped a clump of brush and swept the trail behind them to erase as much of their retreating tracks as possible then resumed the lead as guide to the Point.

Noah continued beaming at his new friend in admiration as they walked.

"You sho is strong!" Noah praised. His arms swung with youthful exuberance. "I ain't neva seen no colud man whump a white like that befo." Kuendela placed an arm around the young boy's shoulder. "He ain't nobody special Noah. Just a man. Remember that. A white man is just that...A man! No more and no better. And so are you. You're just as strong and just as equal. Be them black or white." Kuendela stepped back to observe him. "Even a better man if truth be told. I can tell by looking at you Noah. You gonna be as strong as an ox when you grow up." He shook his shoulders playfully.

"Maybe even as strong as me." Noah's little chest swelled with pride.

"Yeah!! You're a warrior." He stopped walking and pulled the boys chin up so their eyes could meet. "An African warrior," he praised. "I can see it in your eyes."

"A Afican." Noah chided, drawing back. "Yes," Kuendela stated proudly. "An African warrior." He beat triumphantly on his chest. Noah drew back again. This time in confusion. "How you a Afican.?" Noah asked dubiously.

"You talk like a white man."

"I speak as well as any man who knows how to speak Noah. There's nothing magical about being a white man. But being proud of being black, now that's something else. That is something to be proud of. Remember that. No matter what you hear white folks or even some confused Negroes say about who you are. Always be proud. Because you're black. Okay? Promise me you'll remember that." Noah nodded his head absently.

Bessie beckoned for them both to come on. Kuendela kept his arm around Noah's shoulder as they walked. "We Black people were stolen from Africa. Our real home. Stolen and brought here to America. We were enslaved and our names and culture were taken away from us. To keep us enslaved they lied to us and kept us from learning our own history. Knowing our true selves. They fooled us into thinking we were nothing. Less than animals and they were better. But they lied Noah." he repeated simplistically. "They lied. We are God's chosen people. Don't be ashamed of who you are and don't let them fool you. Be proud...Be a warrior. Right?" What Kuendela was saying sounded strange to him. Yet it sounded good. Noah grinned as wide as his mouth would allow. "Right...warrior."

What Kuendela had accomplished or proven, he had no idea. What he was sure of was that this was a perfect opportunity to plant a seed of pride in this young 19th century brother. He saw no reason to be nettled over this violation of protocol. Maybe if he continued planting these idea's...Who knows.

*****

269

A quarter of a mile and a few planted seeds later Bessie, Kuendela and Noah reached the top of Fall Point. Behind them laid a stream divided weald. Before them an empty expanse of sky. Kuendela wondered where they could possibly go from here. All he saw was a cliff that dropped off into an abyss of nothingness. Then to his horror Noah, in youthful exuberance, leaped from the edge of the precipice into that endless abyss. Kuendela's face flushed pale and ashen. Bessie shook her head in amusement at Kuendela's expression then laughed at his angst. She extended her hand and led him to the very edge of the cliff. He shuffled beside her reluctantly and looked over. He was flabbergasted to see Noah standing on a slender berm six feet from the cliff's edge. His arms were folded as he waited impatiently for Bessie and Kuendela to follow. "Come on yall."

"People lookin for freedom have been usin this place for years." Bessie replied to Kuendela's questioning gaze. Carefully they descended the ledge to the granite toehold then entered one by one through the aperture formed in the wall of the ledge. Kuendela had a little difficulty squeezing through the opening. Once inside he paused to look around. A large granite walled cavern laid before him. Outside, the mountains narrow crevice gave no hint to the vastness of the caves interior. He eyed the entirety of it's inner expanse, marveling at the spectacle. A rushing stream sliced through it's earthen floor, emptying into the back of the waterfall giving it an additional air of wonder. The water cascading over the mouth of the cave created a constant roar that, at first, was deafening but slowly Kuendela became inured to it's rumbling. His eyes followed the current's lazy path along the inner stream to where it became a rapid before the sudden drop into the falls. He nodded to himself. Now he knew how Bessie and Noah got caught in the falls.

A supply of faded light poured in through the sides of the waterfall while the unmistakable smell of dampness purveyed the air. Kuendela could see evidence of Bessie and Noah's occupation along the inner stream in the way of sacks bundled together side by side. The remains of a small fire caught and held his eye. Skewered meat hung above it. Hunched over the flame was the figure of a woman tending the meat. A rack of several freshly caught game lay beside her. She eyed the entrants remonstratively as she leaned on a formidable looking wooden staff. Slowly she rocked back and forth on it, eying the trio. Her gaze rested on Kuendela for what seemed like an eternity. It was the same look one gave an unwanted intruder, an invader to a holy sanctuary. Kuendela was parting his lips to greet her when she blurted.

"Wheah on earth yall been Bessie. I been worried ta death bout chall. I almost made myself sick worryin about what happen to ya..." Bessie said nothing. Suddenly struck mute by the woman's tone. "WELL!!" she demanded in a blustering tone. "Speak up!" Kimbe was too angry to even wait for an answer. She turned a scolding gaze on Kuendela and posed her next question. "And who in the devil are you?" she asked curtly. There was hostility in her voice. Her hard brown face shifted from furious to livid.

Kuendela watched the woman. She was an older, harder version of Bessie. Probably, he inferred, Bessie and Noah's mother.

"My name's Kuendela maam."

"Quinn.."

"He saved us Mah," Bessie blurted out. Kimbe turned an incredulous eye toward Bessie. "What on earth chile." It seemed she had dismissed Kuendela's existence all together. Still looking at Bessie she moved in closer to the trio. Kuendela saw her start to limp then maneuver expertly on the wooden staff she used for support. "What you mean Bessie?" she went on angrily, leaning in on her staff. A hard scowl masked her face. She was in no mood for hanky panky. "We got to far to go for a lotta a foolishment. And a lot of work ta do." She pointed to the rack of game beside the fire where the skewered meat slowly smoked over the flames. Then looked back at Kuendela, eyeing him suspiciously. She hadn't forgotten him after all. Nor had she forgotten the choral warning about traitors from Angora. "How you find yo way heah?"

271

"I brought him up Mah," explained Bessie. "Noah an me fell ova the falls and this gentman..." Kimbe flared into a terse rage before Bessie could finish. "Boy!!" she yelled, her staff reproofing Noah. "Didin I tell you bout that stream. Didin I!" Noah cringed under the stick's indictment. Kimbe swung at him. Noah ducked though the swing wasn't close enough to touch him. It was then that Kuendela noticed the petrified nub on the end of Kimbe's right foot. "You coulda drown boy!"

"He did drown," Bessie pleaded. The claim struck Kimbe dumb, freezing her in place. "Bessie what in the name of God..."

"He drowned Mah, honest. But Kendella saved him.."

"Make sense girl!"

"Mah. He stopped breathin. Stopped cold. I was so scared," Bessie choked as she relived the experience, hardly believing the event herself. "Swear to goodness it's true." She slapped her own chest. "I know death when I see it Mah and Noah was gon, sure nuff." Bessie swallowed to compose her shaking voice. "Then he come long. Breathed Gods breath of life right back into em. Mah it's true. You know I wouldn't lie bout such a thing. I tell ya it was somethin else. I ain't neva seen nothin like it!"

"You a colud doctor o sumptin?" Kimbe asked, still doubtful. "No Maam. I'm not a doctor."

"Talks polite enough and educated. Don't he."

"He lookin for his brother Mah." Kuendela stood passively as Bessie played intermediary. After all he understood the woman's suspiciousness. They were on the run and had to be cautious. And Kimbe, he could see. Was no fool. "Where you think he at."

"I think he's captive on one of these plantations."

"Whatcha gon do if ya find him?" Kimbe asked.

"Free him!"

"Well." She almost smiled for the first time. "You gon walk up ta ole Massa and ask fo em. Uh? Demand him? Buy em? Huh?" At least she'd lightened up a bit, he thought. "White man can't sell what he doesn't own. I'll take him.

272

Free him from the devil by any means necessary. The white man won't have my brother." Kimbe allowed herself to come a little more closer to a smile.

"Imma take him ta see if Miss Clara can help him. Maybe tell wheah his brother is. She might..." Bessie spoke quickly but not quick enough. Kimbe raised her staff to cut her off. "Hold it girl," she demanded. "You ain't gon do no such thing. You don't know dis man heah. He only said he come fo his brotha. You go galavantin back ta Riches plantation you gon end up stayin there. And you know what Im sayin."

"I'm just gonna take em ta Miss Clara thas.."

"Chile you don't know this man," she stated again. Her staff now accused Kuendela. "Suh," Kimbe said calmly. "You been kind ta save my boy. But we caint go rushing back into the jaws a dat lion."

Kuendela understood. He had no intentions of getting anyone re-kidnapped by the slavers. Or turned in. But Miss Clara's help was invaluable and Bessie was his sure way in to her. She was a Godsend. The best connection he could have hoped for. Everything he'd found up to now. The watch, the name McPacker pointed to Angora. Providence could not have sent him a better guide to its inside. He had to convince this woman that he was trustworthy, that he was one of them and would protect Bessie. "If Bessie could just introduce me to Miss Clara, Maam. I assure you I' can protect her."

"Protect her!" Kimbe chided. "From the white man. Mistah how you gonna do that?" Kuendela started to say something, she cut him off. "I'm gonna take a chance and tell you sumptin. Hell, you already know wheah our hideout is. Maybe then you'll see why Bessie caint hep ya. We fixin ta leave heah. We gotta meet friends who caint afford to wait on us...Time is somethin we jus caint play wit out heah."

"I can promise you. Bessie will rendezvous with the underground railroad station on time." Kimbe looked at him curiously. She never mentioned 'Underground railroad station'? She looked back to her sister. "Bessie?"

"I tole you Mah. He on the run jus like us. We can trust him and we have ta help him. He come from far off Mah. From Africa. He don't know how ta find Miss Clara. I can hep him."

"So how he gone protect you?" Again the staff commanded attention.

"Besides. Africa!?! Girl you fool? Ain't no colud come here from Africa and runnin round the woods like this. If he is and made it this far then he can find his way theah too!...I'm all fo helpin a body get free. You know that. But this all sounds too funny." Kimbe turned to him. "How you gon keep the paddy rollers offa Bessie." She eyed him victoriously. "AND! How you gon get yo brother out a plantation?"

"All I need is a way in. A way to meet this Miss Clara. She knows everything about everybody. Right? Bessie says Miss Clara may have already seen my brother." Kuendela's tone was strong. He gestured forcefully with his hands.

"To meet Miss Clara, I need Bessie. Miss Clara don't know me from a mules ass. She'll probably distrust me as much as you have. Once I get in with her, Bessie's job is done and I can take it from there" Kimbe's head cocked. Her eyes still burned with suspicion. She slowly drew her words out. "Yea then you bring the law back to Miss Clara and the underground station. Dat ought get yo brother free. Huh? Seem to me a nigger can get in good wit the white folk after given way that kinda prize." Now it was said. Kuendela understood now more than ever. Looking back over the history of insurrection, suspicion and skepticism was a sure standard for continued success. So many attempts for freedom were betrayed by a brother or sister of the race, jockeying for favor from the plantation owners and slave catchers by handing them some brave freedom fighters head on a platter. But then Bessie delivered a clincher. "He caint go to the white man bout nothin Mah. He don already killed Mister Virgil." Kimbe's eyes widened. Almost taking over her face. "The paddy roller?"

"Thas right Mah. He caint go to no white folk."

"Sho nuff. You saw him kill that big ole white man Virgil McPacker?" Now, more admiringly. "Yes um!" blurted Noah for the fist time, "and whumped dat otha white man. Whumped him good too!"

"And beat some ole nigger what tracks colud fo dem peckawoods," Bessie added. "Girl, why in hell didn't cha say that in the first place!" Kuendela looked a lot more favorable to her now. Kimbe's eyes softened for the first time since she'd laid eyes on him. Her smile was wide and genuine. She spoke to him, pitiably. "When I was a young girl our daddy was kilt cause some nigger tole da white man my daddy run." She wheeled around and guided herself to an earthen mound then sat on it. "When Bessie was just a little thing I took her and run away. To Florida. We followed some otha run aways down there. We stayed theah a long while. S'where Noah was bon. His father was a full blood Seminole. One day the US army come." She shook her head. "Chile we fought them soljuhs tooth and nail. Gave em a whoppin too." Kimbe's eyes grew sentimental and misty. "Noah's daddy was kilt in the first battle." Silence.

"We fought on fo what seem like two, three springs comin. In them swamps the army jus couldn't catch us. Many a time the men would spring out from the swamps and dem US soldiers went ta scattin." Her right hand chased her left across the air in front of her as she relived the campaign.

"Just like dat, they scat." She laughed. "Like scared jack rabbits."...Her smile slowly disappeared. "Finely they found a way ta get in dem swamps an wear us down. They always do," she shook her head. "Cause some nigger always tells. Some niggahs led dem peckawoods right into our swamps," she sneered..."Finely, they took us all. All us who was still alive. Some went back to their masters, some went back to the slave block fo sale again. Me, Bessie and my baby manage to stay together. Thank God. Guess we was lucky fo that."

Kuendela listened intently as Kimbe's narrative became choked in her throat. She looked down at her withered stub and scowled. "The white man cut off my foot ta make me stay put." She raised her nub in the air and stared at it before lowering it back to the ground. "From that day on I neva did run agin. Massa figger it was cause he cut off my foot, but it wasn't. Naw. I stayed put to help othas run and bided my time fo my own freedom. I swore, next time I run I was gon stay gon. Then I was sole ta Massa Riches. Thas when I met Miss Clara. Me and her been workin wit the underground fo years. All the while I was plannin. Gettin white folks ta trust me. They jus knew I was finely a good nigger and was gon stay put. Then when me and Miss Clara saw the time was right. Phitt! I was gon and. Well. Here I am." Kimbe looked up at Kuendela and held his eyes. "I almost missed Bessie that first day. I don't plan on that happenin agin. Understand me? Now when you meets Miss Clara you listen to her and you listen good. Ain't nothin bout these parts or bout this game she don't know. And she be glad ta help anybody who want there freedom. But once she tell ya what you need ta know. You bring my Bessie back to me. Now you promise me that."

"You've got my word...Maam."

"Kimbe," she told him.

"You've got my word Kimbe." She relayed her trust by way of another smile and Kuendela reciprocated. "Kanedella...Thas a funny name. African ain't it?" Everyone laughed, even Noah. The tension, thus far, was lifted.

"Bessie, tend ta dat meat." Bessie hugged her sister before complying. Noah followed Bessie to the game hanging over the smoking fire. Kuendela watched his new allies. Kimbe was like a compassionate general. Staunch, tenacious and sympathetic. Bessie was a loyal soldier. Young, strong and dutiful. "Make sure you keep my Bessie safe," she added again. Kuendela nodded in accord.

"Both them paddy rollers dead?" She asked bluntly.

"No. One is dead. The other one is unconscious. Knocked out. So is the black one. The white man will be so groggy when he comes to it'll be hours before he gets himself together enough to raise an alarm."

"How you know?"

"Trust me. What I put on them. Believe me. I know." Kimbe rubbed her chin. "Too bad you ain't finish them off too. It woulda been betta if ya had killed em all and buried em," she added using her staff to pull herself up off the mound. "Well what's done is done...We betta rest up Noah. Me an you'll be gettin on our way tonight. Bessie, you an Kandella wait till witchin hour den slip down and see Miss Clara. Yall ain't goin ta have but two sun downs at most befo dat train ta Canaan. Understand me?"

"I understand Mah."

Kuendela smiled. He had found the kind of people he'd always read about and admired. Formidable allies to have. The people American history tried so hard to discount. The strong, the cunning, the tenacious, the dedicated. Watching Kimbe he imagined Harriet Tubman, Nat Turner, Denmark Vessey all the people he was proud to be a descendant of.

"Ole big bad Mister Virgil uh? Ha ha." Kimbe's snicker broke Kuendela's reverie. Her equanimity in the face of their potential problems impressed him...She wasn't frightened at all. In fact she seemed quite amused.

"Course," Kimbe added while gathering her things. "These woods be full as a pickle barrel come tomorrow. Colud killin a white man gon make em invite people from every county in Carolina. They gon get drunk, talk big and say how its a sin and a shame. Good christen white man gettin killed by some coon. They gon talk bout you and talk bout gettin right on the scent...but they ain't. Times like dis is like a cotillion witout women folk fo dem.

"I've caused a lot of trouble for you all," apologized Kuendela. For the one hundredth time to himself and the first time out loud to his allies. He blushed from the remorse. "Don't be son. Life fo us ain't nothin but trouble anyway. I ain't got no sympathy for that cracker. Onlyist thing is, if they don't get you, they gon get some otha po colud man. But don't you fret that neither. This is life fo us son. It's war. Some innocent folks gonna get hurt," she said glumly. "Always has been and always will be. Till we all gets free. That's how its gon be. Then when we get freedom and equalness we can sit down wit white folks and live in peace." Kuendela thought how ironic those words were. What she couldn't know is that even after getting so called freedom the struggle for black humanity would continue well pass his own time.

"It hurts white folks pride when we fights em. They don't like it. But they tramp on colud folks pride every day." She stamped her staff on the ground.

"So don't you fret none son. Does me good to win a battle." She swung herself around and moved toward the stream. "I'm glad you come long Kanedella. My Bessie and Noah might be daid. O worse back in chains. I been takin care a Bessie so long, she call me Mah instead a Sis. No. Don't you fret none son."

Bessie came over with the meat. Once everyone got a piece Kimbe offered a short prayer. "...Amen. Now," she turned to Kuendela. "Tell us bout where you from." The fresh meat, antiquated from Kuendela's abstracted point of view, was good. Better than any other spartan fare he'd ever remembered tasting. Surviving in the wild was nothing new to him and he could honestly rate this piece of wild game as the best he'd ever eaten. It had a sweetness he couldn't describe.

"Well?"

The meat was good. Juicy too. Wiping his mouth with the back of his hand he looked at Kimbe then to Bessie and Noah, and decided to change the subject.

*****

When Two Willie regained consciousness he was on his back. His legs were spread eagle, one foot resting in the water and his toes poking through the surface. He was groggy. How long had he been out? It seemed like only a second but he was sure it was longer. He managed to sit up, propping himself up on the palms of his hands. The graying sky told him the evening dusk was on it's way. What a powerful nigger that was, Two Willie contended. He himself

278

was no weakling and by no means was it easy to put his sizable black hulk away. But this man who did was well deserving of praise; if one would be honest. he'd done Willie in with one punch. Unbelievable...Two Willie turned around, quickly, as another thought came to him. The man had put Massa Virgil and Luke down...too. Two Willie leapt to his feet and ran to where his master laid and straddled the man's form on all four. "Massa Virgil!!" One look told him his master was dead. Two Willie looked over at the other white man laying several feet from his master's deceased form. Luke's chest heaved up and down slowly. Mucus dribbled from his long hawkish nose and slobber snaked down the corner of his mouth, laying a jagged trail across his scraggily brown stubbled beard.

Massa Virgil's contorted head was turned at a ghastly unnatural angle. His bulging vacant eyes stared into nothing giving him a ghoulish expression which Two Willie purposely avoided. He staggered over to Luke. "Mista Luke, Mista Luke!" He shook the white man's body. There was no response, just a weak nasal snoring. At least he was still alive. Two Willie scurried to the edge of the riverbank and plunged a handkerchief into the water then returned to Luke's side and soaked his face in an effort to shock him into consciousness...No response. In a panic Two Willie repeated the process again and again. Frustrated by now, a thought dawned on him, if Luke dies he could be blamed. He could be the scapegoat. He'd been around these people long enough to know how they vented their frustrations. Finally, after several anxious minutes more, Luke started to grumble incoherently. Two Willie almost leaped for joy at the white man's signs of consciousness. At least this white man could vouch for his innocence he reasoned, rubbing Luke's face in anticipation. Luke groaned and tried to sit up. "Get the hell off me boy!" he admonished to the black man's relief. Two Willie sighed happily. If he wasn't so afraid of swinging from a tree he would have kissed the man.

"Mista Luke...Massa Virgil is daid!" he cried. The look on Luke's face made his blood turn cold. "That dam nigger kilt em?" Luke scrambled to his feet and stood over Virgil's cadaver. "The black bastard," he snarled. "He kilt Virgil. I'm gonna see that black demon bastard hang," he swore at his balled fist. "And I mean swing...boy." He turned to Two Willie. "Go back across the pass and get our horses so we can get outta heah!"

Two Willie fetched the horses. They draped Virgil's limp body over one. Two Willie took the reins and followed on foot while Luke mounted his horse, grabbed the reins of the supply horse and led the way.

*****

By sunset the last remnants of light faded from the caves interior, leaving a ghostly permeation throughout it's expanse. Beside the stream, four figures huddled together against the chill in the approaching darkness.

"Noah," Kimbe called softly. "Come on honey. We gots ta go." Noah awoke against his mothers soft security, sleepily rubbing his eyes.

"It sure would be nice to have some light by the openin," she said to no one in particular. Though she'd done it many times, negotiating the slender berm at night was dangerous. Climbing down onto the berm from atop the ledge was a lot easier. But climbing up required a lot of concentration and attention to navigate the grips and foot holds on the mountain face in the darkness. One slip. One miss balanced step and death would be the tragic result. A torch would make it safer to climb but it's glow would be seen for miles. "No sense goin through the trouble a lightin one," Kimbe reasoned, "We caint use it no way."

"I can help you Kimbe," Kuendela said rummaging through his pack. He removed an eight inch elongated aluminum tube and pulled a translucent cylinder from it. He shook it roughly, causing the chemicals inside to mingle, creating a bright blue light. It's radiant energy glowed from the combining compounds, illuminating the foursome with a shadowy light. Kimbe and Bessie stared at each other. "What on earth is that devilish thing!?!" Kimbe pointed.

"It's called a light source Kimbe," Kuendela explained. "We use it for light when we don't want the light to be seen. It's perfect for what you need."

"Un uh," Kimbe nodded incredulously. "That don't make sense. A light you don't want to be seen. Umpf!"

"Yes," Kuendela laughed. "That's about right. Look," he instructed. "Stand over there." He pointed to a spot yards away from where they stood. Kimbe hobbled there then turned. "Land sakes Bessie. Come look." Bessie and Noah went to where she stood, leaving Kuendela standing alone by the supplies. They looked back at the light source Kuendela held. Neither of them could see a radiance. Just a faint blue amber emission. "Maybe it went out," Bessie reasoned then hurried back to Kuendela's side. "Come here Mah. Come see this." Kimbe and Noah were both amazed. The light, when they got close, was bright now.

"It'll last only a short time but long enough for our purpose. It'll give us some light and no one from far off will see it's glow."

"Land sakes. Africa ain't nothin like what white folk say. They say people in Africa ain't nothin but backward but don't no backward folk got nothin like this!"

Kuendela helped Kimbe with her sparse belongings. The group now made it's way to the small incline leading out through the aperture. Kuendela's pack and Bessie's sack lay ominously behind them in the cave. Kimbe still harbored some trepidation over leaving her sister. She tried to quell her fears with the knowledge that what Bessie was helping him do was worth the risk but her concern was hard to alleviate. Helpful was the thought that FREEDOM, after all, was a duty. Achieving it, as well as helping one obtain it and with this man, she had a feeling. This strange African and she trusted her feelings. There was also, she saw, a sense of admiration and trust growing between him and Bessie as well. She forced a smile and turned to her sister in all sincerity. "Bessie you be careful. Take the forest wit Fall

Point at this side a yo back." She tapped Bessie on her left shoulder. "They say the train a be headin out in a day a so. Know what I mean...Huh?" Bessie nodded. "Thas all the time yall got. I want cha wit me and Noah by daybreak in no less then two days," she demanded, turning to Kuendela. "Not pass daybreak. By!! Daybreak. Ya heah me? Now you got my blessin. Jus bring my Bessie back." She turned to Bessie and gave her directions to the farm. "You let Miss Clara know I'm waitin on you. Now when yall get to the farm there be a statue, you know like the one Miss Clara tole you bout, out in front the house. That be yo sign. You be able to see it from the woods. Now mind what I say, heah. "Yes Mah," Bessie answered obediently. Kimbe lightly brushed Bessie's cheek with the back of her fingers. "No later than tommora now." They stared at each other for a long moment, then Kimbe turned again to Kuendela. "You promise me you'll take care a my sister." It was a command not a request. "You see she get there befo time to leave."

"I'll see to it Kimbe. I promise and thanks for your help. I appreciate it." Without another word she hobbled through the aperture with Kuendela lighting the way with the chemical wand. Noah and Bessie climbed out behind them. Even with her impaired foot Kimbe was as agile as she needed to be. Once outside she could see how well the thing Kuendela carried lit the way without reflecting the noticeable flame a torch would radiate. It was almost like moonlight.

The true moon was full, creating a beautifully lit night. For the average nocturnal traveler that would have been a big help. But for these travelers and those like them a bright moon to silhouette their images could be a dangerous handicap. Together the four stalked cautiously for a quarter of the way along the outer stream then Kimbe turned Kuendela and Bessie back. She and Noah proceeded the rest of the way alone. Bessie and Kuendela watched the two figures move slowly into the night. The light of the moon now no longer provided enough light to see them and they began to fade from sight. "There goes a stomp down sister."

Kimbe's hobbled sway, with Noah attentively at her side, provided an eerie but melancholy scene. "You ready to take me to Miss Clara?"

"Yea I'm ready," Bessie sighed, eying her sister as she disappeared into the woods. She tried to clear the choking emotion from her throat.

"How long will it take them to reach the farm?"

"They be theah twix midnight and sunrise."

"That's about four or five hours," he figured. He turned to look back at Fall Point. The moon was partially obscured by its mountainous silhouetted peak. Thousands of stars framed it with a twinkling crown. Kuendela looked back down the path along the stream winding around and away from the ridge. It was their road to Angora. "Let's go.

*****

John McPacker swung lazily in a hammock behind his cabin. He'd been home for hours enjoying a peaceful swing with no niggers to be broken or chased. Virgil was taking care of that today. For the senior brother this was a rare but deserved day of relaxation. Jane McPacker exited the house adjacent to the cabin, carrying a pot of fresh coffee for her husband when approaching horses made her glance towards the opened gate in the split rail fence. The dogs in the yard began barking as the riders came through. John lifted his head. Riders always elicited the dogs alarm and from that alarm John could tell a riders status. Friend, foe or stranger. The variant in the dogs particular bark was his indicator. The dogs seemed to have a signature bark for every human scent they came in contact with. If it was a regular visitor the dogs gave a happy yelp, in contrast to the gruff, sharp barking growl they reserved for strangers. Virgil's coming had the most unique bark of all. A high pitched, excited yap that construed the dogs happiness to see him. This day's heralding seem to be a mixture of both. Virgil's yap with a little bit of a strangers growl. John wasn't quite sure who to expect. The dogs sound was confusing, maybe anxious or even afraid. That was unusual for these hounds. John McPacker slapped his thigh and rolled off the hammock to see just who it was. He walked around to the front of the cabin and watched the riders somberly trot up the path. From where he stood he could see his wife coming with the coffee. She knew the dogs too and strained to see who had brought about this unusual barking. To her the riders looked like Virgil and Luke to be sure. She smiled. They would, as always, be ready for a hot steaming cup of coffee too. Jane McPacker stopped just outside the door to watch the riders come up the path. They were more visible now. They seemed a bit strange though. Even to John who cocked his head to the side like a suspicious cocker spaniel. Jane McPacker dropped the coffee pot to the ground splashing coffee over the front of her long dress. Her hands flew to her mouth in shock. "Oh my God!!"

John McPacker's jaw dropped. His mouth gaped open. He felt the second twinge of apprehension grip him as he recognized one mounted horse and the other strapped with supplies and Two Willie leading the third with Virgil's body draped across it's saddle. "By the Saints of Eire what's happen!" Two Willie rushed ahead pass Luke with his horse in tow. "It's Massa Virgil," he began. A warning inside shut him up as he took in the looks presented around him. He'd spoken out of place.

"Virgil has been killed John," Luke informed him as he dismounted. His eyes scolding Two Willie.

"Killed? Killed how Luke!?! What happen to my brother?"

"Another a them niggers," scorned Luke. "He was a big un John."

"One nigra!" spat John in disbelief. "Are ye mad, man?" There was no way to fathom a black slave getting the drop on Virgil. Not like this. Not this way. It was just too unlikely. Too bizarre to accept. "Speak rationally. What do you mean another nigger?" He examined Virgil's neck incredulously. "What black slave could have gotten my brother in such a fashion."

"It was a nigger run away John. A big nigger," Luke explained, almost apologetically as he demonstrated topping off an invisible head with his hands to indicate the black man's height. He shook his head disbelievingly. "A hell fired fighter John. I'm still baffled at the way he took us all on. He came out of nowhere."

John pointed at Two Willie. "What about this one. What did he do?"

"He was overcome as well. The dam dog took off like a jack rabbit. That bastard even shot me with some kinda gun I've never seen before. Why it didn't kill me, heaven only knows."

"Aye," John responded dubiously. "Why indeed."

"The damn thing. It had no blasting powder," Luke strained to explain.

"It made a noise. 'Shump' like that." He examined his abdomen. "I could have sworn I was hit I..."

"What sort of madness are ye givin me man!" John lift his dead sibling's head and demonstrated it's pendant-like condition. "His neck is broken. Broken!" John yelled in disbelief. "Broken!!" he said again jabbing a clenched fist toward the heavens.

"What's goin on here father?" John McPacker's two sons emerged from the cabin. Drawn out by the ruckus.

"This black savage will hang. Hang and be dammed!! I swear it!!"

He instructed Two Willie to assist his two sons in attending to their uncle's body. They were equally grief stricken and just as bent on revenge.

"I want you in no part of this affair," John warned them. "Not till we've made some sense of this." They grumbled in protest while struggling with their uncle's body. But they would obey their father and take no part. At least not until their father gave them consent. John McPacker and Luke wasted no time mounting fresh horses and riding off to see the sheriff in Spritton.

*****

285

Kuendela thought about the men he'd left unconscious at Fall Point. They'd be sure to raise one hell of an alarm when they revived. Again he silently reproofed himself for his temper. Killing the tracker was not only a violation of protocol but could well be of serious consequence to Kimbe and Noah. An inevitable mob of avengers would surely rally at the sound of that alarm. Kimbe said it best, 'white folks don't take too kindly ta bein attacked by colored.' And he'd killed one. Meeting Bessie and Kimbe had been a godsend for him. He wouldn't want to repay that good fortune by becoming a curse in their lives. He brooded over the point. Kimbe and the others didn't need the added obstacle of a vengeful posse roaming the countryside nor did it make his mission any easier. Bessie observed the hard lines of concentration on his brow. "What's fretting you?" she asked.

"Nothing," he lied. "Nothing." Fortune or misfortune. No sense in beating a dead horse he reasoned. The dye was cast. He chided the irony of his thoughts. There was no undoing the past while you were in it. Was it?

*****

The South Carolina sky on this 19th century night flourished with bright stars and a full moon. Their mutual luminance afforded adequate visibility for Kuendela and Bessie as they made their way through the hills and forest toward Angora. From the rocky headland where the stream entered the back of Fall Point one could look back across the valley below and see almost the entire county. Kuendela removed a compact pair of high-tech binoculars from his belt. Adjusting the lenses to his face he wheeled himself at a 180 degree arc to survey the county below. A soft high pitched whistle emanated from the binoculars as their optical gears automatically zoomed in and out to focus and digitally compute the distance to it's visual targets and data on the contours of the land. The sight below came to him in vivid reality. Trees, grassland, boulders, woods. In the distance he could see homes and enclosures just barely in range.

Immediately below him there were no signs of movement except for the clear sighting of a nocturnal owl stalking it's prey from it's perch. There were no fires, no man made shelter or horses to be seen between him and their objective. When he removed the field glasses from his face the valley below him returned to a moonlit bathed view of full blackish green tree tops. He took it in for a moment. As yet the peaceful scenery was unmarred by concrete roadways, fabricated homes, satellite dishes or poles with electrical transformers sitting on top. One day though, he thought shaking his head. One day. "What a shame."

"What's that thing?" Bessie pointed to the binoculars in his hand. Kuendela set the optic end of the binoculars to her face and pressed a button on the side. The whirling noise close to her ears startled her. The moving image she saw in the lens astounded her. Automatically the computer driven lenses focused themselves to the tree tops below and followed from memory the recorded data it held from Kuendela's observations. The tree tops seemed to uproot themselves and come directly at her. She could see every gnarled knot in the barks of the trees, every thick elbow like root jutting up from the ground. Patches of grass and naturally sculpted rock came to her in clear sharp focus. Naively she jumped back in terror from a bird that seemed to be attacking her, and dropped the binoculars. The owl leaping from a branch hundreds of yards away appeared to be lunging straight for her. It was all too real. In fact it was.

Kuendela caught the instrument before it hit the ground. "I'm sorry," she gasped. "I, I. The owl. He was..." Her chest heaved and she held a steady hand to her heart as she composed herself. "It only looked that way Bessie," he added with a laugh then explained as best he could the dynamics of telescopic vision. She nodded blankly as though she understood. In any case she was a good sport about it. "Thas really some lookin glass!"

"You've looked through binoculars before?"

"I snuck a look through Massa Riches lookin glass one time. But hisin ain't nothin like yours. Its only got a peephole for one eye." Kuendela laughed. "I've got a lot of things that Massa Richards don't have."

Having observed their route he returned the binoculars to it's case. "Let's go Bessie." She stepped passed him and led the way down the sloping trail.

*****

They trudged cautiously but quickly. Every step was accompanied by the nocturnal sounds of insects and birds. Time, as always, was precious. Kuendela consulted the map Argee acquired from the archives. Aside from the year (2000) stamped in the corner it was an accurate document of the day. The topography depicted of 1852, so far was as it showed. Argee had done her homework. If the accolades hold true, Angora should be only two miles northeast of their present position. Kuendela consulted the illuminated face of his watch. It was 9:05 pm. He figured it would take about two hours to reach the plantation.

Bessie walked a few stealthy paces ahead of him. Kuendela watched her. She was not the slow dimwitted ingenue stereotyped in American literature, shuffling along in fear with mulching eyes. She was a queen. A confident, meticulous warrioress. She moved like a stalking panther through the forest. In the moonlight her muscular legs moved taunt and alert beneath the bedraggled material of her dress. Her cat like sinewy movement wasn't simply walking. She prowled like a tigress. Every step had a purpose. The picture imprinted itself sparking concupiscent impressions of Bessie's naturalness and feminine toughness. He couldn't help wondering how Barbara would handle herself in Bessie's position. The obvious answer amused him. 'No contest'.

"You say somethin? Shh be quiet." Her intonation had the slightest hint of a black southern dialect. She sounded serious. All business. But why not. Taking him back to the very plantation she'd escaped from was taking an awful chance, jeopardizing her freedom as well as her life. There

288

was no way for them to blend into the countryside, no way to maintain a normal appearance or make themselves inconspicuous. This trek was an extremely dangerous situation. Barbara would never put herself to such 'inconvenience' to help another African.. No way...She was very pretty, extremely classy but not very strong. Naw. Compared to Bessie she was lacking.

*****

There was no rest for the weary in antebellum America. And every black body in 1852 America was weary. The odds had long been stacked against Bessie, Miss Clara, Kimbe, Noah, Shai and Kuendela as well in this land of liberty. It was a sad fact of life everyone in this age knew. Now the added factor of Virgil's death was just another turbulent addition to strife. There was, however the people's drive and Bessie, like them, had an ability to weather adversity. In some ways she surprised herself. She was durable. One could say it was the taste for freedom that drove her and her kind. Precious freedom. Freedom that manifested the needed ability to survive. It was a character akin to and passed on to those like Kuendela as well. A sharing strength, mixed with infectious pride and with it Kuendela and Bessie's confidence seemed to proliferate.

She felt safe with him. It was an impression she couldn't explain but felt. Vividly. She stole a glance back in his direction. His sinewy movements behind her showed the same confidence and determination she felt. She saw it. Strength and determination. It dripped from him. She knew nothing would stop Kuendela from freeing his brother. Just as nothing had stopped her from joining her sister...She admired that. She knew Miss Clara would too. She stopped and dabbed at the sweat on her brow with a cloth that was tucked under the rope tied around her waist. "Kendella spossin he got sold away? She whispered. "Whatcha gon do then?"

289

"In that case I'd hope Miss Clara could tell me who bought him. Then I'd go after him." He'd thought of that too. The idea made him shudder. If Shai gets shipped somewhere outside of this county he'd be hard pressed to find him. But he wouldn't give up. The entire nucleus of his aplomb was the belief that Shai was still somewhere in the area.

A bush Bessie released swung back toward Kuendela's face. He ducked. Just in time. Bessie let out a lilting and unpretentious laugh. The first, Kuendela remembered, since they met. It was a pleasing sound.

"Where ya headed afta you find him Kendella."

"We're going back home. To Africa...," he lied. Having to do so didn't sit well with him. "You caint get back to Africa. Can you? How you figger on doin that?" It sounded outlandish and unreasonable even to her. They'd need a ship or something and Negroes didn't have ships. Did they? Kuendela stopped to brush some debris from his chest and face. "Let's worry about one thing at a time Bessie." She nodded her head and continued to lead the way.

*****

It was dark when they reached their destination. Most of the buildings were not fully visible to them yet. But from their vantage point at the edge of the plantation, Bessie and Kuendela could plainly see the rice mill. It sat lifeless and idle in the darkness. It was the first structure Bessie pointed out to him as a reference point. Some yards north of the mill a row of logged and clapboard cabins came into view. "That's where the colud live," she sneered. "Best be careful though. Never know when white folks might be walkin round."

They made their way across the field and took refuge beside an empty wagon. From here they saw the cabins more vividly. They were small wooden shanties. One every 15 feet, in a surprisingly uniformed row. A muddy thoroughfare divided the two rows of cabins pock marked and cratered with footprints and stagnant pools of water. An unattended fire of burning logs blazed bright in the center of the cabin row. It's flickering flames outlined the cabins with dancing reflections of light. All the roofs were slanted with brown tiled clapboards as crackling sparks of light leaped from the pyre to disappear above the cabin tops. In the light Kuendela was surprised to notice a pale white painted veneer to each cabin. Bessie pointed out a cabin at the far end of the row. This one was slightly larger than the others. "Thas Miss Clara's." Kuendela pulled out his binoculars and scanned the area around and beyond the slave cabins. To his delight there were no signs of movement. Black or white. Stealthily they made their way across the remaining distance to the back end of the cabins. All seemed clear. Kuendela crept out between two cabins and swept his eyes up and down both sides of the road. Then on tiptoes he crossed the road and surveyed the rear of the cabins on the other side. They were well inside now. This was the most vulnerable passage in their journey. Crouched down at a quickened pace they hurried down the row of cabins making sure to stay in the shadows, away from the fires glow. Bessie pressed her ear to the door of Miss Clara's cabin then looked nervously from left to right before knocking twice. Kuendela remained crouched behind her. "Miss Clara," she called softly. "Miss Clara."

"Yea. Who there?" An apprehensive voice responded from inside.

"Miss Clara it's Bessie."...Silence...followed by a vituperate reply.

"Bessie?"..."Bessie!?! Come in heah," ordered the raspy voice. Slowly Bessie pushed the door open. It creaked and the raspy voice again beckoned her inside. Kuendela followed closely as Bessie stepped fluidly in through the door. He quickly scanned the cabins interior. A worn and drafty one room abode. A gnarled wooded table dominated the center of the floor flanked by two wooden chairs and a shawl covered rocking chair. Against the wall stood an uncomfortable looking cot with an over stuffed horse hair mattress. A seemingly crude domicile for an old woman. Yet a certain intuitive charm exuded the room. An aura. A result.

Probably due to the old woman's presence. There was no back door. In the corner suspended from the ceiling, opposite the front door hung two wicker baskets. Several sweet potatoes filled one. What appeared to be leaves were stuffed in the other. Turnip greens Kuendela thought. These too lent a singular charm to the drab ambiance. Bessie moved in towards the low fire crackling in the fire place. Coming back here was an uneasy journey for her. Not just for fear of being caught but because returning to Angora was against everything Miss Clara had taught her. After all the danger and planning it took to orchestrate her escape, she was now recklessly walking back into the lion's jaws. Bessie's face was strained in anticipation of the reproof she expected from her old mentor.

"My God!" chided Miss Clara. Bessie's gaze rested on the old woman sitting on a cot smoking a corncob pipe. A thick trail of acrid smoke circled her head and expanded the room. Miss Clara pulled herself from the cot and stood in the center of the floor. The glare from the fire place barely reached the top of her head, eerily casting a dancing headless shadow on the wall. She hobbled over to Bessie and hugged her. She seemed genuinely happy to see her. Then all at once she reared back with an expression of chastisement on her wrinkled face. "What in God's name are ya doin heah!" she snapped. "Ya got my warnin I know! Yall spose ta be on yall way to da underground station." Before Bessie could reply the old woman went on. "Mr. Jim Smith catch you heah he gon whomp the tar offa you...AND ME! You gon moonstruck or sumptin Bessie!" Bessie looked nervously from Miss Clara to Kuendela. Whom the matriarch had yet to acknowledge. But she saw him. Had him in the corner of her eye. She wondered if Bessie had brought trouble to her door. But no. Her faith in the girl inferred not. Bessie took the opening reprieve to speak. "Miss Clara," she stammered, "I jus...uh...remember...I.." She was rarely at a lost for words. "Speak up girl. You betta have a good reason fo risking yo freedom disa way..." Bessie hung her head shamefully for an instant. Finally Miss Clara pointed a gnarled finger at Kuendela. "Who in the name a heaven is this heah,"

"This here is Kendella Miss Clara. I fetched him heah to you, Maam."

"Do tell," the matriarch drawled eying Kuendela up and down. "What you want wit Miss Clara son?" She slowly maneuvered around him, almost completely encircling him as she sized him up.

"I need your help Miss Clara. Help that only you can provide. I need you to help me find my brother. He's on a plantation somewhere in this county but I don't know which one. Bessie tells me you know everybody and everything around these parts."

"She did?"

"Yes Maam she did and I was hoping you'd use some of that knowledge to help me."

"Do tell. Do tell."

"Yes maam." He kept his voice in a subordinate tone. "If there's any chance in hell for me to find him it can only be with your help." Miss Clara backed up to her chair, sat down and took a long slow pull on her pipe. Languidly she began rocking, eying the young couple. "How you know he around these parts?" She eyed him suspiciously.

"He's here Miss Clara. I know he is. He was kidnapped not far from here by the McPacker's."

"Um." She sneered at the mention of the trackers name. "How you plannin on freein him? That is what you aim to do. Ain't it?" she inquired through the smoke. "Gon go to the Masta and ask if he can jus leave, huh? Maybe you gon buy him o sumptin" He ignored her sarcasm and remained conciliate. "No Maam. I'm here to liberate him from the masta. How? I'll know when I find him. Point is I will free him." Miss Clara raised her eyebrows. This attitude was to her liking. "You gon do this by yoself son? You that bad a nigger?"

"Whatever I have to do. I'll do it." He smashed his fist together. "I'm just that bad a nigger. But I can't make a plan or make a move until I know where he is. For that I need you." He didn't want anything in his demeanor to sabotage her trust. He softened his tone. "Miss Clara you know how hard it is for a black man to travel freely. Especially one who has no idea where he is or where to go. I'm a stranger in this land. I know you have to be careful. Trust is not easily won these days. You don't know me. But you know what I stand for." The dull twinkle in her eyes began to give solace. Small, limited, constrained and effective. Miss Clara's network could make the connections. She could organize rendezvous and orchestrate the way north for hundreds of black slaves. It had taken years to put it together and it was Miss Clara's intuitiveness that kept it safe and secure.

Bessie was a girl she helped to nurture since puberty. But even an introduction from this favored daughter wouldn't be enough to gain this matriarchs confidence. Not just like that. Intuition, information and appearance told Miss Clara a lot. She was not beyond grilling someone fiercely before letting them into her confidence. She'd ask a million questions before satisfying her suspicions. Above all, it was her gut that told her true. Her instincts about people were seldom wrong. She knew who was true and who wasn't. So many lives rode on her calls. They always had to be right. A few seconds passed before she said anything else. For Kuendela it seemed an hour. All the while Miss Clara's probing stare remained cold and unflinching.

"Tell me son," she asked slowly. "Why you think this boy ain't take his own freedom. How come he gotta wait fo you. Seems like if he want ta be free as much as you want him ta be. He'd a at least tried by now. Maybe he ain't worth yo trouble. Maybe he don't want ta be free. Won't be the first time a body come here and get loyal to da mastah."

Kuendela bit his lip. He was being analyzed. He sure couldn't tell her the truth. That Shai was from the future and lost and alone without a hope of reaching his own time. This woman could detect a lie or weakness like sonar could pick up sound. He wished now that he'd prepared more of a cover story. "Not him Miss Clara. Not him. He's a long way from home. He's young, lost and alone in a strange land Miss

Clara but he's a true African. He's proud and he knows the white man for what he is. He needs me to show him the way home. I've traveled far to find him and he knows, he knows someone will come for him."

"Jus wheah you and this boy from?"

"Far away from here, Miss Clara...Africa."

"Uh uh," she interrupted again. "No foolishment now." She sat her pipe down and leaned back with her arms folded, staring at him with one eye."

"Wheah yall from?" Kuendela thought for a moment. I hope this old woman doesn't take me for what Bessie called, 'a rat niggah'.

"Miss Clara," he begun uneasily. "We're from Africa..." For the first time an inviting smile crept across her harden wrinkled face. "Shy?" She said, like an electric bulb coming to light. "You sent by Jubilee," she pointed. Kuendela all but leaped into the air. "Jubilee!!...Yes!! Professor Jubilee." She laughed, slapping her knee. "Well I'll be. Soon's I saw dem clothes and heard you talk I knew sump then. I jus had to be sho. Yea. Thas right, Professa Jubilee. Dat poor boy. Thas all he talked bout in his 'lirium' after they beat him. Jubilee come to get me he said...Well I'll be...I never spected somebody come like he said." Kuendela slid to his knees in front of her. "How bad is he hurt. Is he near!? On this row?" "Is he all right?"

"Is he still heah Miss Clara?" Bessie asked evenly. Miss Clara averted her eyes when she told him. "I'm sorry son."

"Sorry? Miss Clara."

"Yes son. He was heah. But now I don't know wheah he is." Kuendela's heart sank to his stomach and sat there like a stone. "I heard Masta Richids tell that paddy roller McPacker he gon make a fine deal wit the boy. Say he smart and gon bring him a good price."

"So he may be sold already."

Sold! The word was like a hot poker. All hope rushed from Kuendela's chest like air from a balloon. "Now I didn't say WAS sold! I said may be." replied Miss Clara seeing Kuendela's dismay. As strong as he was the prospect of Shai being carted off somewhere in antebellum, 19th century America, away from this immediate area laid on his heart of possibilities like a thousand pounds. "What eva happenin to dat boy we gon find out. I just don't know where he at right now. But one thing I do know fo sho he still in dis county somewhere. I'm sure a dat."...Hope returned. "How you know that Miss Clara?" Bessie asked.

"He still here," Miss Clara nodded affirmatively. "Maybe at McPacker's or maybe in town. Maybe even on the otha side o the plantation. But he ain't sold. Cause before he good enough fo sale he got ta be what they calls nigger ripe and he ain't nigger ripe yet." Kuendela's face asked the question. Miss Clara's eyes closed as she thought of the young boy she got to know for only an instant.

"Slave life ain't no good fo nobody. Specially fo a colud boy with free spirit. And that boy got plenty of free spirit. Some boys born inta slavery will take ta slave life with no problem. It ain't no good fo them either but they's ripe to the life they born to. Fo them it ain't as hard as it is fo a boy born free like Shy. I saw it in him. He a proud colud boy. And that peckahwood McPacker saw it too. Tried to beat it out a him. But that boy wadn't soft. No suh. He was strong and he made it hard for McPacker and Masta Richids to brake em. I mean hard." Her lips pursed as she temporarily pushed back the hate she had for the oppressors long enough to tell her story..."When a man like Shy is finely broke he brakes in a lot a tiny pieces. Not all at one time, but little by little."

Kuendela's eyes shut over the images of Shai being violated and destroyed at the hands of the slave drivers. His heart ached for his young friend. Miss Clara shook her lowered head sorrowfully, seeing the hurt in the large mans eyes. She continued her explanation. "When a colud boy broke he ripe for sale, but a boy broke in so many pieces ain't ripe yet. All he good for is ta sit and stare at the pieces a hisself. There's a lot a ways to put them pieces back together an ain't none of em pretty. But when them pieces is back he a miserable wreck of a man and thas jus what the Massa want. A black man who now excepts what he say his station in life is. Cause then he ain't no mo trouble. Ain't high minded no mo. See a colud man born free and high minded like Shy is a threat ta Massa. He gotta be mo than ripe. He gotta be destroyed. Else he serve as the wrong kinda example to the otha men. So it go, high minded then broken an put back togetha is, from the white man's eyes, a good example."

"What makes you think he's been broken. He's a strong black man."

"Son. Many a strong black men be broken. Black o white a man can only take so much. I seen him when they finish wit em. I seen his eyes. That boy is broke right down to his soul. So I know he ain't sold yet. Masta Riches want a lil life back in him before he sell him. He caint sell no weak goods. That's why I know there's time to find where he bein kept. And believe me, when I find out where. I'll get word to ya. I don know yet what can be don bout it. But I think a sumpthin and I will get word to ya." A mixed glimmer of hope and sadness returned to Kuendela's eyes. He couldn't have been any luckier than he was to find Bessie and Miss Clara and Kimbe. God and luck was on his side. Now if God will hold up for Shai they'd soon be on their way home.

Kuendela smashed his fist into his open hand. "I'll wait for your call Miss Clara," he promised. "Then I'm taking Shai home. Just tell me where he is. I'll do the rest." The old wrinkled face smiled again "I know you will son. But tell me. We's all African. Wheah you and Shy from fo sho." That comment surprised Kuendela. Bessie started pacing nervously by the door. They'd been there a lot longer than she'd expected. They were, after all, on dangerous ground. "Yea Kendella, you never did tell us zackly wheah you come from or wheah yall gonna go from heah." There was no way to avoid the question. Should he keep lying, he asked himself.

"Son, I'm an old colud woman who seen a lot a things," Miss Clara added.

"Don't know a lot. Hell white folks think I don't know nothin. But I do know when somebody holdin back...You aint sayin somethin boy. What is it?"

The atmosphere was taking on the tone of an interrogation. He couldn't afford to garnish distrust between himself and this woman. But how could he convince her that he and Shai were really from the future without being judged completely insane. "I ain't sayin you lied, or that you're bad son. I can see pride and spirit in you. Like I saw in nat boy. But this old heart can sense ya got more you want ta say." Kuendela looked into her tired old eyes and imagined the sights they'd seen. The hate, degradation and hardship. The pain and struggle they endured. For those reasons he wanted to tell Miss Clara where he was from. To show her that her efforts and struggles were not in vain. That he and Shai were products of the sacrifices she, Kimbe, Bessie and countless others had made. That SHE was one of many keys to the survival of generations of black people they'd spawn. He wanted to assure her that hers was the sacrifice that made it possible for him and others to be as great as their potential would allow them to be. It wasn't the benevolence of white people but the faith and tireless altruistic efforts of people like her. He and his generation were the living embodiment of the fruits of her labor. She, he knew, would love to hear that. She probably deserves to hear it in spite of protocol. Should he. Could he. Tell her that?

Miss Clara stuck her pipe in her mouth and leaned back in her rocking chair. She kept eyeing Kuendela intensely. It was as though she could see right through him. He felt the depth of her vision, deep inside him, clear down to the bones of his collective conscious. He decided. He had to come clean.

Miss Clara grunted then decided to let Kuendela off the hook. What man, she reasoned, could live in this life and not hold secrets. That thing she felt he was holding. Was it treachery?...No, she told herself. She knew the hearts of men. Especially the heart of a strong man and she could see this man's heart was good and strong. Like the rebellion she saw in Shai. Such young black men did her heart good. She knew these trees by their fruit.

In the interest of evasion Kuendela produced a small box the size of a match book from his utility. Holding it to Miss Clara's mouth he instructed her to speak into it.

"Say what?"

"Anything."

"Lord a mercy. What is this thing fo." Kuendela pressed a tiny button on the face of the box. "Lord a mercy. What is this thing fo." Miss Clara's voice came from the contraption just as clearly as she'd said it herself. She backed up. Bessie retreated beside her.

"The devil you say. That was me...Wasn't it?"

"Yes Miss Clara. It was," he laughed. "It's a log recorder."

"A what? Bessie did you hear that!?!"

"That ain't all Miss Clara," Bessie blurted out. In a recovered voice she recounted Noah's resurrection and Kuendela's battle with the trackers and the light stick that didn't shine, everything she remembered about him that before now didn't seem so incredible then suddenly, a lot more, relevant now.

*****

"Mista Virgil daid huh?' She was delighted by the news. Miss Clara continued staring at him, finding him even more appealing. "That mean that a posse gon be out lookin fo ya. The cave a keep ya safe till we can get ya out a here." She'd taken on the expression of a strategist. Calm and meticulous.

"The station'll be safe but I got ta get word to um ta be mindful...Bessie ya sho bought a handful to my door." She turned to Kuendela. "Son! Don't cha fret none. Ya did what cha had to do. Humph! You know every time a baby is born on a plantation the ole folks like me sit round an ask. Is they da one?...Son you just may be the one." She laugh. "No Maam I'm just one out of many. A black man who's come to free a brother...Something," he added, "you do everyday."

299

They'd been here long enough. It was dangerous. Someone, especially that sneaky looking nigger, could come by and jeopardize Bessie's and Kuendela's freedom. Business Miss Clara didn't take lightly. She stood up after another series of grunts and groans. Kuendela reached out to help her stand but she declined. "Yall better get." Her tone was all business. "Stay in the cave," she instructed. "I'll send somebody out before sundown with a message either way bout Shy. God willin, it be good news." She hustled the couple to the door as she spoke. "Son...Thank you." She patted Kuendela on the shoulder. He embraced her as did Bessie. "I'm the one who's thankful Miss Clara. There's nothing for you to thank me for."

"Son, this business of being colud in America is hard. Helpin folks get free and tryin to hold just a lil bit a dignity round heah is a hard job to do. A body can only take so much. Sometimes ya wants ta give up. But then young folk like yall," she swept her hand by him and Bessie, "reminds ya what it's fo. Lets ya know ya caint give up. Ya just have ta figger out what to do, when you's at the end of yo rope...You know what ya do when you's at the end a your rope son?"

"What's that Miss Clara."

"You tie a knot an hang on." Her lips smiled, her eyes softened. "Thank you son," she said seriously. "Thank you fo tiein a knot at the end a my rope. I know now why I do what I do. And I know everything gon be all right. I look at you and I remember tha ole sayin. You can tell a tree by the fruit it bares." Without another word the door shut and the two were again off into the night.

*****

Contrary to the old adage, the way back seemed longer not shorter. It was still dark and they were tired. The walking and constant vigilance was exhausting. Yet Bessie didn't complain. Kuendela couldn't be more impressed with her. He wanted so bad to tell her some of the things he knew, that he had possibly intimated to Miss Clara. But then there was protocol. They walked and they talked and he decided to take just a step out on a limb.

*****

They pressed on until Angora was far behind them and out of sight. Only their cautious steps through fallen dried leaves could be heard. They were both tired. Bessie, it seemed, far more than Kuendela. "Its so hard bein colud," she sighed moodily. "Why would God let white folks rule among us in such a evil manner." She slowed her pace and stared at the ground. "There was a girl named Sara. She was big wit a baby and she was my friend. When her and four other girls was bout half way along Massa brought them out and made em stand in a circle wit their bellies stickin out ta heah."

"Nobody knew what thet evil man was up to. Nobody but Miss Clara an some a the otha older women. They tried ta make the rest of us scat but me and Jesse snuck back round ta see. Ole Massa made them stand in that circle and he went ta choosin. Finally he picked a girl. Sunkiss, everybody called her, on count she was so dark. As dark as white people are white." Tears began to well in her eyes and her voice was shaking. "He brought Sunkiss to the middle of the circle and one of the overseers came and pulled out a knife then cut her belly open." She was weeping and sobbing now as she recounted the horror of that day. "Sunkiss' baby spilled out right there in front a all them girls who was big wit their babies." Kuendela held her close to him. "It scared them all half ta death and he neva said a word. Just made em watch as he butchered Sunkiss and her baby. Why?" she cried. "Why God let things like that happen. Why do he let the devil rule in his world. Kuendela held her tight without saying a word. He knew what the slave holder had done. He remembered reading the research on how they induced fear in the coming generations of slaves by instilling terror in the hearts of the mothers while they carried their child. He gritted his teeth. Hearing it from an eyewitness was a thousand times more affecting then simply reading about it. His heart went out to the woman he was holding. He wanted to protect her. To assure her of her value.

"It's a curse bein colud," she cried into his chest.

"No Bessie don't say that," Kuendela whispered in protest. "Being black is a blessing. It's being black in this white man's land that's the curse. But even that can be turned around. As long as you remember who you are."

"Who I am." she sobbed. "I ain't nothin." She pounded a fist of frustration into Kuendela's chest. "Nothin. nothin at all."

"You're more than you know Bessie." He pulled her up by her shoulders so that she was looking in his eyes. "You are the mother of the universe Bessie. You're a beautiful, black lost African queen who was stolen from her kingdom. White people know that and that's why they spend so much time trying to wipe the memory of who you are from your mind. Bessie trust me. You have to realize that you are God's chosen one. Not the white folk. It's hard but we will prevail. As long as you remember. You're a queen in search of your kingdom."

"Where in this white world can I find a kingdom."

"You've taken the first step already, when you took your own freedom. And where you build that life of freedom is where your kingdom will be. You teach Noah and the others who come behind you that and you bring them up in a righteous African way. Teach them who they are so that they can build on your kingdom and with each generation we as a people can return to our rightful place in a glorious African way." Bessie simply stared into his eyes. He made her want to be comforted. She felt safe and secure in this strange man's grasp, who spoke such strange words. Strange, but they meant something. She could feel it's meaning much clearer than she could articulate it. But she felt it, she understood it, as though she'd always known it.

"Bessie, take heart. Slavery won't last forever."

"Maybe not," she replied, "but it won't end in my life time."

"Ah Bessie. But it will." She stared up at him incredulously. "In about ten years it will end. It won't be the end of white folks evil but it will be a beginning for you to build that kingdom." In spite of the response he thought he'd get from her, she simply stared at him matter of factly. "The president," he went on, "will finally end slavery...Legally." Kuendela tried hard to look convincing. A chill went through Bessie, conscripting her trust and belief. "How you know its gonna happen?"

"Trust me. I know many things. I want you to believe this if you never believe anything else I say." To her he almost sounded desperate. After all he'd done and shown her so far. Why not trust his premonitions. She smiled at him patronizingly to let him know she was all ears. "In a few years there'll be a terrible war. A terrible war. It's going to start because southern white people want to keep slavery and northern folks want it to end." He knew better. The Civil War was about preserving the Union. It had nothing to do with any altruistic notions of saving the black race from slavery. It only became a cause when it became useful as a means to an end. But for now that explanation would suffice. He hoped she was following. She looked at him attentively. "Before the war is over, slavery will be abolished."

"How long this war gonna last?" she asked.

"Four years," he stated flatly. "But the black people will be able to get away even before the war is over because the north is gonna burn these plantations down."

"Is colored gonna fight in this war?"

"Believe it. In fact, the north won't be able to win without them.

"Before Shai and I leave. I'm going to make sure you and Kimbe are well prepared for what's going to come. But in ten years you're gonna be free."

"Im free right now," Bessie smiled. "But it would be nice ta be legal free. If it happen that way."

"You can't lose anything by believing me and you sure can't lose anything by listening. Just remember what I said. And when I'm gone and ten years from now you'll sit back and laugh knowing that you had this piece of information to remember me by."

"But how," she insisted. He pursed his fingers to his lips to quiet her. "Ten years," he repeated. "Ten years and then...jubilee!.."

"Yea...," she said. "Ten years...God willing. Ten years and you can call me jubilee," she laughed. Lord it would be wonderful she thought. A prayer answered. Like he said, it can't hurt none to go along with his prediction. No harm in that at all. No harm in dreaming. "Oh I'll remember," Bessie acquiesced softly. "And I'll be more than happy to have that laugh because you was right." It was her turn to look serious. "You're a strange man Kendella. I want to believe you. I need to. Sometimes I caint make hide nor hair of what you talkin bout. But it feels right. Yea...You a strange man all right. But you a strong man and like Miss Clara say, you a good man too. I know you brave. And I believe you know things. I may not understand it all. So, if you say we gon be free. Then Mister from somewhere. We gon be free."

"Ten years," she saluted. "Ten years, then jubilee." Kuendela wasn't sure until then if anything he'd said made any sense. But her expression assured him that it at least meant something. They both reciprocated with a smile. Bessie again led the way. "I declare," she offered, navigating the path. "I sure do declare."

*****

Sheriff Abram Pickett pushed himself away from his old wooden desk then heaved a sigh of relief as he found room for his large abdomen. Jim Smith and Clem stood on either side of the desk peering over a map of the forested area around Spittle County. "We'll give them enough time to feel safe and drop their guard," he explained making a sweeping gesture across the map. "Then we'll move in and take them."

Jim Smith had devised what he confidently called a fool-proof plan to corner and snare the whole lot of fugitive slaves. He had little difficulty persuading Sheriff Pickett, Colonel Richards, Mister Belfield or the other plantation owners who supported it with their blessing. To date, Jim Smith's plan was the only strategy, yet untried. Each of the planters were obliged to sign off on the state charter that gave them the authority to draft area men for the operation. Jim Smith and Sheriff Pickett would provide leadership and expected a generous bounty for their part. Every major supporter of the plan had a lot to gain from the success of the operation and more slaves to lose if it failed.

"We have to make it clear to these gun happy rednecks," announced Jim Smith, relaying Colonel Richards explicit orders. "We want as little shooting as possible and only if absolutely necessary. They have to know that this operation is meant to retrieve these niggers. Not to kill em." That was the main concern for the plantation owners. None of the men making up the posse was a slave owner. They were mostly poor farmers and artisans. They were all men who enjoyed hunting and killing, especially black slaves. For them it was sport. A weekend drunken spree of hide and seek where the hiders had more to lose than just being found.

Jim Smith narrowed his eyes. He knew most of them. He knew none of them would hesitate to use a slave for target practice. In a tight spot that enthusiasm would be an asset but in this kind of action that enthusiasm would only serve to hurt his pocket. He couldn't emphasis enough the importance of retrieving these properties alive or the size of the bounty he and Sheriff Pickett expected would be lacking and if he wasn't paid enough, they sure in hell wouldn't be paid at all. A dead slave could only be an absolute necessity. Not fun. He smiled as he admitted to himself that he may have to fight the urge for a little fun himself but he would restrain himself. He had to set an example. This was business. He poked Clem in the chest to drive home his point. "Tell them gun happy hicks a yours to mind. You hear me Clem? Cause if I have to I'll kill one of their asses myself."

"I understand!!" repeated Clem. annoyed.

"A live nigra is worth more money then one a them dumb ass rednecks any day."

"How are we gonna recognize your agent, Jim?" wondered Sheriff Pickett, happy to change the subject. "He'll be wearin a red bandana on his head," replied Jim Smith. "But don't worry Abram, he'll make dam sure he's out of the way when things get goin. But if one of the boys happenin upon him, those fat lips of his will blubber out his station before he gets drug off." They all laughed. "Now. Let's get on to something important." At that moment the door opened. "John?" Sheriff Pickett rose from his desk. Jim Smith and Clem turned to greet him. Luke came in behind McPacker. Before anyone could say another word John McPacker slammed his fist down on the desk.

"My brother's dead Abram." He was almost in tears

"What!" Sheriff Pickett heard McPacker's words but the meaning failed to register. "Dead Abram!!...Dead!!" McPacker's face was twisted into a hateful mask. Not a trace of curiosity could surface above the hate and rage he felt for the black man who did the deed.

"My God!" gasped Sheriff Pickett.

"I can't believe it," expressed Jim Smith. McPacker looked at each man in turn. He was not here to herald bad news he was here for recourse. Revenge.

"My brother is dead. Killed by a heathen fugitive. And by the Saints I want every available man who can handle a gun to join in posse and track the bloody blackamoor down!" There was no doubt each man was in. A negro killing a white man was the highest crime imaginable. But there was a better way. "John. You can count on that," assured the sheriff, snapping his fingers.

"But we're on to something here that..."

"By the Saints! Dam what yer on to. I want to go after this blackguard without delay!" Sheriff Pickett arrested John by the shoulders and shook him forcefully. "Listen to me

John. We all share your grief. You know that. Virgil was a good Christian man. We all were fond of him. I wouldn't dismiss the opportunity to punish the nigra that did him in. You know that. Just hear me out for a minute." John McPacker tried to pull away but Sheriff Pickett's hold was firm. "DAM IT!" he shouted. There was quiet in the room. Convinced he now had the man's attention, Sheriff Pickett lowered his tone. "Jim Smith has come up with a plan and in it I have no doubt it's going to rope in the dirty bastard who killed Virgil and the treasonous abolitionists and ungrateful runaways as well. All in one stroke. It's going to benefit us all."

Sheriff Pickett offered John McPacker his chair and walked around the front of the desk. With the palms of his hands he commanded everyone's attention. Even McPacker was willing to give the Sheriff an ear if it would bring him some justice. He laid out the main points to Jim Smith's plan.

"Saints preserve me!" McPacker's hands went up to demonstrate his confusion. "What does this have to do with trackin down this darkie." Sheriff Pickett spun the map on the table for McPacker's purview. "Don't you see. We're mounting an expedition to corner the fugitives at there gathering point. Don't you think our murderer will be there as well. It's his best hope to get north. This nigra has killed a white man and he knows he's got to get out of the county. And fast. Now, I hate to admit it." He scratched his head incredulously. "These slaves have been giving us the slip through some kind of organized network. Escape route and all. Every nigger run away in the county seems to know of it and I'm sure this nigra knows how to use it. None of the trackers in our county have yet to figure it out." Every ear was tuned in to him as he made his point. "They've been real careful up to now. They've safeguarded their operation." He shook a finger of warning. "But between this nigras desperation and Jim Smith's plan we have em by god. When this killer goes to this network for help it's gonna be a

307

hellava mistake. Cause he's scared and they won't be prepared for him."

"I don't know if this boy's scared," offered Luke. "He was awful fierce." All the men looked at Luke with disgust. "I don't care how fierce a nigger you think he is,' snapped Sheriff Pickett. "He's killed a white man and he knows his black balls are in the fire."

"Even if these niggers are careful. We'll bag em," added Jim Smith eager to give some input. He was proud of his plan and he wanted his credit. "And with this scared nigger mixing things up..." He sliced his index finger across his throat to illustrate his point. "We got em cold because let's face it," he nodded to McPacker, "the reason you and Virgil ain't been able to track down these runaways is cause they got a runaway plan in place. They got communication, warning and intelligence." He counted each point on a finger.

"My plan guides us to em. With the added bonus of this nigras desperation we got em flushed out." McPacker frowned defensively at what he felt was a denouncement of his abilities. "Be damned Jim. You give a few lucky runaways too much credit..."

"John," he interrupted. "Can you deny every runaway you've tracked from Angora, Belfield or the other plantations north of Falls Point have always led southwest toward the falls before you lost them." McPacker shook his head stiffly. Jim Smith began to feel bigger still. "All the plantations south of the falls have em tracked northwest before vanishing." He pointed to Falls Point on the map. McPacker looked at the map but missed the point. "Don't you see!?! Falls Point is the key!" Jim Smith almost yelled. "Every runaway has been tracked there." He slammed his finger into the map on the table. "And now the murder takes place there." He bared his palms in conclusion.

"But there's nothing there Jim," protested Luke, "just water falls."

"Nothing there that we can see. Now that we have the right questions we find us a few nigras and make them talk.

We'll find out just who or what causes these nigras to vanish into thin air on Fall Point."

"Reasoning it may be," agreed McPacker pointing to a place on the map,

"But there's no place here for them to gather."

"That may be, as far as we know. But this is where they vanish. Maybe they're meeting somebody there that helps em. Guides em somewhere from there, I don't know. But Fall Point is the key and my plan will unlock the mystery. And we'll bag that killer to boot."

"He must be shakin in his boots by now," added Clem for the first time. Sheriff Pickett agreed. "That's right. He's got no time to plan. Just run. This network wherever it is, ain't prepared for these kinds of emergencies I'll bet."

"I want to know what happens to em after Fall Point. Where do they hide after they meet there." Jim Smith shook his finger. "Wherever it is, that's where we'll bag the lot of em." Sheriff Pickett extended a hand. "What do you say John." McPacker turned to his new partner by proxy. "What do you think Luke?"

"It sounds reasonable to me John." John McPacker grabbed the sheriff's hand. "I agree, by Eire. Gentlemen, count us into your plan."

CHAPTER 11

Year 1852

George laid in the punishment shack shaking to his very soul. He knew a severe whipping was due. The thought of that cat-o-nine across his back chilled him to the bone. How was he discovered? It baffled him. He could only surmise, one of the overseers saw him or discovered the supplies he'd stashed. Yea...that must be it. Only two others knew of his plan. Miss Clara, the architect and Caesar, a new found friend. In the short time they'd become friends he felt sure enough of the man. After all a fellow bondsman was the last one he'd suspect of treachery. So it had to be, one of the whites found his gear. One, two maybe three days had past since then. He couldn't be sure how long he'd been shackled. The days of deprivation served to increase his confusion. The days and nights all seemed to roll into one, and now with the bits of information he'd been able to pick out of the air about the runaway who killed a white man, his fears had grown even more. He was sure the whites would vent their frustrations on him if they couldn't catch the true murderer. The more he harped on the possibility the more terrified he became. He just couldn't shake the feeling he believed to be the obvious.

When the door creaked open his heart leaped into his mouth. The way it stopped at each creak made his eyes stretch beyond their orbital limits. Someone was worried about the noise. Each movement gave way to numerous possibilities of distress. He crouched his body against the wall. Finally the door opened wide enough for a figure to slip through. The darkness made it impossible for George to see who his intruder was. Perhaps, he thought, when the aberration crossed the stream of moonlight coming through the door he'd be able to recognize them. The figure closed the door quickly and leaned against it. Deliberately the shadowy figure peeled itself away from the door and knelt beside George. George lurched forward in response. His trembling limbs caused his shackles to clang. "Shhh. Hush all that noise." His face came close to George. "Caesar!" he whispered too loudly. "Caesar!...Whatcha doin heah! How in da hell did you get in heah?"

"Shut up fool," Caesar warned. "I'm heah ta hep you get away. Some nigger done kilt Mister Virgil and dem white folks is lookin for a black neck ta stretch."

"Yea I know," George whispered abhorrently. "It's gonna be yourn iffen dey ketch you in heah. Now get yoself up an out a heah man! You caint hep me. Now git...Befo one a dem crackers come. I don't want ta be the cause o you gettin whipped." Caesar sat back defiantly. "It ain't gonna be my neck," he retorted. "Cause my neck ain't gonna be heah. George you know when a colud kills a white ain't nobodies neck safe fo sho. So I'm gonna git but I caint make it wit out you George." George's eyebrows knitted together in confusion.

"What in the hell you talkin bout boy?"

"Look. I knows deys a underground goin north frum somewheah but Imma a new nigga. Nobody tell me nuthin an I don't know wheah the place is to meet. You gotta show me the way George." A premonitory warning tugged at George's intuition. Telling the man of his own plans was one thing but talking about the underground railroad without the express approval of it's conductors was another. Caution was the hallmark that kept the underground so successful for so long. Yet helping all those who needed its help was it's creed. There wasn't reason enough to rebuff his friends request but there remained a lingering vestige of apprehension. He thought of Miss Clara who was the main conductor and an ardent supporter of discretion. "I don't know Caesar.

If you don't already know where it is I ain't sho I oughta be..."

"Dam it nigga! I needs yo hep George." The man sounded desperate. But still. "What can I do. I'm chained up heah. Ain't much I can do but Miss Clara, she could help..."

"George!" Caesar almost shouted. He grabbed George by both shoulders and spoke directly into his face. "I killed Mister Virgil." George reared back in shock. "He caught me tryin ta run." It was a dilemma. George had to weigh the fear in his friends eyes against the integrity of the railroads survival.

"George ya gotta hep me!" Without George's reply Caesar bent over and began working on the locks holding George's shackles.

George pondered the situation as he drew more concerned for his friend than for himself. Surely if he killed the white man he was in dire need of the information he held. "We gotta see Miss Clara," George warned. "No time fo dat. Niggah! Overseer Jim up theah now, askin questions." Caesar said too quickly. "I gotta get frum heah now George! Caint you see dat." Caesar continued working the lock then motioned for George to complete the job. He couldn't see how Caesar unlocked his shackles but he reached between his feet to do his part. George's trembling hands made it difficult to remove the shackles, but finally he did. He stared at Caesar for a moment in the darkness. "Now what," he finally managed to say. Caesar's mouth unfolded into a wide grin. "Now we get the hell way frum heah. Dat dam peckahwood got what he deserve, George. Now dem chains is off you. Ain't nothin holdin ya heah. Now if ya wit me, we as good as gone." He nodded his head in agreement. There was nothing left to ponder as far as George was concerned now. He would guide his friend to the safety of the underground.

With as little noise as possible the remainder of the shackles were discarded. The two men slipped from the shack and dashed across the empty grounds. "Every bodies out in da hills lookin fo a runway killer," Caesar whispered facetiously as they ran. "Pretty smart huh? Doublin back lak dis."

"I reckon so," George answered mechanically. He soothed his anxiety by reminding himself that Caesar was a black man in trouble. The worst trouble a black man could be in. He believed Miss Clara would approve at a time like this.

Warily, they ran across the yard to the rear of the main house, taking care not to fall into sight of those inside. They crossed the grounds into the field and faded among the stalks of stacked rice shoots. Once they'd gotten outside the plantations perimeter George took the lead. He led Caesar north into the night. They wasted no time treading stealthy through the moonlit darkness of the South Carolina forest, taking advantage of the few hours of night left to them. Neither man spoke as they trekked. All their attention remained focused on the journey, their senses heighten and vigilant. Survival and fear of detection keeping them alert.

*****

By early morn the sun had knifed through the am twilight with blades of piercing sunlight. The coming dawn found the two fugitives deposited at the edge of the forest before a sparsely grassed clearing. Some yards ahead stood a rather large farm house. A white brick pathway led to it's front door. Beside it a small brown colored statue of a jockey stood in perpetual vigilance. Behind the farm house, the roof of a tall barn rose above the housetop framed by trees that lay beyond it. George nodded to Caesar. Their journey had ended. A few yards left of their position a white man stood like a sentinel, watching the expanse of forest ahead. Neither George nor Caesar knew if the man had seen them. Caesar removed the bright red bandana he wore around his neck and wiped the sweat from his brow then tied it to his head. "Looks okay out deah, don't cha think?" Caesar tried to judge if George was familiar with the area. "Is dis wheah dey gonna fetch us from? Dat man out dere," Caesar pointed.

"You reckon he don seen us. Looks ta me if he was da abolishment he'da come out ta greet us..."

"Shhh!" George hushed him.

"Will you shush. We wheah we spose ta be. I jus wanna make sho all is cleah. Is dat all right wit you." His tone clearly showed his irritation as he surveyed the area. From a few yards away they were being observed themselves.

Kimbe and Noah huddled down among the bushes watching George and Caesar. Noah had seen them long before the two men reached the clearing and brought his mother's attention to them. Most peculiar, Noah noted, was the man with the red bandana. He seemed to be dropping something out of a bag tied across his shoulders every few yards as they walked. Noah thought the animated motions the man made tossing objects behind his back was a funny spectacle. Kimbe scolded him for snickering. Silence was an important commodity to maintain and too important to compromise with coltish laughter though she had to admit it was amusing. The man in front of him seemed totally unaware of his companions actions.

George was concerned about the immediate business of the house, the sentinel and the carved wooden lawn jockey in front. Even from a distance it's features were discernibly sharp and subtle. Unlike most lawn jockeys this one bore a marked resemblance to a human being instead of the hyperbolic, negative image of a black stereotype. It had no comically exaggerated negroid features. But even more important to George was the bow tie it sported. It was the only feature not painted. It's clear white surface was a sign that all was clear. Together with the former characteristics this was a safe house for runaway fugitives. An underground railroad way station.

Kimbe also recognized the significance of the 4 ft. indicator and instructed Noah to remain hidden while she ventured out into the open.

"Kimbe!" whispered George to his partner.

"That the girl who been gone all this time. Wheah she been hidin George?"

"Neva mind," George scolded. He pointed to the clearing. The white sentinel had begun moving toward Kimbe. He noticed the cane the woman struggled with and quickened his pace to reach her. They met directly in front of the bushes where George and Caesar were concealed. "Let me help you Maam," offered the white gentleman, supporting her under her arm.

"You looking to find your way to Canaan Maam?" he asked in code. It was the second time he called her Maam. An unusual greeting from a white man. Kimbe couldn't help but display a nervous and cautious smile. "Yes sir," she replied finally. "I'm lookin ta go on ta Canaan."

"Well now," he smiled. "You're on the right course. Come this way." He beckoned to her with a light wave of his hand. Kimbe hesitated. "I'm not alone," she said, motioning for Noah to come out.

"Come this way lad. The two of you must be fatigued? Let's get some food and rest into you." He was genuinely cordial to the black woman and child. Suddenly two black men emerged from the woods. Sheepishly George and Caesar greeted the white man. "We headin fo Canaan suh," George called out.

"I was wondering when you all was gonna come out. Come on, all of you," he motioned happily. "You're all welcome." He led the small party to the house. His stout red face was covered with a full black beard streaked with gray. He stroked it constantly. His white shirt sleeves were rolled up to his elbows. Black suspenders lined his shirt front and crisscrossed in the back. The archetype of a rural, rustic man with hard work ethic. Joshua Whitten led the foursome to the front door. A woman, equally stout with a ruddy complexion, met them with a joyous welcoming smile. "Come! Come!" she called cheerfully holding the door open. "Tomorrow an agent will be here," she informed them happily. "There are others waiting as well and you'll all be led north to Canaan." She clapped her hands and looked upward to the heavens. "Tis a glorious mission of God's work that we entreat."

Joshua and his wife Prudence, lived in a modest home on a modest farm with their son Jonah. Devout Quakers from Pennsylvania they lived incognito on their small farm with sparse interaction between them and their southern neighbors who had no idea of the Whitten's religious beliefs or politics. They came three years ago, sent south by northern abolitionist to help set up a freedom weigh station for the underground network to shuttle escaping slaves north. In a clandestine midnight religious revival held by some slaves wishing to worship away from prying eyes they met Miss Clara. Immediately there was a connection that culminated into an underground organization with a complex system of codes, membership, signs and trails. Two years later they had created the most successful underground railroad network to date. Joshua, Prudence and Jonah were crusaders as much as they were abolitionist. The world they envisioned was one devoid of inequality and hatred. Unlike many of their abolitionist peers they saw their African charges as friends in deed, not just inferiors in need of charity and guidance. To the Whittens, the negro people were equal creations of God whose lives and well being was threatened by evil perpetrators. It was a perilous philosophy born of a dangerous occupation. Their home was always open to the absconding blacks who came calling in desperation after being guided there by the encrypted lyrics sung on designated plantations by designated people at designated times. It's three floors were overly furnished with three rooms at ground level and three bedrooms upstairs where a ceiling access led to an attic.

Prudence Whitten led the group of fugitives to a dining room whose walls were wallpapered with garish pink, red and lavender flowered patterns. Along the wall on the far side of the room three rows of shelves were built into the wall. They were filled with delicate cups and bowls situated uniformly across each shelf. Mrs. Whitten unlatched a hook in the corner and swung the entire shelf out on a hinge. Behind it was an open crawl space large enough for a man to crawl through. It led into a large hidden room that housed up to fifteen people. At present it contained fourteen. One by one the fugitives crawled out into the dining room where a doorway led from there to the kitchen. A large pot boiled in a hearth. Adjacent to it another hidden trap door, concealed by an array of pots and pans hanging on hooks. It opened to expel eleven more people. Mrs. Whitten clapped her hands. "All right everyone!" she announced. "Get yourselves some food and stretch those limbs." She laughed heartily with her hands on her wide jovial hips. "You've one more night before the start of your journey." Kimbe and Noah stepped forward. "Thank you Missus." nodded Kimbe, "But my son and me'll jus get some sleep if you don't mind. We been travlin a lot lately and we don ate already."

"Certainly dear." Mrs., Whitten's voice was as light as a bird for such a large woman but suitable for someone with so much mirth. "These crawl spaces will have to air out," she pointed. "Why don't you take them to the barn, Joshua."

Joshua Whitten led Kimbe and Noah through the far kitchen door out into the yard. They walked down to the end of a short walkway to the barn just behind the house. Inside was filled with hay and farming implements. The smell of domestic animals permeated the air completing the milieu. A few chickens and hogs roamed the grounds outside while two horses nibbled on alfalfa in the back stalls. Kimbe and Noah made themselves comfortable in an upper loft. Before long they were sound asleep.

*****

Latimor Winslow propositioned Colonel Richards on the idea some time ago. The noted northern architect surmised that a negro slave with an extraordinary aptitude could be a profitable asset to his business as an apprentice and rentable commodity. Colonel Richards, of course bulked at the very idea of entrusting a slave with any amount of education. Like all the others who heard Latimor's idea he said that such responsibility as architect apprentice heaped upon a slave was blaspheme at best. Besides there is no such aptitude among the negro race. But soon, Colonel Richards was forced to relent to Winslow's financial reasoning. It was a sound investment. The overhead price of acquiring such a slave would be offset by the minimum cost of maintenance it would take to maintain him. Latimor could expect a profit in the first year. The apprentice would never have to be paid a salary and all wages paid for his services would go directly to Latimor. And even if he chose to do such an unorthodox thing as paying a salary it would not be the salary he'd be obliged to pay a white man. The expense of such a condition could be offset by making the negro responsible for his own lodging and meals. For the owner it would be a win, win situation regardless. All he needed now was a negro with the right aptitude and circumstance. He was never satisfied with the learning abilities of the Negroes he'd interviewed so far. But Latimor Winslow was undaunted. He continued to advertise for such human commodity that met the criteria until two free born Negroes applied for the position and had the nerve to ask for dignified salaries. Their aptitude may have been impressive but they lacked one thing...subservience. They were free and presented themselves accordingly...It wasn't what Latimor Winslow had in mind, at all. No.. He wanted a negro slave with a free Negroes ability. Now finally, Colonel Richards has informed him that he was in possession of just such a candidate. One with the right ability at the right price with the right attitude. Colonel Richards had proposed the slave's competence and dexterity at a money back, no questions asked guarantee at an agreed upon price of $3000. A $1500. down payment was made with the balance promised in two installments once satisfaction was established. To Latimor Winslow the deal was quite agreeable. A negro brokerage firm, Winthrop & Company, had negotiated the transaction as middle man. Tomorrow the deal would be consummated legally and the slave Joe would belong to him. Lock, stock and intelligence. Though; Latimor proposed he would change the slaves name. Joe didn't sound dignified enough. Maybe Joseph. Yes, Joseph Winslow.

Joe/Shai was transported, mentally numb and dejected, to Winthrop & Company's holding pens in Spritton, South Carolina early in the morning to await transfer on completion of Latimor's deal. Colonel Richards chomped on a fat cigar, rolling it around in his mouth several times before removing it with one hand. His other hand was jammed into his vest watch pocket. "This boy fills me with reservations Winthrop," he said rocking on his heels. "He's extraordinarily despondent. Winslow won't be interested in him in this condition."

Arthur Winthrop, short, partially bald and portly, sat at his desk absently shuffling papers. He stopped and tried to look confident. "He signed a contract, Randolph. The transactions been made." Colonel Richards lassoed his middle man's head with a thick loop of cigar smoke. "No, no Winthrop. I don't do business that way. I'm a southern gentleman of principles. I promised him a spry and intelligent colored apprentice."

"Don't you worry Colonel," Winthrop assured him. "I'll spark life into him. Post haste. I'm an old hand at inspiring the likes of a shiftless nigra."

"Well. You'd better. He's worth a lot of money and your commission comes out of it." Colonel Richards walked to the door to leave. "Colonel, don't worry. I know how to make these people marketable. It's a technique the Winthrops have been using since the earliest days of the trade." Winthrop walked to the door and courteously opened it for Colonel Richards. "Don't worry." He reassured him with a pat on the back. "I'll try not to," Colonel Richards implied through a ring of cigar smoke. "You just work some of that Winthrop magic on this three thousand dollar nigra and you'll have my full confidence."

*****

Shai sat inside a large cell leaning against a cold brick wall. His arms were chained to two large iron rings embedded in solid rock. Several other slaves sat shackled

319

around him in the same helpless manner. Every face in the room reflected despondence. Shai considered his distress several fold in comparison to his fellow captives. He was trapped in another time and dimension, never being able to return to his own familiar world again. Ironic, he thought. He knows so much about the happenings of the times. More than those who rightfully exist here. From his purview of the era he knew the awful truth of everything that will occur in this tragedy of time. Yet, knowing that bondage in America will one day be remediable provided him with little comfort. If anything it left him more dispirited. It didn't improve his circumstance. He didn't belong here. The rigid inflexible knot in the pit of his stomach reminded him of that constantly. Then he realized...these men, his co-captives, his brothers in bondage, their predicament was no different from his own, after all. Regardless of the differences in his perception and experience, the wretchedness of their situations were exactly the same. They were all captives in an alien world with no hope of returning to the life they once knew. The sights and sounds of the white man's world were as alien, strange and unknown to him as it was to them, and just as frightening. He thought of Argee and Professor Jubilee. He wondered if maybe one day they'd recognize him in some archival photo. An old bent, scraggily bearded ex-slave in some post civil war photo. Or some old bleached out ossified carcasses remains dug up during some 20th century excavation project. Or...perhaps just forgotten and lost to oblivion like the majority of his African brothers and sisters. Lost here in this barbaric American wilderness. He lowered his head and tried to conceal his face as the tears of pain and frustration rolled down his soiled and swollen cheeks.

320

CHAPTER 12

Year 1852

The sun peaked high above the horizon when Kuendela and Bessie entered the cave. They were exhausted. In the cave they silently moved to adjacent areas to bed down until dusk. Kuendela removed a plastic square shaped container from his utility. It contained a thin rubber mattress tightly folded and compressed to fit inside. After unfolding it he spread it flat on the ground then gave a forceful tug to the thin piece of braided cloth in it's bottom corner. This activated a small air pump that quickly inflated it to maximum size. Bessie gathered a pile of linen shreds and leaves to fill a burlap bag. She hadn't noticed Kuendela's preparations nor did she notice him watching her as she made her own. "Bessie." She turned. Chivalrously he offered his mattress to her. She looked puzzled over the unusual looking thing before accepting it. It was light as a feather, she noticed, in spite of its size. She poked at it cautiously as if it would bite her and her fingers bounced back from its firmness. It was 'cushiony' like a five foot pile of freshly cut grass and just as soft as it was light. She didn't just lay down on it she laid into it and found the thing extremely comfortable in spite of its strange appearance. Gratefully she smiled and pulled a blanket over her body. Bessie couldn't wait to tell Mah about the strange contraption or the equally strange predictions he'd made.

Kuendela tried punching the make shift bed of leaves and burlap he'd traded his mattress for into something comfortable with little success. He laid down and tried to close his mind to all the distractions and tried concentrating on sleep. A hard exercise in itself. No matter how fatigued he was, sleep evaded him. He got up and walked a few paces toward the stream and stared at the water. He listened to it's fluid rustling and sighed. Awful images rushed by his minds eye like the movement of the stream itself. Terrible images of Shai laid out on a rack being whipped and tortured. "DAMN!" His eyes shut tighter with each imagined lash. He wondered if he should be doing something right now. But he was, wasn't he? If he had transported here with a cache of modern weapons he could have blasted his way through the entire plantation instead of waiting for the old woman. But would that have been a proper action? It certainly would have been a satisfying one. He smiled, though it was agonizing to do so. The waiting and the uncertainty nagged at him. He couldn't turn his mind off. His thoughts vacillated back and forth between what he was doing and what he wished he could do. Just what was the initial plan? Yes...He was to scout the plantations and find a perch from which he could observe the target areas, keeping surveillance with his high powered vision gear until Shai was spotted. Then formulate a plan to get him out. Shai couldn't have been taken too far from the area. That was the inference. But how sure and efficient would that have been. Whew! Meeting Bessie and getting an in to Miss Clara, an underground matriarch, was a godsend. It, in fact, changed the dynamics of the plan. But waiting was hell. If only Miss Clara would have known where Shai was right then. He could've gone there, kicked an overseers ass and brought Shai out. But it wasn't that simple. Was it? He'd just have to wait. He shook his head and resigned himself to that fact.

Man! I must be tired. Kuendela rubbed his eyes. My mind is racing on all pistons. I've got to get some sleep. Bessie watched him pace in frustration.

"You worried some?' she inquired, braking his reverie. "Huh? Yes I guess I am." He walked back to where Bessie laid. "I worry some bout Mah and Noah too," she admitted.

"That sister knows how to take care of herself." Kuendela bent down on one knee and spoke quietly. "Bessie. You, Kimbe and Miss Clara are the most incredible black women I could have ever expected to meet."

"Gon," she waved, embarrassed. "Ain't nothin credible bout runnin round these woods hidin from white folks." Her face grew serious. "Nothin incredible bout bein nobody. Just a slop bucket for white folks to kick round." Kuendela could barely see her eyes strain in the dimness. "Masta's youngin, Miss Jenny say. Bessie you po thing," she aped the white girl's patronizing tone. "It's jus wretched the way you people have ta live. But God makes a place for everybody Bessie...Humph," she spat. "The more wretchid colud folk life is, the betta white folks live." She looked hard at Kuendela. Tears brimmed her eyes as the magnitude of her plight in life overcame her yet again. "It ain't fair Kendella. Why God make the world such a wretchid place fo colud? We do the work and the toilin and white folk do all the livin. Why," she cried. "It ain't fair." Kuendela held her face. "God has nothing to do with that Bessie. God made the world for us to live in harmony with nature. It's the devil that drives an evil people to take out their fears and short comings on the righteous people of the earth. It's not Gods fault Bessie it's mans. Don't you worry about what Miss Jenny says. Gods only intention was that man be free to find his own destiny. If one man takes that from another man then that MAN has to take it back for himself. By any means necessary and its just what you and Kimbe and Miss Clara are doing."

"Is this my destiny? To run."

"It's your destiny to live and be free for the coming generations. This is the world you live in Bessie. You have to take your own destiny. And if that means running away to be free, then that's what you have to do. White folks have made it difficult I know. But we learn and we grow strong. We make ways to deal with it. God did not intend for you to be a white man's slop bucket."

"Then why? Why am I a..."

"Bessie, your as free as the freedom you take. In your world or mine. It's the same struggle that connects us. I'm a king and you're a queen. We're royalty of a lost tribe. Always remember that. WE are God's people, struggling through the greatest test of humanity and we'll pass if we stay together and stay strong."

"If we stay together," she repeated to herself. "Yes. If we all stay together we could weather the storm of life." She looked at his eyes and her mood changed. She smiled. "Well, this cave is as free as Im gonna get right now." He smiled. "It ain't much, but it's all the freedom we got. When you get north you'll find it a little better. Not a whole hellava lot better. But better."

"Whatcha mean by that?"

"Well. Down here at least you know when white folks is against you. Up there they may fool you. Things may look even on the outside but sooner or later something is going to happen and the outcome of that event is going to depend on you being black and them being white. But at least up north you can get together with other freedom loving black people. Yall can struggle and build a new nation and teach the next generation. You know better than I do that the fight is never over Bessie. Not for you and not for me. But believe me. We win battle after battle." Bessie smiled again. It had only been a day since they'd met. Yet it was as though they'd known each other for years. Their eyes held the story. Their eyes had the answers.

"You know, Kendella. I have dreams," she confided. "I want things. I want a home made out a bricks. Like the houses in Spritton. I been there one time wit Miss Riches. They homes look so nice. They got windows wit glass. I want a family and I want my children to feel safe. I want ta have chickens and a garden. When white girls want them things its they right to want it and they get it. But all a colud gal can do is wish fo it. And they wanna make it feel wrong fo me ta want that. Like I don't deserve it or something."

"Don't believe that Bessie. You have the right and it's your duty to get it. White people can simply want it. Black people Bessie have the duty to get it. It's our duty to make sure we get the things we want so that the children know that it's possible for them to get what they want. What steps we conquer make our children conquer more." Bessie looked at him skeptically. "You think one day we can have it all."

"One day, I'm sure. When that will be I don't know. I just know that we are a race of survivors. To have endured what we have endured in this country is truly no less than a miracle, Bessie."

"I don't see where we endured so much."

"Think about it. People like you and Miss Clara and Kimbe. Yall struggle. Yall fight. You don't let the fight for freedom die. Believe me. One day it'll be better than you can imagine. Not cured. Not fixed. But better. And as long as you stay strong and stay proud and pass it on the struggle will never die.

"Just like freedom comin," she winked. Kuendela smiled. Another seed sown "That's right Bessie. You remember that." Kuendela laid down on the bed pile. Bessie laid back on the mattress and stared at the cavern ceiling. The events since meeting Kuendela took a tempered promenade across her minds eye. With the possible exception of Kimbe, she'd never felt so secure in someone else's company. Maybe it was more than security. Maybe fortitude or the confidence he exuded that had such an effect on the confidence she had in herself. She smiled at it's infectious nature. It was difficult to pinpoint and equally arduous to articulate. He's handsome, she opined, but it had to be more than that. But he IS handsome. She smiled to herself. It didn't explain things but it made it hard not to think of him. She seldom, if ever, concerned herself with the aesthetics of men. Rarely had she entertained amorous thoughts of them. The initial stirrings of womanly emotions usually eluded her but now something bloomed deep inside. Emotions long dormant.

The guileful, flagitious violation of the overseers who forced themselves on slave women had long since dulled Bessie's sense of amorousness. Occasions of love were reduced to a perfunctory humping of blatant frustrations. Any womanly urge akin to love or pleasure had long since been removed from her. But now Bessie felt the blossoming of a rebirth. A resurgence of feelings she had long forgotten. Something inside her had awakened. Something that made her want to give herself...openly...fully...lovingly and sensually to a man. This man...beside her. He elicited a delicious female stirring within her. Something Bessie forgot she had.

Kuendela laid beside her with mirrored feelings. Not feelings withheld but feelings that were just as deep and longing. For him...this was not the time, or perhaps he had no right to feel these things at all...Not now. Kuendela wrestled with this stirring dilemma by combating the attraction he felt growing. He pulled himself to his feet again and began rummaging through his gear. A stilled silence settled in the cave as he withdrew a map and plotted some calculations on Spittle and Aiken counties. "What's that?" Bessie inquired softly. "A map," he replied, perhaps too curtly. He was immediately sorry he'd spoken so sharply. Lying there, her skin reminded him of the unstamped side of a hershey chocolate bar. Smooth, creamy and sweet. Her voice was a husky bird like soprano. Kuendela shook his head. Maybe he should remove the distraction. For its own good. "Bessie," he began slowly. "I don't want you to miss your rendezvous with Kimbe and Noah because of you being here with me. If for some reason they had to leave sooner than planned you'd be left behind. I would never forgive myself if that happened. After all, you've fulfilled your part of the bargain and I'm grateful." He paused to gage her response. She was silent.

"Now that I've met Miss Clara I can wait for her message alone." He was not convincing, not even to himself. "I could take you to meet Kimbe and find my way back here in time to catch Miss Clara's messenger." Bessie raised up on both elbows and stared long and hard at him. It might not have been a bad idea. But the words disappointed her to the point of tears. "You don't need me no mo?" she asked painfully. "You've handled your end Bessie. I can wait for Miss Clara's message."

"Spose they come whilst you gon. Then what?' Kuendela could hear the aching in her voice. "Anyhow,' she inferred, "we need sleep now. Not pushin off through some woods." She laid back down, concluding her point. "Getting to the underground is more important than sleep..." Before he finished she was again up on her elbows. "You finish wit me now..." It was the feelings of a strong black woman he was dealing with now. Neither Bessie nor Kuendela spoke. Not with their mouths, but the truth was there to see...in their eyes. They held each other that way then looked away to avoid each others gaze. "I ain't gonna miss them Kendella. I got time. I don't want to leave. Not now." She pled in a demurall voice. "Anyhow ya caint be sure. You might need me still," she reasoned. "I caint leave you now. Not afta you helped me, saved Noah..." Silence...Her point was well founded. After all, this was a strange land to him. He could very well need her later. So why, he thought, was he trying to get rid of her and why now was he relieved that she didn't want to go. Again he thought...I gotta get some sleep. "I do need you Bessie," he said, too quickly. He looked again to the map. Bessie reached for it and pushed the document away. "Neva mind that now," she said huskily...not smiling...Still staring. He stared back. He found her as impressive as she was the very first time he'd seen her. He couldn't help thinking of the irony. The beauty of a woman who's life and times were so hard, so distant and so far from his. His eyes moved at their own command, across her smooth cocoa brown skin enhanced with long black silken hairs. Kuendela stared transfixed. How sexy, he thought, hair is on a black woman's body.

Bessie found herself drawn in beyond her thoughts. What those thoughts were wasn't important now because she only wanted to...kiss him. An aura surrounded the moment. The intentions they both harbored came to light. He wanted to kiss her and she wanted to be kissed. They drew near, even closer. Then kissed. Slowly and softly at first until the heat of passion spurred them on deeper and harder...Unabated...hungrily and needing, they gave to each others lips. Delicately their lips parted. It became a silent moment that gave way to the inevitable. Sensually her linsey-woolsey slid away. Then without knowing how, she helped him remove his jumpsuit, unzipping it completely. Never before had she felt the true need or want to totally give herself to a man. She felt it now...and she gave. Bessie was feeling love, true love, for the first time...and she loved it. They laid together enthralled in the after glow of each others arms. She felt complete. Not done, thank God, like when a white man forces himself on her. Or a colored man relieving himself by her. No this black man shared and gave himself as he excepted her to do. She could be with him forever. But somehow she knew it wouldn't be. She'd have to except that. The thought jolted her for an instant. Her mind and body moved undulant through space and time. She nibbled nervously on his ear. Somehow she knew she shouldn't, and not wanting to, she asked. "Will you take me with you?" The question effected him in a way she would never know. It left him ashamed. Or sad. Or even confused. The obvious answer would make him feel he was being cruel. She knew it and was immediately sorry she asked. She looked away from him.

Had he brought her more pain? He asked himself. There was no future for them together. Their worlds were dimensions apart. He couldn't understand it but he was ashamed not strong. He'd been selfish and wrong like he'd taken unfair advantage of her. But one look in her eyes and he knew he didn't take advantage at all. She wanted him and he wanted her. His shame was in not knowing how. The aura of this black woman showed him that she excepted him on the terms that were. One look and he knew that she had not felt retrogressively used and he had no reason to feel introspectively irreverent. The air was an aura of intimacy and sharing. No games and no deception. For this instant they had merged their beings and spirits. He looked in her eyes and...it was all right. "I know you don't belong here," she exclaimed. It was not a question but a revelation. "I can feel it. The things you got. The things you do. The things you know. The way you talk. Even the way you look. The feel around you." It was difficult articulating her feelings in this way. She just wanted him to know that she understood. That she knew...

"Bessie...," Kuendela began to say something but she stopped him with finger tips pursed against his lips. She kissed him softly. He reciprocated in kind then reached behind his head and unclasped the gold chain he wore around his neck. He displayed it to her. Attached to the thin gold braided chain was a small circular hollow crystal filled with minute grains of sand. It was the talisman given to him by the elder chieftain during the christening ceremony that graced him with the name Kuendela. The small minute grains were from the Sudanese bank of the Nile River. "This is a piece of Africa Bessie. Our home. I want you to always carry it with you." Gently he pulled her to a sitting position and placed it around her neck. "This is the source of our strength and power and as long as you wear it you can do anything. It's the symbol of what we...have shared and a reminder of all that I've told you. All our memories are here in this crystal Bessie. Whenever you need to remember. Whenever you need the strength and the power to go on. I'll be right here." He touched her chest above her heart where the crystal dangled. "I'll be right here, along with our ancestors to protect you and keep you safe. And when you're free. Kiss it and remember me." Bessie smiled knowingly. "African Kings and Queens at the time of jubilee."

"Kings and Queens Bessie...Always." Bessie kissed him. "Thank you Kendella. It's beautiful." She'd wear Kuendela's piece of Africa and treasure it always. They stared into each other for what seemed like an eternity but only an actual moment. No future, no expectations could they imagine. For however long they remained together, in spirit they would be, forever. Cherished...as their long slow kiss foretold. All pretense and rationality was wiped away in a single moment. They laid together while love and exhaustion consumed them in a blackened blanket of sleep and contentment.

*****

The mission at hand was set aside for a moment while they replenished themselves until a voice aroused them from sleep. It seemed at first like a summons in a dream. Like a voice far off in the distance. "Bessie!" It was a strained voice. Then, "Bessie!" More distinct. "Bessie!...Yall in there!" It was now a strong gruff whisper that tried not to call attention to itself. Bessie stirred awake. "Kendella!" She shook him. "Kendella!"

"Bessie!...Bessie!" The voice called again. This time a little louder.

"It's Hammonds," she snapped. "Hammonds!!!"

"Bessie," he called again. His voice was a deep bassed, friendly tone.

"Hammonds!...Hammonds!," she answered standing. She and Kuendela raced to get dressed. "In heah Hammonds!" Bessie had just finished tying the rope around her waist when Hammonds squeezed through the entrance of the cave. Their visitor stood a little over six feet. His skin was very black and his lips very thick below large flaring nostrils. When he inhaled they pulsated and expanded. His close set eyes gave his appearance a perpetual furrowed brow. The sleeves of his brown shirt were bloused and stuffed into a tight fitting dark vest. It's shirt tails jutted out below and hung over his baggy dusty brown pants. The gray wide brim floppy hat he wore had seen better days. It seemed to be screwed down upon the thick kinky hair jutting out from all sides of his head. Kuendela could see he was very muscular under his shirt. He had the physique one would expect to see on the body of a blacksmith. Hammonds stated his business quickly without further formalities. "Miss Clara sent me ta tell yall that the boy done got sent to da dealers." Bessie let out a startled gasp.

"Dealers?" asked Kuendela. "What dealers?"

330

"Winthrops!" Hammonds stated. "Winthrops, the slave dealers. Massa Richids found a buyer fo him up north."

"Did Miss Clara say if there was any way I could head them off before they moved?" Kuendela's voice conveyed his desperation. Anxiety was etched in both his face and Bessie's.

"Miss Clara sent me ta fetch yall ta town. She say if yall don't make a move befo dawn they gone a cart him north and you ain't ever gonna be able ta hep em." Kuendela snapped to attention. "Enough said on that my brother,"

"I'm heah ta help ya if ya need me."

"Oh I need you Brother. And I thank you." Kuendela slapped Hammonds on the back in appreciation then began taking things from his utility and stuffing them in a smaller waist pack.

"WE!! need jah Hammonds," corrected Bessie. Kuendela didn't reply. He went about gathering his gear. Lastly he slipped something on himself. "Dats a fancy lookin vest."

"It's fancier then you think, Brother Hammonds. It's Kevlar. Body armor," he explained to their amused expressions. "Body armor? Well, what in hell is that thing?" Hammonds pointed to the strange gun Kuendela holstered to his hips. "That's a funny lookin firearm."

"You better believe it."

"I do declare."

"How are we getting there, Brother."

"My wife lives on Wilson's plantation," Hammonds explained. "Mr. Jim Smith lets me take the ole wagon dere ta visit one time a week. Today is my day ta visit," he added cleverly.

"Wilson plantation ain't tward town Hammonds!" snapped Bessie.

"I know dat Bessie," Hammonds returned in his bass tone. "I been savin money ta buy my suga sumptin special. Even a po colud slave husband like me wants ta see his missus in some sto bought finery at one time anotha." Hammonds smiled and winked at Kuendela revealing a row

331

of dull jagged teeth. Kuendela weakly smiled back then added. "We ain't gonna have time to shop, Brother." In response Hammonds pulled a haphazardly folded blue silk dress from inside his vest. It was tied up with string. Kuendela congratulated him with thumbs up. "Good for you Brother Hammonds."

Once outside atop the ledge they descended to a wagon parked by a tree at the base of Fall Point. It was hitched to an impressive looking black horse. A long rectangular wooden crate sat in the rear, almost even with its length. Hammonds instructed the pair to crawl into it. Kuendela crawled inside behind Bessie. "Miss Clara's a sharp lady," He was again impressed with Miss Clara's resourcefulness and ingenuity. She was some kind of agent. Once they were inside, Hammonds covered the crate with large heavy blankets. A smaller wooden crate lay uncovered beside it to further add to the ruse. Hammonds boarded the wagon's seat. With a snap of the reins he signaled the horse. "Giddy up girl!" The wagon lurched once then rolled on it's way.

*****

By mid afternoon Sheriff Pickett and his deputies met Jim Smith and the others at the edge of town. Every member of the posse was there including McPacker and Luke. There were twenty in all, heavily armed with muskets and side arms. A few men brandished bayonets at the ends of their muskets. They were outfitted for destruction.

"You sure your boy marked the trail for us?" Sheriff Pickett asked once more. "Is he reliable?"

"Yea," Jim Smith answered warily. "He's reliable. I reared him for this job myself. He knows exactly what I want done." He then turned to address the others. "My boy is wearin a red bandana on his head. So be careful. I don't want him shot in the ass."

"Wheah else can we shoot em," someone quipped. A few men laughed.

"Pay attention!" Sheriff Pickett ordered. His voice full of irritation. He was not altogether pleased with taking along men he considered gun happy and unprofessional. They were too quick to shoot nigras. Thus too quick to upset his profit margin. Jim Smith went on. "I don't want my boy roughed up none either. You hear!" A chorus of low grumbles affirmed.

Sheriff Pickett raised his arms to signal the posse to his attention. "Men. We're not on a nigger game hunt. We are out to put an end to an abolitionist underground network. Too many slaves have been escaping of late. We're going to choke it off and put an end to their organization." He cast a cold eye on the them. "We're out to return property to good folk. Remember that. We're not out here to have fun. These people expect us to return their property so they may recoup their loses." He watched the faces of the men. Some he knew had been drinking. If they disobeyed their orders he was serious about putting a bullet into the transgressor. Not to kill but certainly to teach. These men would have to learn to respect the mandate of law. He counted out the same demands on each finger. "I want no random shooting, no clubbing, no beating and NO KILLING!...Understand!?!" A variable chorus of acquiescence rounded the group. John McPacker trotted his horse beside Sheriff Pickett's. "I want the nigra who killed Virgil. I want his hide personally. I'll be the one to have him swing, by Eire."

"You got it John," someone yelled. Satisfied, Sheriff Pickett pulled up on his horse's reins. "...Let's move out!" The posse fell in line behind him filtering into a column of twos. Sheriff Pickett and Jim Smith rode side by side, leading the way. McPacker and Luke rode behind them.

"I'm surprised the Colonel's not joinin us," Pickett remarked. "He's at Winthrops arranging the sale of that new nigra he got from John. He rides with us in spirit though."

"I hope that murderin niggra's still akithe here by Eire." Jim Smith turned to the man riding behind him. "If he's not, we'll do one of those heathens in till he tells us where that nigger can be found."

"Make no mistake," added Luke, "these niggers know all the places another nigger can hide. We'll find the devil."

"By the Saints we had better!" With a few hours of daylight left to their advantage a row of ten thundering pairs galloped off to pick up the trail left by Jim Smith's agent.

*****

Pressed together in the small, dark confines of a moldy wooden crate, Bessie and Kuendela were jerked about uncontrollably. Every chuck hole and rock in the road seemed to fined itself in the path of the wagon's wheels while Hammonds' felicitous humming found harmony with the rumbling obstacle strewn roadway. "Whoa...Whoa girl!!" Hammonds brought the horse to a sudden stop. From inside the crate, Kuendela and Bessie heard the sounds of horses approaching. The clumping of hooves and the screeching of voices seemed to fall on top of the wagon itself. Kuendela and Bessie could swear the mysterious riders outside could hear the wild staccato drum beat of their thumping hearts inside the crate. Instinctively they held their breath. "Hammonds!!" yelled a gruff voice. To Kundela it sounded like a terse command, not the prelude to a greeting. Hammonds swallowed hard and tipped his hat to the familiar face of his overseer. He tried to conceal his nervousness as the white man eyed him closely. Hammonds put the thought of the human contraband he carried out of his mind, to ease his anxiety. "Hi do Mistuh Jim Smith, suh." He grinned and removed his hat.

"Hammonds," Jim Smith repeated, his horse bucking slightly. "Why're you headed this way? Your pass is to see your wife over at Wilson's." There was no suspicion in his tone but rather a condescending annoyance over the slave's misguidedness. Hammonds managed his most obsequious smile. "Yes suh Mistuh Jim Smith and dats wheah I be headed soons I go ta town and buy her sumptin pretty fo a present. I been savin a long time ta get my sugar sumptin nice." He hoped he hadn't come across too cute. Balancing

334

the temperament of whites was a skill that took years to perfect and Hammonds was proficient at reading his overseer's egomania. Some of the other riders began to chuckle. The thought of love and sentiment between two Negroes was just too laughable for them to hold in.

"Whatcha got back there, Hammonds?" Jim Smith demanded pointing an askance finger at the back of the wagon. He struggled to hold his restless horse steady. Inside the crate Kuendela fingered the gelatin gun at his side. He struggled to position it outside of the compressed space between him and Bessie. Bessie clutched nervously at the talisman around her neck and prayed silently into fingers pressed to her lips.

"Some wood I scrounged Mistuh Jim suh to build me a..."

"Jim," Sheriff Pickett cut in. "We don't have time to dally with this nigra. We better get on if we're gonna have some daylight left to follow that trail."

"You're right Abram." Jim Smith never took his eyes from Hammonds nervous grinning face.

"Don't get into trouble Hammonds and be back by work time in the morning." He kicked his horse in the side, galloping off without a response.

"Yes suh Mistuh Jim. Yes suh." Hammonds scuffed at the overseer's receding back. He smiled and nodded to the passing riders. None of which reciprocated. Nor had they noticed the scornful curl of Hammonds' lips or the obscenities he mouthed at them as they passed. Hammonds two rear passengers sighed a breath of relief. Kuendela pecked Bessie on the lips. Bessie celebrated back. Hammonds made a clucking noise at the roof of his mouth then snapped the reins. The horse leapt forward. "Get up girl. Come on les go!"

*****

Circular clouds of dust swirled about the riders galloping around the edge of the rice mill. Slaves unaware of the riders sanguineness purpose stopped working long enough to watch them pass the slave cabins. Behind the riders, the main house of Angora faded in their wake as they followed Jim Smith and Sheriff Pickett into the woods. As the woods got thicker they slowed the pace. Jim Smith spotted something familiar up ahead and raised his hand to halt the posse. He dismounted and knelt down. Holding the reins in one hand he picked a painted pebble from the ground and examined it closely between two fingers. "Ha ha! Ole Caesar has come through for us gentlemen. He's laid us a clear path of yellow stones. All we have to do is follow them."

"A yellow stone path eh?" grumbled the Sheriff. "That's right." Jim Smith twirled the marker around his fingers. "Right up to them nigga lovin, nigga stealin abolitionist's door." Sheriff Pickett raised his arm. "Let's go men!" His horse lurched forward. Jim Smith remounted his horse in one smooth motion then joined the sheriff in the lead. They continued at a measured pace. The entire group was filled with excitement and much too much elated anticipation. Jim Smith slowed the procession every few yards as he spotted the yellow stones marking their trail.

*****

Kimbe awoke with a jolt after a restless sleep. Noah slept beside her, snoring lightly. She yawned, stretched and drug herself up by her walking stick. Bessie should have arrived by now. She worried that something may have happened to her. If Bessie is captured again she couldn't imagine what she'd do. There was no way she could go north without her. Unconsciously she began formulating steps she might take to find her should that happen. No. I can't start worrying about that. That kind of worry could put a jinx on her. No she'd just have to have faith that the strange black man will keep his word and bring her sister safely to her.

In light of the feelings she had for her sister she could well realize how Kuendela felt about his brother. The wisdom of allowing Bessie to escort the man still made

336

sense. She closed her eyes in silent prayer before going out to check on things. *I just hope that big nigger don't get my Bessie caught.* A rustling noise in the loft on the other side of the stall startled her. Something over there was hidden from view and moving around. She eased to the end of the stall to peek around it without alarming Noah. Slowly a pair of outstretched legs atop a pile of hay crept into view. She looked further, bringing the entire image within sight and saw that it was a man. His bare back was exposed to her. It was mapped with whipping scars. A feature all so terribly common and familiar to her. This tortured soul could be any one of a dozen men akin to her. She stretched her neck as much as she could to get a clearer glimpse of the man. She could almost see his profile. He turned slightly. She smiled. His bare back heaved up and down slowly as he slept. The rustling she heard must have been him rolling over in his sleep. She tapped his legs with her cane to wake him. "George!...George!...Wake up man! When did you crawl up in heah? I thought you was in da house wit the othas. You like ta give me da histacks" She was happy to see him. A friend and colleague from Angora. A brother in misery.

George moaned himself awake and sat up. Tufts of straw fell around him like broken flower peddles. Squinting his eyes he looked alarmingly at her. Kimbe rocked back on her cane and laughed.

"Wheah's Caesar?" he asked curtly, looking around.

"Who in the devil is Caesar?"

George got to his feet. "Wheah did he get ta? Kimbe guessed it to be the man he came to Whitten's farm with. "Musta gon ta eat wit da rest of em in the house," she reasoned. "Why you worryin bout wheah a grown man don got to, anyway?" George thought for a moment. It was silly to be so alarmed about Caesar's not being there in the barn. After all, during times Mr. Whitten thought were safe, the Negroes were permitted to move from the house to the barn as long as they remained inside. So what was the problem...But there was a feeling, a sixth sense that something was not right. It was an apprehension he'd felt since they'd

337

arrived. He couldn't pinpoint it. So he elected to dismiss it. At least for now. In so doing he climbed down from the loft and started for the barn door.

*****

Jim Smith and Sheriff Pickett's posse followed the yellow pebbles to a cluster of trees at the base of Whitten's farm. There was still light left but the thick brush along the outer perimeter provided enough cover for them to dismount without being seen from inside the farm house. They left their horses a few yards behind and approached the area in front of the clearing on foot, careful to keep out of sight behind the tree line at it's edge. There was no movement around any of the three small buildings on the farm as far as they could see. Suddenly a figure appeared. John McPacker knelt down beside Jim Smith and nudged him in his side then pointed to the negro male creeping suspiciously across the clearing. He was wearing a red bandana. "That's my boy," Jim Smith informed him. "That's Caesar."

Caesar moved nervously, looking from side to side. He hoped his contacts were near. He was anxious to receive the reward his betrayal would earn him. Unknown to him he had timed his masters arrival almost to the second. Entering the tree line, he stumbled over one of the white men. The white man pulled him down and muffled his astonished cry just as Joshua Whitten emerged from his home some 50 yards away. "Massa Jim," Caesar whispered into the man's palm. His bulging eyes scanned the dangerous looking group for his boss. The posseman removed his hand from his mouth. "Here Caesar. Here boy," Smith beckoned. Caesar crawled over to his master, glad to see a familiar face among the armed white men. "You done good," Jim Smith congratulated him. "Now tell me boy, how many white men are in that farm house."

"Just Mister Joshua and his son, suh."

"Any women...? white women."

"Yes suh.. Miss Prudence.

"How many niggahs up theah?"

"More an a litter suh." Jim Smith turned to McPacker. "Alright!...Now that's my boy. Would you believe the yellow stones were his idea."

"Now that's a good one by Eire," praised McPacker. He gave Caesar a patronizing rub on his kinky head. Sheriff Pickett then pulled him by the arm. "Any guns in there boy?" he demanded, not bothering to disguise the scorn in his voice.

"Yes suh. Mr. Joshua tote a musket rifle."

Checking his side arm Jim Smith turned to Caesar. "You better get back there, where the horses are," he ordered. "And tend to em. Bring them up when I call you."

"Yes suh." Caesar, having earned his 'thirty pieces' was already up and on his way down the slight incline toward the horses, still crouching as he ran.

*****

When Joshua Whitten walked out his door he thought he'd seen something or someone dart into the woods. There was nothing in the direction of the aberration now. The agent he was expecting wasn't due, so it could not have been him. Perhaps it was an animal. Stroking his beard he sighed with revelation. It was one of the colored boys. He'd swear to it now. They were so much like children he thought. One has to watch over them at all times. He told them to stay inside and explained how important it was to stay out of the woods. Now, one of them has ventured out there anyway. Joshua started across the clearing to retrieve the wondering charge before he gets himself into trouble. At the tree line Joshua froze in horror. He'd found himself staring down the muzzles of a half dozen muskets. Instinctively he dropped his. One of the men scooped it from the ground then pulled Joshua into the woods. The others took him into custody. "Not a sound you nigger lovin abolitionist bastard or I'll see daylight through your gullet, by Eire," snarled McPacker as the posse moved out toward the farm.

*****

George stepped from the barn and heard a blood curdling scream followed by a rifle shoot. Noah was jarred
awake by the sound and instinctively rushed into his mothers
outstretched arms. Inside the farmhouse the other fugitives
went into action fleeing through doors and windows, trying
to put as much distance between them and the gun shots as
possible. Kimbe shuffled Noah from the loft down to the
barn door. "Come honey. We got ta git." George held his
arm out to stop them. "Wait Kimbe," he warned. "There's
white men out there!"

"No waitin George. It ain't gonna take em long to search
heah. We betta git in the forest whilst we can." George
understood but thought it smarter to move with caution. He
knew the others were running wildly into the arms of the
paddy rollers. There would be men waiting in the woods to
cut off their retreat. He didn't want to make the same
mistake. If they would take it slow he thought they'd have a
better chance. Kimbe thought it best to high tail it into the
woods away from the gunshots as fast as they could. She
pushed the door open with her cane and peeped out.
Knowing her severed appendage would be a hindrance to
Noah's ability to reach the forest quickly she pushed him
ahead of her. "Run boy!!" she commanded. "But momma."
His eyes filled with tears. "But nothin boy. Git! I'll ketch up
wit you in the woods." Noah ran into the woods adjacent to
the barn as fast as his legs could carry him. Out of the corner
of his eyes he saw the white men converging on the house.
They didn't see him. They were chasing screaming slaves
around the farm in all directions. Noah reached the tree line
and dove into a thicket then burrowed deep into it. His
mother and George struggled across the clearing away from
the direction he'd entered the forest. He saw them from the
foliated vista he crouched in. George was helping Kimbe
hobble along in spite of her objections to leave her and save
himself.

Jim Smith and Luke exited the back door of the house and spotted the struggling couple. George was quickly overtaken by the two white men. Who in turn, were joined by two more. As Jim Smith reached for Kimbe, George was able to throw himself at the white man in her defense. With the back end of his musket, Luke butt George in the head and knocked him down. George tried to recoup from his attackers only to be smashed in the head again. This time rendered unconscious. Jim Smith tried to dodge Kimbe's walking stick but caught it across the side of his face. She quickly turned to feigned off an attack by the other white man and caught him across the back of the neck causing him to drop his musket. She was surprisingly adroit in spite of her impediment. Her momentum was slowed when Luke smashed her on the side of her chin with a fierce blow, knocking her to the ground. Jim Smith snarled in anger as he uncurled from the blow he incurred. He stood menacingly over Kimbe's prostrated figure, breathing heavily. He found himself aroused by her feisty audaciousness. His sensual excitement was a surprise even to himself as it inflamed his encroaching sadistic desire.

"You black heathen she-devil," he gasped, hardly recognizing his own voice. He turned to Luke with his chest heaving. "This wench has caused me more trouble than she's worth," he gasped remembering her arrogance at Angora. It excited him then and excited him even more now. Especially now that she dallied beneath him. Completely at his mercy. He always found her erotically attractive for an elder colored woman. The arrogance...The violence...His breathing continued deep and husky. His own devious thoughts erected an amusing and sinister smile on his face. He handed his musket to his comrade and snapped his fingers as the idea emerged. "I'm going to teach this wench some humility once and for all." He unbuttoned the front of his trousers. The other two held her down as he straddled her writhing body and forced her legs open. Jim Smith yanked her dress high above her thighs, up to her face, over her nose. Leaving her eyes exposed. His breathing was heavy and erratic. Jim

Smith forced himself into her. He bucked and grunted like a wild beast until he growled in spent climax and fell limp atop his victim. Luke jumped around them cheering on the spectacle of the merciless gladiator defiling the helpless female. The ordeal was a pitiful performance. The sinister act would have been laughable to her had it not been so spiritually demoralizing. Kimbe was thoroughly appalled at the savage affront to her dignity. Even more painful was the despondent stare from the eyes she could plainly see from the vista in the thicket just a few yards away. She hoped the distressing plea in her eyes registered enough to make Noah stay put. Tears of transference ran down both sides of her face settling in tiny pools in her ears. The ravaging lasted one long insufferable minute but seemed an eternity. Jim Smith pulled himself off her. The second he got to his feet Kimbe dragged herself to a sitting position. Just as she began to rise from the ground Luke slapped her hard against the side of her face. The force of the blow spun her head around. Just as quickly she brought her face back to spit in his execrable expression. She was determined that his turn would not be so easy. She sprung fully to her feet and smacked Luke's face with a force that caused a snakelike mixture of blood and mucus to slither from his nose. Shock mounted with rage, sprung into his face. Blaring some incoherent obscenity he lift his bayonet and plunged it into her chest. When he withdrew the vile weapon the wound remained dry for an instant, long enough for her to look down at the hole in her chest. Then all at once shear horror erupted on her face as the wound turned into a gushing red stream of blood. Her mouth opened. She eyed her attacker, then dropped without a single cry of pain. She was dead as soon as she hit the ground. Her eyes still open wide in horror.

"You dam fool," Jim Smith yelled in wild reprobation. "You dam stupid fool bastard." Luke reached down and felt the silent pulse of Kimbe's carotid artery. "She's dead you ignorant jackass! Dead...! and payment will go to Colonel

Richards on your account. You fool it's gonna take you a year to pay this off. She was worth a $1000. at least."

"I'd bet against that. Not with that foot of hers," Luke replied arrogantly. "Besides," he explained. "She struck me. You saw it Jim. What about yall?" He turned to the other two. They shrugged their shoulders as they walked away.

"Bastards!" Switching gears he added, "What about you. Raping her. I ain't have nothin to do with...that."

"Save your breath," defended Jim Smith defiantly "You dam sure wanted to. Besides. Rape! That's nothing. But killing her, now that's a horse of another color. Somebody's got to make good on her value."

"Some friend you are Jim."

"You must reap what you sow my friend. Come on lets get this one." Jim Smith and Luke each took a side of George and pulled his unconscious body across the ground by his shirt collar. They casually made their way back to the group while they continued their debate. When they reached the front of the farm house Sheriff Pickett, John McPacker and the others were corralling the fugitive slaves into a circle.

"Luke," called McPacker. "By the Saints, man come here and point out the murdering heathen who killed Virgil." Luke obeyed quickly, dropping his side of George to the ground then racing over to scan the line of worried faces.

"Turn this way...dam you," Sheriff Pickett ordered one of the captives.

"Well Luke," he implored impatiently. "Which one is it. Is he here."

"He ain't here," growled Luke, kicking a small frustrated cloud of dust.

"By the Saints, have a look at em again."

"He ain't here!" Luke piqued. "Shit! He was a foot wider and taller than any of these niggers here."

"By the Saints!" McPacker yelled in frustration. "I was sure the blackamoor would be among em!" He paced back and forth angrily before the lot of frightened chattel. Their eyes followed him nervously. His meaty neck surpassed his face in a race to flushing red. By now the prisoners were all aware of what the ruddy faced white man wanted and they feared what could happen to them if he didn't get it.

Caesar approached the scene with a few riders and dismounted horses trotting along behind him. George was just coming to. He struggled to his feet and caught sight of his Judas friend. The earlier apprehension he'd felt now came to focus. "You dirty rotten ass nigger!!" You Judas bastard. I should a knowed." It took several possemen to restrain him. Sheriff Pickett found the outburst amusing enough to laugh.

"Hold it!" snapped Jim Smith shaking an accusing finger at George. "This nigra here knows something, I bet cha."

"Dam right I knows somethin," yelled George through sneering teeth. "He the nigger who kilt Mister Virgil." He pointed to Caesar. Every nerve in his body strained against him for revenge. "He kilt em! He did." Jim Smith found the claim dubious. But the accusation was enough to make Caesar's eyes widen in fear when he perceived a vengeful glare come to life in McPacker's eyes. Jim Smith saw it too and rushed to Caesar's defense. "No John. He's not the one."

"Massa Jim!...Tell em!...Tell em," Caesar blurted. "I tole him that fib sos he bring me here...Tell em!...Massa Jim.

"Luke?" entreated McPacker. "Naw," Luke replied, shaking his head. George though defeated enjoyed the spectacle of seeing Caesar squirm with fright from his supposed benevolent master. It was worth telling the lie and what ever else came next. Only the big white man believing his accusation could transcend the moment.

"It's all right Caesar...calm down." Jim Smith placed a reassuring palm on his shoulder. "If you'd had done it. Luke woulda fingered you long ago. And you'd be dead by now. No. Our killer's still out there somewhere. The Point more than likely." Sheriff Pickett turned to McPacker. "I'm sorry John. I was sure we'd bag em here." He turned to George and grabbed him by the scruff of his neck. "Tell me boy,' he ordered. "What's up there at Fall Point. Why're you people

344

always runnin. up there...What is it? Who meets you up there?"

George sweated profusely. He was caught but he wouldn't tell. With nothing to lose, George fell silent, then obstinate. Strangely he began to swell with arrogance. Sheriff Picket watched him and observed the metamorphosis. It only made him grimace and grow angrier. WHAM!! the sheriff violently back handed George knocking him back a few steps. Two deputies pulled him back. WHAM!! George fell to the ground. Sheriff Pickett straddled him. "Who's up there nigger?" he shouted.

"What cha gettin at Abram?" Pickett never took his eyes from George's face. "You said it yourself Jim. They're always starting in that direction. I'll be dam if there ain't somewhere for them to meet or even a hidin place up there and I betcha this nigra knows where it is."

"Saints of Eire!" rejoined McPacker. "You may have something. Let me have a go at this one."

"Be my guess." The sheriff stepped aside. John McPacker now loomed over George. His eyes dared the arrogant runaway to move. Without taking his eyes off his charge he instructed a deputy on what he was going to need.

"Fine," contended Pickett. Meanwhile we'll get this lot into town and hold them at Winthrop's. Their owners can claim em there." He cupped his hands over his mouth and yelled to the men in the farm house. "Bring em out." Two deputies appeared with Joshua, Prudence and Jonah Whitten. There hands tied securely behind them. "Harboring fugitives is a serious offense here in the south Mister Whitten. You'll wish you stayed in Philadelphia with the rest of them Quakers and abolitionist." His lips were curled into a sneer. His top lip rose with every word of intimidation but Whitten remained unscathed.

"Do what ye must," he dared, "But you'll not hold back the wave of freedom. This land was founded on that principle. For EVERY MAN!! Pickett stared at him queerly. What a disgrace he opined. White men such as this remained a complete mystery to men of Pickett's ilk. The nerve, placing the coloreds on a par of freedom with white men. Then to risk their own lives to defend them. The irony of his own thoughts were lost to him. Whitten shook his head as he returned Pickett's stare. The irony was not lost on the abolitionist, just his faith in his fellow countrymen.

The deputies roped the slaves together hand to hand. The young men of the lot were secured with metal vistees then connected to one another with ropes. McPacker, Jim Smith and Luke stayed behind with George as Sheriff Pickett and the remainder of the posse led the miserable caravan to town.

*****

Noah remained in the thicket the entire time, paralyzed with fear. His knuckles strained against the skin of his clenched fist while he stared into the lifeless eyes of his mother just yards away. He was frozen in horror. Unable to move. His emotions laid siege to his young mind, filling him with rage, grief and an insatiable hate and contempt for the men who walked leisurely away from the carnage they left behind for his innocent mind to imbibe. What he saw conceived a force that he'd feel for the rest of his life. It manifest into words that dripped from his lips, defining a way to articulate his soul. "I HATE them people," he moaned. The phrase ruminated over and over. chanting inside him, hardening deep within his young existence.

From somewhere inside the farmhouse the sound of a man's terrible screams reverberated throughout the entire area. Noah covered his ears but it did no good. With all his eyes had taken in now his ears were immured in even more depravity.

*****

Long after the white men in the farmhouse had gone, dragging their unfortunate reamed captive away, Noah could still hear George's screams. The sun disappeared behind the

346

barn and the beginning of night grayed the sky around it. He would remain in his concealed clump alone...all night.

"I HATE em!" he pledged. "I hate white people!" With the coming of night his tears blurred the scene before him as he continued his refrain.

"I HATE em! I hate white people!"

Nothing else was visible to him except Kimbe's eyes. They were still stretched wide in horror, staring without life. Their eeriness burned into his conscience. Forever in his memory, echoing the culmination of this tragic event. "I HATE EM!" he cried. "I HATE WHITE PEOPLE!!!."

CHAPTER 13

Year 1852

Sunset found the streets of Spritton empty except for a few scurrying figures. It was the end of a working day for good Christian citizens and those still in town were making their way home. Midtown, where Peach street met Apple Orchid Lane, the Winthrop Negro Brokerage Company building bared witness to sparse activity. The towns reputable Negro Dealers housed a sales office, show rooms and holding pens that took up an entire block on one side of Peach street. A sign over the front entrance professed the finest dealers in Negro sales. Peach street and Apple Orchard lane was the center of Spritton's mercantile district. Across the street various shops and stores were closing. Proprietors and customers alike were abandoning the district leaving empty stores to the night. But in Winthrops Negro Brokerage Company three guards and a night watchman remained vigilant over it's operations until business the next day.

At the east end of the street Hammonds' wagon sat motionless and inconspicuous. He moved around, pretentiously fussing over the horse and wagon while waiting for the last shop owner to close for the night. No one who saw him paid any attention to the dusty Negro with the wagon loaded with a long crate. When the last proprietor vanished into the darkness at the western end of the block Hammonds whispered into the slightly ajar end of the wooden crate. "All cleah." Slowly the crate lid opened and Kuendela slinked out. He extended a helping hand to Bessie as she did the same. They both stretched to recirculate their blood after being cramped up for so long.

"Where's Winthrops?"

"That's it," Hammonds pointed to the building. "Up dere is the way in." He swept his hands toward the sign on the building at the opposite end of the street. Kuendela's eyes rested upon the large wooden sign proclaiming the Winthrop Negro Brokerage Company. He read the sign aloud and a wave of anger washed over him. To the bonded blacks in the county and the free blacks from out of town who'd heard of it but never saw it, the sign above Winthrops elicited an ominous feeling of dread and distress. The very words "Negro sales" and "dealers" struck their hearts numb bringing to mind a sense of hopeless depravity. Blacks, whenever in town made a conscious effort to go a block out of their way to avoid it. In it's vicinity they avoided even looking at it. Providence and the black population knew it was wrong. A span of a century in time separated Kuendela from it's terrible reality but it did nothing to quell his feelings. He'd seen hundreds of historical pictures depicting auction blocks, posters of slave sales and buildings such as Winthrops and felt the anger that those antiquated images elicited in black people of his time. But to actually be here and experience the ambiance emitted by such arrogance and hatred was too much for his sensibilities. The sight of the sign and all it represented was such a source of discomfort for him he fell against the wagon with his eyes closed. It took a minute for him to compose himself. "You okay, Kendella?"

"I'm all right Bessie.." he replied shaking off the creepy feeling. He turned to Hammonds. "Drive slowly up to the alley beside the holding pens brother. I'm going in. After I do, you and Bessie wait for me to come out." Bessie began to protest, she wanted to go in with him. Kuendela waved her off. "You wait out here Bessie," he ordered sternly enough to ward off any further protest. Hammonds climbed aboard the wagon with Kuendela and Bessie. He drove up the street, slowly as he was instructed. The horse's hooves clopped on the cobblestone street. Their hooves echoed throughout the isolated thoroughfare from end to end. Hammonds pulled the wagon to a stop directly in front of the alley entrance. Here was where the slaves were led in and out of the building. Kuendela and Bessie hopped off after Hammonds pulled the wagon into the holding pen alleyway. Once he came to a stop a night watchman spotted the negro wagoner from a doorway at the end of the alley. The tall thin white man stepped from the building to confront the intruder. "Hold on there boy," he challenged. "Just where the hell do you think you goin wit that wagon!" There was more irritation than alarm in his query. He'd never given serious thought to a nigger being anything back here but a nuisance. Someone trying to liberate a slave from the pens was as ridiculous a thought as he could have, especially a negro rescuer. Since they were employed to watch over those who were already housed in the pens there was no concern to watch out for those who might try to get in.

"Move on there, now boy." he ordered, "before I come over there and tan your hide." He waved the negro away but the wagon didn't move. The failure to comply with his command irritated him further. He stepped toward the wagon to deal with the obstinate Negro, maybe even give him a good thrashing. When he reached the steadfast driver he was suddenly grabbed from behind. He turned around to face his attacker and found himself face to face with another, larger negro. The big black man eclipsed the thinner white man in size as he held a strange looking side arm to his forehead.

"What goes on here..."

"Shut up," ordered Kuendela. The watchman saw a seriousness and determination he'd never seen in a black man's eyes before. Abruptly, he fell silent as his inner gut warned him this nigra was not to be toyed with.

"Now," Kuendela ordered in a slow measured tone. "Tell me. How many men are inside?"

"What! You crazy boy? You better..." Kuendela seized his throat with a free hand and choked off his words. The watchmen's eyes bulged. He could feel the blood pulsating behind his eyeballs. Kuendela loosened his grip enough for a reply to squeeze through. "Ta...two," the watchman stammered in an airy whisper. "If you're lying. I'll kill you," Kuendela promised. There was no hesitation in his words.

"Two!.. I swear. Two."

Kuendela lowered the gun to the watchman's abdomen and pulled the trigger. The sound it made was the last sound the watchman would hear for hours. It was like the thumping of an arrow striking a stuffed leather target. The watchman fell to the ground unconscious. Kuendela rushed to the doorway to make sure no one was coming before he drug the unconscious man inside the entrance. "Wait here," he advised Bessie and Hammonds. "I'll check inside. Then be back for you." He formed his fingers into an OK circle before disappearing into the building.

A short hallway extended from the doorway's entrance to a closed door in the back. Kuendela laid the unconscious man inside the entrance way then crept down the hall and placed his ear to the door. Hearing nothing he twisted the knob and found it unlocked. Quietly he pushed it open and squeezed through. It was an office. A desk and chair were pushed against the far wall. Next to it was a small metal safe. Adjacent to that was a door. Portraits and religious symbols hung on the wall. At the opposite wall was another closed door. Kuendela crept across the floor and pressed his ear to it. He could plainly hear the laughing voices of more watchmen. Faintly he could hear the clinking of chains. Bracing himself he held his breath then thrust himself against the door. The force of his momentum sent the door flying off it's hinges and crashing to the floor in the next room. Two startled white men turned toward the fallen door. One of them sitting in a chair leaped forward while instinctively reaching for a shotgun propped in the corner. The other man, closest to the door, leaped at the intruder. Kuendela crouched under and fired two successive darts into him. The man was unconscious before hitting the floor. The other watchman leveled his shotgun and pulled the trigger. The blast caught Kuendela squarely in the chest and knocked him to the floor.

The front of his jumpsuit was ripped and clawed open from the peppering of lead shot. But aside from a tremendous soreness in his chest, the body armor's absorption of the blast left him unscathed. The shooters eyes widened in disbelief as he witnessed the black mans resurrection. He knew he'd killed him. He saw the man take the full blast of his weapon, yet he rose to his feet in spite of it. Before he could fire again Kuendela nailed him twice with gelatin darts. The watchman's eyes were still wide with bewilderment as he dropped to the floor, unconscious.

Bessie had rushed into the room just in time to see Kuendela cheat death at point blank range. Her mouth was still agape in disbelief when Kuendela turned angrily to reproof her. "I told you to wait outside Bessie!" Her only response was the wide eyed awe of seeing him take a full load of shot and get back up unharmed. If ever she'd contemplated his strength and invulnerability she was sure of it now. This man was some supernatural being. But the immediate danger was over and Kuendela's anger abated into mere irritation. "Bessie." He held her in place with his eyes. "Stay behind me honey, PLEASE!." 'He called me honey,' her eyes exclaimed. She nodded while feeling the ragged material of his shirtfront. When she felt the pellets embedded in his vest she withdrew her hands quickly in surprise. "Take the keys from the watchman. Kuendela ignored her response and pushed open the heavy rusted gate that led into the holding area. Cautiously he entered the large room. It's roughhewn dirt floor was a far contrast to the wooden floor of the guard room. It's bare brick walls held a dank and musty odor that penetrated the nose. At the far end of the area were four cells. Their heavy wooden doors were reinforced with iron. A small slit near the top provided a view of the room inside. In each cell, five to six black men languished in chains. Those who's chains permitted them to reach that far were pressed against the cell doors with their backs to the violence coming from the front of the holding pen. When silence returned they turned toward the door and was too stunned to speak as the eyes of the black man peeking through the five by five inch barred opening scanned the length of their cell. Kuendela didn't see Shai among them. Around the corner were another row of cells. These held one or two slaves a piece. Their occupants strained to see what was going on. Anxiously, Kuendela went from one cell to the other, looking for his lost associate. In the last cell a lone slave sat on the floor, apart from the others. He looked battered and weak. He was the only slave who seemed not to be interested in the melee. He looked familiar in spite of the chains and sallow expression "Shai!" he called to him. Bessie ran to Kuendela's side and peered into the cell. "Shy?" The man turned slowly. His eyes were glazed and hopeless. Kuendela recognized him even in the battered shape he was in. A pang of pity immediately gripped his heart as he again yelled for the young brother. "Shai!!" Slowly Shai looked at the man with dull expressionless eyes. He wondered who he could be. For an instant he thought he knew the man. But how could he? Who could he know in this time and place. But there was something about him. Was it a dream. I've finally lost my mind, he told himself. A tear rolled down his cheeks. His eyes jumbled as the thought of insanity engulfed him. Then a slow veil of recognition replaced the vacuity in his eyes. It came to him! The face was real. It was the face of a friend. A friend from his own time, his own century. He could scarcely believe his eyes. It looked like Calvin...NO...Kuendela. Kuendela! The name reverberated. All the emotions he'd suppressed over the long days and nights poured forth. He wept openly while Bessie gave Kuendela the keys. Shai struggled to his feet, trembling, straining against the length of chain. His shackles clanged with each movement as he gripped the bars of his cell. He could barely control his excitement. "Kuendela!...Kuendela!! Is it really you brother!?! All man! I can't believe it!. I can't fuckin believe it!"

"Hold tight brother. Let's get this door open."

Elated tears flowed. Kuendela tried each key from the ring until the lock sprung open. Inside the cell he repeated the process with Shai's shackles. They fell open, hitting the floor with a bang. Shai and Kuendela embraced while Bessie looked on. She smiled at the true expression of manly emotion they demonstrated for each other. Kuendela noticed the gap in Shai's mouth. "Your tooth man!" It was an awfully painful looking sight. He looked into the young mans eyes. "You look like shit man. They really put it to you. You've been through a lot but you're safe now brother. Shai fell against his liberator and wept openly. "They put it on me no doubt," he cried. "It was terrible man. They broke my ass. Man, those motherfuckers stole my tooth, my dignity, my self worth. Everything man." His voice trembled. "Kuendela, man. This slavery shit is horrible. More fucked up than anyone ever imagined. It's terrible brother. Terrible. They're fucking barbarians! You wouldn't believe what I've seen them do to us man. What they've done to me. They even forced me to..." he choked. Kuendela stopped his testimony and embraced him "Save it Shai. We've got work to do brother. Don't worry about it. I'm returning your self worth right now. This shit is over for you brother. You're goin home!" Shai tried to exhibit more strength than he felt. He pulled himself together for Kuendela's benefit.

"You ready to get out of here?"

"You better believe I'm ready." He noticed Bessie for the first time . "You had help?"

"The best. A real black woman. This is Bessie. I couldn't have done it without her man. Her and a lot of others. Shai there's no wonder we survived in this racist ass country. I've seen first hand the stock we come from."

Shai looked at his fellow captives eyeing the scene from their cells.

"What about them?" Shai asked rubbing the soreness in his wrist.

"Shit! We can't leave them here. What do you say Brother?"

"Let's do it!" They went about unlocking the other cell doors, then unshackled the bondsmen. They didn't force anyone to leave. They left the decision up to them. To their astonishment, some of the slaves chose to remain. Those who wanted their freedom took it. But to all, the two men wished good luck.

Shai leaned weakly on Kuendela and Bessie as they made their way through the holding pen and through the first door then into the office. Before reaching the outer hallway Kuendela and Shai simultaneously took in the safe sitting along the wall beside the desk. They looked to each other and smiled.

"Shai. I know some good folk who could use a stake in the north."

"No doubt." Bessie had no idea what they were talking about. Then she too saw the safe. Taking freedom was one thing but braking into the white man's safe was a little unnerving. She kept her reservations to herself. Kuendela and Shai examined the safe. It was secured by a simple metal pad lock. Kuendela pulled a square package from his utility that contained a length of surgical wire. "This thing can saw through anything."

"Yea," Shai agreed. "Especially anything in this day and age."

Bessie looked on amazed, as the men proceeded to apply the thread. It sliced through the pad lock like a hot knife through butter and in seconds they had the door open. Inside were three shelves. The bottom shelf was the largest. A metal strong box sat tightly in it's space. On the second shelf two small piles of paper currency sat side by side. Legal papers were stacked neatly on the top shelf. Shai picked up the currency and at a quick count announced the total. "$4000. dollars. A lot of cash in this day." Kuendela took the money then turned to Bessie. "A tidy sum for you and Kimbe to get north." Bessie smiled but wouldn't touch it. Kuendela put it away.

"In a couple years that tender won't be worth shit," reasoned Shai.

"Yea I know. But it may come in handy for bribes. What's in this box?" Kuendela pried the rusty metal lid open and both men looked at each other in pleasant surprise. "Gold coins!"

"Look at the seal," Shai pointed.

"But this is only 1852," Kuendela protested. By his estimation it was way too soon for this. He rubbed his fingers across the under side of the lid and felt the raised metal letters. C.S.A.

"They started planning secession long before the war," explained Shai.

"This is a war chest man! These guys are on the inside planning for the Confederacy."

"It's a lot of gold but hardly enough to start a government," Kuendela commented. "They're just beginning to save this shit up," Shai reasoned.

"Well," Kuendela laughed, closing the lid. "There's a monkey wrench in their plans now."

"Taking it won't hurt em but it sure won't help em," chaffed Shai.

"No. But I know who it will help. That paper may not be worth a dam in a few years but this shit is always valuable tender. Anywhere." He continued his examination. "Hey look at this." Kuendela removed a large caliber sidearm he'd spotted on the shelf when the chest was removed. It was in mint condition. "I'm keeping this baby." Shai took it from Kuendela's hand and turned it over, examining the heavy wooden stock and thick metal barrel.

"It's a 44 Colt. A precursor to the peacemakers Samuel Colt made during the Civil War. See this on the stock. It's for attaching a rifle stock." He broke it down. It swung on a hinge like a miniature shotgun. "It's loaded."

"Good," Kuendela replied taking the weapon and handing it to Bessie.

"Let's get the gold and roll!" The chest wasn't very large but it was heavy. It took both Shai and Kuendela to carry it. Bessie followed behind mutely, clutching the gun to her bosom. While the trio removed the chest from the building the slaves who elected to emancipate themselves filed past. Kuendela, Shai, and Bessie came out behind them and made their way to the waiting wagon. Hammonds greeted the new comer with an extended hand.

"You must be Shy?" His nostrils flared with a deep breath. "You okay Bessie?"

"Yea Hammonds. We just freed everybody in the pen," she laughed.

"Yea I seen em," he nodded. "Miss Clara will be glad ta hear it but she gon cuss when she hear they ain't got no plan."

"They had they choice Hammonds. Some us would rather die on the run then let a chance at freedom go by."

"Amen," agreed Hammonds. "What's that yall carryin." He turned to the two men. "We just made a sizable withdraw my brother," Kuendela laughed.

"Brother." Shai took Hammond's hand. "I'm certainly glad to meet you. I appreciate the help."

"We ain't out chere yet," Hammonds warned." Tell me that when we's safely out a town," Hammonds' motioned them toward the back of the wagon. They placed the chest inside the crate then hopped in the wagon beside it. It was a tight squeeze. Hammonds draped a large canvas over them and jumped into the driver's seat. Beneath the blankets Kuendela could still see the bright almond shapes of Bessie's eyes staring reverently at him. He wondered idly if he should be worried about getting her to Kimbe in the midst of the alarm their actions most assuredly will create. He lift the edge of the canvas and peeked out. "The quickest way out, Brother Hammonds." Hammonds turned onto the street and headed out of town via the nearest exit.

*****

On their way through town much to their satisfaction they saw no one except the run aways on the streets. No one in town, it seemed, heard or responded to the shots inside Winthrops. Once outside of town Hammonds steered the wagon toward the cover of the forest. Kuendela, Bessie and Shai emerged from beneath the blanket and smiled at their

357

success. Then to their dismay gunshots rang out in the distance. "Sounds like the alarm has been raised."

"No doubt," Shai agreed, "I hope none of those brothers'll get killed man. You know their chances are next to nil. Long shots at best."

"I Know. But a small chance is better than no chance at all. Whatever happens I think they've decided it's worth the risk. Those who took it are hip to that." Kuendela shook his head. "The suffering never stops in America does it?" "

"I just hope we haven't released the frogs just to fatten the snakes. They're too easy to detect and probably don't no which way to go."

"A find time to think of that. But I saw their faces Shai. They were happy just for the shot at freedom." He looked at Bessie. She remained silent.

"We read about this shit, Brother, but there's a lot we've forgotten about the experience." Shai revealed.

"We've been snoozed by the little progress we've made. If only our people in our time understood the reality of the sacrifices our forefathers have made...Are making," Kuendela corrected himself on the tense. "Not just acknowledgment of their history but the true gist of their struggle, man. They deserve constant recognition. We've forgotten a lot and have taken much for granted Shai."

Hammonds gritted his teeth. "Them white folks gonna catch em all befo daybreak." Bessie looked at the two men. The quartet rode on in silence. Each in their own thoughts as the town faded from sight.

*****

A night sky filled with stars hung vigilant over the horse drawn wagon as it rumbled without incident down a lonely dirt road. Shai could feel the cool night air on his face. He inhaled deeply. For the first time since he'd been stranded he had a smile on his face. His ordeal seemed just about over. He was sure, at least that from this point on he would die before going back to slavery. "Our people haven't forgotten what these folks went through. They remember the event. They just lost memory of the pain. The spirit of the struggle has been lost to our time. Too many of us think this part of our history is irrelevant. We've gotten complacent in our nitch in the white man's world. You know? In fact. We've settled for our world being white. The commonality of experience has held these people together. That's what's gone from our time man. The common experiences that bind us together are gone. Too many of us have abandoned unity for acculturation." Kuendela looked at Bessie in response to Shai's statement. "I'll never forget it. I've learned a lot here Shai. A lot more than I'll ever be able to read in a history book." Kuendela shook his head in sincerity. "What the brothers and sisters of our time need to do is visit this era in history. Take an excursion. You know? Just to observe what's going on. Or better yet, maybe they should experience it the way we have."

"Yea. Maybe the 19th century white man's lash on their ass instead of on their 21st century minds would wake them up."

*****

It was after midnight when they reached a furrowed fork in the road. Kuendela scrambled across the back of the wagon to the front seat. Hammonds brought it to a stop. The sound of insects performing their orchestrations in the night accented the silence while the two men stared at each and Kuendela tried to find the appropriate words of appreciation. He intended to dismount with Shai and Bessie so that Hammonds could push on to keep his date with his wife. But to his surprise Hammonds hopped down from the wagon. "You folks keep the wagon. Miss Clara said for me to see that yall is takin care of. Ain't nothin more I can do frum heah but I can make sure ya get a good start to where ya goin."

"Thanks Brother Hammonds." Kuendela wondered about his safety.

"What about your boss? Won't he question you about the wagon? I wouldn't want you jammed up."

"Don't worry bout ole Hammonds. I know how ta handle Mr. Jim Smith." He faked a startled expression. "Well I be. Looks like somebody done gone and stole my wagon in town. I be doggone." He laughed. Kuendela leaped to the ground, grabbed Hammonds by the hand and shook it gratefully. "I won't forget what you've done for us Hammonds. You really done good tonight. Good luck my brother."

"Good luck to yall." With that he turned and sprinted off in the night. His smile faded as he trekked through the night. He'd spoken with more assurance than he felt, still he saw it necessary to grant them the appurtenances of the wagon. It was good to help his fellow bondsman it created a feeling of satisfaction all it's own.

Hammonds was still in sight when Bessie and Shai climbed down from the wagon. "Your turn Bessie," exhaled Kuendela. "I promised Kimbe I'd get you to the underground station." He turned from her eyes and climbed into the wagon seat then grabbed the reins. "It's been a rough day for you Shai. Climb in the back and get some rest." Bessie climbed aboard beside Kuendela and laid her head on his shoulder. Kuendela whistled, clucked his tongue and flicked the reins twice. No response. "How do you start this dam thing." Bessie giggled. "You caint drive a wagon!?!" He shook his head no. Bessie laughed then took the reins from him. After two clucks of her tongue and a snap of the reins they were off to a slow and easy pace. Shai raised his eyebrows coltishly at the couple sitting together in the driver's bench. It was easy to see that deep feelings had developed between them. Something beyond platonic or alliance was bursting at the seams. He shimmied into a comfortable position in the back of the wagon and closed his eyes.

"I'm going to miss you Bessie," Kuendela confessed at a whisper.

"Im'a miss you too Kendella." Her voice trembled. She clutched the talisman around her neck. "I know where you'll always be though. Right here." She patted her chest where the talisman hung. After a long moment she finally asked. "Kuendela," she began sheepishly. "Why caint you come wit us..."

"Shhh.. Bessie." He covered her mouth with his fingers. "It's impossible, baby." He'd called her baby and it made her smile. "You must believe me," he continued. "I'd love to come with you or better yet take you with me. As much as I want to do these things, baby. I can't." He stumbled over his words. "I don't belong here in your time Bessie and you don't belong in mine."

"My time?" wondered Bessie.

"What I..." It was Bessie's turn to stop him. "Don't say nothin else Kendella. I believe you. What's more I believe in you" She could see his pain too. "Somehow I know if you could you would...This all seem to be happening for a reason. I don't know why but it's all right. Everything is all right." There was still disappointment in the understanding she professed. There would always be an empty space in her heart for the man she'd only known for a score of hours. Though time enough to fill her heart with wonderful memories. Memories of many lifetimes. They kissed. Sweetly. "I'll always remember what you taught me." They rode on in silence. There was no reason to explain further. An inexplicable pact had developed. It would grow and be passed on for generations.

*****

By dawn the roadway had disappeared. They now navigated the forest on spec over untrampled ground. At a tree line before a clearing Bessie stopped the wagon and hopped off. She was tired. So very tired. Kuendela too. He hopped down to stand beside her. Shai was stirred awake by the wagon coming to a halt. He sat up. "What's up?" Kuendela and Bessie stared straight ahead, saying nothing.

Something up ahead had stopped and stunned them in their tracks. Shai looked in the direction of their stare. Now he saw it too. Billowing smoke swirling skyward from what had once been Whitten's farm. Kuendela and Bessie started moving towards the scene. Shai leaped down from the wagon to join them. "What in the hell happened here? Is this the place?" asked a worried Kuendela. "I don't see anyone." The pained look on Bessie's face answered his question. "Ye.. yea," she stuttered. "Th.. this is the place." Secretly she hoped by some magic it wasn't. But it was, and she knew it. Tears welled in her eyes. Kuendela felt bad for her. He wished there was some way he could ease the pain he knew she was feeling.

"Dam!!" observed Shai. The sight of more destruction filled his eyes with angry tears. "Dam! Dam! Dam!" He smashed his fist against the side of a tree. They walked slowly through the destruction. There was no one to be found. Living or dead. Inside the house it was the same. In one room a gaping hole in the wall revealed the hiding place once used by the fugitives. Inside that small clandestine space a chair sat in the center of the floor. Spattered blood stains radiated from it in all directions. Beside the chair Shai picked up a box dripping with molasses. The awful ordeal of Joe the slave caused him to stagger. "Someone was tortured here," he told them. "How you figure?" asked Kuendela. Shai's eyes glazed over with the horrible memories of the bug box. "I'll tell you later." He tossed the box to the floor. All through the house broken furniture cluttered the rooms. Dishes were sprawled over the floors. Shai went through the back door. He saw the burning barn and something stretched out on the ground between the barn and the woods.

"There's a body out here!" An intuitive pang of revelation stabbed at Bessie's heart. She raced through the house and out the door to the body. The anguish started deep in the bowls of her gut and mushroomed to the tips of her lips when she saw it. "Mahhhhhhh!!!" she wailed. Her hands clasped to her face muffling her scream. "Mahh!!" She fell to her knees beside Kimbe's body. Kuendela stood consolingly behind her. He was helpless to do anything to help her now. He gently caressed her shoulders as she wept uncontrollably. Her shoulders heaved with every sob. Her first meet with Kuendela came to mind. She remembered how he did something that brought Noah back to life and the way he recouped after taking a fusillade of lead shot. Shots that tore other men in half, Kuendela had brushed off like flies. And Noah she thought excitedly. Noah, Kuendela breathed life back into him when he drown. She spun to Kuendela with despair laden hope in her eyes. He instinctively knew her expectations. It was all in her eyes to read. The desperation and hope, the very confidence he hated to impede but he knew it would be a useless endeavor. Kimbe was too far beyond the veil of death.

"Kuendela!" was all that escaped her lips. He felt utterly helpless and inadequate. So much would he love to restore the ether of life to Mah...for Bessie...But it was useless and now...Bessie knew it. It was in his eyes for her to see. "Oh God," she cried, extending her arms to the heavens.

"God," she pleaded. "Rain down on me and give me strength." She was helpless, hopeless. Lost to what she could do. Her whole world was sprawled out on the ground of Whitten's farm. Behind her the barn continued to blaze. The crackle and pop of fire did nothing to drown out her sorrowful pleas. It only bathed the saddened scenario in strobe like brilliance. "Help me...Help me Please," she continued to cry, shaking her balled fist toward heaven. Behind them Shai spotted the small boy's head peeping through the bush. The little boy stood up and walked trance like toward the trio. His small expressionless face hedged a rueful lump of sympathy in Shai's throat. Premonition identified him to Shai as the dead woman's son. "How he must hurt," grieved Shai. He was reminded again of all the pain and grief he'd witnessed since his sojourn in antebellum America. Bessie raised her head and saw Noah. She ran to him. "Noah, Noah!" she sobbed. She held him tight. Noah never changed his expression. His face remained numb and featureless. Deadpan...In shock.

All the inimical scenes they'd encountered came to Kuendela's mind as he watched the two grief stricken relatives. Bessie turned to Kuendela, her face awash with tears. "Kendella. If anything happens to me. Please promise me you'll take Noah with you." Kuendela's protestation was only facial. He could not form the words to speak against her request. Finally all he said was, "Bessie I..."

"Kendella. If something happens to me promise you'll take him with you. Noah will be alone. I want him to grow up where he can be a man. If a colud man can grow up to be like yall it got to be a betta place than this. Promise me please." Kuendela nodded his head. "Yes Bessie." He could not say no.

"But we'll make sure nothing happens to you."

"You caint promise that honey. Please don't try." Noah lifted his head from Bessie's chest. The gist of their conversation dawned on him. "I'ma stay wit you Bessie." His face was covered in tears and mucous. "Noah you do as I say. Somethin might happen ta me. It's a awful truth chile but it's somethin we got ta be prepared for. There ain't nothing but dyin here. And if I get killed. I want to know you in good hands. So if thing come ta worse you go on with Kendella like I say. You hear me."

"Yes Bessie." The weight of the violence that is antebellum bared down on his young mind. Pulling his innocent soul apart.

*****

Kuendela and Shai went about the sad task of interring Kimbe. They dug a shallow grave and placed her body in it then covered her with soil. Bessie said a brief but emotional prayer. Kuendela decided they should return to Fall Point. There they could decide what to do to help Bessie and Noah before he and Shai transported back to their own time. With the gold and the money it was, at least, a foundation for a plan. The mourned quartet boarded the wagon. They made the entire trip in silence. Kuendela struggled with the pendular urge to take or not take Bessie and Noah back to his time. But there was the protocol. He had to decide against it with all the pragmatic will he could muster.

*****

Upon discovery of the break out, Sheriff Pickett raised the alarm throughout Aiken County. Twelve slaves were recovered and returned to the holding pens almost immediately. Three more were shot and killed. Two were still at large. Never in the history of antebellum had such an outrage been committed upon a broker/dealer holding establishment. Every slave holder in the county was completely flabbergasted by the incident.

It had been a long night. By the time things had settled down the white men were all dead tired. But for Sheriff Pickett there was no time for rest. Not yet. His investigative nature needed satisfaction and it would not be put to rest until he had some answers. He elected to interview Winthrop's watchmen while the events were still fresh in their minds. It was really more of an interrogation. Sheriff Pickett found many particulars intriguing with respect to the description of the attacker. But he was very interested in the white men he knew had to be at the heart of this outrage. He was sure more abolitionists were at work here, advising and stirring the Negroes to rebellion. Far more than the Quaker abolitionist already known to them. There was too much violence involved for him to be a part of this particular affair. No, these agents, whoever they are, and the entity they represents could not be taken for granted. They were organized, resourceful and dangerous.

Jim Smith and John McPacker returned to town with George in tow. They threw him into Winthrop's pens with the other slaves captured at the farm. George staggered across his cell. His body ached from the pain of torture and exhaustion but his honor remained in tack. McPacker's methods had proven unsuccessful in getting George to reveal any information. He may have been broken in body but he was redeemed in spirit. George had stood up to the best that McPacker could inflict. Now he laid on the stone floor in a cell along side the other recaptured slaves, hurting from head to toe. George's fellow companions were tired and sore from their trek back to town as well. The return to bondage had left them dispirited. But the anger the white men displayed over George's resistance offered the apprehended slaves, at least, a bit of solace. George's resolve gave him some relief from his aching back and torn purulent feet and he finally drifted off to sleep.

Jim Smith and McPacker drug their weary bodies to the office where Sheriff Pickett apprised them of the events that had gone on at Winthrops while they were out raiding the Whitten's farm. "By the Saints," complained McPacker. "How much more of this devilment can we take, Abram? Nigh Jim Smith's boy kithed. We are at a lost."

"Well," Sheriff Pickett added flatly. "We can add robbery to the blackguards sins." Everyone turned towards the sheriff, not sure of what he meant. "They stole the holdings from Winthrops safe," he reported. "Just when it seemed we'd broken the back of this epidemic, this malady is added to the broth."

"They won't last a fortnight now that we have the white traitorous dog that's been leading them."

"No," replied Sheriff Pickett. "This Whitten's not the one. An agent perhaps but not the leader of this conspiracy. No Jim, he's just the neck. We have a little more reaching to do to get the head. Somewhere in our county these nigras are receiving refuge. A cave, a swamp. There is someplace where they hide until signaled to rendezvous. There is some place where this abolitionist dog has found sanctuary and I want to know where it is."

"We'll find it," proclaimed Jim Smith. "We're getting close. I know it. This white man, whoever he is, will soon reap the wrath of his victims. Has the council been notified about the breakout? The Colonel and the others will be hell bent on ravaging this dirty dog even more now."

"My man should be back at his estate by now and Winthrop is on his way." Sheriff Pickett leaned against the wall with his arms folded. "Here's something that should interest you McPacker." He beckoned to one of the watchman, waiting patiently on the side. "Tell him Seth. Tell him about the gun." Seth, the first watchman who'd been overpowered by Kuendela approached them dizzily, still groggy from the effects of the gelatin projectile. "Well Mr. McPacker," he began slowly gathering his thoughts. "It was the darndest thing ever happen to me. That nigger shot me. Or so I thought." He lifted his shirt and pointed to the red and swollen area on his abdomen. "He shot me right here with some fool gun with no blast. But whatever it was it put me out. Like that." He snapped his fingers. "The devil you say. It's the same heathen blackamoor who killed Virgil. Has to be. Tis the same weapon."

"That's right," nodded Sheriff Pickett. "It's the same kind of weapon Luke described. It's the same damn thing he was hit with."

"What do you make of this boy, Abram?" Jim Smith wondered. "You think he knows that this gun of his doesn't work and that he's leaving witnesses?"

"Couldn't be that he doesn't want to kill..."

"By the Saints NO!." McPacker pounded the table. "If that be the case my brother would be alive. Aye!" McPacker's eyes fell upon Burl Johnson, the other watchman sitting quietly in the corner. "What of his testament to the affair." Sheriff Pickett looked at the man contemptuously. "He has nothing to add that would aid us." The man lowered his eyes to the floor. His recollection of blasting the black man to the floor with a full load of lead shot only to see him rise unscathed was just too preposterous an account to hear again. Sheriff Pickett had completely discounted his claim. No one else had witnessed the act. Though the shotgun was found to have been fired, Sheriff Pickett assumed the man simply fired blindly before falling unconscious from the same unusual weapon that befell the others.

"It's a strange affair in any case," Sheriff Pickett inferred. "This blackguard of ours is blessed with a wealth of resources. He's getting a lot of help and not just from the nigras. We have to locate this leader. By God he'll have the whole population of nigras in revolt. There is no way to keep all this quiet. We've got to find someone who will reveal this bastard to us." All the banter suddenly drove a spark of revelation to Jim Smith and he snapped his fingers. "That sly devil," he said more to himself than to his colleagues.

"You have something Jim?"

"I'll say," he smiled. "Remember that nigra on the road with the wagon."

"Yea," Pickett said. "One of yours wadn't it."

"That's just it," he said. "One of mine. And it seems that ONE OF MINE is always somewhere in the midst of these outrages. Trails to Fall Point. Caesar's trails to Whitten's farm. Now this breakout in town on a night when one of my nigras is riding into town. Always one of my nigras somewhere near. And," he walked to the wall where a map of the county hung and pointed. "...through it all Angora sits in the middle. Just like a base of operations. Look at it with a military eye." Arthur Charles, the senior watchmen from Winthrop's, broke out in raucous laughter. "Something funny, Arthur?"

"Ah come on Jim. Ain't no white man on Angora helpin these niggers. If that's their base of operations then some nigger has gotta be leadin em. You give these coloreds too much credit."

"I think you don't give these nigras enough credit. I think we're gonna have to have a talk with ole Hammonds."

"Ah come now," insisted Arthur the unbeliever.

"No, no," waved McPacker. "No! You haven't trailed these buggers as I have. Tis the only way to look at it that hasn't been employed as yet. By the Saints you're right again Jim Smith."

Sheriff Pickett stepped forward. He too was interested in the idea though he held to his theory of a white master planner. Yet he admitted, this Hammonds could be the best link to the elusive white man thus far. For now there was time to rest. Pickett was tired as were the others and he wanted to be sharp in this coming interrogation. Having the authority to decide he spoke up to champion the thoughts of all the men. "Why don't we all grab a few hours sleep. Then we'll meet at Colonel Richards and put this boy to the rack. We have all the time we need now to end this thing once and for all."

"Good idea Abram."

*****

Word spread fast throughout the region. By mid-afternoon the nights developments were known to everyone in the county. Most disturbed by the affair were those immediately affected. Winthrop, Colonel Richards, Henry Clanston, Thomas Belfield and the rest of Aiken Counties most prominent slavers were all personally affected by what was now being called a northern abolitionist conspiracy. Though most of the fugitives had been captured the breakout at Winthrop's holding pen bore a bad mark on it's reputation and the security of the township. The rash of escapes in the county were bad enough but now saddled with news of the Winthrop breakout and Virgil's death, panic now spread across the entire state. It seemed the coloreds now displayed an unmitigated audacity and gaul in liberating county slaves directly from the county's pen's. And the worst of outrages, county money from the county's most prominent slave dealing institution. Very, very bad for business, observed Winthrop. Equally bad for ones reputation, Colonel Richards observed further.

The small group of men converging on Colonel Richards front portico were some of the wealthiest men in Spittle County, the elite of the slave holding community. A few of the men sat around the marble table as the availability of chairs allowed. Others stood. "I just can't believe these darkies could formulate such an intricate undertaking," Colonel Richards protested. "Especially my niggers. NO they have help from some misguided white fool. I'd bet a years harvest on it." He went on, spitting on the tip of his cigar to secure the ashes. "The confiscation of our secession holdings would implicate to me absolutely, that we're dealing with northern abolitionist. I believe a northern conspiracy is the main problem afoot here." He looked around to see if they were taking in his theory. "There's no way to convince me that these nigras could commit such atrocities alone without the help of some white man. They are innately incapable of aggregating the necessary components to network." He seemed to be trying to convince himself. Jim Smith's theory that the epidemic's base of operation could be centered at Angora was a further stain to his opinion and reputation. He looked around the room for allies to support his protest. "Would you agree Major Jackson."

Major Clive Jackson, a stout, beefy faced, gray bearded plantation owner responded with a nodding affirmation. He fancied himself a student of anthropology and long held the belief of the Negroes inferiority. So any opportunity to confirm it had his full support. Jim Smith rolled his eyes, silently opining evidence to the contrary. He held his comment to himself.

"With all that has happen here to fore," spoke McPacker incredulously,

"I'm not sure how far I'd underrate these heathens, by Eire."

Colonel Richards sat at the table between Winthrop and Thomas Belfield lighting a second cigar. Being the proprietor of the meeting place and the most respected and affluent among them he emerged as the unofficial leader, or at the very least the conscience of the concerned parties.

"Gentlemen," he stated standing. "There are several considerations before us." He took a long pull on his cigar. "We all know what's at stake here. Our business. Our way of life and our families welfare. We're faced with grave outrages bound to burgeon into atrocities that will threaten the very fabric of our southern way of life Gentlemen, if we don't put an end to this affair. Now Sheriff Pickett and Jim Smith here," he indicated each man with a wave of his hand, "are close at determining that end." He walked through the gathering of men to the edge of the portico and leaned over the railing eyeing the layout of his beloved Angora. "It's a grave business indeed. They've influenced our slaves, murdered a citizen and ransacked our savings toward liberty. That gold was our seeds to secession. To liberate ourselves from the accursed northern abolitionists." He pointed with his cigar grasped firmly between two fingers. "All this!!" he yelled, "is in dire need of redemption." He turned back to face the men. His grim face was a tight mask of contempt. All eyes followed him as he returned to his seat. "This must end...NOW!!"

"Here! Here!" shouted Henry Clanston. His small plantation had lost several slaves in the last six months. "The seditious white man who has aided these Negroes to go about traversing the county absconding our slaves will burn in hell when we've seized upon him. No expense is too great to obtain his apprehension."

"I think we make too much of who is at the center of this affair," commented Thomas Belfield. His plantation was as large as Angora but he owned only ninety three slaves. "Be he black or white, what is important is that we cut off the head of this conspiracy. I can hardly sleep at night knowing that their might be a rebellion brewing among the slaves on my own land. Slaves who I've given all the freedoms a Christian man could grant and holds my family's very lives in their hands."

"It's insurrection is what it is," cried Arthur Winthrop in his high whining voice, proving to be more of an example of hysterics then anything else. Since he'd learned about the brake in his building he'd exhibited every emotion of consternation including crying and hiccups. The war chest's disappearance during the brake upset him the most, seemingly more than the breach to his dealership. Being absolved of responsibility by his colleagues seemed to be of little compensation to his wounded southern ego and pride.

"Colonel Richards is right," added Major Jackson whose tobacco plantation had lost three slaves thus far. "The coloreds could not come up with this type of outrage alone. Not without the guidance of those dam abolitionist anarchist!" He pounded his fist curtly on the table. Cigar smoke snaked a trail around and over Colonel Richards head as the meeting went on. "Sheriff," he beckoned with a flippant wave. "What do you make of this weapon this niggra's been usin." Sheriff Pickett placed a coffee cup on the table. He pushed back the sides of his waistcoat. "I had discounted Whitten's involvement in this part because of his beliefs but this weapon forces me to amend my thoughts of this whole affair," he stated matter of factly pointing an index finger to target his point. "Whitten's a quaker. They abhor violence. Somehow they've rigged some sort of blow gun sedative to avoid actually killing someone.."

"If that's true," someone added. "What of Virgil's death."

"These nigras are unpredictable," replied the Sheriff. "They caint be depended upon to apply civil restrictions."

"Seems to me, a lot of trouble," remarked James Belfield. "Unnecessary trouble to boot. Besides, if they are so God fearing why would they give so much time to these blasphemes acts of stealing our property in the first place."

"To me that implies the hand of a northern white anarchist," replied Colonel Richards still defending his theory. "Who else would recognize the importance of our holdings."

"Here, here. But what of this weapon?" reiterated Winthrop. "It intrigues me, And what kind of sedative could cause unconsciousness so...so suddenly," he whined.

"It may be some kind of vegetable alkali," lectured Major Jackson. "When I was in England I attended the lecture of an explorational society. There I heard an explorer of the eastern jungles of Africa speak of such a thing. It seems that a tribe of eastern natives dipped their arrows in a concoction made from some local plant secretions that had the properties of rendering the animal pierced with its mixture, unconscious." Winthrop broke in with another question, remembering the incredible incident told to him by his watchman. "What about Burl," he sputtered. "He claims to have hit the black devil with a solid round of lead shot. Burl says he brushed them off like they were fruit flies."

"I think Burl might have overstated the events some," interjected Sheriff Pickett. "I mean come now. I admit there are strange doings here but common sense has to account for something. I think Burl just missed his target."

"From just a few feet!?!"

"Repose yourself Winthrop," reproofed Major Jackson angrily. "Are you buying such dribble that we have been violated by some preternatural niggah? Sir please."

"Quite right," agreed Colonel Richards, "A strange fellow this nigra but hardly supernatural. Besides it would hardly do to have such prevarication spreading through the region and exciting the imagination of the good people of our community. They have enough to worry about without the added burden of spotting a preternatural blackguard behind every cupboard. Nor do we want to enable the nigras with the same superstitions. They are a gullible race but it is only useful to us if we fabricate the guile." He spit on the end of his cigar. "Yet I will admit just between us that this nigra like my nigra, whom he gambled so much to abet, intrigues me. He is smart, agile and has little fear of white men. It's as though he and his cohort are alien to the land and neither of them seems to know his station."

"Strange, unholy or no," averred McPacker. "He and his cohorts are answerable for the murder of my brother. And they're all to pay."

Colonel Richards turned to the one person whose plans had brought them this far. "Where is this refuge located," he demanded looking to Jim Smith. "I understand Mister Whitten died before any useful information about it could be obtained."

"Yes. It seems his constitution could stand no more."

"We have a theory as to its location," Sheriff Pickett interjected after a sip of coffee. "Our reckoning leads us to believe it lies in the vicinity of Fall Point. We have a nigger in mind who might be able to shed more light on it's location." He nodded to Jim Smith "That's right Colonel. He's the only nigra accounted for that night. So that makes him our prime suspect." Sheriff Pickett nodded his head in agreement.

"Okay Jim,' stated the Colonel. "You said we were near the end of this affair. Let's have it." Jim Smith's expression was confident. Ever the schemer he was way ahead of them. He wondered about the sighting of Hammonds that night. The man's trek into town on that night, at that time, bothered him. Spritton, though known in the area for it's contemporary fashions and willingness in some cases to allow negro patrons with proper passes, was a considerable distance in the opposite direction. Even though circumstances would explain why a colored would elect to travel so far out the way. Hammonds just didn't strike Jim Smith as being one of such sentimentality. He began his inferences thoughtfully. "I believe Hammonds is next key to our problem gentleman. That ole niggra's being in town last night just gives me an itch I can't scratch." He pounded his fist in his hand. "What part he plays in it I am unsure. But I will get the location of the nigger refuge out of him and when I do we can bag the whole affair."

"You've said this before Jim."

"I did Colonel. I admit. I too underestimated the depth of this conspiracy. I thought we had the thing done. But now we are on the top rung of the ladder. All we need do now is step aboard. I'm convinced that once we lay siege to the location we will have back the gold. We will have the killer and any niggers at large and the captain of this ship of conspiracy." He smiled at his own maritime analogy. "Have faith," Jim Smith implored. "I will get the location of this dam refuge out of Hammonds or there will be hell to pay."

"The cost may be yours Jim," warned the Colonel between puffs. "But we are with you. Let's interrogate Hammonds and see if we can scratch that itch of yours." Standing up and pulling back his chair Colonel Richards invited the group to follow. He led them from the portico, across the grounds askew of the mansion until they sidled a row of work houses several yards from the field. The small group proceeded across the plantation at a leisurely pace resembling an afternoon promenade of friends parading the grounds. Their relaxed countenance was just the opposite of their blood lustful purpose.

"He's a valuable smith," admitted Colonel Richards watching the fire in McPacker's eyes, "but cooperation is the only thing that will save him from the gallows."

"Nothing will save the murderer, though. Nothing," stated Sheriff Pickett.

"This contumacious rascal has guile whoever he is," Major Jackson continued on Pickett's theme.

"The abolitionist bastard abetting him will burn in hell for his turpitude," Colonel Richards insisted, throwing his cigar to the ground mashing it beneath his foot. .

*****

In spite of the languishing misery there was still reason for exhilaration in what they'd accomplished thus far. Shai expressed it best when he first peaked into the sanctuary at Fall Point. "Damn! This is tight!" He barreled through the aperture scanning the expanse like a child looking over the toy section in a department store. "Historically this is a significant site!" he exclaimed. "One hundred years from now the artifacts here will be priceless in historic value." Kuendela could hear his voice from the ledge. It was well to see that Shai was shedding more and more of the despondent cast he'd worn in the slave pen. Though; Bessie's slow gait and Noah's despondent shuffle worried him. How much atrocity can a person withstand he mused. "Fucking dirty racist bastards," he spat the words out like a bad taste. Shai returned to the berm to help Kuendela with the chest. One look at Bessie left him rueful over his enthusiasm. Kuendela kneeled to the ground with the metal box and pushed it until it teetered on the crest of the ledge as Shai supported it from below. After jumping down beside him they pulled the chest unto the berm and dragged it through the aperture to a far corner near the stream where he and Shai decided to bury it.

"Have a look at this Bessie," Kuendela called. Bessie approached as Shai pulled back the lid and Kuendela guided her eyes toward it's contents. "Thas gold?" Her mouth dropped open like her chin was weighted with the gold itself. "You better believe it. And it's all yours and Noah's." Bessie put her arms around Noah as he straggled beside her. The sight of the precious metal had no effect on him. Her mind, however, went into high gear. Keeping the white man's gold was an added burden she wasn't sure she was ready to carry. Kuendela touched her face. "Don't worry Bessie. They'll never find it here and they'll never know that you have it."

The two men began digging behind a calcified pile of rocks. Using Shai's knowledge of history, they'd already formulated a plan for them. They gave Bessie enough incidental and geographical information to stay out of the clutches of slavery and how and when to tender the gold. "You can't travel with this gold yet," Kuendela instructed. "Remember I told you a war was coming." She nodded mutely. "Well, you're going to leave it here until then. Just a few years. When it's safe you and Noah can come back and be set for life." After a few exhausted grunts he stopped digging momentarily. "Bessie. You still believe in me. Don't you?"

"Yes Kendella I believe in you," she nodded.

"Good, baby. Then believe me now when I tell you that the white folk will never find this gold. Even if they find this cave they won't get this gold. They're gonna be looking for somebody to spend this gold but they won't find anyone because you're going to leave it here for ten years."

"Ten years!?! Kendella I caint just stroll down heah afta ten years." He held her hands again. "Bessie yes you can. Trust me when the war starts..." He waved off the obvious outburst. "You and Noah can reach Fall Point safely because we're going to tell you just how and when to come get it."

"You gon come back and show us."

"No Bessie I'm going to tell you now."

"But how you gon..."

"Bessie." She fell silent. "You believe in me?" Bessie lowered her eyes then looked at him again. "Yeah," she replied softly. "It's gonna seem like a long time but you'll both be young enough to use it and enjoy it. So do exactly as I say." She shook her head consensually. Noah's face remained buried in her stomach. "When you're ready to use this money no one will be able to touch you. The gold will be yours. No one will be able to trace it or prove otherwise. It'll be enough to carry generations of Bessie's and Noah's," he smiled.

"It ain't enough to stop the pain Im feelin now," she said seriously. He embraced them both. "I know. But it will help you and Noah fulfill Kimbe's dream." Bessie looked up at him and began weeping in heaving sobs.

*****

In less than an hour the hole was completely dug. The chest was placed in, bordered with shale, then covered with dirt. Kuendela poured water over the freshly covered mound to even it with the terrain. "We should get some sleep. There's nothing else we can do now." Shai gathered some of the rags and a blanket brought in from the wagon and laid down on it. Bessie had long pulled out the still inflated mattress Kuendela gave her and carried Noah to it. He was fast asleep. Then Bessie sat on the ground beside Kuendela where he'd prepared a cushion of rags and blankets. "I've got an idea," he whispered slowly. "The watchmen at the pen never saw you. The white folks are gonna be searching for the brothers who escaped the pens and dam sure'll be too busy looking for me to pay any attention to a young woman and a small boy in a wagon doing errands for their master." He waited to see how she was taking it. "You've got $4000. dollars cash to travel on. In the morning I'll show you where to hide it and how to spend it. In small amounts," he added. "If we go north and get out of Aiken and Spittle County we should be all right," she reasoned finally sharpening up for her survival like Kimbe would expect her to. Kuendela was glad to see her old self emerge. "Maybe you can keep off the roads.."

"No," corrected Bessie. "No, we'll stay on the roads. White folk don't expect that from colored wit somethin ta hide."

"Is that Kimbe or Miss Clara talking."

"Both," she smiled. Bessie was filled with a rekindled confidence but she still worried about Noah who, as though to illustrate her fears, stirred from his make shift bed and began pacing along the edge of the stream. He stopped and stared into the quiet running water, still unable to erase the ghastly image of his mother's death from his mind. Kuendela came up behind him and embraced his shoulders. "It's not your fault little brother," he said quietly as if reading the young boy's mind. "You couldn't help her Noah. But you can do what she wants you to do." Looking up at Kuendela, Noah's eyes begged the question. "She wants you to be free Noah. She wants you to fight. Not give up and die. She wants you to grow up and raise a family of proud african warriors and teach them what she and Miss Clara and George and Hammonds taught you. And tell them what they all did in this war with America." Noah shut his eyes tightly but the image remained. His eyes filled with tears. "I hate em, I hate em!" he cried.

"I know Noah. But don't let the hate kill you. No. Let the hate sharpen you. You're a fighter lil man. Use that hate to keep you going." Noah turned away from Kuendela. He'd idealized the man from the very start. He turned back to face his hero then fell into his arms, crying. "Yes young brother. That's right. Let it out. Let it out." Kuendela removed his knife and it's sheath and gave it to Noah for a keepsake. Noah gripped it close to his chest and promised to treasure it. "I know you will Little Brother...I know you will. Now get some sleep. You've got a long way to go in the morning." He saw the first smile of the day struggle to find it's way to Noah's face. Then fail.

CHAPTER 14

Year 1852

Naked from the waist up Hammonds stoked the fire in the hearth of his blacksmith's furnace. Sweat dripped from his forehead and rolled down his face and chest to the rope around his waist. He picked up a section of quatrefoil to examine it. One of the leaves was broken, probably by one of the Richards children he assumed. Hammonds decided to solder the leaf then give it to the white workman to replace on the portico railing. So engrossed was he with his work he never heard Caesar enter the shop until he turned to dunk the hot metal in the water bucket. Hammonds sneered when he saw him. It may or may not have been warranted, he wasn't sure. But Hammonds distrusted him immensely and Caesar's duplicitous smile did nothing to mitigate his unwanted obtrusion. Their relationship had been casual at best and not much to formulate upon. Hammonds knew nothing of Caesar's machinations with Jim Smith. His distrust, however, was too instinctual an inclination to dispel. Yet Hammonds decided to return his smile on pretext. Then just as quickly his expression changed as he opted to freely display his scorn. "Whatcha want heah nigger?" Caesar's smile took on the character of a snake. "Jus wanted to do ya a fava boy," he slithered.

"Don't waste yo time," Hammonds snapped tersely. Caesar put his hands on his hips. "I know ya hepped dem niggers run away boy. And da Massa know it to." Caesar then leaned in close to Hammonds ear. "One a dem boys kilt Mista Virgil, you knows dat. Iffen ya tell me wheah dey is.

379

Me and you can split the reward money. Dey pay alot fo dat nigger. Mayhaps you get da money ta buy yosef free." He slapped Hammonds on the back. "Whatcha say ta dat." Hammonds pounded his hammer down on the anvil after sloughing off Caesar's unwanted touch. "I say git yo black, Judas, niggah ass out a my face. I don't know nothin bout run aways and if I did I wouldn't be sellin em out ta the white man. I don't know how you sleeps at night niggah harpin thoughts lak dat. But if you don't git yosef away frum heah Imma put yo Judas ass ta sleep rite naw." Hammonds perpetual furrowed brow was even more pronounced. His nostrils flared with rage. "I sleeps jus find nigga." Caesar retorted through curled lips. He started to leave, then turned to add. "It's dumb niggers like you who make white folks treat colud bad. I'm givin you a chance ta do right but ya jus don't knows it." Caesar backed up towards the smithy opening. "Yall gon rile up the white folk so till dey takes everthing dey gives us away." He threw his hands in the air for one last pitch. "God Almighty tell me wheah dey is an we splits the reward and make Mistah Jim Smith happy. We be in his fava from now on."

'Mister Jim Smith?' the name was an arrow through Hammonds instinctual heart. He had cause to worry now. This Judas bastard clearly worked for the overseer. Perhaps his story to Jim Smith the night before wasn't so convincing after all. Seeing Hammonds anxiety Caesar laid on a knowing smile. "Otherwise you mayhaps be facin Massa's wrath."...There it was. Hammonds had one of two choices. Stay and take his chances or run. In an angry panic, Hammonds opted for the only clear path to survival and pushed Caesar aside. "Get out a my way you Judas niggah." Three steps toward the open door he collided with the white bearded face of Colonel Richards. His tilted mouth was blowing a stream of thick cigar smoke skyward. Hammonds followed the smokey aberration with his head until Colonel Richards brought his eyes back with a haughty condemnation. "Nigger I hope you know I have the power of creation and damnation over your worthless soul. And by God I'm not going to fiddle with queried manipulation. So to the point. If you don't tell us what we want to know." He raised his colt pistol to the side of Hammonds' sweaty face. "I'm going to put a hole in your black wooly head!" Hammonds froze in fear. Finding his voice he managed to eek out a response.

"Suh I, I, swear I don't know..."

"Liar!!" the Colonel yelled and slapped Hammonds roughly across his face. Hammonds was reeled off balance and grabbed on either side by Clem and Jim Smith. Colonel Richards snatched Hammonds by the nape of his neck and placed the colt hard against his temple. "You black bastard. You're gonna tell me what's up there at Fall Point. Those unholy nigras are up there hiding and I want to know where. WHERE!!, blacksmith! Tell me!"

"Colonel!" Jim Smith snapped his fingers. "Wait a minute. Blacksmiths have ta be trained, if you know what I mean. We can't afford to get rid of ole Hammonds right now. In deed, we'd have to train another nigra to blacksmith. But now old mammies," he said slyly, "are expendable." The awful meaning to it's deadly conclusion was not missed on Hammonds. Sweat poured from his head like a faucet. Jim's proclivity for foresight provided them with a leverage chip. He understood the loyalty these coloreds have for their matriarch. He cued two of his subordinates to summon Miss Clara to the scene. In a few minutes they returned with the old woman between them. They snapped her to attention before Hammonds and roughly rocked her from side to side for affect. Jim Smith held a symbolic gun in the form of an obtrusive finger against Miss Clara's temple. Colonel Richards smiled menacingly at Hammonds distress. "Boy I'll ask you again." He drew the words out slowly. "Where's that murderin nigger and his cohorts!" His lips were curled in mock rage. "If you don't tell me or even if you don't know, say good bye to your dear Miss Clara. There's no survival for her save one. Which is it to be boy?" Feeling utterly helpless Hammonds came apart. He looked up in one last hopeless appeal to God but got no satisfaction. Miss Clara's eyes remained anchored to the ground. With no miracle from God, no respite from providence, Hammonds opened his mouth to speak but a sudden sharp look from Miss Clara made him turn his head. The two men flanking him turned his head back.

"Don't you say noth..." Miss Clara's frail body was knocked violently to the ground before she could complete her warning. A wrenching ache twisted Hammonds stomach into a knot as Clem proceeded to kick the old woman repeatedly in the groin causing her to scream out in agony. Seeing her helpless and in pain was a heavy burden. Hammonds broke free from the two men holding him and flung himself atop Miss Clara, to shield her old withered body from the attacks. "No suh! Stop," he yelled. Jim Smith knelt down and placed his pistol to her head. "Enough play Hammonds," he threatened. "Now! Or I kill her." Hammonds rose and stammered in a barely audible, tremulant voice. "F, Fall Point."

"What niggah!!"

"Fall Point. Theah a cave..."

*****

Kuendela and Shai's ordeal seemed close to an end. One obstacle remained though, the few miles between them and the ARC's pad and to see Bessie and Noah safely on their way. His plans for the fugitives journey north was far from fool proof but workable. It was a chance. Sneaking back to Angora to contact Miss Clara was out of the question. It was just too risky, now. Bessie and Noah were on the verge of a new beginning with the money and gold. Their long hard quest for freedom seemed closer to being gained than being lost. But at the moment timing was not a calculable commodity. There was no way to ascertain the possible dangers that loomed for them outside. Kuendela pondered the question. Should they wait until they gathered some intelligence on their imperilment or act with celerity and make a move. Bessie, Shai and even Noah seemed to be looking at him for a decision. "We'll hold up here until tomorrow," he decided. Fall Point thus far had provided them with relative obscurity. There was no reason for a capricious dash into the night. Shai yawned and the act passed from one mouth to the other. In deed, the weight of the last 24 hours bared heavily on all their shoulders. They were exhausted. Kuendela stood at the bank of the stream and stared at the rushing cascade blanketing the open face of the cave and worried for Bessie and Noah. Their future. Strange, he thought. He felt responsible for them but could do nothing to assure their security. He'd known Bessie but a few days yet he loved her but could do nothing to foster it further. He wrestled to understand. This woman exists in a time before he was born and he was going to miss her.

Bessie stood at the far end of the stream beside the buried gold. She held Noah tight against her and blinked away a tear. She loved Kuendela and grappled hard to understand why they had no future together. She could at least, she reasoned, hold on to faith and feel assured that they'd carry their feelings for one another in the realm of heart and mind but would that memory be enough to sustain her? She looked at Noah through the blur of tears. She'd be strong for him. Be strong because Noah needed her to be. Because Kuendela wanted her to be. Poor Noah, she thought. For him there was only grief. Maybe with God's prayer he'll come around and live again.

Shai laid upon his bedding with his eyes shut, afraid to open them. Afraid that Kuendela was just a dream. If he'd open his eyes he would find himself in the damp dingy cell of the slave pens. The roar of the cave stream and waterfall, though, refuted his fears. He smiled. He was going home. He'd rest now and on his return to his time he'd have much to tell.

*****

Miss Clara cried out in agonizing ululation, stricken by more pain then the heel of Clem's boot could ever hope to inflict. Hammonds opprobrious disclosure, as noble as he may have imputed, was a dagger in her heart. It was the end. Paramount to the death of an era. The hidden cave had been a proven operation providing sanctuary to courageous fugitive slaves for years and NOW!, it would be no more. Destroyed by the very people it was designed to outwit. Her heart ached. She would have rather died than to have it's existence forfeited. She looked at Hammonds scornfully, knowing it was his treachery that was going to kill her precious underground's most vital center. Her eyes grew cold but it didn't last. The anguish in Hammonds eyes began to warm her revulsion. The matriarch and mastermind of the most successful underground operation of the time just couldn't foster a shameful vendetta against this man. A loyal and trusted ally. She felt as bad for him as she knew he felt for himself. Her pity though, would never over shadow his own commiserated guilt. Hammonds, after all, had to live with himself from this unfortunate day on.

*****

Colonel Richards sat behind a large brown mahogany desk staring at the cigar he twirled between his fingers. A victorious sneer emerged from beneath the gray speckled beard on his face while his impromptu council stood around him. "We have them gentlemen. We have them." At just that moment Sheriff Pickett entered the room with a sheet of paper in his hand.

"Caution Colonel. We must move with caution." He laid the paper on Colonel Richards desk. "I took the liberty of bringing this along. It's a formal request to the county seat to call up the volunteer militia and release arms from the county arsenal. We can't afford to use a posse of town tenderfoots."

"I'm with Abrams, Colonel," added Jim Smith. "We got all but two runaways from Whittens but we don't know how many more fugitives are hiding out there at Fall Point. Nor do we know the kind of resources this wraith has." Colonel

Richards spun the paper around and signed it without reading it then handed it to Major Jackson who signed it then gave it to Thomas Belfield. All the signatures required to submit.

"How long will it take Abram?"

"We'll be upon them by morning."

A knock on the open door turned everyone's head toward the intruder.

"Excuse me Colonel. Jim, what do we do with the two nigras?"

"Lock em up in the punishment shack."

"The old one too?" Jim Smith looked at the Colonel and received a nod.

"Yea...The old nigger too. We'll take Hammonds here, with us in the morning. And Jim," added the Colonel, "suspend all work and passes today. Confine the nigras to their cabins and arrange for a guard. Gentlemen I suggest you issue orders of the same at your plantations. We can ill afford even a squeak of our revelations or plans. This rebellion is crushed!"

*****

Hammonds and Miss Clara were tossed into the shack with less care than a sack of potatoes. The old matriarch had hardly stopped rolling when Hammonds rushed to her aid. "Miss Clara, what have I done!?! What have I done!?!"

"You give up our sanctuary fo my life Hammonds is what you done." Miss Clara painfully pulled herself to a sitting position with Hammonds help. "Ain't no way ta warn them youngins out there." She groaned with each word. "It's in God's hands now." Hammonds began to bawl like a child in misery. He buried his head in Miss Clara's bosom. His head heaved violently as he sobbed. She held his head tight against her breast cutting off his spastic movements and stroked his head. "Be no greater gift than ta give yo life fo yo fellow man Hammonds. You remember that. Id'a rather died than ta give them peckawoods our sanctuary. But it be done now." A tear rolled down her strong wrinkled, weather

385

beaten cheeks. "We gon have ta start all ova agin cause Fall Point is gone and them po, po youngins gon die."

*****

Kuendela stared at the fading translucent semblance of daylight shining through the waterfall. He hardly noticed the soft touch of Bessie's hand on his shoulder. He turned around. She was staring into his eyes. Kundela reciprocated, looking deep into the soul behind her wide almond shaped brown eyes. There was something there. From her depths an emission of energy emerged, filling him with a surge of collective consciousness. In her he saw a million years of Nubian existence and with that apercu, realized in a cosmic second the cosmogonical reality before him. Bessie returned his gaze and found herself swept inside him. Truth detonated before her in divine revelation and in the twinkling of an eye she understood the higher calling of her African existence. Before her lay the apocalypse of just who she was. She was a Queen. They kissed long and hard and held on to each other for an eternal moment.

*****

Kuendela's moderate snoring hummed in unison with the movement and soft roar of the inner cave stream. It had been a rapturous night. Bessie watched him breath and listened to him snore. She found it amusing and thankful to have something to cheerfully muse over. She got up careful not to rouse him and checked on Noah. He'd spent a restless night beside Shai and now sat by the stream idly staring into the water. Black life was so difficult for a child in America she thought as she hugged him. Like Kuendela said, 'the hardness of life in America can swallow you whole and destroy you if you let it. Or the adversity can make you strong. All you have to do is draw on the things that exist inside you.' An adage of truth, she inferred. Something she could pass on to Noah. She pulled him to his feet and guided

386

him toward the aperture. A walk outside the cave, in the fresh air, would do them both some good while the men slept. Afterwards they could say their goodbyes.

Bessie and Noah crawled out onto the berm then onto the ledge. It was a cool morning, serenaded by melodious birds circling above and perched on the trees abreast the outer stream. Bessie made note of a slight overcast. They started slowly along the precipice while Bessie talked soothingly to Noah. In a soliloquy worthy of an orator she weaved a sermon of healing and confidence, all the while hoping her words would set in motion a process of healing for her distraught nephew. It wouldn't make things right but it could help him come around. After all was said, a moment of silence lingered then passed. "Looks like it's gonna rain, huh Noah?"...Silence. "Things'll get betta fo us honey. Jus wait an see. When we get up north we gon get us a little house up theah in one a them neighborhoods wheah theah's lots a people like us."

"What you mean Bessie?" Glad to hear him speak, she hugged him. It was the first sign of healing. "What you mean Bessie?" he asked again. More insistent.

"Kendella and Miss Clara say up north theah a whole lotta people like us who run away from slavery and there's places where they all live together. In Philadelphia, in Baltimore and Boston. We'll pick one a dem places ta live. Up theah folks get along with each other. Even some white folk." Noah's faced hardened into a scornful mask. "No Bessie. Don't want nothin ta do wit white folk. Nothin!!

"Hush now Noah. It's all right. Theah some decent white folk up north," she assured him, wiping a blade of grass from his forehead. "I don want nothin to do wit em." He was adamant. Bessie didn't push it. "We can organize and help other fugitives." Noah flashed the first smile in days. "Mayhaps we can hep other people git north Bessie." She smiled then agreed.

"Like Miss Clara?"

"Yea, dats what Kendella would do," he stated. "An Im'a be jus like Kendella and hep free colored people and whump any white men who try an stop us."

"My, my, my," smiled Bessie. "You turnin out ta be the warrior. A tear rolled down his ashy cheek. "Yea but I couldn't hep Mah." He started weeping softly. "I couldn't stop thet man frum..."

"Don't think about that Noah. Jus member the good things bout Mah and be strong. You heard Kendella Noah. Weren't nothin you coulda don. Now don't go beatin on yo self. You got things you can do now fo Mah, like live and live free, grow ta be a true and strong colored man, like Kendella."

"You mean a strong BLACK MAN Bessie!!" Noah corrected.

"Yes Noah." She smiled. "That's just what I mean. A strong black man." She stared at him. He'd grown well beyond his years in the past few days.

"It's a shame..." Bessie began in sentiment when she was distracted by a loud clamor rushing toward them from the hillside. She looked back towards the refuge. She hadn't realized they'd walked so far. Bessie listened to the noise. It was easy to tell. There were men on foot in the lower path. An obstreperous posse of marauders rushing vociferously toward them. Noah and Bessie froze. They could hear the men coming but they couldn't see them. Noah pulled himself together and pushed Bessie toward a pile of rocks and brush for cover. The men were still out of sight but their commotion grew louder, clearly announcing their advance. Bessie grabbed Noah and looked for better cover. They hadn't been spotted yet but they soon would if they couldn't find a more adequate hiding place. Nothing would do. Bessie gestured to him. "Run!" she ordered. They'd have to make it to the cave.

"We got ta warn Kendella and Shy." They made a dash for the berm just as the men had them in sight. The posse stepped up it's pace, changing a siege into a pursuit. Bessie pushed Noah in front of her and tried to out distance the men but she couldn't effectively navigate the rocky terrain. She just wasn't fast enough. Noah's youthful and agile body exploited the ground expertly. He sprinted along like a gazelle. Bessie looked back to see the men closing in on her and tripped. She grunted as she tried to get back up. Noah heard her and turned to see Bessie on the ground. He started back for her. "Run Noah! Gon! Run! Tell em. Tell em what..." One of the white men overtook her before she could say another word. Then another and another. Noah's heart sunk. His hope of saving his aunt were dashed beneath the swooping élan of pursuing white men.

"Run!!!" Bessie cried out again before her voice was muffled by the hand of one of her captors. From beneath her restrainers Bessie saw more men rush pass to catch Noah. He quickly out distanced them with ease. He wasn't afraid, he was angry, anxious and hate filled. The mixture added wings of adrenaline to his quest to warn the two men in the cave. Kuendela would save her he knew. He'd even beat and kill the white men in the process.

*****

The posse of militia volunteers left their horses at the base of Fall Point and surreptitiously trooped the moderate hillside to it's top. Jim Smith was surprised to see anyone out in the open, especially a child. Now that child had spotted them. It would diminish the element of surprise he knew. But there was a benefit to the chase. The burden of searching for the cave opening was lifted now that he had someone to lead the militia to it. One of his men almost closed in on the little nigger but Jim Smith quickly reined him in to allow the boy some distance.

*****

As the militiamen pulled her to her feet Bessie watched Noah disappear and silently prayed he could stay out of the white men's grasp long enough to alert Kuendela and Shai.

Where had they come from, she wondered. How did they find the refuge? It was a puzzle. The question was agonizing. Their refuge had always been secure. Now it was compromised. How had they come upon them so quickly.

*****

Noah ran so fast he was almost unable to stop himself from running off the edge of the cliff. As he climbed over the ledge he had a mature revelation and wondered if he'd made a mistake. He was leading the white men to his friends. But he needed Kuendela and Shai, desperately. Bessie needed them. He positioned himself at the ledge to jump down and one of the possemen took a shot at him as he leaped off the berm. Kuendela and Shai sat up in alarm. "Dey comin...," Noah yelled, running to the bank where the two men stood. "Dey comin and dey got Bessie." Kuendela grabbed him.

"Who's coming!?! Who's got Bessie!?!"

"The paddy rollers. Dey comin and dey got Bessie. Dey's right behind me. Right now." They were trapped. Each of them scouted out a vantage point to better defend themselves against the coming threat. Kuendela drew his gel gun set on automatic. Then pulled Noah behind him.

John McPacker had seen Noah leap from the mountain precipice and thought the little colored boy jumped to his death before he could put a bullet in him. But when he approached the edge and looked over the side he was astonished to find a ledge. One that had eluded them for years and existed as a welcome mat for fugitive slaves for just as long. It was the source of their elusiveness. Sheriff Pickett came abreast of him and remembered the very year the first slave jumped from the ledge into legend. Now, looking down on the berm it seemed so elementary now, All they had to do, so long ago, was simply to look over the edge. Kismet had garnished freedom for the coloreds and made a fool out of the slave hunters for all these years. The revelation only added fuel to his anger and sanguine anticipation. "Can you beat that." Jim Smith stated as he sidled up to the Sheriff. "All this time," added Sheriff Pickett. "All this time them nigras been hiding here. Right on top of us. Otis go down in there," he ordered the man standing behind him. Deputy Otis Thebideux looked at the sheriff in a brief show of protest before obeying his order and climbed down with the help of an associate. Sheriff Pickett signaled the other men to follow. One by one they helped each other onto the berm and began filing through the narrow opening.

Otis and Jake were the first to enter the cavern. Shai and Kuendela had just stationed themselves defensively when the intruders appeared. Seeing a pistol in the black man's hand, Otis raised his rifle to fire on him. Shai, out of Otis' view, pulled the rifle from his grasp. Then used the weapon's leverage to threw Otis over his hip. Otis slammed to the ground then rolled over trying to raise himself on all four. Shai brought the rifle down across his back, stunning him with the force of the blow. A second blow broke the rifle in two and knocked Otis out. Shai threw the useless weapon across the unconscious man just as Kuendela dropped Jake at the opening with a barrage of chemical darts. The third man following Otis and Jake emerged through the aperture in time to suffer the same fate. His and Jake's body formed a pile blocking the cave's entrance. "Get their rifles," Kuendela shouted.

Someone outside was pushing the human obstacles out of the way while Kuendela went for the third man's rifle. The next man to squeeze through the aperture had Kuendela dead in his sights. "Kuen!" Shai warned as he leapt for the man but reached him too late. A shot rang out causing them all to stop and stare at one another in dreaded anticipation. Suddenly the white man dropped to his knees and stayed there for a moment. Then Jim Smith slumped over dead, falling across Jake's unconscious body, his eyes still wide in recognition and disbelief. Noah stood before him holding Jake's' musket. An avenging column of smoke slowly trailed from the mouth of the barrel. Kuendela gathered his utility pack and swung the long strap across his shoulder then pushed Noah toward the water's edge. "Let's get the hell out of here!"

*****

Colonel Richards flipped his cigar to the ground. "Get your asses back up here! We'll have to expand the entrance. Bring up the grenadier and blow it open," he shouted to Clem standing in the rear. "Two of the small ones should be enough." Sheriff Pickett ordered the other men off the ledge as Clem came forward with a saddle bag. He crawled down on the ledge and cautiously neared the entrance and peaked inside. He could see the fugitives making their way to the water. He rolled Jim Smith's body clear of the entrance and set down two small hollowed balls filled with explosive black powder. He lit the short fuse then scampered back up on the ledge. "Stand clear!" Just as the men on the ledge backed up a moderate blast exploded, widening the entrance just enough for the men to enter two at a time. And enter they did, pouring through in armed pairs. Some of them brandishing bayonets.

Kuendela waded out to the stream where he could feel the current pulling toward the falls, Noah in his arms and Shai close behind. The riflemen, giving chase, splashed clumsily into the water after them. "I want em alive," yelled Sheriff Pickett, too late to stop a couple men from squeezing off a few shots that missed their targets. The fleeing black men allowed themselves to be whisked away by the rapid force of the water. In one swoop they were swallowed up by the cascading falls. The possemen watched in disappointment as the fugitives vanished into the roaring abyss of the water fall. 'Bang!' Clem fired a shot into the curtain of water covering the mouth of the cave. "You're just wasting ammo Clem," complained Sheriff Pickett from the bank. Clem slammed his musket in the water in frustration. "Them dam darkies done it again Sheriff."

"Way to go Clem. Let's get the hell out of here."

*****

They tumbled in and out of roaring sheets of water. Centrifugal forces caused Kuendela to lose his grip on Noah sundering him from his grasp. They all hit the water In intermittent splashes. Kuendela was the first to brake the surface. He spun around in a frenzied search to locate his companions. He spotted Noah, splashing frantically to stay afloat but going under. Kuendela swam the short distance to him and held the boy above the water then paddled to the bank. Shai, swam behind them. All three crawled out of the water gasping for air. Shai tried to pulled himself erect but fell back down wincing in pain. "Kuendela," he called breathlessly. "I'm hit."

*****

The pursuers splashed their way back to the cave's inner bank. They were hardly prepared for the escape the fugitives managed to orchestrate and none of the men were about to follow them into the falls. By now the cavern was filled with white men who set about inspecting the cave. Several of the bags of supplies were kicked around in angry frustration. John McPacker banged the butt of his musket on the ground in disgust. "By the Saints! These are the most wily devils to boot."

Colonel Richards entered behind the last man and stood for a moment, stunned by the interior. "What the devil is this place!?! Look at it's size!" Sheriff Pickett, kneeling over Jim Smith's body, stopped what he was doing to observe. During the chase he hadn't paid much attention to the scope of it's size. The expanse of its interior and it's stream were a complete shock to him. Colonel Richards stepped deeper inside and removed his hat and wiped his brow. His head pivoted slowly from side to side as he took in the magnitude of the Negroes lost sanctuary. This is the end of the epidemic he told himself. He was sure of it. "By God!" he slapped his thigh with his hat.

393

"They'll not escape. Back down the point to the horses men." Sheriff Pickett was way ahead of him. He ushered his men out of the cave and boosted them one by one up on the ledge. Then held his arms up to be assisted himself. One of the men lost his footing in his zeal to get up on the crag and fell screaming to his death. The unfortunate mans companions continued without so much as a glance.

*****

Kuendela sat up quickly. "Is it bad man?" Shai checked himself. "No...No ..I don't think so." Kuendela checked him. No bones were broken. No vital organs seemed to be hit. It was an apparent flesh wound but he was bleeding profusely. Kuendela extracted a sterile battle dressing from his utility bag then wrapped it tightly around Shai's thigh and taped a smaller one to his side. "Good thing these packs are water proof? How's that Brother?" Shai struggled to his feet and hobbled around in a small circle to test his agility.

"Fine my brother. Thanks." Except for a slight limp he was all right. It just ached a little. Kuendela turned his attention to Noah. "You all right little brother?" Noah sat up coughing water. "Yea.. yea," he said between coughs. "I'm okay." All three were soaked and dripping wet.

"What now man?" Shai asked.

"What bout Bessie?" Noah pled, frantically looking from Kuendela to Shai. Kuendela unholstered his gel gun and checked it's reserve then cocked it once. The sound was sharp and metallic. "You go to the Aeon Pad," he told Shai without looking at him. "I'm going to take Noah back to Bessie." Shai grabbed his arm. "And do what man!?!" Kuendela pulled away and started in the direction of the hillside. "What the hell do you think!?!" he exclaimed over his shoulder. "Them whiteys ain't going to give her to you then escort you to the pad brother. At best you're gonna have to kill them all. At the least they'll kill you. At worse they gonna put shackles on all your asses." Kuendela stopped. He knew Shai was on point. He was being led by his emotions again. The feeling of helplessness came. It was torture not being able to alleviate the situation. That terrible feeling of defeat, that he hated, overcame him. "I just can't leave her to those wolves Shai." Shai stepped up to Kuendela whose back remained to him. "Brother, you're going to have to kill them all to get her out of there. You don't want to do that. And we can't take her with us. I hope I don't sound selfish man. I know you went through a lot to free me and I know Bessie helped you. But how far are we going to go with this brother. We do have a protocol to follow and we've interfered enough all ready." There was that matter of pragmatism again not to mention the conscious fact of protocol. It was a hard call to make on some hard cold facts but in his heart he knew Shai was right.

Shai waited to see if his words had taken effect. Kuendela's slumping shoulders confirmed when penetration was made. Shai felt bad for his friend and rescuer. He understood the rage Kuendela had for injustice. He knew well his propensity for protecting his people. He'd known Kuendela long enough to know his character. Leaving someone in distress, left to these barbarians was not an easy nut for him to crack. Especially a black woman. And especially this woman. He'd seen the way they looked at each other. He'd seen enough to know that the big brother's judgment was jaded, clouded by the war raging within his conscience. It was all there to see in those big broad constricted shoulders. "I'm sorry man. I know how you feel about her. But what can we do now? At least you know she won't be killed and with what she knows if she bides her time there's still that nest egg waiting for her in the cave." It wasn't much but it was something to cling to. In those words there was at least a kernel of hope. A semblance of justification. At least for Bessie. Kuendela finally turned to look at him. He inhaled deeply. "You're right brother...You're right." His voice trembled but he managed a half hearted smile. "I'm being dangerous, man. I'd fuck around and get myself and maybe even you killed."

"No you're being heroic and loyal brother. It's just not our call."

"I feel guilty man," Kuendela replied matter of factly. "I've interfered too much. Way too much." But inside he was already planning. Maybe there was a chance he could return to 1852 and free Bessie. He'd be dam if he'd leave her here in chains.

Shai looked at Noah. "What about little brother here?" Kuendela but his arm around the boy. "That's where I draw the line," Kuendela averred. "No way I leave him here to those motherfuckers." He thought for a second to rationalize his actions. "If I hadn't performed CPR on him he'd probably be dead anyway," he reasoned. "So protocol is void where he's concerned." He waited to hear Shai's protest. Shai shrugged his shoulders. "I hear you brother. There's no drastic effect to history here. If anything it'll be put right."

"That's settled. Let's get the hell out of here." Kuendela grabbed Noah up in his arms. "Those paddyrollers will be here before you know it."

*****

It was a short while before the posse reached the bottom of the hill where their horses and captives were tied. Bessie saw the anger beaming from their faces as they mounted their steeds and correctly assumed her comrades had gotten away. Colonel Richard's rage was especially evident.

"Dammit!" he spouted. "Dam, Dam, Dammit!" He pointed to Bessie, huffing and buffing from his trot down the trail and gave Clem a breathless order, "You and Luke put this one on a horse. We're taking her along." He turned a piercing eye to Hammonds. "Him too!" Luke grabbed Bessie by the binds on her wrist and pulled her to a horse. After placing her in the saddle he mounted behind her, grabbed hold of the reins and snarled in her ear. "Try anything funny wench and I'll cut your heart out!" Bessie made no response. She was staring at Hammonds. Her eyes narrowed at the trance like state he was in. Since the moment Bessie had been brought down from the Point Hammonds avoided looking at her. His shame kept him riveted to any object that would anchor his eyes away from hers. But averting his eyes did nothing to escape Bessie's accusing gaze. The sense of accusation gripping at the back of his head was almost palpable. It was impossible to avoid her any longer. Hammonds turned his head slowly, forcing his eyes to meet hers. As soon as their eyes locked Bessie saw the grief and sorrow in his soul. And something else. Something that caused her initial anger to slowly dissipate into a rueful pity. Her own spirituality bore his torment before her and helped her to gage the degree of despair in his heart with one deep penetrating look.

Hammonds opened his mouth to speak but the sense of the men around him struck him mute. Bessie's eyes relayed to him, there was no need for words. She knew something significant had to have happened for him to give away their most guarded secret.

*****

Colonel Richards ordered her secured to the horse with intentional coarseness. Bessie was still able to smile in spite of the rough treatment and it bugged him. "What the hell is so funny? I'll knock that contemptuous sneer off your black face!" To her surprise he didn't strike her. He just went on, huffing in exasperation. Praise God!! They musta got away. Kuendela and Shai was giving them white men fits. Bessie put her head down to smile and lifted her bound hands through Luke's grasp to touch the talisman dangling from her neck. "Thank you Jesus," she mouthed under her breath. She closed her eyes and prayed silently. "Please keep them safe."

Colonel Richards mounted his horse. He had trouble holding his stead steady. "Sheriff! Take some men around the western approach and follow the stream. We'll take the road northwest through the woods and snare the blackguards between us!" He turned his horse so that he was facing the men now mounting their steeds. "I want these devils gentleman and I will have them. DEAD...OR ALIVE!"

"The big nigger. Alive if ye can," added McPacker pulling up beside the Colonel. "By Eire hanging him will be the sweetest of pleasures. But!" McPacker slid back the lock on his musket, purposely affecting a loud metallic clasp. "If justice be dealt in the woods by the gun, by Eire. So be it!"

By west and northwest the posse and militia volunteers thundered off to hunt down the fugitives the gold and the money. Virgil's slaying and the humiliation of the brake out fed the flames of vengeance that could be heard in the thundering hooves and burned in the hateful heart of each man as they rode. By the time the two groups were out of sight of each other Kuendela, Shai and Noah trotted toward the transmission pad at a measured pace. Noah's weight and the weight of the body armor created an enormous load for Kuendela. The irritation caused by his wet clothing added to his burden. He had to stop and remove his vest. He gave it to Shai. At no time was he unsure of where he was going. His memory served him well. For twenty five minutes, with Noah on his back, he led Shai on an intermittent trot and jog through the uneven terrain of the forest toward the wooded area where the Aeon pad awaited. Their sodden, mud laden pants chaffed their legs amplifying the strain and anxiety growing with each irritating step. But on they trudged until they reached a clearing where they stopped and Kuendela put Noah down. Before them stretched a wide open field of grass. On the other side a long line of trees beckoned to them from across it's expanse like a line of imposing sentinels guarding the entrance to the thick wooded area beyond. "Right across the field," Kuendela pointed breathlessly. "Yes. I remember." Shai panted. "Over there is the path where I saw that sister killed. She chose death over going back into bondage." The memory made him shudder. "Blessed are those," recited Kuendela, "those who died oppression is worse than the grave. It's better to die for a noble cause than to live and die a slave."

"No doubt."

Noah stared from one man to the other. "Where we goin Kendella? Is we gon back fo Bessie?" Kuendela's blood went cold. He swallowed hard and bent to one knee shaken by the eyes that met him on the way down. He bit his lip as his eyes searched Noah's face for an inkling of credence but found only a modicum of inculpation. Kuendela discerned there was no easy way to mitigate another of Noah's many pains or compensate his mounting loses. But he would try. Kuendela was going to trust the strength of the bond they nurtured and the intuit of purpose Noah inherited from his mother. He would explain to Noah that there was no way to overcome the posse and liberate Bessie and that he, Kuendela, had made a decision to take Noah across the barriers of time with him and Shai, away from all that he knew, to a new existence. Kuendela asked himself, could he assume the right to choose for this child. Could he postulate the authority. He sighed. Fate, he reasoned. Fate and an inherent patrimony gave him perquisite and domain. He could and would save this child. "No Noah," he began slowly. "We can't go back for Bessie." Noah tried to break free of Kuendela's embrace. He'd save her. He'd go back and overpower the white men with their guns and their bombs and their bayonets and horses and he'd...he'd...The magnitude of it all fell upon his tiny shoulders like the unfair weight that it culminated. He could only protest the inequity with the only means his young life afforded, Noah fell limp and cried. He cried hard, with heaving sobs over the awesome inequality of his black life and the utter helpless- ness that life endured. "I know, Noah. I know man. It's not fair, little brother, but we got to go on. Finish what Bessie and Kimbe started." Kuendela's voice cracked. He too felt the utter helplessness of black life that Noah felt. He knew, though centuries apart in consciousness, they shared the same inadequate fate thrust upon them by others. He too felt the strain of invisible shackles and the pull of virtual chains dragging him away from his true inalienable calling in directions not of his own choosing. Not of chance but of cruel necessity. A survival imposed by the unprincipled dominance of those who gave not a care for his humanity but only recognized him as a commodity or a whim. Denying him destiny, directly or indirectly forcing him to take preternatural actions. Even in so unlikely a realm as fulfilling his god given duty to protect one of his own. His woman. With difficulty Kuendela straightened his back. "We've got to keep going Noah. We've got to finished what Bessie and Kimbe. George and Miss Clara and Hammonds sacrificed themselves to start. To get you free...One day we'll come back." he shrugged.

"Den free Bessie!"

"Then free Bessie little brother. But right now, we got a mission to finish." He looked into the boys eyes. "Noah, there's always danger in the struggle for freedom. It shouldn't be. There shouldn't even be a need to struggle for what god gives us by right. But it is. You know that?" Noah nodded mutely but his youthful gaze never lost their petitioning hold on Kuendela's eyes.

"Bessie told me once that Kimbe taught you what being black in a white man's country meant. She told you that life for black people here in America is a war and getting freedom is a day to day battle where the liberty of one person is sometimes sacrificed to gain liberty for the rest. Remember Noah?"...A nod. "She told you that sometimes a body falls behind to help the race move ahead."...Noah nodded again. His upper lip trembled and his eyes filled with tears. Kuendela looked sorrowfully at this child who's eyes had seen so much misery in so short a life time. Hardships and pain he's endured by virtue of his black existence. Kuendela lamented. He's known asperity, no white child of any era, has ever known in an entire lifetime. Kuendela pursed his lips in anger. If there were ever any doubts over his decision to take Noah back with them, the look in his eyes erased them completely. Now Kuendela's eyes filled with tears. He tried blinking them back but it was no use.

"Bessie and Kimbe want you free, little brother. They want you to grow up to be all you can be and I promise you Noah, you'll do just that. I'm gonna see to it. We're taking

you with us. Where we can rear you into a strong warrior."
Kuendela unconsciously wiped a tear from Noah's cheek.
"Bessie'll be fine Li'l Brother. I promise you. And she'll be
free one day. I promise you that too. But for now! We're still
in the fight and so is Bessie. Can we count on you to fight?"

"Like a...African warrior?"

"That's right Li'l Brother!" He hugged Noah tight.
"Like an African warrior."

To their rear, Fall Point hung above the trees like a silent
witness, committing the events to memory. From a distance
it loomed, reserving the right to pass judgment. Kuendela
stood up and turned raising a clench fist toward the
mountain. "Be strong Bessie." Then at a quick turn and a
step Kuendela took Noah's hand and started out across the
clearing with Shai close behind. "I'll be glad to get the hell
out of this place!" Shai exclaimed. As soon as they entered
the woods Kuendela began looking for the landmark X's
he'd carved into the trees. It took only a minute to spot the
first one. Then something stopped him. He cupped his ears to
listen. From the woods on the other side of the clearing
they'd crossed, a growing clatter of horses hooves
crescendoed to a thunderous roar. Kuendela, Shai and Noah
advanced their pace to a sprint as the sight of the horsemen
emerging from the woods put speed in their heels. Gun shots
rang out from the group of angry pursuers galloping
furiously to ride them down. Kuendela led the way dragging
Noah by the arm while he looked frantically for the
remaining X's.

When the posse entered the woods Kuendela was running toward the last landmark. Several yards to it's left laid
the Aeon platform. The three Africans ran for it at break
neck speed. Kuendela slid to the pad on his knees while
simultaneously removing the OCP key from his utility. He
felt around the Aeon Pad until he felt the perforations on the
transparent platform's edge. His steady hand guided the key
into it's insertion slot and locked it in place. Colonel
Richards hand flew up to halt the group of horsemen a
hundred yards from the fleeing trio when he saw them stop

running. From his purview it appeared they had given up. Finally, he inferred to himself, they showed some sense. Exhausted and seeing themselves surrounded they rightly decided not to go on. He smiled a sinister grin. The big one showed the good sense to give up on his knees, to boot. Obviously a plea for mercy. Mercy he will never receive. He leaned to Sheriff Pickett. "A touching show of prayer and submission. Eh Abram? But it won't save the villain. It won't fly. Take them!!" he ordered. The horsemen sidled into a skirmish line and unsheathed their muskets. How ironic, Colonel Richards thought, for them to have come so far only to be taken in such a surprisingly reprehensible act of cowardice. Astoundingly it disappointed him. He really expected more of a fight from these blackguards. The respect Jim Smith had for their resourcefulness and prowess may have been grossly overrated. "Come here and surrender yourselves," he yelled...Only silence permeated the woods save the sound of muskets being swept into place.

Bessie sat nervously on the horse with Luke still behind her. The scene before her brought beads of sweat down her back. She feared the three of them would be executed before her very eyes or, worse, apprehended. What could she do? Create a diversion. With all the strength she could muster she threw her head back into Luke's forehead. It wasn't enough to throw him from the horse but it did cause him to jam his spurs into the tender under side of the horses thigh. That action made the horse rear up. Luke tumbled to the ground as Bessie grabbed the reins and bolted through the woods.

"Get that wench!" someone yelled. Clem shifted his sights from the cornered trio to Bessie's fleeing back. Hammonds swung his horse around to rear up at Clem causing him to fall from his horse. Clem pulled out his revolver and squeezed the trigger. Fire spewed from it's barrel hurling a mini ball at Hammonds, drilling a hole into his head. He fell dead to the ground never hearing the shot that killed him.

Kuendela stood erect and lifted Noah into his arms. Shai stepped up on the transparent platform and threw his arms around Kuendela sandwiching Noah safely between them. Kuendela looked to his aligned pursuers just in time to see Hammonds fall and Bessie being targeted by Sheriff Pickett. He reached for a weapon. This time it was the pistol he'd found in Winthrops safe and raised it.

"Drop that gun!" screamed Colonel Richards. "Drop it I say or die!" He turned to see the object of the black man's weapon while Kuendela took aim. In that split second of indiscretion Colonel Richards heard the shot but was unsure where it landed until Sheriff Pickett wavered and fell. A well placed round from the colt smashed into his shoulder. The thud like sound of metal hitting flesh came to him as he fell wounded from his horse. "Fire!!" ordered Colonel Richards at the top of his voice. The entire posse fired simultaneously. A thunderous roar went up in the woods as their volley exploded in tandem. A fusillade of lead blasted into the triple aberration upon the Aeon Platform. The din compared to canon fire. Never before had any of the men heard a sound like that emanating from their thirteen rifles. The roar was strangely bombastic and ear shattering. The blast, the fusillade of bullets seemed to explode and utterly demolish their targets into infinitum. The three figures huddled together were ripped apart into shreds of nothingness. For an instant the entire woods seemed to be consumed by a hell storm of fire. When silence finally prevailed, some of the men turned their muskets around and incredulously examined their barrels. Except for gasps and the sound of their gaping mouths, nothing else was heard. Finally John McPacker, in his own words, expressed the amazed emotions of them all..."By the Saints Of Eire...!!!"

CHAPTER 15

Year 2000

Professor Jubilee stood over his station at the central controls. "Where in hell is Professor Lewis!?!" His face was haggard. He'd spent long restless hours at his station waiting for signs of Kuendela and hopefully Shai's return. Argee had, on several occasions, enlisted Professor Kobolongo to persuade him to let someone else man the controls while he got some much needed rest. He was exhausted, he was agitated but he refused. Professor Lewis had been sent to Quad A headquarters earlier in the morning and was expected back an hour ago. Doctor Belton eyed Professor Jubilee's uncharacteristic ire. He'd expressed mild intolerance for Professor Lewis' slow procrastination in the past. This time he was angry. In her expert opinion, Professor Jubilee was transferring his fear and anxiety to his eccentric colleague. "We're all worried about Kuendela and Shai, Pressman. All we can do is wait and pray." Professor Jubilee grimaced. "I know Ida but it's tough waiting and wondering. I can't stop worrying about their welfare, their condition, their fate. But you're right Ida. You're right."

"Kuendela's a strong brother, Pressman." she added. "The ancestors will guide and protect him. They will guide and protect them both and bring them back home to us." Doctor Ida Belton placed a consoling hand on her association's doyen and friend's shoulder. The strain of the mission and exhaustion wore heavily on his face like a morose mask. She too felt the strain and wondered if it was so evident upon her own face. Kevin walked onto the platform to relieve Doctor Belton from her monitor. "You know Professor Lewis," he tried to assuage then made that sound of clucking his tongue against the roof of his mouth. "He probably got side tracked in the archives or something."

Argee stepped up to relieve Bilal. "I'll take over Bilal. You need a brake," she offered. Her voice was hoarse and dark circles ringed her heavily strained eyes. Bilal shook his head. "No, sister. It's okay. She looked to Professor Jubilee for support. He wearily nodded his approval of Bilal's decision with a weak smile. He was proud of the dedication and love that exuded from his young scientists. The old ones as well. Even that tardy ass Professor Lewis.

"It's been a long three days my brother." Professor Kobolongo rubbed his eyes. "You can say that again Ohoolu."

"Yes, brother. We must trust our ancestors and the creator to watch over them."

For three days the monitors on the Aeon Retrogression Chamber's platform had been manned constantly and monitored for signs of retransmission. Each program member rotated in turn to watch over the scientific devices. Stress and anxiety were high as was the nagging pressure of suspense. But no manner of tension was enough to overshadow their hope and anticipation. Suddenly a blinking cursor on Argee's screen infused her with a jolt of energy. Her eyes widened as the sudden deluge of electronic data on the screen gave her an indication of activity. Someone had activated the Aeon Platform and was attempting retransmission. "Somethings happening!" she announced. From his station, Bilal began hitting buttons and swiveling in his chair from monitor to monitor. "Yes. I've got it!" All at once the languorous platform was now a beehive of activity. Professor Jubilee tilted his monitor up towards his face. Then quickly looked around at his team. Everyone was on hand...except Professor Lewis who was now 90 minutes late. "Is it a confirmed retransmission?"

"That's affirmative," Professor Kobolongo responded gliding his seat toward Bilal's terminal. "There is a definite surge, building up to a transmission threshold." Professor Jubilee quickly pecked at his keyboard, transposing a block of data to Argee's screen. "Guide in on that signal at 75^, Argee."

"Yes sir."

"Ohoolu..." Professor Kobolongo furiously pecked at his controls. "I am on it Pressman." The sound of moving gears and an electrical hum filled the platform as the glass enclosure was activated. Slowly the large glass panels embedded in the ceiling above began their descent and in seconds the entire platform was enclosed in a protective shield of laminated glass, protecting the team from the physical emanations generated by the ARC's surge to power. All eyes shifted from their prospective screens to the ARC as it came to life. Gradually threads of electroluminescent energy began to spin their way from the crystal peaked obelisks, leaping from tower to tower, accompanied by a low vibrating hum. Broadening bands of energy reflected from crystal to crystal. They seemed to engulf the ARC, enveloping the entire structure in electrical ribbons of energy until they burst into an orange red brilliance. The explosion that followed was both deafening and unexpected. "There on the pad!" yelled Argee pointing to the translucent figures vacillating on the Aeon platform. The images of Kuendela and Shai were momentarily visible for just a few seconds at a time then disappeared when a sudden hale of projectiles replaced their strobe like images. The bullets bounced off the glass enclosure like raining pelts of lead. Some of the occupants inside instinctively ducked for cover as the lead balls pinged off the glass partition. "What the hell!" Bilal stood up from his terminal.

"Keep to your task," ordered Professor Jubilee. "We're losing them."

"Oh my God!" exclaimed Doctor Belton as she tried to stabilize her biological fix on the returning subjects. Professor Kobolongo worked frantically at the keys to maintain a cohesive interface between all devices.

"If we lose them they'll be trapped in a dimensional abyss forever!" he proclaimed as the possible consequences became clear to him. "We'll never be able to resurrect them." His voice was broken and filled with emotion at the possibility of them being trapped between this realm of reality and some neither word of unknown dimension. His shaking hands worked his keyboard while the awful image of the unimaginable filled his minds eye. The obelisk to the left of the wheel had been struck hard by several lead balls that ricocheted from the glass partition. The force of the bullet pushed a crystal off it's peak ever so slightly causing the band of energy emitted from the wheel to lose it's calculated alignment. The worse of unexpected fears were happening. A deflected band of electro lasered power scattered across the laboratory in a frightening display of rampant energy. Its laser like precision flung it's rays wildly about the room slicing wires and gashing scorched inch wide trenches in the walls. A wayward lased beam found it's way along the starboard wall severing the cabal leading from an electrical box to the circuitry panel that controlled the glass partition, trapping the entire team in the enclosed platform. "Oh shit, no!" cursed Bilal when he saw the enclosure's icon on Kobolongo's screen disappear to be replaced by a flashing 'Power OFF' icon. There was no contingency plan for what was happening.

"How can we get out to realign the tower...Shit!!"

"The access panel in the floor," snapped Professor Jubilee. "It's our only hope to regain control."

"What the hell was that?" asked Kevin crouched beneath his terminal for cover. "Bullets," informed Professor Kobolongo swinging out of his chair.

"Pressman there's no time to access the emergency panel. We've only got minutes to stabilize their retransmission." He lifted his metal swivel chair and held it back ready to swing at the glass partition.

"Professor Lewis!!" Argee yelled pointing. "Professor Lewis!" Doctor Belton also saw him enter. She stood at the glass panel banging for his attention. Professor Lewis stopped in the doorway startled by the melee and confusion he'd entered upon and ducked. Doctor Belton banged hysterically and pointed toward the misaligned tower hoping he'd understand her. Professor Lewis made his way to the platform crouching below the searing hot beams of energy. He could barely hear the shouts of the people inside but he did managed to understand. Quickly, he made his way to the ARC. Here he was safe from the wild beams while he accessed a small panel at the base of the tower. A few pressed keys and still nothing happened. The crystal would have to be aligned manually.

Professor Jubilee had Bilal lower himself down into the belly of the laboratory to regain control of the glass partition. As his young assistant descended the ladder he thought of Professor Lewis' tardiness. This time it may have come as a blessing. Professor Lewis stood on his toes to reach the base of the crystal. Surprisingly, he felt little heat emitting from it in spite of the close proximity to his hands. But he knew if he came into contact with a beam, even slightly, it would slice off his hand. With some difficulty he was able to turn the base of the crystal enough to realign the orbit of power. An orange red burst of power exploded around the ARC announcing the regained alignment. The sharp force of the beams coming back together threw Professor Lewis to the floor. There was now retransmission for the time travelers. Like flickering strobes their figures vacillated from visible to invisible, back and again until finally they came to complete reformation. Kuendela and Shai were still embraced with Noah snuggled securely between them. All at once the transmission activity came to a halt. The laboratory was bathed in complete silence as the partition went up into the ceiling. The scientist poured off the platform like the crowd that must have come out to receive Mohammed Ali after the Liston fight. Kuendela and Shai with Noah still between them melted to the floor. Instantly they were swooped up by the team and carried to makeshift recovery rooms down the hall. Kuendela in one. Shai in another.

The sight of the small boy caused all to throw confused glances at one another but this was not the time for speculation. Argee tenderly took the boy in her arms. His eyes danced wildly about the room while Argee checked him for injuries. He'd come through without a scratch though the osmotic shock he suffered during transference must have been traumatic to his young mind. "What's your name young brother?" Her voice was so soothing and clean. Like Kimbe's when she was cooing. Or Bessie's when she was being sweet. He missed them both. Noah stared around in awe at the sudden and spectacular changes in the environment. The events of the last few minutes were bewildering to him. One moment he was standing in the forest and the next he was here. For him it was clear and simple. He, Kuendela and Shai were dead and now resided in heaven. Maybe he could find Mah here. "Im Noah," he replied as Argee led him to the recovery room. "Is dis heaven?" he wondered out loud in child like amazement. "Is we dead?" He looked up at Argee with a widened gaze. Her long braided hair, usually tied behind her head, today hung in a frame around her face. Noah was entranced by her rope like tresses. He never imagined an angel would be so beautiful...and black. In the background he saw Bilal moving about. His large black muscles strained against his sleeveless tight fitting shirt. He recalled the Richards children boasting about the illustrations in the bible. How they showed a white Samson slaying enemy legions. He wished they were here now to see that Samson was really as black as he was. He remembered what Kuendela said about the noble kings and queens of Africa and spoke out to him in remembrance. "You was right Kendella...GOD IS COLUD!!"...And God was right here in the room wearing a white smock and they called him JUBILEE! Argee held back her amusement and hugged him tighter. Noah's presence there was without question accepted, though an explanation was eagerly anticipated. Still the boy was welcomed. And he felt it. He was welcomed and accepted and...loved. So in spite of his difficulty in grasping it all and because of what he could feel, miraculously, he was not afraid. He let himself be taken along by the friendly, heavenly angel that seemed to take a special liking to him. "Don't be afraid, young brother," Argee cooed. Her voice was like a warm and secure blanket. These people were like Kuendela and Shai he thought. They even seem to know them.

Inside the room Kevin applied a dressing to Kuendela's temple where he'd been grazed by a bullet. Noah started towards him but Argee held him back.

"Let them finish, Noah." She used his name for the first time. He relaxed in her embrace and waited patiently allowing himself to be comforted. Kuendela looked at the boy and smiled. Professor Jubilee stood over him with his arms folded. "I can explain the little brother Professor. We really had little choice," he began but was cut off by a wave of Professor Jubilee's hand. "Not now," he commanded. "I'm sure I'll get it all from your audio log." He held out his hand. Kuendela reached inside his utility pocket and hand over the small voice recorder. Professor Jubilee took it. "Let Kevin finish up. Then I want a full report." He looked over at the child. There'd better be a good explanation for affronting the most sacred aspect of protocol.

Professor Jubilee trusted this man. "There'll be plenty of time for explanations. I'm sure you did what you thought best," he nodded then added sternly. "You better make it good though." When he said it better be good. He really meant, it better be good. But for now he lauded his praise. "I'm proud of you son. You've done a fine job. We were all worried about you and Shai. I just looked in on him," he sighed. "Ida gave him a transfusion and a sedative. He's lost a lot of blood from that leg wound. He's also taken two hits in the side. But he'll be all right. He's a survivor."

"No doubt, Professor. You can't imagine what that young brother has already been through."

"Oh. But I can imagine son. He's been through the worse that America has to offer. So have you."

"You can say that again."

Kevin tapped him playfully. "Don't talk while I'm working please."

"Shai really looks bad. He has a lot of injuries," Professor Jubilee declared softly. Kuendela thought he detected some shades of guilt in the Professors voice. "They must have really put him through the ringer...But he's safe now."

"He's a strong young man, Professor. He held his own. He'll certainly have one helluva story to tell when he's ready."

"Okay. I'm done." Kevin patted Kuendela's shoulder. On his way out the room he stopped to pinch Noah tenderly on the cheek. "He's handsome."

Argee guided Noah to Kuendela's bedside. "I thought he'd be more comfortable in here with you big brother," she winked. Noah's eyes darted around nervously Though he was comfortable to be near Kuendela again, he was still bewildered. "Come here warrior." Kuendela stretched his arms to receive him. Noah sat on the edge of the bed still taking in the environment and its people. Professor Jubilee watched the two silently.

"Everything's gonna be all right Noah...You're free now man. The way Kimbe and Bessie wanted you to be."

"Is Mah here, Kendella?" Noah asked sadly. Kuendela swallowed ruefully.

"Mah's gone, Noah. But she'll always be with us..." He pointed from his own heart to Noah's. "Right here."

"Bessie too?"

"Bessie too," Kuendela agreed. "There's a lot I have to explain to you Noah. Man you have the opportunity of several lifetimes. You've got a lot to learn. So many sad and wonderful things." Kuendela gently stroked Noah's back. "Mah would be mighty proud of you Little Brother." He could only imagine Noah's confusion. But he'd make sure his transition would be as smooth as possible. He knew the others would do their part to help. In some ways he envied Noah. He was to discover a world of enormous opportunity and with all the resources he knew these people would put at his feet he'd grow into a remarkable young black man. He didn't know it yet but the Quad As' entire institution was at his disposal. There's a lot we can probably learn from him as well. In time the hurt of the losses he incurred would heal, at his age probably sooner than one would think, and all of the pain would be behind him. But not forgotten.

"I know this all seems strange to you Noah. It's going to be hard to understand. But I'm here with you and in time you will. We'll make sense of it together. Right, warrior?" Noah stared at his hero. Kuendela gently swiped him across his chin. Noah nodded his head.

"Professor, you know if there's a logical heir to the potential of the ARC, it's him. He's got to be the most unique young brother on this planet. Like Noah in the bible," he laughed. "Only the charges on his voyage will be two sets of history. What's true and what's bull." Noah continued to look at him without the slightest notion of what he was talking about. One day however, he would. Thus began Kuendela's soliloquy into his report. Professors Kobolongo and Lewis entered the room followed by Doctor Belton and Bilal. Kevin remained next door with Shai. They listened intently for sixty five minutes as he recounted everything from meeting Bessie and Noah at the falls to the last time he'd seen her riding off to buy them a few precious moments to escape. Argee took notes. When he finished Professor Jubilee put his arms around Noah. "Welcome Noah," he said with a smile. "Kuendela we prayed for you and Shai everyday." He reached into his shirt and withdrew the necklace he wore at all times faithfully. "I kept my faith in this sacred talisman," he explained. "It's a source of comfort for me. My grandmother gave it to me right before I left for college." He remembered her explaining it's meaning to a young white woman who had come to write about Tentu's stories. "Whenever we need the strength of our fathers, she'd say, pray to the crystal. It's our connection to our ancestors. That's what Grandma Tentu always told me," he remembered fondly. Kuendela eyed the necklace languidly. He'd never noticed it around the Professor's neck before. Then recognition widened his eyes in disbelief. "Let me see that

Professor?" He reached for it to get a better look. Professor Jubilee removed it from his neck and handed it to him. "She got it from her mother," Professor Jubilee explained. "My great grandfather gave it to her." Professor Jubilee's eyes were veiled by the wonders of the past. "Grandma Tentu never saw her father, never knew his true name. But she was told he was an African prince killed by slave chasers. She said that it was the source of our power and our heritage and that it was a piece of our homeland. It's given me strength in times of need." Kuendela held it tenderly in his fingertips and a tear rolled down his cheek. It was a small crystal talisman on a thin gold braided chain. It was filled with minute particles of sand. Noah rested his head on Kuendela's chest and he too began to shed a tear as he thought of his Mah and Bessie. "Kendella, do you think Bessie got away all right?" Kuendela continued looking at the crystal talisman. "Trust me Noah," he said still tenderly handling it between his fingertips. "Bessie made out just fine..."